Cold November Rain

NICOLE WARREN

Cold November Rain is a work of fiction. Incidents, names, characters, and places are a product of the author's imagination or are used fictitiously. Any resemblance to actual events, locales, or persons, living or dead, is coincidental.

Copyright © 2015 by Nicole Warren. All rights reserved.
Cover Design by Sarah Ayres

No part of this book may be reproduced in any written, electronic, recording, or photocopying form without written permission of the author.

ACKNOWLEDGEMENTS

Laura and Kristen, thank you for your keen editing and proofreading skills. You were both so great to work with. You made the process smooth and easy, and dare I say fun! Also, I'd like to say thank you to Michael. I received your round of editing in lightning speed as promised, along with a generous amount of tips, helping me to learn along the way.

Sarah, I love the cover! You are madly talented and a sweetheart to boot! Thank you so much for all of your work.

And lastly to my friends and family who supported and encouraged me since the beginning. Special thanks have to go to Cassie, Nick, Shanna, and Tiffany. Whether this was your genre or not (wink, wink, Nick and Shanna) I appreciate the time you all took to be the first to read my story, even before any editing took place! Your enthusiasm for what I created kept me going and I'm forever thankful!

"We have indication of movement."

"Who? To where?"

"Charlotte. Malibu, California. Along with her daughter. It appears to be permanent."

"Hmmm…it has been a year. She's finally done licking her wounds, is she? This is interesting, very interesting. Well, if she's ready for some fun in the sun, then let the games begin. Keep me posted and stand ready for orders."

"Will do, Boss."

"How about we call it a day, Asa? I don't know about you, but it's six o'clock at night, and I think it's time for some fresh air," Charlotte said to her caramel-colored Pomeranian, who didn't understand what she was saying but was excited nonetheless. Charlotte had been unpacking boxes since five thirty that morning. For over two days straight she'd been working alone to get her daughter and niece moved into their new condominium.

The cousins had just graduated from high school and were on a celebratory first-ever road trip. Aubrie Elle, Charlotte's daughter, had been accepted to Pepperdine University in Malibu, California, and Chloe, the daughter of Charlotte's sister, would be attending Santa Monica College. Since fall term would begin in just two short months, Char was happy to handle the move so the girls could enjoy a little freedom before buckling down to their studies.

Charlotte was also unpacking some of her own belongings. She had begrudgingly agreed to come with Aubrie, at her behest. Whether or not it would be permanent remained to be seen. Permanent or temporary, a move from a small town just outside of Portland, Oregon, to Malibu at the age of thirty-nine was quite a transition.

A widow for nearly three years, Charlotte had good reasons for agreeing to the change, yet Aubrie still had to work hard to convince her to make the move. Char's personal life had been a mess since the passing of Beau, her husband of eight years. Aubrie had shared she was afraid to leave Charlotte isolated and alone. She insisted Char needed a change of scenery and begged her to come at least try it out for the summer. Reluctantly, Char agreed.

The prospect scared her on more than one level, and she knew a hike would be the perfect distraction from her worries.

"You ready to go for a walk, Asa?" Char asked her expectant pommie as she skipped down the stairs with him. Unfamiliar with Southern California, she had searched great hiking spots online and picked Solstice Canyon Trail. At first glance, she had thought it was called Solace Canyon, and that was what she felt she needed: a sense of comfort and reassurance that accompanying Aubrie had been the right choice. She hoped she was finally ready for a change, that she was truly ready to get out and start living again, as scary as it still felt.

She locked the front door and heard the sound of jangling bells coming up from behind her. Char turned and saw a tall woman in a sherbet-colored caftan, wearing several long necklaces and a jumble of bracelets. She looked to be in her midsixties. Her hair was shockingly white with dark roots, styled in what might be called a tousled pixie cut. Tousled it was; it looked to Char as if she'd taken thick wax, raked it along her head once or twice, and called it good.

Her eyes were an electric blue, set off by eyelashes thickly coated with mascara, giving her a wide-eyed expression. She had deep crow's feet around her eyes, Char assumed from many years of smiling and laughing.

"Ohhhh, hello, you must be my new neighbor. I saw the commotion of movers the last couple of days, and I've been anxious to come introduce myself—but thought it best to let the activity simmer down before bombarding you. I understand I can be a bit much," the neighbor said, laughing heartily at herself.

"Nice to meet you. My name's Char, and this is Asa." She offered her hand, which the gregarious neighbor clasped warmly with both hands. Her fingers were laden with many baubles, and she shook Char's hand vigorously; then, strangely, the woman held on for an extra moment or two. Char thought she saw a flash of concern cross the woman's face. Char was about to jerk her hand away, but just as suddenly, the neighbor let go. She bent down to Asa with a big smile as if nothing strange had just happened, bracelets and necklaces tinkling and jangling. She tousled Asa's fur as he bounced up and down and wagged his tail.

"He's a bouncing ball of fur, isn't he? Well, pleasure to meet you two as well. Char's your name, you say?" she said, standing and putting her hands to her hips. "What is that short for, Charlyne? Charla?" she asked with gusto.

"Charlotte, actually."

The neighbor crossed her arms and tapped her cheek before she clicked her tongue decidedly. "Oh, Char doesn't do, no siree. I think you're a Charlie. Yep, that's right. You don't mind, do you? If I call you Charlie?" she said, peering at Char, waiting for her reaction.

Char nodded in disbelief but deference and replied, "Sure, why not. Actually, some of my closest friends call me Charlie." She gave the woman a pursed-lipped smile, wondering how her new neighbor could have guessed her childhood nickname.

"Then we must become best of friends! I'm Morris, Morris McCall, if you must know, but you can call me Moe," she said with another guffaw.

"Funny, Moe was the name of my pet cat growing up," Charlotte said, while eyeing Moe almost suspiciously.

"Oh, don't look so surprised, Charlie. God of the universe definitely intended for our paths to cross. Synchronicity, my dear! Oh, how fun." Moe clapped her hands in front of her face, her eyes even wider with excitement.

Charlotte felt taken by Moe's energy in that moment. It was honest. Moe was carefree, something Char yearned to be herself.

They exchanged phone numbers and said their good-byes after Char promised to have Moe over as soon as she was settled in.

Char made her way through the complex's low-ceilinged parking garage to her white convertible, a purchase her daughter had insisted she make, saying, "It has to be a Mercedes, Mom, seriously. We'll be in LA, and I'll have to borrow it on occasion!" Char laughed at how easy it had become over the past several years for her to be swayed by her daughter. *A mother's guilt,* she thought, opening her driver's side door. Asa hopped inside, jumped to the passenger seat, and waited patiently for Char to buckle them both up.

She had just started her car and was pulling out to the main road when her phone rang. She pushed the button on her steering wheel to answer. Her heart skipped a beat when she heard her son's voice coming through her car's speakers.

"Hey, Mom, whatcha up to?"

"Blake, honey, how are you?" Her son would be a senior at NYU in September and was interning on a movie set in Canada; his goal was to become a director one day.

"Good, doing really good. Learning tons and having a blast, despite the millionth voice mail reminder from Grandma Pam that her birthday's coming up."

"Oh, that's right." Charlotte wouldn't be receiving a call from her mother, nor would she be making a call to wish her a happy birthday. They hadn't spoken in quite some time. Charlotte preferred to keep intact what little self-esteem she had left, and her mother enjoyed breaking it down.

"What kind of grandma does that? You could have done a little better by us in the grandma department, Mom. I mean, come on."

Blake had a long-running joke with Char, teasing her for giving him the most challenging grandmother ever. Of course, he didn't really blame his mother. No one can pick family, but it was a way to ease the tension that always came with any contact with his grandmother.

"I can't say I'm surprised, Blake. But I can say I'm sorry. You deserve better," Char said with a sigh.

"Mom, you know I'm joking. It is what it is, right? Anyway, I was able to sneak off to a grocery store to send her a card, and I called in a flower delivery for her too. That should quiet her down, though she probably would have preferred a bottle of gin. Either way, I won't hear from her until Christmas, so that's something." Charlotte could hear the disgust in his voice and it made her sad.

"I know you don't mean to sound so cold-hearted, Blake. But I understand Grandma hasn't made it easy on any of us."

"I shouldn't give you a hard time, since you got the brunt of it. She's your mom. I couldn't imagine." Blake was a sweet boy with a big heart. Char smiled to herself, though it was a smile with a shadow of pain that would likely never abate.

"That's in the past, right, Blake? I have you and Aubrie Elle. What more could a mom want?" she said as she came to a stop sign, pausing to look both ways before driving on.

There was so much in her past she wanted to hide from, but it would always be in her memory. What she could do was everything in her power to make sure the past would never repeat itself, especially with regard to her children. Her kids had always been her number one priority. She would fight the past and win this time. She had to.

"You may not have hit the lottery on the parent front, but you sure did on the kid front."

Char could practically hear Blake's smile, and she knew he was joking, but she agreed wholeheartedly. "I'll second that. What a lifesaver." She laughed through the pang she felt deep in her chest. She loved her kids so much it hurt. They were her everything, and she knew how lucky she was; they kept her going when nothing else in the world could.

"Thanks, Mom. Aubrie and I do what we can. We just want to know that you're okay, you know?"

"I'm fine, honey. Don't worry about me. You just focus on learning all you can with your internship."

"Speaking of, sorry, Mom, I actually should be getting back. Call time's in a few minutes."

"Oh, okay, sweetheart. It was wonderful to hear your voice, Blake. Call me again when you can."

"I will. And, Mom, I love you."

Char put her hand to her heart and smiled. "I love you too, Blake."

She pushed another button to hang up the phone, and blinked away tears. Despite the pain and trauma she had endured at times, she knew she was blessed. Her kids were her rock, and she wished her parents had felt the same way about her.

She tried to focus on her drive but realized she kept returning to thoughts of her mother. She suddenly felt empty. Even though she was able to joke cavalierly about her childhood with Blake, doing so would invariably send her back to a plethora of unhappy memories she'd sooner forget.

Before even being born into this world, Char had suffered loss. She had never known her biological father, due not to death but to abandonment—and according to Charlotte's mother, Pam, it was all Charlotte's fault. Pam had made no secret of it.

Pam had become pregnant with Charlotte a month after delivering Charlotte's older brother. It was too much, too soon for Char's father, and he filed for divorce. Pam loved to regale the story of how her ex-husband only fought for custody of his son, and how, when he lost, he left town, never to be heard of again.

Pam remarried soon after Charlotte was born, and her second husband had been a violent man who resented being a stepfather—until he also divorced her. From an early age, Charlotte was well aware she had been an unwanted pregnancy and an unwanted child.

As Charlotte matured, she began to question her mom's story. Maybe her father hadn't run away from her but from her mother. Though she never quite convinced herself she wasn't to blame, she did develop a feeling of kinship with the dad she never knew; they both shared the desire to run away.

"You have reached your destination," declared Char's navigation system. She was thankful for the car's command snapping her from the past before she became mired in it yet again.

As she pulled in to the parking lot, she furrowed her brow—she wasn't sure if there were any parking spaces left, but then she finally found one, so narrow she'd nearly overlooked it. "Very last one; we lucked out, Asa," she said, smiling down at her pup.

Charlotte had read that Solstice Canyon parking was limited, so she'd hoped that going during the workweek, on a Monday no less, would make it easier to find a spot. As soon as Char pulled in, Asa started pawing at his seat. "Hold on, Asa, we'll be on our hike soon. Just let me throw my hair up. I'll be quick." She loved Asa's enthusiasm and was grateful how easy it was for him to put a smile on her face.

She pulled down the visor and flipped open the mirror; her light-green eyes weren't happy with the mess staring back. She fished a hair band out of her bag and worked her fingers through her thick strawberry blond hair, making the best ponytail she could muster without a brush. Her peaches-and-cream complexion was sensitive to the sun's rays, so she dabbed sunscreen over the bridge of her small, straight nose and made sure to make a few quick sweeps over her delicate cheekbones.

She knew she was a little pale, which was normal for a Pacific Northwesterner, and one of Irish descent to boot, but she hoped to turn from a creamy white to a golden peach after a few weeks in the warm California sun.

She grabbed Asa's leash, threw her small saddlebag over her shoulder, and got Asa buckled up in his harness, which was no small chore, with his enormously fluffy coat and incessant bouncing. As Char walked through the parking lot toward the trailhead, a black sports car caught her eye. It looked eerily similar to her late husband's prized custom Italian coupe. She wondered if a similarly egotistical man owned the car.

She laughed to herself, remembering her husband Beau's unapologetic sense of entitlement. He had worked hard and fairly for his success and made it a point to reward himself as he saw fit, no matter how ostentatious. He was a man who always got what he wanted. Just like his love for her, he had been a force to be reckoned with. While she had plenty of painful memories, the majority of her time with Beau was not part of them.

She reminded herself again that she wasn't there to delve into the past but to forge ahead with her future. She gently forced herself to shelve her memories in favor of focusing on the present, and soon she was lost to the beautiful surroundings of the tree-and-boulder-lined trail.

She and Asa came around a bend to find the remains of an old homestead that a sign explained had burned down years prior. Her stomach turned, and she squeezed her eyes shut for a moment. Searing pain came out of nowhere. Heartbreak, betrayal, fear. On wobbly legs Char fled the scene, desperate to outrun her most painful secret.

Asa kept at her heels as Char ran from the memory. Her eyes, blurry with unshed tears, marred her vision of the narrowing trail. She lost her footing off the edge of the trail and instinctively let go of Asa's leash to prevent taking him down with her. She fought to stay upright but twisted her ankle and fell down the sharp slope, scraping her hands and hurting her left wrist before rolling to a stop several feet off the trail.

Charlotte sat dazed and dizzy for a few moments before searing pain brought her around. Ignoring her injuries, she called out to Asa, who at this point was God-knows-where, as she struggled to inch back up to the trail using her elbows and uninjured foot. The effort winded her too quickly. She realized she needed help.

She checked her phone, and of course it had no reception. Not that she had anyone she could call locally. She could have called 911 maybe, but her injuries weren't dire. She waited for what seemed like forever and was about to lose hope of anyone coming by when, to her relief, a man came around the corner with Asa in his arms.

She gasped, thinking she recognized him. *That can't be Ash.* He was walking under the shadow of a sycamore tree. She couldn't see if it was really him, but regardless, her heart started beating out of her chest. Her stomach turned, and she wished she could run. *Oh my God, it's him.*

As he came through the shadows, relief flooded over her with the realization she was mistaken; it wasn't her ex-lover. Her racing heartbeat calmed, and she felt she could breathe again, but the scare had put her guard up to high alert.

As the man neared, Char could see how she had gotten confused. He too was tall and athletically built, but then she could also see the differences. This man was wearing a ball cap on backward—something her ex would never do—was more thick and muscular, and had light eyes. She couldn't yet tell if they were blue or gray. They were similar but with enough difference to not make her jump out of her skin. What they had most in common was the attraction factor. Char would be willing to wager this man could have the attention of any woman he wanted. *Except me,* she told herself.

"Hey, what happened here? Are you okay?" he asked as he navigated down the ledge.

"I'll be fine, thank you. That's my dog. I lost my footing, and he got away from me." She was curt but relieved on the inside that Asa was safe and sound.

"He didn't push you down the hill, did he?" he said jokingly.

Char didn't reply. She didn't want to seem too friendly.

"Sorry, probably not the right time for telling jokes. Are you hurt?"

He had a deep voice with a hint of an accent. *A Southern drawl, Texan maybe,* Char thought. Another man with an alluring accent—all the more reason to be on high guard.

"I don't think it's serious. I was about to get up—I was just catching my breath." Char was embarrassed and uncomfortable. She was loath to be sitting there helpless and tried in vain to push herself up with her good foot and hand.

"Whoa there, you don't want to risk making your injuries worse; can I take a look before you try to get up? I'm Emmett, by the way. And you?"

He set Asa down, and Asa leapt into Char's lap, panting as if he had run a marathon. She hugged him to her, grateful to have something between herself and Emmett.

"I'm Charlotte, and this is Asa." Reluctantly she let Emmett approach to take a look at her injuries. He gently held her wrist and carefully assessed the swelling.

"Nice to meet you, Charlotte. Sorry we aren't meeting under better circumstances. You too, little guy." He smiled and ruffled Asa's head.

"I'm not a doctor, but I've had enough injuries of my own to make a basic assessment," he said confidently. Char noted he seemed almost proud to claim his injurious past.

"You didn't hit your head anywhere when you fell, did you?" His eyes met hers to check the size of her pupils, and for a moment Charlotte's desperate need for isolation inexplicably vanished, and she found herself lost in his beautiful gray eyes. Before she knew it, his hand was reaching for her cheek, and she flinched back, startling both of them.

Emmett quickly dropped his hand and leaned back. His cheeks flushed. "I'm sorry. You've got some leaves in your hair." He pointed to her ponytail.

Her guard went up again, and she looked at him warily as she picked the leaves out and gave him a sharp thank-you.

He cleared his throat and refocused on her ankle. "At the least, you've got a couple of bad sprains, Charlotte. You definitely shouldn't put any weight on that ankle. I'm going to need to carry you out of here."

She could feel her cheeks burn red-hot with embarrassment and apprehension. "What? No. I appreciate your help, but I'm sure I can make it out myself." Char knew she was lying to herself and to him. She was in a lot of pain. She needed his help, but her two most pressing needs were diametrically opposed.

"Hey, I get it. You don't know me from Adam. I'm sorry about that. But here's my cell phone. I've got my mom on speed-dial. You can call her for a character reference if you'd like."

"Nice thought, but there's no reception up here. I already tried." Charlotte didn't know what else to say. All she knew was that she was so uncomfortable she was breaking out in a sweat.

"Look, I promise I don't bite, and your little guy here seems to think it's an okay idea." Asa had jumped out of her lap and begun bouncing up to playfully nip at Emmett's face. He laughed and tried to settle him down. It wasn't lost on Char that Asa did seem to like him; he was usually leery around men.

She grabbed Asa to stop him from jumping at Emmett and held him in tight, like a security blanket. "Thanks for catching Asa. I appreciate all of this, but I don't know." Char looked around and wondered if anyone else might come by, a group of women maybe. But Emmett was still the only one around, and she found her eyes settling on him for a moment. His smile was magnetic, with dimples set deep. His square-set jaw and the hint of a cleft in his chin added to his masculinity. His eyes exuded a kindness that was almost palpable.

He smiled at her and took a deep breath. He tilted his head to the side and spoke softly. "Charlotte, listen, you need my help, and while it's pretty clear you want me to take a hike, no pun intended, I'm not going to just abandon you here."

Char pursed her lips together and prayed to God she wouldn't cry. Besides her son and doctors, she hadn't so much as spoken to a man in nearly a year. She wondered how on earth it was that the first man to have a conversation with her was saying exactly what she had once longed to hear, yet it was coming from a complete stranger.

She mused at the painful contradiction, then realized maybe it wasn't a contradiction. Maybe only a stranger would dare stand by her. Maybe there really was something wrong with her, and this was the proof—but she snapped herself out of her brooding to make her decision on the here and now. She looked into his kind eyes and managed to give him a nod of acquiescence.

"There we go. I knew you'd come to your senses." He bent down and swept her up with little effort. She winced at the pain in her ankle. She didn't want to admit it, but she was thankful he had come to her rescue.

She was pressed against his chest and completely out of her comfort zone being cradled in his arms. She hadn't so much as shaken a man's hand in over a year, yet here she was thrust into the embrace of a complete stranger, enveloped in his scent, a mix of spring-scented soap and perspiration. She was awash in his pheromones, and she fought all the way down the hill not to become intoxicated by it.

They made small talk on the way down, and Asa behaved on his leash, sensing it wasn't time for fooling around. Char wondered at Emmett's ability to carry her for so long without needing a break.

She could tell he was doing his best to keep her mind off the pain, chatting her up and attempting to make her laugh. She appreciated it, but couldn't allow herself to come out of her shell, though she knew if she were a different person, she would have been swept off her feet both figuratively and literally.

"There's my car, thank you." Char felt a sense of relief as they made their way to the parking lot. She was happy to be able to get out of his arms. So many difficult thoughts and emotions swirled within her in such a small amount of time. Even this was too much for her.

"Careful, easy does it," he said, gently setting her down by her car, so she could lean on it for support. His strong hands held her hips, and Charlotte gripped his arms for stability before subtly pushing them away. On her cue, he let go and stepped back. Glancing up, Charlotte thought she caught a glimpse of a smile.

"Is there someone who can come get you? I don't think there's much chance for you to be able to drive with that ankle, let alone your wrist. If not, I'd be happy to take you to the hospital."

"No, thank you, but I'll be fine. I'm sure I can manage."

Emmett pulled at the back of his neck. "Come on now, Charlotte, you've let me help you this far. Are we really going to have to argue this? Clearly you're in no condition to drive. And who will watch Asa while you're being seen?"

Char knew the practical thing would be to accept his offer. The pain in her ankle was only getting worse, and if she were being honest with herself, she knew she wouldn't be able to put enough weight on the pedals to drive. What *would* she do with Asa?

"You're right; I can't do this on my own. Thank you."

Emmett smiled.

She gave Emmett her car keys, and he got Asa's carrier and seatbelt harness out of her car, then told her to sit tight and he'd pull his car out for her, as the cars were all parked mere inches from each other. Char shook her head when she saw which one he got into. Of course his was the sports car she had noticed earlier.

Before he pulled out onto the main road, Emmett called one of his friends at the hospital. "Hey, partner, got a favor to ask. I have a friend, Charlotte, who's fallen into a bit of trouble. We're out at Solstice Canyon, and she took a tumble. Her ankle's not looking so good. Great, bud, thanks. We're heading out now; be there in twenty." He smiled at Charlotte. "We'll be met at the door."

· · ·

On the way to the hospital, Emmett continued his attempts to make small talk. He shared that in his younger years he'd been the proverbial bachelor with a commitment phobia, and was still in awe that he had somehow ended up married to his first wife for a full ten years.

She noticed he had said "first wife," which meant there must have been at least a second, but Char knew better than to pry. She had learned over the years that asking personal questions of someone invariably opened the door for them to respond in kind.

"That marriage was tough. I wasn't ready, but out of it I became a better man, in part thanks to my twin boys, Kai and Noa. They'll be sophomores at USC this fall. They're in Europe for another month, taking a much-needed break from college life. Seems like yesterday they were running around in diapers, and now I'm Skyping them from across continents." Emmett rubbed his brow and tugged at the back of his ball cap. Char could tell he missed his boys deeply. She knew the feeling.

He looked over at Char with a bright smile and changed the subject. "But enough about me. How about you? What's your story?"

Char settled on the one subject she was always happy to discuss, her two kids, but she kept it short. She saw no sense in getting to know this man she had no intention of seeing again once she got home to her new condo.

When they reached the hospital, as promised, an attendant was at the entrance, ready with a wheelchair to help her inside. Emmett parked the car and was at Charlotte's side by the time she was finished with the paperwork. He had Asa in his carrier and let her know he'd taken him for a potty walk. Though she was in a lot of pain by then, she managed a thankful smile.

"Perfect timing. Here's Lou now," Emmett said, as a handsome doctor with an olive complexion and dark eyes dancing with energy greeted Emmett and Charlotte in the lobby.

"Emmett, hello, and this must be your friend Charlotte." He looked at her chart for her last name. "Flight. Great last name, by the way. I'm Dr. Samuel. Emmett here knows me as Lou." He smiled at Charlotte and shook her hand. "You took a fall on your hike? Let's see what we can do for you."

He looked at Emmett. "Thanks for calling me, Emmett, I'm happy to help. We won't be too long, but looks as if you've got someone to keep you company anyway." He nodded to Asa in his carrier. "Don't get too comfortable. We'll get Charlotte out of here in no time," he said over his shoulder as he led Charlotte and a nurse through the doors to an exam room.

Dr. Samuel got right to work assessing her injuries, but it didn't take long before he started making small talk. "So, you and Emmett, have you been dating long?"

Char was nervous about being in an ER again; it brought back memories she'd rather not revisit. But Dr. Samuel's presumptuousness took her by surprise. Were doctors supposed to be so familiar?

"We're not dating; he just happened by after I slipped on my hike. We've literally just met." She pursed her lips and looked anywhere but at the doctor.

Dr. Samuel ducked down to meet her eyes, a smile escaping his lips. "I'll tell you, you lucked out with the likes of Emmett happening by. One of the kindest guys I know." He took a moment to type something into his computer. "I've ordered a scan for your ankle; now let's take a look at this wrist."

Despite the doctor's nosiness, Charlotte was grateful that Emmett had called Dr. Samuel. She had never been in and out of an emergency room so quickly in her life. All told, Char had a grade-two ankle sprain, which required a walking boot and crutches. It was serious, but could have been much worse. After three to four weeks, she'd be able to get the boot off and put weight on the ankle again. Her sprained wrist wasn't as bad as her ankle and only required that she wear a removable splint for several weeks.

A nurse wheeled her back to the lobby with Dr. Samuel following. Emmett jumped up to join them. "We have an all-night pharmacy where you can get a set of crutches. If you want to fill your prescription now, you can also do that, but this should be enough to get you through the night," he said as he gave her a small envelope. "But be sure to take it with food. You'll be able to switch to an over-the-counter pain medication in a few days. And don't forget to call one of the physical therapists on the list I gave you as soon as possible. Good therapists' schedules fill fast."

He thanked Char for being a trooper of a patient and wished her a fast recovery. Charlotte thanked him too. Emmett and he said their good-byes and made plans for a barbecue at Emmett's soon.

They went to the pharmacy to fill her prescription and pick up a pair of crutches. Charlotte wanted to walk out on her own accord, but Emmett insisted she use the wheelchair and promised her she shouldn't be in any rush to start depending on the crutches.

Getting into Emmett's car was even challenging with the protection of the wrist splint and boot, but they managed. Emmett reached over and helped buckle her in. Despite the pain she was in physically, Char was chagrined to be responding yet again their close proximity.

Char shoved those feelings down and revisited all the reasons why she couldn't be involved with another man, even though Emmett seemed like a great guy. Meeting a good friend of his, an orthopedic surgeon no less, who gave him a shining recommendation, corroborated her instinct that he was a decent man, but then again maybe she was just convincing herself of that since she was in dire straits and needed his help.

"There's a fast food place right around the corner here. I know you've got to be feeling some pain right now. Let's take care of it."

They were at a drive-through in no time, and while Emmett tried to insist she order a burger like he did, Char had no appetite due to the pain. She ordered only coffee with extra cream and a bottle of water for her medicine.

Before pulling out of the drive-through, Emmett turned to her. "So, where do you live?"

As he piloted over the cityscape, his eyes saw but didn't register the beauty of the eclectic and energetic mix of buildings rising from the busy streets. Nor did he really see the multiple bridges that arched over the sparkling Willamette River, not even the majestic snow-capped Mount Hood in the distance ascending the cloudless blue expanse. He could barely hear the rapid thud of the propeller overhead while he struggled to stay focused enough to safely land his helicopter on the helipad perched atop a building in downtown Portland. He was returning to this office from a meeting in Seattle. He had the sense that it had been quite productive, though at the moment he couldn't even recall what it had been about and hadn't a clue how he'd gotten through it.

Charlotte was on his mind. To his chagrin, it would be one of those days, a struggle to the end: a struggle to stay focused, a struggle to maintain self-control, and a struggle to forget her. On the outside, no one would be the wiser. He was quite adept at maintaining scrupulous control, never allowing anyone to witness the utter weakness of what he might be struggling with deep inside, be it fear, uncertainty, or, God forbid, sorrow.

He landed his helicopter and walked the few blocks to the only high-rise in the city to provide on-site concierge services. He nodded to the security on duty in the main lobby and stepped into the elevator. He absentmindedly hit the button for his firm's floor and then fixed his eyes on the opaque panel and submitted to a retinal scan, a safety measure required to gain access.

Julian catered to the uber-wealthy, providing personal security services that entailed everything from outfitting homes and businesses with state-of-the-art security systems to intelligence gathering and private security detail. He also provided other services that, for legal purposes, couldn't be officially documented or advertised.

Despite being the son of a wealthy British diplomat, whose well-heeled footsteps he could have followed in, he craved adventure, and after university he chose to serve in the British Army's special forces, earning top honors there. He then moved to the British Secret Intelligence Service, where he also excelled. His service gained him a wealth of knowledge, though people who knew him best were surprised he'd stayed within the confines of government bureaucracy as long as he had. However, he had bided his time and, at the apex of opportunity, entered the private sector and propelled himself to the top of his field.

Once it reached Julian's floor, the elevator cued its TV panels to display the lobby. Seeing nothing amiss, he pushed the all-clear button, and the doors opened. He walked with authority through the lobby of his firm and nodded to the receptionist, whose cheeks flushed at the sight of him—a common occurrence, despite the fact she'd worked for him for nearly three years. She managed a meek nod back; he had that effect on women.

To say he was handsome would be an understatement. He was mesmerizing. His height alone would catch anyone's eye, but at six foot four, with broad shoulders, a toned physique, and a confident air, he not only caused heads to turn, but drew stares from men and women alike. He kept his silky, dark-brown hair trimmed short, parted to the side. His dark and delicately arched brows, reminiscent of those painted on a Hummel figurine with a fine brush, protected his intelligent brown eyes. There was a near elegance about him, but his aristocratic nose and chiseled jaw gave him an air of superiority, and his strong persona didn't betray the impression.

He made his way down the hall toward his office and waved off his executive assistant Mara, whom he didn't doubt had several pressing messages for him. He slammed his door shut and leaned against the double doors for a moment. He chastised himself, reminding himself to get a grip.

Usually at the most inopportune times, confusion would come over him, his head would spin, and he'd suddenly be wondering whom he was and where he'd been and why. Most disturbing for him were the times he would feel as if he were dropped into the middle of a conversation. Now he felt another episode coming on, but refused to be sucked into the rabbit hole yet again. He knew from experience all he had to do was focus on anything else but the creeping sense of madness.

He focused on his office, a place he'd spent much time in the last few years, since moving from London to open a satellite office in the States. He let his eyes scan the perimeter of his office, and as he focused on the details of the architecture, furniture, and décor, anything to distract him from the chaos within, he slowly felt himself regaining composure. He took in the beauty of the glistening mahogany built-ins and noted the colors in the prisms cast on the floor from the sunlight beaming upon the clear, sparkling crystal decanters embellishing his bar cart. He appreciated the tall wall of glass that overlooked the Willamette River and welcomed the sun. With much relief, he found that his exercise had worked and he was again anchored to reality.

He took off his suit jacket, threw it onto a side chair, and set to work at his desk. He'd recently received more disturbing news. Not only was he constantly battling his past, but he was also battling a corporate enemy he and his team were still working furiously to identify.

Someone was trying to take down his company, destroy his reputation. Whoever it was had committed crimes against them, felonies that could put them away for a long time.

He knew he couldn't go to the feds for help in the investigation and risk public scrutiny, or worse, be implicated in crimes of his own. He was little worried about any investigation into his firm; they were experts at covering their tracks, but he was worried about word getting around that they were having security issues. It would be a death knell to his firm's reputation if it were ever revealed they were struggling with keeping their own company safe from attack. Trust was everything in his business, and clients would drop them in droves if they knew what he was dealing with.

Julian wasn't giving up, and he had every confidence that he'd prevail. Once he caught the culprit, he'd enjoy making his enemy pay, one way or another. In the meantime, he'd hired a PR exec to formulate preemptive counters. So far she had proven successful at keeping a tight lid on their internal problems and projecting a strong front to the public and their peers.

He heard a knock at the door, and it frustrated him to no end. He pushed the intercom and barked to his assistant, "Mara, have you bothered to look at your phone to see the 'Do not disturb' light is on?"

The door opened anyway, and in came his public relations executive, Taryn. She was tall and slender, five foot ten, with dark-brown shoulder-length hair that hung in loose waves. Julian noticed she was smiling mischievously. "Good morning, Boss. I came to bring you a couple of those reports I've been working on, and to tell you happy anniversary." She tossed some folders onto the console but stayed at the closed double doors and leaned against them. She had seduction in her eyes. He could tell she wanted to play, but he was in no mood. For her own good, she needed to leave. Today he was Mr. Hyde, not the amiable Dr. Jekyll. He fought to maintain his cool.

"Anniversary. I don't understand," he said in his proper British accent, his voice deceptively even.

She smiled confidently at him as she unbuttoned her fuchsia silk blouse, untucked it from her black figure-hugging skirt, and threw it on top of the reports, revealing a black lace bra.

"We've been seeing each other for six months as of today, and I think that calls for a celebration," she said with a laugh. He could see she was just living in the moment, carefree and fearless, but today he wouldn't be appreciating her zest for life.

He pushed out of his chair and made his way to her. Her eyes widened, and he could see she felt a rush of heated adrenaline, anticipating a passionate interlude. He towered over her, and she put her hands to his chest and craned up for a kiss, closing her eyes. He looked down at her angular, beautiful face for a moment and felt nothing but frustration. As alluring as Taryn was, she wasn't who he wanted her to be. He stiffened in resolve, grabbed her shirt off the table, and pulled it around her shoulders.

Her eyes flew open. "Julian, is something wrong?"

He wanted to tell her yes, everything was wrong, that he was making a big, selfish mistake, that he shouldn't be with her, that he wasn't who she or even he thought he was, and that she should run because he was dangerous and couldn't be trusted, but he knew better than to reveal himself. To survive, he played the part he needed to play, a successful and busy corporate CEO who was always in control.

"Taryn, my doors were shut for a reason. I'll have to dock Mara's pay for letting you in."

"You know, if I didn't know any better, I might accuse you of seeing someone on the side, the way you're so hot and cold toward me." Her voice carried a challenging tone.

Now she wanted to argue. He felt his day couldn't get much worse.

He sighed. "Taryn, we agreed to be exclusive months ago. I don't go back on my word. It's quite offensive that you would accuse me of doing exactly that. Must I remind you of my distaste for stormy relationships?"

He saw Taryn was incensed but trying to quell it as best she could. He'd made it clear to her throughout their relationship he wouldn't tolerate any outbursts, and that for her to have one would be a firm deal breaker. In a previous life, he wouldn't have been so cold, but he just didn't have it in him to be patient with anyone anymore, no matter how lovely.

Taryn didn't look at him and focused only on buttoning her shirt and tucking it back into her skirt. "No, no need to remind me."

"I appreciate the overture, I do, but not today, darling. Now, you really must go. I've too many irons in the fire at the moment." He reached around her and opened the door, making clear there would be no more discussing it. He kissed her on the head, an afterthought. Without another word, she left with head down, her arms wrapped around herself, and he shut the door.

He squeezed his eyes shut for a moment before he turned on his heel and sucked in a deep breath. He exhaled in a low growl and made a beeline for his bar cart to pour himself a stiff drink. He gulped half of it down before he reached his desk and slammed himself into his leather chair, doing the same with his glass to the desk. He leaned over, elbows on knees, and buried his head in his hands and pulled at his hair.

Before thinking better of it, he sat up and finished his scotch and welcomed the pain.

Today would be a struggle.

Damn Charlotte.

God damn himself.

Birds were chirping and sunlight was boring through Char's eyes, and so was a throbbing pain in her head, wrist, and ankle. *Good God, what's going on?* Charlotte opened her eyes and threw off the covers in a panic. She had no idea where she was.

She looked around the room. The walls were a light caramel color, and dark wood blinds were allowing the sun in through the barely open slats. The bedroom set was sleek, and the décor was minimal.

She then saw the wrap on her ankle, and it all came back to her, the hike, the fall, Emmett. *Am I in Emmett's bedroom?* She figured she must be, because the last thing she remembered was leaving the hospital with him. Why wasn't she at her condo? What happened? And most important, how did she get into one of his T-shirts? Even if it was as innocent as him getting her out of her grimy hiking clothes, a sickening thought still washed over her. Did Emmett see her scars? She couldn't go there unless she wanted to come apart at the seams, so she closed the thought down as best she could.

The bedroom door was open a crack, and Char could hear the familiar scratching pitter-patter of Asa running down the hall. She called to him, and he came bouncing in, trying to get up to her. She had to hold him. She put her good foot down and slid out of the bed onto the floor. Her ankle was pounding, but thankfully Asa took her mind off the pain. He jumped into her lap, licking and nipping at her face. He seemed to be saying, "I'm glad you're alive!"

Just then she heard a soft knock at the door. Char startled. "C-come in."

It was Emmett. He stepped inside, sporting a wide smile and carrying a tray of coffee, which he set on the dresser. Char had thought he was attractive the day before, but that morning he was simply breathtaking. He had on linen pants that accentuated his long legs and trim waist. His crisp light-purple shirt with two buttons undone highlighted his broad shoulders and toned chest. She hadn't been able to tell the day before because of the baseball cap, but Emmett had curls in his hair, to her surprise. She decided they gave him a boyish charm. His whole look was quite a change from his athletic T-shirt and cargo shorts from the day before. Despite her fear of how she got into his bed, she couldn't help but be stirred by him.

"Morning—how you feeling? I'm going to assume you're only on the floor to greet Asa and that you didn't fall out, right?" Emmett flashed his dimples, teasing her. While his smile did work to put her at ease, Char still kept her guard up. She gripped Asa.

"How did I end up at your house in one of your shirts? I want an explanation. Now." She tried to look authoritative—in vain, she could only imagine—sitting on the floor in his oversize T-shirt and with a messy bedhead to boot.

He looked down at her, and his dimples tugged at a smile.

"Well," he drawled, crossing his arms, "I had a lady in my car last night who was in quite a bit of pain, who also apparently took a double dose of her prescription. Whether that was by design or not remains to be discovered. Anyway, before said lady could finish her coffee, she had passed clean out, and I was left with only partial directions to her home. As a matter of fact, I had to circle back to the hospital so my buddy Lou, Dr. Samuel, could alleviate my worry that she'd just overdosed. So, with a second clean bill of health for the night, I was given the okay to just let her sleep it off. And since she passed out before being so kind as to give me her home address, I was given no other option but to take her home with me. And so you know, it was my live-in housekeeper, Anna, who got you into my T-shirt. Scout's honor," he said, holding up his fingers.

Char had never been more embarrassed. That is, until she was horrified to feel heavy tears escaping down her cheeks left and right. Charlotte wasn't a crier, but they were angry, defensive tears, so that had to count for something.

She had to defend herself. "I would never abuse prescription pills, and I'm mortified this happened. But thank you for taking me in. If you need to be reimbursed for anything, I'll see to it that you are, and I'm sorry for the inconvenience." Her shaky fingers flicked away one tear after another.

A look of anguish washed over Emmett's face as he knelt down. "Hey, no, Char, I'm sorry. I'm just joking. Of course you didn't mean to knock yourself out. Please, this is no imposition at all. I'm just happy you weren't alone, that I could help you." He reached out as if he wanted to wipe away her tears, but quickly withdrew his hand, perhaps having thought better of it, and sighed.

"Listen, Char, I actually have to make a quick run to my office. But Anna is here. She should be bringing you some breakfast soon. If you need anything, don't hesitate to ask. I won't be long, and when I get back, I'll be happy to take you home." He stood for a moment and seemed to relax when he saw Charlotte relax.

"Here, let me help you up," he said as he held his hand out and helped her back up to the bed. "I brought you some coffee. Anna will be in soon with breakfast. Afterward, she can help you with a shower." This time Emmett blushed, and he suddenly looked guilty. Charlotte wondered if she had caught him with a not-so innocent wish to help her himself, and hoped that was not what she saw in his eyes.

"That is, if you're comfortable. I mean, if you think you need to." Emmett stammered as he took another step back toward the door. "Anyway, Anna washed your clothes for you too. We've already taken Asa out twice, so don't worry about him. He already seems to think he has the run of the place." He babbled nervously. "I have to warn you, though, Anna has fallen in love with him already, so she may not let you take him home." He rubbed his neck and blushed as if he'd wanted to say something else but thought better of it. Instead he mumbled a quick good-bye and left.

Char wondered what the abrupt exit meant, but before she could give much thought, there was someone at the door again.

"Knock knock, señora?" Charlotte heard a lilting, feminine voice come through the door and welcomed her in. A slight-figured blonde woman, probably no more than ten or fifteen years older than Char, with huge brown eyes and a pleasant smile, came in. She was carrying a plate of eggs and fruit.

"You must be Anna?" Char eyed her, looking for any sign that Anna had seen her scars when helping her into Emmett's shirt the night before, and relaxed when she didn't sense any uneasiness.

"Yes, señora, how do you feel? You must be hungry; get settled in bed, and I'll bring the coffee tray over."

Charlotte did as she was asked, and Anna fussed with the tray, shifting things around to make it all fit. Then she fished a bottle from deep in the pocket of her work smock.

"You gave señor Emmett quite a scare last night. Here's your medicine. Emmett wanted me to help you in case you weren't sure how much to take." Anna winked at Char with a mischievous smile. She seemed oblivious to the embarrassment Char felt.

Char thought better of taking more codeine and asked instead for ibuprofen, with the hope it would be just strong enough to take the throbbing away. Anna went to fetch some.

When she returned, Anna said, "We don't have a shower chair. It will be easier for you to take a bath, and it will soothe your bruises from your fall. While you eat, if you like, I can start you a bath, and then help you in?" She chuckled as Asa bounced after her to the bathroom to draw the bath, not waiting for Char to answer.

Char knew better than to decline her offer. Bathing was going to be a difficult proposition for the next few weeks, so she figured she'd better take the help while she had it. She also knew that to accept Anna's help, she would have to set aside her fear of allowing anyone to see her without clothes on. Granted, she still couldn't be sure that Anna hadn't already seen her back, but regardless, it was still a scary proposition. Char had vowed to keep her dark past locked away forever, but the scars that still felt so new would forever threaten to betray her.

Char tried to keep her towel wrapped around her until the last possible second before sinking into the tub, but she couldn't stay completely covered. If Charlotte's scars shocked Anna, she didn't let on. Char thought perhaps Anna was too busy talking about Asa and her plans to keep him at Emmett's with her to notice the scar on her side that went from the bottom of her rib cage up to just under her arm, or the many marks on her back. The one just under her eye wouldn't mean much to the casual observer until what she could hide under a shirt was exposed. Char held her breath, waiting for Anna to ask, but she never did.

Sinking into the water, Char was able to let go and relax into the steaming water. For the moment, gone was the guilt for having imposed so much upon Anna and Emmett. With one leg hanging over the tub and an arm propped up with towels under her elbow, she enjoyed the view from the big picture window. A flowering tree with several birds fluttering around its branches reminded Char that she was in beautiful Southern California. Soon enough, she'd be back at her new condo, Aubrie and Chloe would arrive, and life would return to normal.

Charlotte wondered, though, if her life had ever been normal. With so much strife and struggle, all she could focus on now was avoiding any and all drama. She knew without a doubt that men were the number one cause of most of her life's troubles.

She also knew she had much to fight against herself. Despite all the pain and anguish caused by the men in her life, she wondered deep down if she'd really be able to write men off permanently. If she couldn't, she wasn't sure when she'd ever be ready to give in once again or how it would even be possible.

For her the problem was the more macho the guy, the more attracted she was. It was a recurring cycle of hers: to wind up chastising herself for falling for the most enigmatic, type-A, control freak. Why couldn't she fall in love with a placid accountant who wouldn't hurt a fly? No, she wanted the guy who pushed the limit, had something to prove—but it always turned out that what they were pushing was her; what they were proving was their power over her.

"Knock, knock, señora, I've come back," Anna called in her singsong voice through the bathroom door. Char smiled and called her in, and she helped Char out of the tub.

She got dressed and was thankful Anna had had the foresight to wash her clothes for her. She sat on the edge of the tub, across from the bathroom mirror, briskly running her fingers through her hair, and did her best to put it up in the least messy ponytail she could. She frowned at her reflection, noting the slight hollowness under her eyes, and wished she had her makeup with her. She couldn't help but want to look halfway decent in front of Emmett. She rolled her eyes and admonished herself to get a grip.

Anna called to Charlotte that Emmett was back from the office and ready to take Char to her condo. When she got outside, Char was surprised to see her car in Emmett's driveway. First thing that morning Emmett and Anna had gone back to retrieve it, and now Anna and Asa would follow Char and Emmett back to the condo.

As Charlotte sat not in his sports car but in a luxury sedan, she wondered what it meant to Emmett to have these cars that made such a statement.

"You have exceptional taste in cars, Emmett. What are you trying to prove by having these kinds of toys?" As soon as she said it, Char regretted it. She knew she sounded snippy and accusatory. *Oops.*

Emmett looked at her sideways, yet he said with a smile, "Actually, Char, I don't think my having a couple of fun cars qualifies as any kind of agenda. I'm a man. I like power and speed; it's not about trying to prove anything. I simply enjoy these cars."

"I didn't mean to come off like that. I shouldn't stereotype you—that was unfair of me." Char hoped he knew she was being sincere.

"Thank you—I appreciate that. But before we head out, I have to ask you an important question. Is it time for you to take your medication again? Because this time, I'm going to get your address into the navigation system before you take it, if you don't mind." Emmett was being facetious again, and thankfully Char could tell this time. She laughed and explained to him she'd be forgoing any more codeine for ibuprofen instead.

"I'd say that's a good plan. We've only known each other twenty-four hours, but I can say with confidence that you, ma'am, are a lightweight."

She laughed again. "I actually reread the bottle this morning, and

I'm sure I took the prescribed amount last night. I even counted out each pill to make sure."

"No need to defend yourself. I'm sorry I gave you such a hard time earlier. I meant nothing by it, I promise you," he said with a bright smile.

Emmett's easygoing nature put her at ease, and she surprised herself by broaching a personal question. "So, you must not be from here?"

"Why do you say?" Emmett deadpanned; then he let out a chuckle. "No, you're right. Born in Texas, but not entirely raised there, which is why my accent's not very strong. I came to California in my early teens. And you're an Oregonian, right?"

"I'm from up near Portland—Wilsonville, actually. I've vacationed down here on and off, taken my kids to Disneyland quite a few times. We love it. It sure beats the weather up north nine months out of the year. But I have to say, I'm feeling pretty out of my element here."

"California, the Beverly Hills way of life, can be difficult to get used to. I know the drill, but the whole status game…I don't play."

"I'm not so sure about that, Emmett," Char playfully chided. "You've got the mansion, the expensive cars, the requisite Rolex. I'm not sure you can really claim to not be playing the game." She smiled as she spoke.

"I concede that it could appear that way. But here's the thing—my house, a mansion? Compared to others in this neighborhood, it's a McMansion. The cars, well, regardless of where I lived, they'd be in my driveway. And the Rolex was a retirement gift. Playing the Hollywood game? I don't think so."

"Fair enough, but retirement? Aren't you a little young for that? And I thought you said you went to the office this morning."

"I was a kicker in the NFL for fifteen years. From *that* I retired, injury induced, unfortunately," he said, patting his knee, "but now I have a production company. We handle a lot of professional sports projects. I love it; I stay busy and have been able to remain in this industry I'm so passionate about. But the real question is, why haven't you recognized me?" Emmett asked with a laugh.

"That would be because I hate football. I don't begrudge anyone else who enjoys it, but I just can't feel good about watching young virile men hurt themselves for my entertainment. It's disgusting." Char shook her head, trying to erase the disturbing vision from her mind's eye.

"Whoa, darling, those are fighting words. 'Disgusting'? I can appreciate your concern, but entertainment value aside, men love to crash into each other regardless of who's watching. Do you have a problem with men exercising their God-given desire to pummel each other once in a while? It's all just fun and games." Emmett eyed her, looking ready to gauge her reaction.

Charlotte cast her eyes down. She sighed and spoke softly. "No, Emmett, I'm well aware of a man's need to indulge in his most primal of activities, namely, violence." Catching herself, Char took a deep breath and added, "But I digress; to each his own, right? Please don't take offense—football just isn't for me." She smiled brightly, hoping to dodge any melodrama.

"That's a pretty blanket statement about guys and violence. Care to share a little more about what you meant?"

Char couldn't believe she'd led him right there. "No, forget it. That came out wrong. I think the pain is getting to me, sorry. I'm just a little stressed about this whole situation." She hoped he'd drop it.

"No worries. I told you a bit about myself, what I do for a living. How about you?"

Although the conversation had turned toward her, Char was thankful for the change in subject. "Well, I was a young mom. By the time I should have been graduating from college, I was instead the mother of two. They are and always will be my pride and joy, so no regrets there. But after my divorce from Aubrie and Blake's dad, I did my best to make up for lost time, buckling down to work and school, and by the time I married again, I had my bachelor's, and my husband supported my going further, so I got my law degree as well."

"You're a married lawyer? Good for you." The disappointment in his voice betrayed his response, and he looked as if he could kick himself as soon as he said it.

"Oh, no, I'm sorry. Beau, my husband, died a couple of years ago." Char still marveled at her ability to talk about him without the pit in her stomach she thought would never go away. It took time, but the pain had subsided like everyone promised it would.

Emmett offered his sincere condolences.

"Thank you. It was tough, and I had to take over at my husband's firm upon his death. It was a lot to deal with." Char took a deep breath, knowing she was making the understatement of the year. "But I've been on sabbatical and am just now getting more involved again. Thankfully my role now as legal advisor doesn't require me to be physically present; Skype and e-mail are usually sufficient."

Char's cell phone rang. "It's the office. Shoot, I know why they're calling; we had a conference call early this morning. I need to get this," she said as she accepted the call. "This is Charlotte. Hi, Jonathan." She filled him in on what had been happening but implored him to keep it to himself—she didn't want any of her personal business to become general knowledge at the office. "I'm so sorry I missed the conference call but send me what you have, and I'll look it over and get back to you soon. Thanks, Jonathan." After getting off the phone with Jonathan, Char looked up and saw they were nearing her condo. "Up here, take the next left."

"Wow, nice neighborhood, Char—what a surprise."

"Surprise? What do you mean by that?"

"Oh, it's just I didn't have you on the radar as being—"

"The radar of being wealthy? I value my and my children's privacy. As soon as people discover you're wealthy, they suddenly think they know your type."

"Kind of like being a football player and being stereotyped as a violent, superficial jerk?"

"Touché," Charlotte said, tilting her head and mock saluting him. "But it takes time to get to know someone. I choose the when and the how much. Like you, I don't like being stereotyped for any reason. So, yes, I do choose to fly a bit under the radar," she said confidently.

"So, you don't like people butting into your business—I kind of got that about you," he said with a sly smile.

"You could say that," she said, shifting uncomfortably in her seat.

"So, if you guard your privacy and don't want to be judged by your assets, then why the multimillion-dollar condominium? You know, a few miles down from here is the Malibu Beach Trailer Park, if you really want to talk living under the radar." Charlotte glared at his suggestion, and he roared with laughter. "I'm just trying to be helpful; you could save a pretty penny by moving down the road a ways."

She smiled. "This property has the best security. It helps keep people out."

"Hmmm, interesting," he said, eyeing her once more.

Charlotte cringed, but didn't dare ask what he was thinking. Instead, she gave him the gate code and prayed she wasn't making a mistake trusting him.

He pulled through the gate, with Anna following in Char's convertible. Once they parked, Emmett walked Char to her front door. She stood there with the door open behind her for a moment, suddenly feeling awkward. *How do you say good-bye to a stranger when you just stayed the night at his house? What's the proper thank-you?*

Anna came up with Asa's carrier. As Charlotte set it inside the foyer, Emmett burst out laughing, startling her. She looked at him, utterly confused, and then he pointed incredulously at her entry. "Char, no way in hell you're staying here for the foreseeable future. Are you kidding me?"

"What are you talking about?"

"Stairs, Char? Really?"

She stood stunned for a moment as she looked into her foyer. Of course he was right. Her entry was only large enough for three people at best before stairs led the way up to her two floors. She felt foolish she hadn't thought about that in the first place.

"*Dios mio*, that will not do, no, no, no," Anna said, shaking her head in disapproval.

"Well, then, it's settled. You have to come back with us, Charlotte." Emmett snapped his fingers decisively.

Char shook her head before doing her best to try and convince Emmett and Anna that she'd be fine in a hotel for a few weeks, but they wouldn't have any of it. Anna reminded Char what a pain it would be taking Asa out for his walks and potty breaks in a hotel, and Emmett added what a help Anna could be to her for meals and baths.

Char felt pressured, but while she couldn't know Emmett that well yet, something inside her was telling her she could trust him—but who was she to trust her own instincts? Until now, they hadn't really panned out too well for her.

"You two have been so great to me, but I just can't see imposing upon you for three or even four weeks. That's a long time, Emmett." Char felt pretty worn out from the whole ordeal. She didn't feel like arguing, and they were partly right—she wasn't sure how she was going to make it on her own.

Emmett stepped closer to Char and put his hands on her shoulders. She was surprised at herself that she didn't step back. He lowered his voice and looked straight into her eyes. "Please, Charlotte, let me do this for you. I'd hate to think of you struggling out on your own until you're healed."

Emmett's touch should have triggered Char's defensiveness, but his low, tender voice and the sincerity she saw in his eyes diffused what would have been her typical reaction thus far. Her shoulders slumped; she was on the brink of giving in.

As if sensing her resolve weakening, Emmett pressed on. "And, if it makes you feel any better, I have an out-of-town assignment about a week from now. I'll be gone for several days, and you'll have the house to yourself. It's no big deal. Time will fly, and you'll be back in your own place before you know it."

"Señora, come to your senses," Anna implored.

Char looked at their pleading faces and hoped she was making the right decision. "I, I guess you guys have made some good points. I'll do it for Asa. He doesn't deserve to be holed up in a hotel room for weeks." She hoped Emmett's was a kindness without any twisted control issues. Was that even possible?

Emmett celebrated with a loud whoop, and Charlotte nearly jumped out of her skin. Laughing, Anna patted her shoulder and said, "Don't worry, you will get used to his exuberance."

"Ma'am," Emmett said to Charlotte. He held his arms out for her, and without any protestation, she allowed Emmett to sweep her up to her room on the third floor. She packed her bags while Anna gathered Asa's things.

Once back at Emmett's, Anna helped settle Char into his master bedroom, the only bedroom on the first floor. He assured Charlotte he was happy to take one of his boys' rooms upstairs. Emmett told her to relax and make herself at home. Char couldn't believe she was agreeing to the whole thing. She felt as if she were just going through the motions and figured in a few days it would all sink in.

For the first couple of days at Emmett's, Char found herself staying out of the way and simply observing. She would wait until the last second to come out of her room, even though he would greet her with the biggest smile, his dimples flashing each time. She realized she enjoyed listening in on Emmett's morning routine, whether it was hearing him chatting up Anna as she made their breakfast, their laughter coming through her bedroom door, or his whistling as he gathered his things to head out to his car. Joy emanated through the house and inevitably made Charlotte smile.

When she would finally venture out to the living room, without fail Anna was right there helping Charlotte get comfortable on the couch with the TV and her laptop, her foot propped up on a few pillows and with an assortment of things she might need at her fingertips: pens, the remote, drinks, and even snacks.

Char's firm thankfully kept her busy, since she never was one to waste a lot of time watching TV. She asked for as much work as possible to be sent her way, and they didn't disappoint. In the evenings, the three of them shared dinner prepared by Anna. Emmett, ever the gentleman, would help Charlotte to the table and insist she not help with the dishes.

After a few days, when Char's ankle settled down and the pain subsided, she was desperate to get out of the house. By Wednesday night, it was as if Emmett could read her mind. "What do you say tomorrow I take a half day and come get you for lunch? You've been stuck here for days. You'd probably like to get out."

"I think that's a great idea, thank you." Char hadn't wanted to ask him to take her anywhere; she felt she was asking too much with everything they were already doing for her, so she was thankful for his perceptiveness.

The next day Char was just finishing getting ready when Emmett returned to pick her up. She knew he was just helping her out, but she couldn't help but worry he might think it was a date. However, then she panicked, realizing she'd dressed up as if it were a date. She had on an airy yellow skirt and tight white scoop-necked silk tee and had put extra effort into her makeup, something she hadn't done at all over the past year.

Charlotte almost winced when Emmett's face lit up in a bright smile, and he told her how nice she looked. She felt the pang of regret for getting so dressed up, but as he helped her into the car, he immediately put her at ease with his casual air.

"I called ahead to a beachside restaurant. We can sit looking right over the ocean. It's beautiful."

The restaurant host, with gray hair lacquered into place, stood looking bored until he noticed Emmett approaching. His beach-weathered eyes lit up, and he stood a little straighter. "Mr. Waterman, pleasure to have you and your guest this afternoon. Two for lunch? Right this way, please."

They were seated at a table overlooking the water, and a waiter appeared to take their drink order before saying he'd be back soon with bread.

The warmth of the sun on her shoulders and the light ocean breeze lifted Char's spirits. When she lived in Oregon, each time she returned from a trip to California with her family and was greeted by the cold and cloudy Pacific Northwest, it would always take a few days to readjust and remember why they continued to live up north, but she had known why. It was a part of her, the dense forests, the lush greenery, and the misty and foggy days, the need to bundle up in cozy sweaters when heading out, seemingly more often than not. But as always, when in California, she'd fall in love all over again, taking in the alluring flower-and-ocean-scented breeze, enjoying watching the waves crash onto shore with seagulls seeming to hover in place over the ever-lapping water.

Sitting across from such a handsome man also did much to lift Char's mood. As Emmett perused the drink menu, Char took the opportunity to indulge in his looks. She studied him and realized what made him so attractive. *He's a happy guy.* He seemed to be smiling just reading the menu. Char was so used to intense, almost pensive men. She realized it was going to take some getting used to, just like the beautiful sun- and ocean-kissed surroundings. She told herself to just take it in and enjoy.

They placed their order after their drinks were brought over, Emmett's a red wine and Char's a lemon drop martini. Then Emmett asked what she'd been thinking about. She couldn't tell him she'd been studying his happy face. "I'm just feeling grateful to my daughter, Aubrie, for convincing me to accompany her. It's just breathtaking, isn't it? Thank you for taking me here. I love it." Char beamed from ear to ear.

"Well, you're very welcome, and I'd like to throw my hat in too, to say I'm also thankful to your daughter for bringing you with her. How about we toast to Aubrie?" They'd just clinked their glasses when someone sidled up to their table and interrupted them.

"What are we toasting to, Emmett? Anything my lawyer needs to know about? And who is this?" asked a beautiful black woman who wasn't looking at Emmett but had her eyes fixed on Charlotte, smiling and looking her over scrupulously. Char cringed; she didn't trust that smile.

She saw Emmett stiffen at his recognition of the stunning woman. "No, nothing you need to be concerned about, Leann. Char, this is Leann, my soon-to-be ex-wife. Leann, this is my friend, Charlotte." Char could tell he was as uncomfortable as she felt. The last thing she wanted was to be caught in the middle of a lovers' quarrel. *Well, ex-lovers,* Char corrected herself.

"Pleased to meet you." Char extended her hand to Leann, who didn't reciprocate. Emmett rolled his eyes and heaved a sigh.

"Pleased? Were you toasting the demise of my marriage, which you now feel gives you rights to him?" Leann's voice rose and caused fellow diners to surreptitiously glance their way.

Char was embarrassed and cast her eyes down, not knowing what to say. She wanted no part in this and knew better than to come back with any retort, especially since it appeared Leann was drunk.

"Leann, I think you should go now." Emmett kept his eyes straight ahead and refused to make eye contact with her. Charlotte noticed he had gone red from his chest to his neck. She prayed things wouldn't take a turn for the worse. "Don't take this one for granted; he's a real gem," Leann said to Charlotte, reaching out to brush her fingers over Emmett's temple. Emmett recoiled from her touch. Thankfully, just then Leann's lunch date, a large older man with an oversized ring on, came to tell her their car was ready. He took her by the arm and gave Emmett an apologetic nod and, to their relief, escorted her out of the restaurant.

"I'm so sorry, Char. This is really embarrassing." This time it was Emmett who avoided eye contact.

"Divorce is never easy, Emmett, no need for apologies. This must be a sad time." She wondered what their story was, but wouldn't dare pry.

"No, actually, it's okay. I'm truly over Leann. What's sad is we've been separated longer than we were married. After all she's done, she still doesn't understand why I filed for divorce," Emmett shared. "We'd made plans to start a family together, which, looking back, should have struck me as odd since she'd been doing all she could to come between my boys, their mother, and me. The whole deal was bad news. I don't know when I would have wised up. But I didn't have to, thanks to her jealous boyfriend she'd kept on the side. As soon as he saw our wedding announcement in the paper, he came to me and told me everything, including the fact that she'd had her tubes tied years prior. Needless to say, it was pretty devastating." He scrunched his eyes before he took a generous gulp of his drink.

"Emmett, that's an awful betrayal. Unfortunately, it's those closest to us who can hurt us the most." Char reached out and touched his hand. She felt compelled to impart some comfort to him.

They looked into each other's eyes, and if she hadn't known better, she would have said the two of them were connecting. Charlotte wondered why they'd held each other's gaze. Surely it didn't mean anything. Of course it didn't. She couldn't afford to allow it to.

"A wedge salad for the lady and a Reuben for the gentleman. Can I get you anything else?" asked the waiter, breaking the moment between them. They both quickly snapped out of it, and thankfully there was no awkwardness. They continued to enjoy the rest of their meal and soon were on their way out.

Back in the car, on their way home, Emmett suggested they stop and rent a few movies. "I don't know about you, but while it's been a beautiful day here in sunny Malibu, I feel like holing up on the couch and watching a couple movies. Comedies, definitely." Char couldn't agree more. They pulled into the grocery store, and since her ankle had started to throb again, she decided to stay in the car and soak up the sun.

A few minutes after Emmett went in, a man with a large camera appeared literally inches from Char's face, snapping pictures. "Excuse me, what are you doing?"

He ignored her question and instead, said, "Come on, honey, smile for the camera. Can I get a quote about Mr. Waterman's infamous package? Come on, sweetheart, if you're dating Mr. Waterman, you've gotta have a story to tell." He pulled the camera down long enough to fish a business card out to hand to Charlotte. "Here, if you don't want to throw me a bone for free, give us a call. We pay top dollar, and here's a hint; the dirtier the story, the more we pay," he said in a low, guttural voice.

Charlotte didn't take the card. The guy shrugged, completely unfazed, and started snapping pictures again. She was creeped out but didn't know what to do. She thought about the struggle it would be to get out of the car in her crutches and felt as if that would only encourage him, so she decided to stay put. "Please, can you just go away?" Char was pleading and trying to shield her face from the camera when the guy suddenly yelled, throwing his hands up to deflect red projectiles that exploded into a pulpy mess upon impact.

"My camera! All right, all right!"

Charlotte looked around to see who was gunning for him. It was Emmett, and he had a confident stride about him. What stood out most were his muscular shoulders undulating as he made a beeline for the guy.

"The lady asked you to go away, and I suggest you politely oblige her request." While Emmett spoke in his calm voice, he continued to walk toward the guy, never losing eye contact with him. It only took a few seconds for the guy to cower back and run off, well before Emmett came within arm's reach of him.

Emmett stood watch, making sure the guy was gone, then ran to Charlotte. Putting his hands on the car door, he knelt down to her.

"Char, look, I'm sorry about that. Are you okay?" He cringed when he saw she was crying. Emmett picked the goo out of her hair and tucked some strands behind her ear. "Sh, sh, sh. He didn't hurt you, did he? Because if he did, I'll run him down and pummel him to the ground this time."

"No, he didn't touch me. He was just saying crude things, and I was stuck. I couldn't really go anywhere. I didn't know what to do." Char held her breath to stop crying and regretted having a martini at lunchtime.

"No, don't apologize. I understand you had to be scared, but don't worry, he's just one of the pathetic paparazzi. Unfortunately, I've dated some pretty public ladies. One of whom, to further her fifteen minutes of fame, decided to start dishing about our, um, private moments, and not to miss out, Leann got on the bandwagon and sold a few stories too."

Emmett rubbed the back of his neck; Charlotte could almost feel the embarrassment written all over his face, which was turning redder by the minute. "But it eventually blew over, and I learned a tough lesson, that I need to be a little more discerning and not so quick to trust. But, Charlotte, I don't think this will happen again. I've never seen that guy before. I'll bet he's new and missed the memo that I'm old news." As Emmett waited for her to reply, Charlotte could see the hope in his eyes that she'd be able to take his story in stride.

"Well, you don't have to worry about me. I'll keep the details of our lunch to myself." Char gave him a wry smile and did her best to lighten the mood.

Emmett let out a breath, rounded the car, and slid behind the wheel, tossing the DVDs onto the center console. He looked at her sheepishly. "So, you're not completely repulsed by me?"

"That's your personal business, not for me to judge. It's obvious to me you didn't want any of that made public. And thank you for running him off. What exactly did you throw at him anyway?"

"Plums, three for a dollar." Emmett got a laugh from Char before becoming serious again for a moment. "But there is something I want from you. Can I see your phone for a second?"

Char drew her brows together.

"Trust me, please."

She handed her phone over somewhat reluctantly. He tapped in some information and handed it back.

He leaned closer to her with his arm on the back of the seat. "You have my number now. If you ever end up in a situation like this again, or stranded anywhere, I want you to call me and I'll be there, okay?"

Before she could blush or say anything, Emmett grabbed his phone. "And what's your number?"

She gave it to him, and once it was saved to his phone, he leaned back with a wide grin. "That's a good first step, thank you."

"First step?"

"To your safety. Char, as soon as you're healed up, we need to get you in some self-defense classes. And pepper spray. Come to think of it, you didn't have any with you on your hike, did you?"

Charlotte looked away, shaking her head no.

"Yeah, that's got to change too. No use being a sitting duck. We're going to get you proficient at self-defense. You seem a bit rusty."

Emmett wouldn't realize it, but he was bringing Char to a very dark place. "Thank you for the offer, Emmett, but you have your way of dealing with things, and I have another. Sometimes it's more dangerous to fight back. I'm not interested in learning how to provoke an attacker."

Emmett was about to start the car, but he stopped to look at her. "Charlotte, that's probably the stupidest thing I've ever heard. You're saying you'd prefer to let someone attack you without trying to protect yourself?"

Charlotte could see his neck getting red again. His heated reaction made her uncomfortable. She shrank down in her seat and turned away, keeping her gaze out the window. "Emmett, you have your way, I have mine. Can we change the subject?"

His voice softened. "For now we can, if that's what you want, but this is something I'll change your mind on. Believe me."

Charlotte knew Emmett meant well, so she didn't want to argue, but his insistence felt invasive. To his credit, she wondered if he might be right. Maybe her stance on things was all backward because of all she'd been through. It scared her to revisit why she felt the way she did, so she forced herself to focus her attention out the window and out of her own head. She settled in the seat and took a deep breath, realizing she felt exhausted.

They went home, and after dinner Emmett insisted Anna come to the couch with them to watch a Bradley Cooper comedy. Charlotte felt like escaping to her room after the day's events but knew that would only continue the awkwardness from their earlier conversation, so she joined them for the movie. Emmett made popcorn and opened a bottle of wine. With them all in their sweatpants and T-shirts, they each found a spot on the couch or one of the recliners to relax into. When Anna sat down, Asa ran up to her lap.

"Wow, Asa, guess I see how I rate. I'm hurt," Char joked, focusing on turning a corner on her mood. Anna laughed in her singsong way and assured Char it must be because she was the one currently giving him his walks, and not to worry.

"Well, don't feel bad—that little guy acts like I don't even exist," Emmett said as he tossed Charlotte a throw.

"No, that's actually a huge compliment. He's leery around men and has been known to snarl at them. So his ignoring you is a sign he actually likes you."

"Yes, he'll come around, señor Emmett, give him time," Anna said as she stroked Asa's back.

"Well, let's toast to that." Emmett motioned his glass toward Char and Anna.

They all enjoyed the movie, and Char couldn't imagine how lonely she would have been in a hotel with just her and Asa. She was grateful that Anna and Emmett were so welcoming and helpful. She trusted now that Emmett really was a nice guy, but she hoped he wasn't going to keep prying into her private life. She'd never had so much to hide before, and from someone so inquisitive. She worried whether she was well enough prepared to keep her past under wraps from the likes of Emmett Waterman.

• • •

Char was up first thing in the morning. She had begun to feel at home in Emmett's house, so joined him for coffee. He looked messy in the morning, but in a sexy way. He liked to eat and have coffee before showering for the day. Surprisingly, Charlotte appreciated his scruffy look. She'd over the years become accustomed to highly groomed men. She'd forgotten how sexy a five o'clock shadow could be.

He looked a bit sleepy but smiled brightly when she made her way to the kitchen. "Good morning. Can I get you a tea or coffee?"

"No tea," Charlotte snapped before she could stop herself. "I mean, no, thank you, coffee would be great." She hated to remember the time in her life when she'd loved passionately not only tea, but also the man who got her into the habit.

"Whoa, hardcore coffee drinker, are we?" Emmett laughed, took a gulp of coffee, and rubbed his scruff before stretching out of his seat to grab her a cup.

"I guess I am, thank you. No sugar, just cream—lots of it, if you don't mind," she said, smiling weakly.

"So, a little coffee with your cream." He eyed her as he made his way to the fridge for the cream. As he poured her a cup, she couldn't help but notice how each muscle flexed and bulged. He was in good shape, retired from football or not, and she could even make out his six-pack through his T-shirt, but what was most captivating were his eyes. They danced with joy, and it relaxed her.

"I think I might drink coffee for the routine of it, not necessarily the taste." Charlotte was beginning to appreciate his laid-back vibe. He was a happy-go-lucky, straightforward, this-is-who-I-am kind of guy. It was refreshing.

Emmett brought her coffee as her phone rang.

"Oh, it's Aubrie Elle. I bet she's heading out on the road again today."

The last few days she and Aubrie had only communicated by text, but Char texted her the night before and informed her that in no uncertain terms, by that morning, Aubrie was supposed to call her. Char missed her terribly, even though she'd only been on her road trip now for just over a week.

Aubrie told her all about her and Chloe's adventure thus far, making it to Seattle and spending a few days with some of their friends who had also just graduated. They planned to spend the day taking turns driving to Boise, Idaho, where Chloe had family from her dad's side. Aubrie apologized but said they had a long road ahead, and she wanted to keep it short. Char understood and thanked her for calling like the good daughter she was and told her to drive safely.

When they got off the phone, Char took a sip of coffee and said, "So, Aubrie and Chloe will be driving all day, to Boise. I can't believe I let them do this. Sometimes I wonder what I was thinking. But so far, so good. They're definitely enjoying their freedom right now," she said with a feeling of satisfaction.

Emmett was topping off his coffee cup, his back to her as he spoke. "I couldn't help but notice that it didn't sound as if Aubrie asked you how you've been feeling since your fall."

Char bristled. "She had no reason to."

He came back to the dinette and sat down, leaning back casually in his chair, legs wide, clearly at ease, though Char felt quite the opposite. "Is that because you haven't told your kids about your fall and everything that's been going on because of it?"

"No, actually, I didn't," she snapped.

"Why not?" he asked and sat up straighter, scrunching his brow.

"Not that it's any of your business, but what my children don't know, they can't worry about. They shouldn't be dragged down by my baggage."

At her words, Emmett's eyes went wide. "Char, what happens to you is hardly baggage. Your kids love you, I'm sure. My God, you're in a new town, hurt, with a guy you just met. At the least they should know where you're staying." He was smiling, but his tone was incredulous.

"Look, I didn't ask for this. And I agree it's a crazy situation. My kids would freak, and rightly so. But either I've made the right judgment about you, that I can trust you, or I haven't. That's on me. But don't tell me I'm hurting my kids, when I know damn well I'm protecting them." Grabbing her crutches, she got up and backed herself up a few steps from the table.

"Charlotte, after yesterday's conversation about the paparazzi, and now this, I'm beginning to feel like you think you're disposable or something. Where's your basic sense of survival? I mean, if you don't care about yourself for you, how about for your kids?"

Emmett had hit on her worst insecurity, being a bad mother. The truth was, she had caused her kids a lot of pain in their young lives, and she was intimately familiar with the pain caused from resenting one's own mother. Char hated her mother for all the abuse she'd suffered as a child, yet to her utter disappointment, Char felt maybe she hadn't done much better.

For Char it boiled down to choices: marrying an abusive alcoholic, putting her kids through the subsequent bitter divorce, escaping into the arms of a distant egomaniac, only to have him actually bond with her kids and then be torn away from them because of selfish pursuits, and then the worst of all…but Char couldn't allow her thoughts to go there. She knew Emmett really did have her pegged. She was a horrible mother. His words cut her like a knife.

"I don't know who you think you are, but you are way out of line. I don't have to put up with this. Thank you for your hospitality, but I see now a hotel will suit me much better. Asa! Come!" Char headed down the hall to get her stuff.

Emmett got up from the table to follow. "Oh, come on, Charlotte. I'm sorry, it's just…I think you should be a little more open with your kids."

"And I just think you should mind your own business. Asa!" Char went to her room and grabbed her two bags.

Anna came downstairs and told Charlotte Asa was napping in the laundry room. "I don't have the heart to wake him. I'll bring him to you later, I promise, señora."

Charlotte pursed her lips and looked at Anna, wondering if she was just trying to delay her leaving, but she trusted Anna and at that moment decided nothing was going to keep her from leaving. "Fine, Anna, thank you. I'll let you know which hotel I've checked into as soon as I get my room number. And you'll bring him right to me?"

"Of course, señora." Anna took the two bags from Charlotte and helped her to the car.

"Charlotte, come on, what are you doing?" Emmett followed Char out to the garage.

"I'm driving myself out of here. You've done more than enough, and I'm done with imposing. I'll handle getting myself to a hotel."

"Please, Charlotte, let's cool it down. No need to run off like this. You're not going to be able to drive with that boot on."

"I'll manage, thank you." She frantically searched the walls for the garage door opener, finally got it open, and made it to her car.

"Oh, this should be great," Emmett said under his breath and walked out to the driveway to watch.

Charlotte started her car fine with her foot on the brake, but when she put the car in reverse and tapped the gas pedal, it was more like a stomp. Her car lurched back with such speed Char panicked and slammed the brakes so hard the seatbelt locked, and she whipped forward. She looked into her rearview mirror and saw, to her chagrin, that Emmett stood there laughing.

Charlotte was infuriated that he seemed to be enjoying the show. She knew she'd have to give up on her plan, so she turned the car off. She was dealing with too many emotions: anger at herself, because she knew Emmett was partly right, that she shouldn't be keeping her injury, and its aftermath secret from her kids; frustration because she was already having some sort of feelings for this man, which she knew was totally wrong; and fear that she ultimately wouldn't be able to turn away from him. All she could do was break down.

Her car door opened, and Emmett spoke quietly. "Char, are you okay?"

She looked up and tried to compose herself. "I'm sorry. I'm such a wreck. I know I'm overreacting."

"I'm the one who should be apologizing, Char. I came on way too strong, not one of my best attributes. I didn't mean to sound so judgmental. It's just, I know how much I love my mother, my brothers and I, we're very protective of her. I wouldn't be able to forgive myself if she ever had to go through anything like this alone."

"My kids and I have a different relationship. They understand that as their mother I don't want them taking care of me."

"I respect that, Charlotte, I do. But I wouldn't sell your kids short. I bet if they had the opportunity to step up to the plate for you, they'd do it in a heartbeat."

Charlotte already knew that was true, but she doubted his mother had gallivanted around town with a new boyfriend soon after the loss of her husband, thinking she was invincible and putting herself in harm's way. Char felt she needed to protect her kids from herself; not that she would reveal that to Emmett, though.

"You're right, they would," she said meekly.

"And you know why? Because you're worth it."

Char gave a huffed smile.

He held out his hand. "I'll get you believing it sooner than later, but until then, can we put this argument behind us?"

She knew the easy way out would be to vilify Emmett and still run, but she couldn't do it. He was right, and he cared enough to tell her how he felt. As hard as it was to hear the truth, she valued his bravery. She had to admit she didn't want to leave and answered him by putting her hand in his.

Emmett helped her out of the car and grabbed her crutches for her. He stood facing Char and rubbed her shoulders. "I really am sorry. You're in a stressful situation, and I shouldn't have added to it." Char barely heard what he said; she was too focused on their close proximity.

Char felt a spark between them. She was in awe of this man's humility. What really struck her was his admitting he was wrong, apologizing. It didn't make him appear weak—just the opposite. To her it showed immense strength and confidence. The pull she felt toward him caused her to instinctually step back. Emmett dropped his hands, but didn't step away, and kept his eyes fixed on her.

Charlotte stood there fiddling with the padding on her crutches. "Thank you for that, Emmett. I needed to hear you say it. I am just doing the best I can for my kids."

"Yes, you are. Now, are we good? Are you still on board with my and Anna being at your beck and call until you're all better?"

Char thought for a moment before answering. She pressed her lips together as she thought over his proposal, and Emmett smiled down at her.

"Not sure about the beck and call thing, but yes, I accept your apology. I guess if you'll still have me after all this, I'm a lucky girl," Char said with a shy smile.

"No, I think I'm the one who may have lucked out, finding this damsel in distress in the Malibu hills," he said, cocking his head toward her. "Listen, I was thinking earlier, it's Friday, and I need to put in a full day at the office, but how about this weekend we hit the road? Spend Saturday up north and Sunday down south? Nowhere I want to take you is too far. We can come home Saturday night. I'd love to show you some of my favorite spots within a couple hours of here. What do you think?"

Charlotte agreed. With the time they'd spent together, she knew they'd have a great time, as friends, and the fact that they would come home Saturday night was reassuring.

Emmett finally got ready for work, and she went back to her room to sleep off some of the stress of the last few days. She hoped that by the next day her ankle would be calmed down and she would be refreshed and ready for the adventure.

By morning Char's ankle was feeling much better. Emmett unexpectedly had to go to his office before heading out. He had to meet with his crew to go over a story. Charlotte was happy to go with him and see where he worked. Seeing the film equipment made her think of her son, Blake. They hadn't talked since Monday, just before her fall. They'd texted since, but it was Saturday. She couldn't believe nearly a whole week had gone by. She found an empty office to give him a call.

"Hi, Blake. Oh, I've missed you. How are you?" Just hearing him say hello warmed her heart.

"We've been slow to start today, which is great. We've had some long nights the past few days. How about you, Mom? Are you settled into the condo?"

She thought about her argument with Emmett and knew she should come clean with Blake about her ankle and all that had gone on the past week.

"Well, actually, honey, when we last talked on the phone I was on my way to a hiking spot, and I got into a bit of trouble. I slipped on some rocks and hurt my ankle, so I've been slowed down some getting moved into the condo."

"What do you mean? Are you okay?"

"I'm fine, but I have to wear a walking boot for a few weeks to a month. Nothing broken, just a grade-two sprain."

"Still sounds kinda serious. How did you get to the hospital, Mom?"

Charlotte swallowed and forced herself to answer truthfully. "A hiker came by and helped me out. If Emmett hadn't come by, I'd probably still be there." She forced a laugh, trying to make light of the situation. "Actually, you might know him. He played in the NFL for years, Emmett Waterman. He's a pretty great guy. He's kind of been helping me out since the accident."

"No way, the kicker? So the very first friend you meet there in Malibu is a retired NFL star? Way to go, Mom."

Charlotte laughed at Blake's enthusiastic approval. "I guess that's LA for you."

"I was excited when you decided to go to Malibu with Aubrie and didn't stay holed up all by yourself back home. So, are you doing okay, Mom?"

Charlotte tensed up. She knew the direction their conversation was headed. "Blake, the last thing you need to be doing is worrying about your mother. I'm good, I promise."

She could hear Blake heave a sigh; she hoped of relief, not doubt.

"Well, good, I'm glad to hear it, Mom. I'm sorry for all you've been through the last year. I'm sorry about you and Ash. You guys had it great, from what I could see. I still can't help but hope you two might get back together. He made you happy. None of what happened made any sense to me, Mom."

Charlotte bristled, then peeked into the hallway to make sure no one was around to hear her conversation and quietly shut the door.

"Blake, it's never going to happen. We've both moved on. So let's do so with this conversation." Charlotte pressed her lips together, angry with herself. "Blake, I'm sorry. I didn't mean to snap at you."

"No, Mom, you don't have to apologize. I know better than to even ask. But it was hard being so far away when it all went down—your accident, then breaking up with Ash, then Aubrie trash-talking him. Sometimes I wish you would tell me more about what happened, Mom."

"I did tell you, Blake. It's just Aubrie's misguided chatter clouding the facts. I was in a car accident, and during my recovery I had time to think about where I was in life, and I decided to end things with Ash. As sad as it can be, sometimes relationships just end. There doesn't always have to be some big reason why."

Charlotte felt like she was reading from a script. She hated to lie to Blake, and to Aubrie for that matter, but it was in their best interest. The less they knew, the safer they were. The mental burden of knowing what had really happened would be more than she'd ever wish on her kids. They already knew too much about her abusive childhood, thanks to family rumor and innuendo. Blake still maintained vague memories of his violent father, memories Charlotte pleaded with Blake to keep to himself, for Aubrie's sake. There were many secrets Charlotte worked to keep hidden for everyone's benefit, and at times the weight of them took their toll on her, but she was willing to pay the price.

"You're right. I'm sorry if it sounded like I was accusing you of lying. I believe you, Mom; it's just I forget sometimes I'm dealing with Aubrie. I love my sister, but she can be such a drama queen sometimes."

Charlotte laughed. "That's our Aubrie. She means no harm but doesn't realize that her hyperdramatization sometimes causes a lot more trouble than she intended."

"I just want to know you're okay, Mom."

"I am. The only thing wrong right now is I miss you. Aubrie too, but she hasn't been gone nearly as long. I haven't seen you in months, honey. I miss you so much."

"I miss you, too, Mom." Charlotte could hear someone in the background shouting to Blake to get a move on. He groaned. "Hey, looks like I gotta get going. I'm glad you're okay, Mom. I love you, and I'll talk to you soon."

Charlotte was pleasantly surprised that Blake took the news of her fall in stride. It felt good not adding to her list of secrets, and she was grateful toward Emmett for pushing her to be forthcoming. When she came out of the office, she could hear Emmett talking near the reception area and looking for his keys. It was time to go. She was excited to hit the road and spend the weekend sightseeing instead of drowning in the past.

The official start to their weekend that afternoon was sunny and beautiful. They took his convertible with the top down and soaked up the sun. They headed north up the Pacific Coast Highway to the small town of Montecito, a favorite community of the A-list celebrities. The drive was like no other. Char literally ached at the beauty of the breathtaking beaches. With the wind in her hair, the smell of the beach, and the warm sun on her face, she couldn't have felt happier.

After driving up a narrow winding road lined with sycamores, they dined at a luxurious boutique hotel nestled in the foothills of the Santa Ynez Mountains that boasted many Hollywood legends as guests. With views of the ocean in the distance and the smell of the hotel's lavender-lined garden blowing through the breeze, Char thought she was in heaven.

"Emmett, do you come here often? It's absolutely stunning."

"Only when I have a special someone to share it with," he said with the sweetest smile Char had ever seen, but like a stern schoolteacher not to be swayed by the charms of the class clown, she kept her guard up.

"Emmett, I thank you for that, but keep in mind you don't know enough about me to say I'm anything special."

"I don't know about that." Emmett looked as if he was going to continue, but the waiter came to their table.

"Would the lady or you care for another drink?" he said expectantly, looking to Charlotte first.

"Thank you, no, I shouldn't."

"I'd love another scotch on the rocks, thank you," Emmett said to the waiter before looking at Charlotte. "You don't drink much?"

"I've gone through periods where I have and haven't. Since Beau passed, I haven't, really."

"Ahhh, sounds to me like it depends on who you're with, am I right?" Emmett teased, not realizing he was closer to the truth than Charlotte would want to admit. "Was Beau not much of a drinker?"

"No, that's not it, really. He never skipped his nightcap. I've just learned I prefer to keep my wits about me." She couldn't explain that it was all courtesy of her most recent ex. *Forget about him, Char.*

They enjoyed a long dinner together, and Emmett regaled her with some of his most memorable football follies, ones that had riled his fans the most. He shared it had been tough back then, but was proud to finally be at the point of not really caring what others thought about him.

They talked over a wonderful meal and agreed to share a crème brulée for dessert. Emmett insisted on giving her the first bite, and Char protested it was much too big of a spoonful, so she got him back by scooping as much as she could into his mouth. Char tried to remember if she'd ever been able to completely relax and be goofy in that way. She couldn't remember that she ever had, but she discovered she liked it.

Their waiter interrupted their revelry by approaching and pointing out an elderly couple getting up to leave. He was holding a bottle of fine wine and said the couple wanted it sent to them with their compliments; it was a thank you for bringing them back to the time they were much younger and falling in love.

Char blushed, and Emmett smiled without any hesitation and turned and nodded to the couple. She self-consciously waved and mouthed a thank you.

"Shall I pour?" Char and Emmett looked at each other and just laughed. "You can't reject a sweet old couple's gift, now can you, Charlotte?" Emmett's eyes twinkled.

"Now you're making me feel guilty. Fine, one glass," she conceded, telling herself to forget the mantras of her past.

An emptied bottle of wine later, the waiter discreetly brought the check, and that was when Charlotte realized they were sitting under candlelight. When had their waiter lit the candles on their table? There were only a couple of tables still occupied, and it appeared the staff was starting to clean up for the night.

"I think we're going to need to stay here; that bottle of wine sent me over the edge. I'm not one to risk it on the road. Not my style." Emmett fumbled with the pen and did his best to sign the tab.

Char agreed, but she was panicking inside. She wasn't about to share a hotel room with him or anyone. As if he could see she was getting the wrong impression, he interjected, "Separate rooms, of course."

Charlotte relaxed and let Emmett help her out of her chair. Putting her hand in his felt right, but she told herself to remember it was wrong, very wrong.

The front desk was able to get them two cottages side by side. It was a beautiful night, and although they were both fuzzy in the head, the romantic air wasn't lost on Charlotte. The scent of orange and lemon trees filled the night, intoxicating her senses, and she wondered if Emmett was similarly affected.

Emmett walked Char to her door. She allowed him to hold her steady at the waist as she fumbled with the key.

"Here, let me." He put his hand on hers. Char looked up and caught her breath. The soft glow of the porch light highlighted Emmett's broad shoulders and cast shadows that played over his cheekbones and jawline, shading in every rugged feature. Instead of intimidating her, it mesmerized her. She watched as his eyes seemed to take in every detail of her face before settling on her mouth. Leaning in, he gently put his lips on Charlotte's; their hands were still clasped together.

The kiss was soft. It felt nice, but she fought the feelings, reminding herself she couldn't afford to be foolish. Even when drunk, she tried to maintain control. Before it was too late, she snapped her head back.

"Emmett, this was a fun day. Dinner was lovely, but let's not ruin it. We barely know each other." *True*, she thought, *but I'm broken, bad news. I'm doing you a favor, Emmett.*

She got the door unlocked and patted Emmett's arm as if to apologize but also say, "but please go away," as she stepped in and closed the door, leaving Emmett standing there looking blank. For a moment she had to lean against the door and tell herself she did the right thing.

The bright sunlight poured through the picture window, which was surrounded by climbing flowers, and onto Char's bed. There was nothing better in Char's opinion than waking up to bright happy sunshine and the sound of birds waking up for the day. Even better, she felt no ill effects from over imbibing the night before. She noticed the room's phone was blinking with a message. It turned out to be the front desk saying that there was a package at her door.

She hobbled out to the porch and found a basket with every toiletry imaginable and a comfy sweat suit from the lobby's boutique. There was a note from Emmett saying he thought she'd appreciate starting the day fresh, and to please meet him for breakfast as soon as she was ready. Char smiled at his thoughtfulness; she was happy to see her brush-off hadn't dampened his mood.

Once bathed and dressed, Char felt refreshed and looked forward to seeing Emmett. She was headed out the door when, to her astonishment, she saw Leann coming out of Emmett's cottage. She had rumpled hair and was holding her heels. Char's heart sank. *Are you kidding me? He wines and dines me, kisses me, and then has his supposed future ex-wife come stay the night? What a pig.*

"Oh, good morning. Charlyne, right?"

Charlotte was too stunned to correct her, staring disbelieving at the woman Emmett swore he was done with.

"Isn't this place beautiful? It's one of our favorite weekend fuckation spots. I guess being here really got to Emmett. When my husband calls, I come. Again, and again, and again."

Leann's smug face disgusted Charlotte, and Charlotte wasn't sure why she was giving her an audience.

"So, dear, Emmett and I are going to stay on for the rest of the weekend. He wanted me to tell you he called you a cab. See? It's pulling in right now." Leann stood there, hands on hips, legs wide, with a smeared lipstick smirk on her face. Char was repulsed by the both of them.

Wow, Char thought. She realized Emmett must be a sex maniac. *See, Charlotte, you never can see it coming, can you?* He must have planned this all along, to bring her to this secluded ranch, then come up with a lame excuse to have to stay the night—but then when she turned him down, he was so desperate to get his rocks off that he called his ex, someone he claimed he couldn't wait to be divorced from. *Whatever,* she thought. *Just get into the cab and go.*

She had to go dangerously close to the restaurant to get to the cab. She hoped Emmett didn't see her. How did he expect to have breakfast with her while Leann waited in their cottage? It didn't make sense, but she wasn't going to wait around for his lies. She looked straight ahead and prayed he wouldn't see her getting into the cab. She wasn't so lucky.

Charlotte jumped when Emmett knocked on the glass. His voice was muted, but she could still hear him. "Charlotte wait, let me explain, please."

She wasn't up for conversation; she kept her eyes fixed straight ahead, refusing to even look at him. "Can we pull around those cars?" she asked the cabbie.

"It's tight, but I'll try," he said in broken English.

As Emmett waited for her to roll down the window, the cab drove away, and he jogged alongside of it before it gained speed, and he gave up. He was still trying to call to her as the car left the grounds. When her cell phone lit up, she simply turned it off.

By the time the cab dropped Charlotte off at Emmett's, she'd had plenty of time to think over the situation, and though her mind went round and round at first, she ultimately concluded she'd overreacted. She and Emmett weren't a couple. She had told him she wasn't even in the market, and that was true. Why had she reacted that way? Well, he did kiss her, then go romp in the sheets ten minutes later with his ex, which was gross; but it wasn't as if he were cheating on her. *We aren't in any kind of relationship, so what's the problem? There isn't one,* she told herself.

Charlotte grabbed the key from the hiding spot Anna had shown her days before and opened the front door, and Asa came running to greet her. She knelt as best she could to pet him. "Hi, buddy. I'm so happy to see you too. You want kisses? You're the only one I trust to give kisses to." Asa wagged his tail furiously and did his best to jump up and playfully nip at her face.

"I don't blame you, Char. Asa, you're a lucky dog."

Char turned to see Emmett standing in the alcove, looking rough. His eyes were bloodshot, and his clothes were rumpled. He looked handsome nonetheless, but she refused to get lost in his looks.

"Charlotte, I'm sorry—"

"Look, Emmett, it's fine. I had time to think on the way back. While it was a BS move to kiss me, then take your ex-wife—" She paused and held her hand up before adding, "No, wait, let me correct that, your *wife*, to bed within five minutes of each other, it's all a moot point. We're just friends. I rebuffed your kiss, if you remember. No harm, no foul." She set Asa down and grabbed her crutches. Emmett held his hand out for her, and she begrudgingly obliged. They went to the living room.

"I need to tell you what actually happened, Charlotte." His voice was tired and raspy.

"Please, no need to explain. Your personal business is just that, personal. It really has nothing to do with me." Char reveled in the strength she felt when she put up a wall.

"Char, can you have a seat and hear me out? None of what happened is what you think."

"Emmett, didn't you hear me? Moot point? We're not anything, so why should I care?"

"For one, I'm a man of integrity. I don't want my reputation ruined on account of a crazy and dishonest ex-wife. Pulling a stunt like the one you think I did last night, yeah, maybe in my early twenties, but not now, and definitely not to you."

Char avoided his eyes. "And the second point?"

He took a deep breath. "Well, to be honest, Charlotte, I don't believe you when you say you don't care. I think you do. I think your first reaction is the truth. I could see your face in the cab. You were hurt. And why? Because maybe you're starting to have just a smidge of feelings for me." He held up his finger and thumb, demonstrating a tiny space between.

He looked so sweet and vulnerable. There was a feeling inside her that wanted to come out, but she shoved it down. "Emmett, you've gone above and beyond helping me out, especially since you *barely know me*," she said with purposeful intensity, "and what I feel toward you is gratitude and appreciation. I think we're forming a friendship, and that's great, but that's all it is." She spoke with clinical professionalism.

He winced as if her words stung. He seemed to think for a moment, and then took a big breath. "Char, I didn't sleep with Leann.

Apparently a friend of hers texted that she saw the two of us at dinner. And believe it or not, she dropped everything and drove two hours to stalk me. When I answered the door, I thought it was you. She came barging in, and we argued for hours. She wouldn't leave. So finally I did. I got another room. That's it. That's all that happened."

Their arguing all night would explain Emmett's raspy voice, and he sure looked unhappy, just as he had when they ran into Leann during their lunch. For some reason, Charlotte felt relief, and most importantly, she believed him. "So, what, she's just going to stalk you up and down the coast, making you miserable?"

"No, I took care of it. I told her if she wanted to continue working as a broadcaster, she'd have to stop harassing me once and for all. Otherwise I'd destroy her name in the industry. And I could. Give me five minutes to make a few calls. That bitch'd be done." Emmett crossed his arms; Charlotte could see his tendons and muscles tensing.

She didn't like hearing men cursing at or about women, but she cut him some slack. He'd had a miserable night, and Leann had said some disgusting things to her, so she understood his anger, but figured it'd be best to keep the specifics to herself.

"For your sake, I hope she does. I don't understand how some people seem to feed off drama."

He relaxed and put his hands into his jean's pockets. "Thank you. Can we not let Leann win this one? I'd still love to show you around Orange County, if you're still up to it." He bent down to look her in the eyes, and Charlotte could tell he was hopeful she'd say yes, and it made her smile.

"I think I can agree to that."

Happy to be moving forward with their plans, they wound their way south to a resort along the bay, where Emmett told her they'd be having lunch. "We have aunts and cousins in the area, so I spent many summers here with my family even before we moved. We had a blast. My parents love the water, so it was only natural for us to all follow suit." Pulling into the portico at the resort, Emmett helped Char out, and they made their way down to the docks. "I thought we could take a Duffy boat out for a picnic lunch. What do you think?"

She looked at the small canopied boats lined up on the dock. Just big enough to hold a small group of people, they looked adorably like the jungle boats at Disneyland. She looked at Emmett and smiled brightly. "I'd love to."

Emmett swept her up into his arms, helping her into the boat. Every time he had to pull her into his arms, Char would feel a little flutter, one she pointedly ignored.

Laid out on the small table in the boat was an exquisite array of fruits, cheeses, and sandwiches, along with a bottle of champagne and a bottle of orange juice. Obviously Emmett had planned ahead. Char wondered if this was appropriate friend behavior. She wasn't convinced it was, but she refused to brood on it, intent on enjoying a beautiful day just like anyone else. She found that easy to do with Emmett.

Emmett took to the wheel, and they putted all around the bay. Several seals glided by, which was a real joy for Char. She took lots of pictures and worked to get the perfect one to send to Blake and Aubrie, with a caption: "Wish you were here!"

They toasted to the beautiful day and enjoyed their afternoon picnic as paddleboarders, kayakers, and an occasional fellow Duffy boat passed by.

"I couldn't imagine having this as my summer hangout as a kid. It's just so beautiful," Char said as she looked out over the dimpled blue water.

"I do feel pretty blessed. I didn't see any kids out today, but if you think these Duffy boats are small, you should see the training dinghies. They'll get kids as young as five out here in sailboats just their size. It's quite a sight." Emmett laughed at the thought before asking Char, "How about you? How did you spend your summers growing up?"

"Not frolicking out on any beach anywhere, that's for sure." Char smiled. She wasn't averse to discussing her childhood. Over the years she had honed her glossed-over story. She knew how to dodge certain details that would pique any real interest into her past.

"Once I was a teen, I preferred to forgo any family trips to stay home and make money, working odd jobs all summer, anything from babysitting to gardening to clearing brush." Char did her best to be nonchalant.

"You did manual labor? Clearing brush? I think if I were your parents, I wouldn't have allowed it." Shaking his head, Emmett poured her another mimosa.

She, of course, didn't tell him her parents could not have cared less. "Actually, I'm grateful for the experience. It helps build character. To tell you the truth, I actually enjoyed working outside. At least during the summer. Now, in the fall, when it was time to work on my family's property, that was another story. November's the worst for working outside. It's cold, but not so drastically cold like in January to keep you indoors. And the rain. The cold November rain. Your clothes got soaked through; you'd get chilled to the bone. It was miserable," she said as she wrapped her arms around herself, almost feeling the chill.

"Cold November rain, huh? Wasn't that a song?" Emmett laughed.

"Yes, I guess it was, but back then, I don't think I was lamenting a lost love." Inside, Char thought twice about her statement. If she were to have lamented anything back then, it would have been the absence of love from her parents. That was a loss she worked hard to get over through loving her own kids as much as she could. *Stay focused. Don't get caught up in sad songs and sad memories,* Char admonished herself.

"Well, take heart, babe, it's not a cold November rain out here today," he said, sweeping his arm out, looking over the bay. "You're right where you should be, so here's to a beautiful day with beautiful company." They clinked glasses. Char couldn't help admiring Emmett's smile and the way his eyes exuded such a pure happiness.

She had to admit there was growing attraction between the two of them. Why did she have to have met him now? It was much too soon. She knew in her heart she'd have to use extraordinary strength to resist him. "To beautiful friends," Charlotte toasted back, hoping to send a message to Emmett and herself.

They continued putting around the water, taking in the changing sights, and soon the sun was making its way down to the horizon, casting a beautiful mix of pink and blue hues throughout the evening sky.

"As much as I hate to, it's time to head back to the docks. I want you to know how much I enjoyed this time with you today. Thank you for agreeing to come with me, Charlotte."

"I can't remember a more fun day in recent history. All in all, this was a beautiful weekend. Thank *you*, Emmett."

Emmett didn't take his eyes off Charlotte.

She had to ask him. "What?"

"It's just, the sunset's reflecting on you, and you're…it's beautiful."

Charlotte looked down at her arms, and sure enough, they were radiating a glowing pink, but in fact nearly the whole boat was filled with the glow. It felt magical; there was no denying.

"Come here, I want to see how you look with a pink glow." Charlotte pulled Emmett closer. His white button-down shirt first glowed a soft pink, then slowly turned crimson. "I think pink becomes you too. It's very pretty."

"Pretty? I feel like a pink Oompa-Loompa. Not sure it's my best look. You, on the other hand, here, smile for me." He got his phone out and took some pictures. Charlotte posed haughtily for him, giving him a good laugh, then returned the favor and took some pictures of him as he did his best to look cool. He nonchalantly sat next to her so they could get a shot of the two of them together. Charlotte let him, but told herself it didn't mean a thing.

Once the sun set, they were left in the twilight, and the air began cooling off. "It's getting dark. Now we really need to head back in. You look chilled—here," he said as he grabbed the throw on the seat next to him and wrapped it over her shoulders. "Is that better?" He held on a bit longer than he had to as they looked into each other's eyes.

Charlotte knew it would be so easy for her to let him kiss her in that moment, but she fought to stay strong and abruptly turned her back on him, pulling the throw tight around her shoulders. She looked over the rippling water catching blue and white reflections from the evening lights. "Thank you. It's amazing how quickly it can turn cold," she said, hiding behind her clipped tone.

"It is, and it's a shame, really."

At four thirty in the morning, as always, Julian's alarm went off. There was a time he used to enjoy waking with the first light of day to the sound of early birds chattering and working, but not anymore. He could tolerate no reminders. His curtains now worked to shut out any sliver of light and any hint at the past.

He was about to roll over and shut it off, but he felt a jolt next to him and then remembered Taryn had stayed the night, and she was sitting up to grab his phone.

"I got it, Julian," she said, and he heard her fumble to shut it off. She rolled over to snuggle next to him. He smiled in the dark and pulled her in close. It had severely tested his patience to get back on track after he blew her off the day she'd tried to seduce him at the office, but he'd worked hard to refocus on the present and to mitigate the hurt he'd caused her, and it had worked. On his good days, he could see clearly what attracted him to Taryn and why he was with her. He had to move forward in life, and with her assertive and carefree attitude, she was helping him do just that.

"Good morning, Taryn. Thank you for staying with me last night," he said as he nuzzled her ear. He actually meant what he said, and the freedom of it pleased him to no end.

"Thank you, Julian; you definitely made it worth my while." She wrapped her legs around him before he swiftly pulled her up on top of him. She let out a small gasp. "Again? What will that be, three times in twelve hours?"

"Let's just say I want to really make it worth your while."

• • •

Julian drove them to the office in bliss after their morning together. He liked to get an early start on the day, and despite the carnal detour, he was pleased they would still make it to the office by seven thirty.

Taryn went to her office, and he made it to his and immediately poured himself into his work. He had taken on a new high-profile client who traveled extensively and needed around-the-clock security. He had little time left to get the details in place before the contract would start.

His assistant, Mara, buzzed in Taryn at one o'clock that afternoon, and he figured she was coming to invite him to lunch. He barely looked up from his reports. "I'm sorry, dear, I'm knee-deep. I'll have to have a salad at my desk today."

"Who's Charlotte?"

Julian felt his body go cold. He kept his head down, fearful his countenance might betray him. He blinked furiously as he calculated how to handle her. He took a controlled breath.

"I'm sorry?" He could only look at his hand as he deftly twirled his pen. He willed himself to maintain his composure.

"I asked Ron to send me the basic files on Chevere. I know they've been one of our best clients and thought we could do a campaign featuring them. Instead, he forwarded me a file on a Charlotte. I thought I was familiar with most our clients. It looks active; there were entries as late as last week. I don't understand. Who is she?"

Julian's pulse quickened, and on instinct he let his anger drive the conversation. He dropped his pen to look her in the eye, knowing his only move was to put her on the defensive. "You know you're not to have access to restricted files. How dare you rifle through them."

Taryn crossed her arms, and her voice rose. "At first I didn't realize they weren't what I had asked for."

"Key words. *At first.*" Julian's eyes bore into Taryn's.

"Who is she?" Her voice shook.

He remained stoic, but his voice was laced with poisonous anger. "You're quite out of line, Taryn. This is an egregious breach of trust."

He'd be damned if he was going to answer her, and Ron would get his for making such a rookie mistake.

"You want to talk trust, Julian. I don't trust *you* right now." She glared back at him.

He'd hoped to intimidate her out of his office, and he marveled at her bravery. He desperately wanted to tell her to trust her gut, that she shouldn't trust him. He stayed silent.

"There were no billings attached to the file, Julian. I've put some thought into this. Either she's an indigent, and you're doing this pro bono, and of course that's preposterous, or she's an ex, and you're stalking her."

"You're pulling all of this out of thin air. It's really quite ridiculous, Taryn."

"Julian, remember when we first got together, and I found that shattered picture behind the side table at your condo? That picture I found all those months ago, I'd put money on it that it's the same woman who's in that file."

"Taryn, essentially I'm in the spy business, of which you're well aware. Now, you and I have a good thing here, and I've enjoyed our time together, but I've made clear to you that the nature of my job precludes us becoming overly serious and also precludes my sharing with you confidential client information. There are no two ways about it. I've been as up front with you as I possibly can. If that no longer satisfies you, I'll understand if you want to end our romantic involvement, but please know that's not what I want."

He watched Taryn and knew her mind was racing, with her arms still crossed, hands clenching, and foot tapping in bottled frustration.

"So that's it. You're not going to say one thing to allay my suspicions. Fine. We're through." Taryn turned to make for the door.

Julian realized he should have been suspicious waking up feeling so free. When had he ever been free in the last year? He knew he had a choice to make, a big one, but which woman was driving the decision, he couldn't know, and was terrified to find out. He pushed the dangerous thought aside. "Taryn, wait."

She turned around; her cheeks were tearstained.

"I can tell you this. That's an old file. It should have been deactivated a long time ago. I'll notify Jameson." Jameson had served alongside Julian with the British special forces, where they'd become close confidants. He was Julian's first hire when he started his company and someone he trusted implicitly, and they knew each other better than anyone.

"If you don't want me to walk out that door, notify him now."

His heartbeat quickened. He hesitated, but did the right thing, something he should have done long ago. It felt like slow motion as he picked up the phone and called Jameson to his office. Much too quickly, Jameson was there, both he and Taryn looking at Julian, waiting for him to give his order.

"Jameson, there seems to have been a mistake. There's a file, on a—" He cleared his throat. "A Charlotte that should have been closed months ago. Please deactivate it and transfer the men on that detail to Mr. Kyomoto's assignment once he's Stateside."

Taryn watched the two of them with rapt attention.

Jameson didn't blink. "No problem, Boss. Sorry for the confusion. Anything else?"

"No, that will be all, thank you."

Jameson left Taryn there with Julian.

"Are you satisfied? Can we put this little tiff to the side now?" He gave his best forced smile.

In answer, Taryn rushed his desk and threw herself on top of him. Before he knew it, they were making love. He imagined actually being free from his chains and wondered if it was finally happening. Was it finally over? He wondered if that was why Taryn had come into his life, to free him from his desecrated past. Only time would tell.

. . .

"Thank you, Julian," she said softly, and blew him a kiss before leaving.

"Thank you, Taryn." With all the hope in the world, he meant it. An instant message beeped on his computer. It was from Jameson.

Boss, that was a decoy order to abort Charlotte's detail, correct?

Julian's fingers hovered over the keyboard.

Damn it. He should have known his feeling of freedom would be fleeting. Who was he kidding? The room began to spin, and his fingers shook. He arched his pained face up to the ceiling and slammed his fist onto his desk.

When Monday rolled around, Charlotte asked Emmett if he could drop her off at the condo. She would leave Asa with Anna and get a full day's work in. She still had so much to do. Her fall had thrown her off track in preparing the condo for Aubrie and Chloe's arrival.

They stopped for a coffee on their way to Char's place. "Are you going to be okay stuck in that condo all day? You're going to be like that princess stuck in a tower, though your hair's not quite long enough for an escape."

She smiled. "I think I can manage."

"How about this? I have an eleven o'clock appointment, but afterward I can swing by and take you out to lunch."

Char appreciated Emmett's thoughtfulness. "Ha-ha, a lunch break rescue? No, that's so sweet, but I have so much to do, the day will fly by." The idea of having lunch with him did appeal to her; he looked so handsome. He was clean shaven and wore his hair parted on the side with a little pomade in its waves. With his fitted linen suit, he looked quite different than he had on Sunday morning, after his night of hell arguing with his ex.

At the condo, Char unlocked the door and found she was looking forward to him carrying her up the stairs. She couldn't wait to feel his strong arms around her.

"My lady," he said playfully as he held his arm out, her cue to let him sweep her up. Char changed her expression to say, "Oh, gimme a break."

She thought she had her coffee secure in her hand even with the brace on, but her own leg bumped it when he picked her up, sending a splash of caramel-colored coffee right down the front of his button down and all over her white blouse.

"I'm such a klutz. I'm so sorry," Char said, wanting to die of embarrassment.

He set her down at the top of the stairs and assured her it was fine. His eyes swept over her soaked shirt before he blushed and turned away. "No worries, Char. I think I can get this out. Where are your towels? I'll grab you one too. I think you got the worst of it."

Charlotte sensed the change in the air, so made a beeline for the utility room just off the kitchen. She leaned against the wall to catch her breath before she called back, "Never mind the towels. Let me see your shirt. I'm sure I can get the spots out."

He came around the corner with his shirt in his hand, and Char's heart leapt into her throat. He'd never looked sexier than right then. She took in his broad shoulders and toned pecs. His sun-kissed abs cut perfectly to his waist. His silver belt buckle glinted, beckoned.

Their eyes locked as he stepped close. She grabbed his shirt, and her hand touched his. For a moment, neither took their hand away. The connection startled her. She had to pretend the energy between them wasn't there. She broke their gaze, jerked her hand away, and turned on the faucet. Head down, she set to work on washing the spill out.

"What a way to start a Monday," she said nervously, trying to break the spell.

"I think we can fix that." His voice was soft and low. He took his shirt from her and turned off the water. *Uh-oh*, Char thought, and before she knew it, Emmett had her turned toward him. He pushed his hips into hers. He caressed the back of her neck and pulled her close as his lips took control of hers.

Char was conflicted. Her body was asking for one thing and responding in kind, but her mind was screaming no. His lips on hers, his warm embrace, the feeling of his strong chest against her. She knew she could be easily carried away with passion, but she knew it wasn't right. It couldn't be right. She faced an internal struggle her body was about to win.

His hands were at her hips and slipped just under her shirt, reminding Charlotte of her scars. "No!" She knocked away his arms and, forgetting she was in her boot, tried to make a run for it and instead fell to her knees in pain.

She came to her senses immediately and knew she'd blown it. She had no idea how she was going to brush off the scene she'd just made. She rolled over to face him, and her heart sank when she saw his shock and confusion.

He rushed to her side to help her up. "Char, what just happened?"

She grabbed her crutches and stepped away. She couldn't go weak now. "What the hell, Emmett. I mean, we just talked about this after the debacle with Leann. I thought I made it clear that we're just friends."

"True, you did, but I'm sorry, that's not the vibe I was getting from you until you suddenly freaked out," he said as he crossed his arms. "Listen, I'm not one to throw unwanted advances."

Of course he was telling the truth, but she didn't have that luxury. She thought quickly to come up with a plausible excuse for her abrupt change of heart.

"I'm sorry, it's just, it's only been a couple of years since Beau died. I'm not ready to be in any kind of relationship besides friendship."

He rubbed his temple and cast a doubtful look her way. "At the risk of sounding insensitive, you do know you're free to move on with your life now, right? Two years, Charlotte? What's holding you back?"

Char didn't think she'd ever get used to Emmett's probing questions. As controlling in other ways as the men in her past were, they didn't hold a candle to Emmett and his demanding questions. She decided that was a comfort she missed.

"Are you sure you're not an investigative journalist? Maybe you should switch from sports to sleuthing." She rolled her eyes in frustration. "It's complicated, Emmett. I just feel better off alone. Let's just leave it at that." Char wasn't going to answer his questions, but she also didn't want to start an argument.

Emmett leaned against the sink and was silent for a moment. Finally, he said, "I'm sad for you, Charlotte. We've all got issues we need to work through from our past; that's just part of life. Being all alone isn't the solution. You have to work it through. I'm willing to work through those issues with you, whatever they are. You can feel safe with me."

He tried once more to step closer to her.

Char took a step back and wondered at his need to always be so physically close. "More often than not, men have been the complication in my life, Emmett." She didn't know why she revealed that. Frustrated, she bit her lip, knowing she'd better put the brakes on her sharing.

"But maybe the reason is because you haven't found the right man just yet." He tried again to close their distance.

She managed another step backward. "I've been hurt, time and again. I just think I do better on my own, Emmett." Charlotte felt conflicted. She did agree with him, but it wasn't that. She had nowhere near the strength she'd need to be completely honest with him, and even if she did, she'd then be betraying those who helped her during her greatest time of need. She still felt hostage to her past, unable to move forward, and here was this man asking to be able to stand by her side, and she couldn't let him.

"Well, I think you could be pleasantly surprised, Charlotte, if you let your guard down."

His voice was low, and as he looked down at her, she couldn't help her eyes sweeping down his frame. The gentleness of his voice softened the masculine strength his body exuded. Instead of intimidating, it was frustratingly alluring. But she shut out the physical attraction to focus on the cold, hard facts.

"You might be right. But for so many reasons, I just can't. Not for the foreseeable future anyway." Charlotte didn't have the heart to tell him it could never happen.

"I can be patient. I'm enjoying building this friendship between us. But, Charlotte, please know, you don't have to shut me out. I don't scare from much; you just keep that in mind."

She felt so guilty misleading Emmett, but by time she had fixed his shirt and they said good-bye for the day, she had convinced herself it was for his benefit as well. Time after time, Emmett consistently proved he was worthy of far better than to end up with someone like her.

. . .

The time flew by, and Charlotte was shocked to see it was already five thirty in the evening and knew Emmett would be there any minute. Right on cue she heard the key in the lock. She'd given Emmett the keys, so he could let himself in. He called up, "Hi, Charlotte, it's me, and I sure hope you haven't been snacking all day."

"Why?" She came to the top of the stairs and looked down at him suspiciously.

"Well, the esteemed, as he put it, Dr. Samuel e-mailed to let me know without right of refusal that he and his wife, Katena, would be coming to call tonight. He's requested a bottle of my best wine and filet, al fresco." He looked incredulously at Char as he made his way up the stairs.

"He invited himself over tonight? That's a riot." Charlotte was happy it seemed there would be no awkwardness between them after her earlier outburst. She was surprisingly comfortable in his arms again when he carried her down the stairs.

"Yeah, well, it's par for the course for my buddy Lou. So, are you up for a barbecue tonight? You'll like Katena; she's a beauty, inside and out. She's from Eastern Europe, a no-holds-barred kind of woman, but I think you two will get along great."

"I'm game. Sounds like we're in for a lovely evening."

Locking the front door, Char turned around to the sound of familiar jangling. Emmett turned too.

"Charlie! There you are! Oh dear, yes, you really did a number on your ankle now, didn't you?"

"Charlie?" Emmett said in a whisper, confused.

Ignoring his question with only a sideways glance, Char instead introduced Moe to Emmett.

"You're not Emmett Waterman, are you? You were my late husband's favorite player, almost as much for what you did off the field as on. What a pleasure to meet you."

Emmett smiled proudly, evidently used to the kind of accolades Moe was showering him with. "Well, thank you. Pleasure to meet you, Moe."

Charlotte wanted to ask what Moe meant about his work off the field but knew they were pressed for time with their guests on their way to Emmett's. "Moe, we have to get going. I'm sorry we haven't been able to get together just yet like we'd planned."

"You take your time healing. You're in good hands until then.

We'll get together soon, Charlie." Moe gave them a knowing wink and jangled off to her condo.

Emmett smiled at Charlotte. "See? Even your neighbor can see you're safe with me. I'm here for you, Charlotte, as a friend or otherwise."

Charlotte believed Emmett, but also knew their relationship could only go so far.

They found Anna in a frenzy when they came through the door. Asa, doing his best to keep up with her, barely acknowledged their arrival. Anna was hurrying back and forth from the patio to the kitchen with Asa right behind. The table was set beautifully with a flower arrangement of coral and yellow roses, candles were lit, and a bottle of red had been set out to breathe; a bottle of white was chilling in a bronze wine bucket. Char thanked Anna profusely and explained that, had she known earlier, she would have figured out a way to come back to help her.

"Oh, no, no, it's my pleasure. You were working hard at your condominium. Please take your time to get changed. Let me know if you need help. Dr. Lou and his Kat will be here in twenty minutes. I'm almost done." She hurried out the French doors with a large platter.

Emmett said he wasn't going to change, that after this late notice from Lou, Lou had better take him as he was. He needed to heat up the grill anyway. Anna could have cooked for them, but Emmett preferred to do the grilling himself.

Soon enough, Emmett called to Char that their guests had arrived. As Charlotte was making her way around to the side gate, she saw that the backyard was gorgeous. Flowering hedges lined the side yard to the wrought-iron gate, with flowering trees strategically placed throughout.

"Seven o'clock sharp; here we are as promised," called Lou. He was even more gregarious than Char remembered from when he was treating her in the ER. He was wearing a loud Tommy Bahama Hawaiian shirt, but had paired it with tan silk slacks and Gucci loafers. His wife, Katena, towered over him by at least six inches in her sky-high wedges. She was thin and graceful, with ice-blue eyes and dishwater-brown hair cut in an angled bob. She had on an ice-blue maxi dress that matched her eyes. She was stunning, and it made Char feel downright squatty, limping on crutches in her basic black wrap dress with a clunky boot on one foot and a strappy flat on the other. *Ugh,* she thought.

They said their introductions at the gate, shaking hands. Lou asked Char how her ankle was feeling, and she thanked him, saying there were no issues. They all turned, and as Char went to follow everyone in, there was a loud sound, like tearing fabric. The group turned to see what had happened. Char looked around too, but didn't see anything. Then Emmett said, "Your dress, Char."

Char looked down and saw that one of the loops in her wrap had caught the hook on the gate, tearing the seam. It exposed much of the scar on her side. Their eyes met, and Char could see the horror on Emmett's face. He was standing directly in front of Char—and she hoped he was blocking the view from Kat and Lou. They seemed calm enough, so Char prayed it meant they had not noticed the scar.

Anna appeared at her side and quickly gathered the dress together. "Oh dear, oh dear. We be back, we be back." She ushered Charlotte back through the gate, leaving the group to continue to the back patio.

Charlotte glanced back only to see Emmett staring blankly after them, concern written all over his face.

Char heard Lou call out to him, "Come on, Emmett, you need to pour me a drink, stat. I'm sure Anna can fix her dress right up."

Anna stayed by Char's side. "Señora, I'm so sorry. But I don't think anyone saw your scar."

Char closed her eyes and took a breath. "No, Anna, I know Emmett did. I saw the look on his face. I don't know what's worse, his look of disgust or that now he's sure to ask questions." Char was being more forthright with Anna than she'd intended.

"Señor Emmett is a man who cares. And he doesn't judge. You can trust him, señora. I promise."

"I don't doubt that, Anna. I'm discovering every day how kind and patient he is. But it's not about him. It's about me. I can't have that conversation with him." Char felt clammy as she tucked a loose tendril behind her ear. She realized her hands were shaking.

Anna must have noticed too, as she began rubbing Char's back soothingly. Her voice was soft and even as she said, "Well, I talk with him, I tell him, 'You don't push this kind lady. You have patience with her heart.' Don't worry, señora. It'll be okay, I promise. You put on another dress. Don't think no more and come back out for a nice evening. You'll see."

Charlotte looked up at Anna. "You said that to him? When?"

"After I help you the first morning," Anna said shyly.

"Oh, thank you, Anna," was all Charlotte could say as she grabbed Anna's hand. It warmed her heart to know that Anna had been immediately protective of her.

"Come now, your guests are waiting. I would stay with you, señora, if I was leaving you with anyone other than Emmett, but it is way past my shift, and you'll be fine, I know, truly. Have a wonderful evening," Anna said, setting two dresses onto the bed for Charlotte before giving her one last calming smile and slipping out the door.

Charlotte tried not to feel abandoned, knowing it was a childish response, and obeyed Anna and threw on another dress. But she didn't know why she bothered. All she wanted to do was hide under the covers and never come out. She still worried whether everyone had seen her scar or just Emmett. *"Just" Emmett,* she thought. Was this the beginning of the end? She wondered why she couldn't be left in peace.

Emmett knocked at her door. "Can I come in?" he asked softly.

Char thought quickly and jumped up to open the door. She used her crutches to take a long step past Emmett.

"Charlotte, wait, shouldn't we ta—"

"I can be such a klutz sometimes, right?" She interrupted Emmett and put on a show of feigned incredulity. She figured her best strategy would be to not let him get a word in edgewise. She stopped at the French doors to look back at him. "You coming?"

Before she knew it, he was at her side, gently grabbing hold of her elbow. "Charlotte, please, can we talk first?" His eyes were kind as they swept over her.

She continued on, and he walked beside her out to the yard. "Emmett, tonight's been embarrassing enough, and it's just getting started. Please, I just want to get through the night without it being completely ruined."

He let go of her elbow, letting his fingers trail down her arm. Charlotte shivered. "You're right—let's enjoy the evening. Sorry about your dress," he said sincerely, but Charlotte saw in his eyes he wanted to say much more.

She looked away and saw Katena and locked eyes with her. To her chagrin, Charlotte knew Katena had been watching their exchange. Charlotte put on a brave face and made her way to Katena while Emmett huffed a breath of resignation and joined Lou at the grill.

Katena poured a glass of wine for herself and Charlotte and carried their drinks to the fire pit. While they made small talk, Charlotte couldn't help but glance Emmett's way on occasion. As she watched

Emmett and Lou talk, she hoped it wasn't about her.

After only a few minutes of benign small talk, Katena seized the conversation. She looked over her shoulder, eyeing the men like a spy undercover before turning back to Charlotte.

"Charlotte," she began quietly, methodically, "something is on my mind, and I must get to the point. We've known our Emmett for over a decade. We've seen him get hurt in relationships many times. We're done with the carnage. I think he may carry hope in his heart for you. But you seem closed. You must trust. He is, besides my husband, the kindest man you'll ever meet. But he bears his heart whole. He can't expect less in return." Katena's eyes narrowed at Char while she awaited a reply.

Charlotte couldn't have been more shocked. Kat was as intrusive and presumptuous as her husband had been that day in the ER. Thoughts raced in her head, and she worried that Emmett had been spilling the beans about their relationship—*friendship,* she corrected herself.

"Katena, I appreciate your looking out for your friend. I agree, Emmett's a great guy, but believe me, there's nothing…there's no way. I mean, no, we're just friends. Has he been talking to you about us?"

Kat's eyes danced at Charlotte's reaction, and she gave a sly, knowing smile. "Call me Kat. No, Emmett is a fairly private person. But I see how you two look at each other. His heart is open to you, but you seem apprehensive. If there's something in the way, you must work it out. He is a patient man, but don't wait too long. A man's heart can only take so much."

Charlotte stared into her wineglass as she twirled it this way and that. "I don't want to hurt Emmett. He's a wonderful guy. I've told him I can't be in a relationship with him. I've been quite clear." She looked back at Kat.

A gust of wind swept Kat's hair forward, accentuating the sharp angles of her cheekbones even more. Her cool eyes narrowed as she leaned toward Charlotte. "But your eyes betray you. I see you care for this man, Charlotte. I do hope we may be friends. But if you hurt Emmett, that would become an impossibility." With that, Katena scooped up both their wineglasses and sauntered over to the wine bucket. Without looking back, she waved Char over with great command.

Charlotte stayed put and called over, "Oh, no, I shouldn't. I have a one-drink maximum. Thank you, though."

Kat snapped her head toward Charlotte. "What kind of nonsense is that? You must. That's the second condition to us becoming friends. Drink up." Kat filled Charlotte's glass without hesitation and brought it back to her.

While she was happy Kat had changed the subject by offering to pour her a glass, it was still her reflex to turn down subsequent drinks. However, in that moment, Char decided to oblige, grateful for any elixir to dull the stress she was under. Looming over her head was the distinct possibility that later Emmett would ask for an explanation for the scar on her side, and then to have Katena grill her like that—she felt the pressure mounting. It seemed everyone around them was hinting about their being a couple. With Moe saying, "He's a keeper," his soon to be ex-wife making a crack about Char being ready to pounce on him, and now Katena pushing her, it was almost too much.

She had to remind herself of the productive talk they'd had earlier after their awkward kiss. She had made it clear to him that it wasn't going to happen. If it continued to get too hot, she told herself she would definitely leave, but if she were being honest with herself, she hoped she wouldn't have to. Emmett made her feel safe, as long as he did so from a safe distance. They could be friends and friends only.

The meal itself was wonderful. Anna had made way too much to accompany the filet: lemon Caesar salad, a creamy risotto with mushrooms, and a balsamic watermelon salad. Everyone agreed it was all delicious. Emmett razzed Lou about the list of demands he would send next time he expected Lou to host dinner. Lou retorted that if, at the least, Char would bring a peach pie from his favorite bakery, all would be even. Charlotte cringed. *There goes another couple comment.*

Emmett only laughed, saying, "Well, we'll see about that." Char blushed; she couldn't look at him, but she definitely felt his eyes on her.

"Speaking of the pie, would you like me to serve it now?" Katena asked as she got up to grab plates.

"Yes, absolutely," Lou said heartily.

It was getting late for a work night, so Kat and Lou took their leave after the dessert. "Thank you for having us, dear Emmett. My Lou may have been a bit pushy, but if he goes too long without seeing you, he can get pouty. We thank you for your hospitality. Tell Anna the food was delicious. Charlotte, a pleasure to meet you. I hope we may have lunch together soon." She gave Charlotte a proper hug and a kiss on each cheek.

Char understood Kat's double meaning. She also had no desire for Emmett to be hurt. "I hope so too. It's nice to see Emmett has such great friends."

Lou shook Emmett's hand and gave him a hearty pat on the back, his dark eyes dancing as usual. "Bye, buddy. Our turn to play host and hostess next, deal? And, Char, thank you for the wonderful evening, and it was a pleasure seeing you again. You take it easy on that ankle, and hopefully in a couple of weeks you won't need the boot anymore. Then we'll have a good excuse to celebrate!"

After Lou and Kat left, there was the elephant in the room, but Emmett and Char both played innocent.

"I'm regretting not asking Anna to stay late," Emmett grumbled jokingly as he surveyed the cleanup that still needed to be done.

"I'll start on the dishes if you bring them to me," Charlotte offered.

She tried to sound light, but was feeling uptight and trying to think up ways to avoid talking about her scar. There was no doubt in her mind that he'd bring it up, and she knew Emmett was persistent and had the sinking feeling she wouldn't be able to get out of this one.

Once he was done cleaning up outside, Emmett sidled up to Char at the sink with a towel. "You wash and rinse; I'll dry and put away." Charlotte and Emmett were mere inches apart again. The last time they'd stood so close at a sink, there were tears and tense words. She winced at the recent memory. Of course, Emmett, ever the optimist, didn't seem the slightest bit put off and was his usual smiling, cheerful self.

"So, what did you think of Katena? Looked like you two hit it off," he said as he made quick work of drying off several serving spoons.

"I liked her. She's sincere. And seems like a good friend to you. I think she respects you," she said to his back as he sorted the utensils into the silverware drawer.

"We have a mutual respect for each other. Katena's been through a lot in her life, suffered greatly. Her tenacity is truly something to be admired. She refused to let her past rob her of her future."

Charlotte couldn't know for sure, but felt Emmett had purposefully let that statement hang in the air. "I could see that. She seems like a determined person." Char wanted to know Kat's story, but couldn't risk asking for fear it would be his segue into delving into her own past. She needed to keep this conversation short and deflect as much as possible.

"It was her story that inspired me to get involved with her charity to combat sex trafficking. I'm on the board, mainly to help bring in donors. Kat's the real workhorse, traveling the globe, bringing awareness. But people don't understand it's happening right here in the US. Take the I-5 corridor, for instance, from Canada all the way to Mexico. Any city with so much as a truck stop off an exit is playing a part. It happens anywhere and everywhere. Women and kids, exploited all around the world. That evil knows no boundary."

"What does your organization do exactly?" Charlotte turned toward him, truly interested but also thankful for the conversational detour.

"A big portion of our funds goes to rescue and rehabilitation. We and a lot of other organizations also work to put pressure on governments to face the issue head-on. We're making great progress, but there's still a lot of work to do." Emmett paused to rub his forehead. "Look at me, I sound like I'm giving a call-to-action speech at one of our auctions. 'But you can do something today! Write that check. Big or small, we'll accept them all!'" he said in a mock game-show-host voice.

She chuckled at Emmett's self-deprecation. "I'm proud of you. You could have just listened passively to Kat's story. But you didn't. Instead you went into action, helping create something so meaningful for so many." Char's eyes welled up. *What a beautiful human being.*

Emmett smiled and gave her shoulder a warm squeeze. "I've never been one to sit idly by when I see someone in need." Charlotte cringed inside.

Emmett folded the dish towel and tossed it onto the counter. He turned, leaned against the counter, and looked at Charlotte. "Well, we're done here in the kitchen. Thanks for the help." He looked down the length of Charlotte's body with what she hoped wasn't a look of sympathy before settling on her walking boot. "How's your ankle holding up so far?"

She tried to stay upbeat, though she felt in her gut the conversation was slowly turning to the topic she dreaded. "Besides annoyance at the utter inconvenience? I'm fine, really. The pain is minimal. I have a doctor's appointment this Wednesday, and I'm hoping to hear news as to when I can get this thing off."

"Remember, I've got that out-of-town job coming up, but I don't leave for Denver until Thursday. I'm happy to take you to your appointment, Charlotte. I'd like to be there for you." His voice was gentle, low—there was an unmistakable tenderness that Charlotte wished weren't there.

Instead of making protestations, she knew it would be better to just play it off and accept his offer like any friend would. "Oh, I almost forgot you were going out of town. Yeah, thank you. I'd like that; you're a good friend, Emmett."

As soon as she said it, Charlotte bit her lip, knowing she failed at trying to play it cool. Emmett nodded knowingly at Charlotte, and she could sense he was on edge but trying to hide it, and it had her wanting to flee the scene.

As if sensing her uneasiness, Emmett suddenly changed his mood, and he gave her a big smile. "Well, look, you've got to be tired, standing all this time. Here, let's have a seat. I'll get you a drink."

Oh no, here comes the elephant. Without a second thought, she decided to feign tiredness. "Ohhh, you know, actually, I think the wine is starting to get to me. It's all Kat's fault. Did you notice I had three glasses tonight? That's much too much for me. I really should hit the hay."

"Ohhh, come on, I insist. Take a load off," he said as he motioned to the bar stools at the island. "I'll be just a minute with a decaf—lots of cream, just the way you like it."

From the tone of his voice, Charlotte knew that Emmett knew she was putting him on and that he was willing to go match for match. Her gut told her she wouldn't win this one without making a scene. With sad resignation, Char capitulated. "Um, sure, thank you."

Charlotte sat at the island with bated breath while Emmett loaded the coffeemaker with a pod and water. Asa ambled up to paw at her chair. Emmett brought her coffee and gave Asa a lift into Charlotte's arms. She smiled and breathed a little more easily, thankful to have the little guy nestled in her arms, her security blanket when she needed it.

With his coffee in hand, Emmett sat next to her, putting his forearms on the counter. He let his head hang down and sighed before he tilted his head up and just looked at her for a moment. She wanted to shrink to nothing and felt certain Emmett could see her heart beating out of her chest. It felt as if they sat there forever.

Finally, Emmett broke the silence. "Char, I know we've only known each other now for barely over a week. But we've spent a great part of this time side by side. If you think about it, we've been on the equivalent of probably thirty dinner dates. That's nothing to sneeze at."

"If this is your lead-up to, 'Char, you know what they say about fish and guests: after three days, they both start to stink,' well, I get the hint." She tried her best at humor *and* changing the subject.

Emmett chuckled before rubbing his face and letting out a labored sigh. "You know that's not what I'm getting at. The thing is, Char, and you know we just talked about it this morning, I hope you know you can trust me. You know I'd love to have more than a friendship with you. But you say for now that's all you're comfortable with. And I want us to be friends, but I get the sense you may not allow a friendship to develop, and that would be a shame."

"How am I not allowing us to be friends? We are friends, aren't we?"

"Yeah, we are—don't get me wrong. But by this point in time, I just feel like maybe you should trust me a little and let your guard down."

All Charlotte knew to do was play dumb, stall for time. "I don't know what you mean."

"I'm saying maybe you should let your guard down and, say, for instance, tell me about that scar on your side."

Char's whole body went numb, and that was when Asa decided to take his leave. He squirmed to get out of her arms. Emmett helped him down, to Char's dismay. She watched Asa run down the hall and wished she were doing the same. Instead, she was sitting face-to-face with Emmett, whom she hadn't expected to be so blunt.

Her mouth opened as if she were going to say something, but then she snapped it shut, knowing it was too dangerous. If it had been her only scar, she knew she could find it within herself to tell him, but it wasn't, and she couldn't be sure that it wouldn't somehow lead to questions about the others, and she could never explain those. She gathered her strength and stood. She wasn't going down the road of revelations. She wasn't that self-destructive.

With resolve, she grabbed her crutches, and Emmett stood, shaking his head in disappointment. "See? One personal question, and you're outta here. You need to trust me, Char. You can tell me just about anything, and I'm not going to run, not as a friend or otherwise. This morning you said you'd try. Here's your opportunity."

Charlotte was already walking away from him, but turned to answer. "Did I really?" Char honestly didn't remember their conversation going that way. "Well, it's not going to happen this way. This morning at my condo you intimated that you'd never push yourself on a woman, but that's exactly what you're doing to me right now. No means no, Emmett."

Regret landed like a stone in her gut before she even finished her words, but she had to make him stop. She couldn't allow him to chip away at her secrets, taking a piece of her with each new revelation until there was nothing left of the fortress she'd built. She couldn't allow him to see the truth, the ugliness that surrounded her, and the darkness that she attracted. No, she wasn't suicidal; she wouldn't lay bare her secrets and risk her very survival.

Emmett looked as if he'd been slapped in the face. As her words sunk in, his shoulders slumped, and he stared at the floor.

Charlotte wanted to take it back, but she didn't know how to rewind what had just happened. She could only watch as he put his hands up and walked backward. "Fine, Charlotte. You win. I'll let go."

Char was racked with guilt and confusion and had a miserable night's sleep. She blamed the wine for why she kept waking up to the worst dreams, which vacillated between Emmett coming after her in an angry rage and him turning his back on her, walking away. When she woke up, she wasn't sure which had been worse.

She thought back to their evening and felt awful for how the conversation had ended. She wanted to somehow make it right—of course, make it right without trading her privacy. Her heart almost ached for him, and that confused her. Her best guess was it was a longing. Was it a longing to love him? How could she? To love him, she would have to bare her soul. That just wasn't a possibility; she felt she'd die if she did. That was the honest truth.

Going to the cupboard for a coffee cup, Char noticed a note taped on the cupboard.

> *Charlotte, something's come up, and I need to leave for Denver today. I'll be back Sunday. Anna will stay through the weekend and can take you to your doctor's appointment and anywhere else you need until I get back.*
>
> *Take care, Emmett.*

. . .

He was leaving for a week instead of a few days. Char suspected that what came up was his intense need to get away from her. She was so disappointed in herself. Katena's warning marched through her mind, and she knew she had already failed.

She texted him that she was sorry they weren't able to have a conversation before he left. She told him to have a great week and that she hoped it would prove productive.

He responded with a curt thank-you and nothing more.

. . .

One unforeseen consequence of Emmett being out of town was Char not being able to get up the stairs to her condo. She hated the prospect of so many days going by without getting any more work done, but to make the best of it, she caught up on busywork. It wasn't pressing by any means, but some of the firm's standard contracts needed updates, and, while it was a bit tedious, it would be a good distraction. Anna took Char to her doctor's appointment, which not only helped pass the time, but also lifted her spirits; her boot was coming off in two weeks.

Her first thought was to text Emmett the good news, but since he'd been practically ignoring her texts, she decided not to. She had tried to keep a text conversation going with him, but his short answers made her wonder if their friendship was over. To confuse her more, he'd always end the text by saying things like *Take care* or *Hope your day's going well* or *Throw Asa a ball for me*, as if maybe he still cared, but she didn't know for sure what was going through his mind.

One afternoon, as had become her routine since she was alone with Anna, who'd already seen her scars, Char went out in her swimsuit to lie by the pool in the warm afternoon sun and get some work done. After several hours, she started to feel eyestrain. She was on her stomach with her foot propped on a folded beach towel, just about to close her laptop, when Asa came running up as fast as he could to say hello. He always made her laugh when he would take off toward her like lightning, as if they hadn't seen each other in days. Laughing and trying to deflect him from completely devouring her face, she didn't notice for a minute that someone had come into the backyard. But when Asa turned and alerted with warning barks, Char looked up to see Kat staring down at her with a steely gaze.

"Katena, I didn't see you. Asa, it's okay," she said, sitting up and quickly grabbing her wrap.

"Oh, don't bother covering up, dear Charlotte. I saw every last one of your scars."

Kat's brazen disregard for Char's self-consciousness stung deeply. "If you're here to see Emmett, he's in Denver for the week. He'll be back Sunday," she said, sounding even icier than Kat.

"No, actually I came to see you. I'm feeling disappointed that perhaps we won't be friends after all. Lou spoke with Emmett last night. I'm happy I stopped by. I feel I'm getting a better picture of what's going on," she said, giving Char another once-over, "and I need to tell you that you're making a coward's mistake." Kat loomed overhead, her long, graceful body casting a shadow over Char.

"I'm sorry you think you know me well enough to make such an assumption. I respect that you're looking out for your friend, but whatever's going on is between the two of us, alone. I have no interest in allowing you to play referee. So, if you'll please—" Char waved her hand toward the side gate, refusing to meet Kat's glare.

Katena sniffed and stayed firmly planted. She pulled a book out of her oversized Louis Vuitton and tossed it down to Charlotte.

"Here, you must read this, and keep in mind the story is mine, yet I have the love of my life, a career, beautiful friends. I engage the world with no need to hide. If after you read my book, you still don't feel like talking with me, then fine. But if you do want to talk, then we will be friends, and we will go to lunch together this week. I do hope to hear from you." With that, she strode out through the gate.

What a piece of work, Char thought. She let out a groan. She reluctantly picked up the book and looked at the cover. It was a picture of Kat in a white ruffle-collared blouse, wearing large teardrop sapphire-and-diamond earrings. She looked stunning. The title was *Victim to Victor: Katena Volkov-Samuel,* and the bottom read, *A survivor's tale of human trafficking's evils.*

Charlotte could only imagine the horror Kat must have gone through and wondered how someone with such beautiful armor to hide behind could dare to take it off and reveal the ugliness she had experienced.

With nothing but time on her hands, Char felt there would be minimal risk to reading the book, and while she wasn't the least bit confident that Katena's book or anyone else could help her change her mind about her and Emmett, she was willing to see what Katena had to say. She settled herself under one of the flowering trees and, feeling brave, dug in.

Just a few pages into Kat's autobiography, Char stopped, knowing she'd need a drink to get through the book. Anna was happy to oblige and brought out a chicken salad for dinner and a small pitcher of mimosa punch. Char was grateful; it was just enough to get her through the few hours it would take to complete Kat's book.

Throughout the book, Char cringed, cried, and finally, at the end, celebrated. Katena's story was horrific and heartrending. Her family had lived in a small war-torn village in Eastern Europe. Katena's mother had been a prostitute, one of the only ways in which she could help support her extended family. While alive, her mother doggedly kept Katena out of prostitution, but once she died, her uncles, desperate to honor their sister's wishes to protect Katena, scraped up what little money they could to pay a man who promised to take her far away from their hellish existence.

Instead of placing her with a family she could work for while also getting an education, the man subjected Katena to the very life her mother had fought so hard to protect her from. It took years before Kat was able to break free, and she lost much in the meantime, but something her mother used to tell her had become her mantra, her hope, and her source of strength. She had instilled into Kat that it would be better to die fighting for her freedom than to live like a trapped animal. Her refusal to give up was ultimately her ticket to freedom.

Katena wrote that she knew sharing her story would be invaluable in helping change the perception that trafficking victims were criminals; she knew it would encourage many who had previously cast judgment to instead hold out a helping hand in one way or another. Charlotte was touched.

What spoke personally to Char was that, throughout her struggles, Kat had maintained a steely determination to overcome the odds. Her perseverance could be inspiring to even the most hopeless of hearts. Char felt it. She was thankful to Kat for insisting she read the book, and she understood why Katena had written it. She wanted to inspire others to overcome their pasts.

Kat's story didn't help Char realize anything that she didn't already understand about herself. She knew her self-esteem, self-confidence, and trust in others had been unduly damaged, and that she was severely stunted in her ability to move forward, but Kat's book did help boost her resolve to regain her strength. Kat had everything in her life; she lacked for nothing, despite her harrowing past. Charlotte wanted her everything too, and in taking the first brave step, she felt the thrill of hope as she admitted to herself that her everything included Emmett.

Lost in thought about her own life's story and the work that needed to be done, Char was brought out again by the cool breeze. Looking around, she saw the sun had almost set, and the crickets had started their nightly communication. She looked through the patio door to see only one dim light was left on in the house. Anna must have turned in for the night. Now Char wanted nothing more than to snuggle into Emmett's bed and think about how to make it right between them. She hoped her chance wasn't long gone.

• • •

As soon as the sun rose, Char was up and getting ready for the day. Once it hit a decent time for a morning call, she called Kat and told her she'd read her book and was hoping to lunch with her soon.

"Excellent. I'll pick you up this morning at eleven sharp," Kat said, then hung up. Char stared at her phone and told herself she'd just have to get used to Kat's blunt communication style.

Katena was right on time, and they made small talk on their way to lunch, saving the serious talk for later.

Once there, at a small but chic restaurant near Rodeo Drive, Kat asked to be seated in a private corner. They each ordered salads and decided they would ignore the clock and order cocktails. Char, as always, had a lemon drop martini and Kat an extra dry martini, two olives.

"So, what did you think about my book?" Kat wasted no time getting right to the point.

"I loved it. What you went through and that you came out whole on the other side—it's amazing. You're an inspiration, Kat."

"And what about you personally? Could my story be an inspiration to you?"

All of the wind in Char's sails suddenly vanished. She'd been prepared to talk frankly with Kat, but as soon as it was actually happening, Char felt her cemented resolve turn to mush.

"Um, well, yeah, I think metaphorically, like I said, your story's an inspiration. For anyone who feels they're trying to overcome the odds, whatever they may be." She played nonchalance as she fiddled with the lemon wedge hanging off her glass.

Kat wasn't fooled. "Oh, cut the bullshit, Charlotte—surely you didn't call me for lunch to blow smoke," she said blankly.

"I'm sorry?" *I'm sorry I'm such a chicken and can't be straight with you.*

"Charlotte, it's perfectly clear that you've been through some trauma in your life. It's getting in the way of your happiness. You have the privilege of knowing one of the most generous, kind-hearted men around, yet you're pushing him away. So what was it? What are you afraid of?"

Char was flustered. She respected Kat and her forthrightness and wished she could emulate her bravery, but when it came down to it, she just didn't think she could. Her eyes began to burn, and she could feel tears welling up, her throat tightening.

"Oh, dear, let's try not to do that," Kat said in her thick accent as she snapped open her clutch. She handed Char a tissue. "Let's have another drink." She motioned to the waiter from across the room.

Kat told Charlotte, "Perhaps we shouldn't jump right into your story. You read mine, but there is still much more that wasn't printed. I have scars too, Charlotte. Not ones that can be seen, no, but scars nonetheless. My husband wanted to have children, but I'm unable to carry a child. My past made that impossible. We could adopt, and perhaps someday we will." Katena pushed her drink away and sipped her water. Her eyes seemed to go vacant for the briefest moment, the only sign that she was at all affected by sharing her pain.

"Katena, I'm sorry," was all Charlotte could say.

"Thank you. I did not want to share the truth with my husband. I was afraid he would no longer be attracted to me. The amazing thing was it brought us closer. That is what I hope for you, Charlotte. But I believe you need someone to talk to before you go to Emmett with your truth."

Composing herself, Char rallied. "Katena, I thought I could come here and be honest with you. I really would love to talk to someone, a friend. But I think it's just too much; it's too painful. And even if I could, I wouldn't know where to start," she said honestly, managing to hold it together.

"Ahh, these Americans, so emotional. Listen, the way I tell my story is I don't focus on myself. I'm not the ugliness that other people perpetrated *against* me. I'm telling a story about the depravity and evilness that exists in the world. That's on them. I have nothing to feel guilty about." Kat paused and narrowed her eyes at Charlotte. "That's it; you have guilt. Why do you carry other people's burdens? It's a waste of time. You're a good person; you love your children, no? You're a good mother?" Kat asked zealously.

"Yes, I really do. I try to be a good mom, but I've made some serious mistakes. You don't know the choices I've made in my life, and you really don't know me, Kat. How is it that you feel so confident about what you think my situation is?" Char took another sip of her martini to help calm her nerves.

"Because not only did I see the scars on your body the other day, but I see the scars in your eyes. You've been hurt, very badly. With the life I've lived, I can sniff out the hardened criminals, the opportunists, the liars a mile away. You're none of those," Kat said frankly.

Char spoke softly and refused to look up. "I've done some selfish things in my life."

"Is selfishness against the law? It's not; get over it. Better yet, another book for you. Read Ayn Rand. Selfishness serves as self-preservation. If you sacrifice yourself until you're dead, then what good are you to anybody?"

"I can think of a sacrifice or two that was well worth it."

"Of course, but then it's not a true sacrifice if what you're giving up is truly worth less to you than the reward you'll get in return. I tell you, selfishness is the way to go. But we digress. Come on, please tell, how did you get all those scars?"

Char looked down again and felt her heart begin to race. "If I were brave enough to tell you about each one, we'd be here a while, Kat. And some, I just can't, brave or not."

"What about the little scar there, on the side of your eye? Is that a safe one to ask about?" Kat pointed to the corner of her own eye.

"Courtesy of my alcoholic first husband. In anger, he shattered a mirror a few inches from my face."

"Bastard. And the one on your side?"

Char took in a breath. "Suffice it to say, my stepfather was an angry, violent man. There were quite a few—I'll call them 'accidents'—around our house growing up."

"I see. I never had a father. I couldn't imagine what that must have been like. What about your mother? Did she try to protect you?" she asked, curious.

Char went crimson. "Uh, no, she usually was the instigator to my stepfather's rage toward me. She was abusive too."

"So you have trust issues, with men and women. It's a miracle you're sitting here talking with me. Amazing. See, there's much hope for you," Kat said with pride. She continued. "The scars on your back; did your stepfather do that to you too?"

"Kat, you asked me to talk about what I was comfortable with. I did so."

Kat smiled. "This is good. You're strong. You'll get there. I won't push. But, for now, we've made good progress. Have you shared your childhood with Emmett?"

Char looked as if she had tasted a lemon. "Kat, I nearly died when he saw the scar on my side that night. Of course I'm not going to tell him all about it."

"So, you do want to pursue a relationship with Emmett, but you don't want him to see your scars or to share your past with him. But you do understand that there's no relationship if there's no intimacy, do you not?"

Char's eyes welled up again, and she nodded to Kat.

"Oh, dear God, not again. Here, maybe you need water now." She slid Char's water glass to her. "All is not lost, my dear Char. You know Emmett is worth fighting for. Don't surrender. Look at all you've overcome already. You have the strength. You can do this."

Charlotte thought for a moment while Kat waited patiently. "You're right. I'll take this step. When Emmett comes home, I'll answer his question; I'll tell him about the scar on my side." Char smiled and, taking a deep breath, felt strong and determined.

"There you go. Very productive lunch. Very good, Charlotte."

When Sunday finally made its appearance, Charlotte's stomach was in knots, and when Emmett called Anna to tell her he was coming home on an earlier flight, Charlotte nearly had a panic attack. Since her lunch with Kat, Charlotte's mind had been consumed with the talk she would have with Emmett, and she had begun to feel confident with the prospect, but the reality of actually having to go through with it hit her when Anna headed out the door to pick Emmett up from the airport.

She was afraid to have the conversation, but nevertheless was committed to following through. Equating his wanting to know the real her with pushing himself on her had been a low blow, and she wanted to make it right. She thought back to her conversation with Kat and knew opening a small part of her past to him wasn't a sacrifice. She wanted to do it. She just had to garner up the nerve to follow through by the time Emmett came home.

She bit her lip in nervous anticipation when she heard Emmett and Anna coming from the garage into the kitchen. "Hi, you're back early," Char said meekly, suddenly feeling awkward. It felt like forever since she'd seen him.

Emmett still looked almost as dejected as he had the night before he left, and it was tough for Char to see. He looked like a hurt puppy. She wanted to make him feel better and have him know that the things she lashed out with weren't really how she felt.

"We finished ahead of schedule, and I was able to get an earlier flight." Emmett seemed unsure of himself and didn't quite meet Charlotte's eyes as he spoke.

"You look like you could use a drink. I made margaritas; do you want to go out on the patio with me?"

His eyes seemed to brighten just a bit. He looked pleasantly surprised. "You know, thank you, yeah. That sounds good. Let me take a quick shower, and I'll be right out."

She was hopeful and told herself to stick to the plan and not chicken out. She fussed with the table to busy herself until Emmett returned, meeting her with a smile. "This looks great, Char. Wow." He was leaning against the open patio door, wearing loose linen pants and a pale blue button-up with the sleeves rolled. His hair hung in wet curls.

Char guarded her eyes as she looked up to him for fear he'd see how captivating he was to her. She was thankful for the distraction of handing him a drink as they sat down. "For you," she said softly. "So, does it feel good to be home? How was Denver?"

His fingers brushed hers as he accepted the drink. Stammering, he said, "Thanks, um, uh, yeah, work was a strain. Eighteen-hour days. It was tiring, but we got a lot of good footage, so it was well worth it. But yeah, I'm happy to be back." He eyed Charlotte and took a drink of his margarita. "So, to what do I owe this warm welcome home?" he asked with genuine surprise in his voice.

Char swallowed. "This is a thank-you for all you've done, and an apology for the awful things I said to you. Emmett, I lashed out and made accusations that I don't even believe. I was just scared by the direction our conversation was going. I got desperate for it to stop," she said looking down, afraid to make eye contact.

He inched closer to her, their knees touching under the table.

"Charlotte, you shouldn't be the one apologizing. You were right. I was out of line, and I pushed too hard. It's just I can't pretend not to care. And every day that I get to spend with you I care even more." He took her hands into his.

Charlotte felt a warmth spread throughout her whole body and bring a smile to her lips. It gave her just the boost she needed. She took a deep breath and began. "I've come to care a lot about you, too. And after you left, it scared me that I might have ruined our friendship, and I want to right the ship. You've proven in more ways than one that I can trust you. This is a starting point for us, so I want you to know I'm ready to talk about the scar on my side." Char wondered if Emmett could even hear her; she felt as if all the air had somehow been sucked out of her lungs, making it hard to speak. She pursed her lips together unconsciously, trying to clamp down on the pain of what she was about to share.

Emmett shot up from his seat. Charlotte could only sit there, looking up at him, scared. She assumed he was going to walk away from her. If he didn't want to hear it, she knew she'd have to accept it, but instead he reached for her hands. He pulled her to him.

"Char, I don't want to pressure you. You've got stress written all over you. I can tell the way you purse your lips; your dimples show when you're uncomfortable," he said as he gently reached up and brushed her dimples. "You don't have to do this," he said, his voice low and comforting.

"Yes, I do." Her voice cracked and her pulse was racing. She was scared yet determined. "I..." she said, but nothing else would come out. Char panicked. *Where did my voice go? Will it come back?* She was desperate for it to come back.

Emmett looked racked with guilt. He pulled her close, his head lowered to her ear. "It's all right, Charlotte." As he bent down, she reached up. She felt relief for the pause he was giving. When their lips met, she melted into the kiss, allowing him to embrace her fully.

Charlotte reveled in how soft and full Emmett's lips felt on hers. He wrapped one arm around her to pull her in tight, his other hand at her neck, his fingers entwining her hair. She felt safely wrapped in his protection. Surrendering to his kiss this time gave her comfort, not anxiety. He pulled back and lifted her chin to search her eyes.

"I wasn't planning on that," he said, anticipating her response.

"Neither was I, but I think we can call it a pleasant surprise," she said softly.

"Thank God. I can't risk you pushing away from me again."

Char gave a shy smile. "No, you haven't pushed me away."

"Earlier this week, after what happened, I wasn't sure you'd even be here when I got back. Lou had to keep reassuring me, saying Kat and you were working together to fix what I had done."

Emmett had reminded her of the problem left to be resolved. She took a deep breath and focused on completing the task at hand. "It wasn't you, Emmett. This is on me. That night you asked me a reasonable question, and now I'm going to answer you. Like you said then, if we're going to have any chance at all, this is it. Katena helped me this week to be honest with myself. And the truth is, I do want a chance with you. I want to do this."

Emmett searched her eyes. "Really? You're ready for more than friendship?" When she nodded, he pulled her in for another kiss. "I wasn't expecting this. I thought I'd ruined everything." The pain in his voice spoke to Charlotte, telling her he really did care for her.

"Let's talk first. I want to get this out. Then you can see if you're still so excited for us to move forward." Charlotte was scared, but willed herself to press on.

"Let's go inside and get comfortable. I'll be right there."

Charlotte sank into the couch and pulled a throw over her, helping her feel a little less exposed. Emmett sat next to her and gave her a mischievous grin as he gave her a refilled margarita. With gratitude, she took a gulp of courage before starting.

"Emmett, I'm sorry I've been so combative. It's just…there's a lot that's gone on in my life that's given me great pause when it comes to the idea of being in any kind of relationship. But talking to Katena and reading her book has been such an inspiration to not let my past rob me of my future, and to do that, I have to let you in, and I'm willing to work on doing just that."

Emmett sat on the edge of his seat. Charlotte could tell he understood the gravity of the conversation. "I appreciate this, Char, but I did a lot of thinking this week too. I was wrong. I don't want to push you. I hope you understand that."

"I do, but you're right, and I think sharing the story of the scar on my side is a good starting point for us." Char felt strong. She felt she could go forward because of the man Emmett was. She knew she could trust him. It was a small step, and there were many more to take, but she felt ready.

She gripped her margarita glass, and though it was ice cold, her cheeks began to flush. "I just…I had a difficult upbringing. I know I told you I liked to stay out of the house. Of course, a lot of teenagers crave independence, but the truth is, I was running away from a bad situation. My parents were abusive: verbally, mentally, physically." Char stayed stoic and matter-of-fact. To get through it, she couldn't look him in the eye. Instead, she focused on the condensation trailing from her thumb strokes and falling like tears down the icy glass.

She heaved a breath and continued. "So this scar on my side really isn't that dramatic of a story. I mean, it was an incident around our house like any other, but sometimes there were unforeseen consequences. As I told you, we lived a rural lifestyle, and we did a lot of outside work around the property. Sean, my older brother, and I were doing yard work with our stepdad—Keith was his name. Sean did something ridiculous to set Keith off; maybe he left the hose running or something, not that it really mattered. His reaction was never warranted either way. So Keith started charging after him, which was nothing new, but the particular look in his eyes that day scared me to death. I just had a sense that he was really going to hurt my brother that time. So I yelled at him. I don't even remember what I said, but I felt like a matador waving the red flag, trying to get his attention. Anyway, it worked, and instead of going for my brother, he made a beeline for me, cussing and spitting his way toward me. I started walking backward, putting my arms up, thinking, *Oh no, I'm really going to get it this time.* He hit me, and I stumbled backward into our rickety wheelbarrow. It had wooden handles, and when I fell into them, one split. It cut me from the ribs up. He was still going at me, but when he saw the blood, he finally stopped." Char paused. "But, boy, was he angry."

"He was angry you were injured?" Emmett could barely get the words out.

"In a way. He was angry that I needed stitches. I would have to go to the hospital, where doctors would ask questions. My brother and I had been coached from an early age how to play off our injuries, but it was still a risk every time."

"What a sick SOB. What about your mother? Where was she in all of this?" he asked with a look showing he was certain Charlotte's answer wouldn't be anything good.

Charlotte answered with a shrug. "I don't remember that she was there during that incident, but she was during plenty of others. Either way, as much as she hated Keith, she never failed to take his side.

Regardless of what happened, it was always my fault.

"Char, not that it really matters, but how old were you when this happened?"

"Eleven, twelve maybe. When they eventually divorced, it had nothing to do with how he had failed as a father." She set down her glass and grabbed a pillow to fold into. She wondered where Asa was. She usually would have his warm furry body nestled against her in times like these. She hoped Emmett would maintain his cool, but prepared for otherwise. She felt guilty for dumping her negativity onto him and suddenly regretted her decision. She avoided eye contact and awaited his response. She knew if she looked up, she'd see anger or sadness or, worse, sympathy, so she played with her fingernails or laced and unlaced her fingers and straightened out the fringe on the pillow, anything to keep from having to see the look on his face.

Emmett reached out to lift Char's chin. She willed herself to meet his gaze. His eyes were tender and thoughtful, thankfully without any hint of sympathy.

"Well, you know what? All that is over now. You never have to go back to a place like that again. I can personally promise that. You're beautiful, wonderful, brave, and smart. And don't forget strong."

If there was ever anything that made Char squirm more, it was being paid compliments. She believed being put on any kind of pedestal only served one clear purpose: giving one a higher perch from which to fall. "I don't know about any of that, Emmett. I've worked so hard over the years to remove myself from my past, but I've made so many mistakes. As much as I try, I just find myself taken right back there again and again." The lump in Char's throat was burning; she had to stop talking if she wanted to keep it together.

"Charlotte, listen to me. The kind of trauma you were put through, no one deserves that. I don't care what you say about your past; it's not your fault."

"I'll need your patience, Emmett. There's more, there's a lot more." Charlotte had been proud of how strong she was being, but just hinting at her deeper pain broke her down. She put her hands to her face and sobbed. There was nothing she could do to hold it in.

He drew her to him. Realizing how fragile she still was, she knew she needed to get one more point clear, the most difficult to broach.

"Emmett," she said into his chest, not wanting to look up at him.

"Yes?" He ran his fingers through her hair.

"All of this we're talking about. Remember how I reacted to you at my condo when we kissed?"

He nodded. "Mhm."

"I just…if we could, I'd like to take our intimacy slowly. I can't…I don't like my back touched at all. I'm going to need time. I don't know when."

"I promise you, I can be patient. I'll be honest; I look forward to the day we can be intimate. But days, weeks, even months. Don't worry about that. I'll protect you, and I'll be patient for you, babe, I promise."

Char knew in her heart that she couldn't hold Emmett to his promise to protect her, and how patient could he be? She didn't know how much time it would take to let him in more. As much as this moment was a turning point for them, she knew that her deeper scars still threatened the bond they were forging.

Emmett held her tightly, and she enjoyed their comfortable silence until Asa went to the front door and gave it a few scratches, letting Emmett know he was ready for his evening walk.

"Guess that's my cue. If I could, I'd stay with you on this couch all night."

"Thank you for taking him out. And thank you for tonight. I felt safe talking to you." Char felt a tingling go through her body, a strange sensation of both elation and still some embarrassment. It hadn't been easy opening up to him. No other man had pressed her about her past, but he did because he cared enough to want to know.

"Thank you for trusting me. I think you know now that I'm here for you; whatever you need, I'll stand by your side." He pulled her in for a kiss, sweet and gentle.

Char enjoyed his lips on hers and the feeling of his strong arms surrounding her. As much as she wanted to stay there forever, Asa needed his walk, and she was tired. "I'm going to say good night to you. It was a long day anticipating your return," Char said, feeling shy.

Emmett got up from the couch and held his hand out to Char, pulling her close.

"I bet it was. You took a huge step for me. And I hope you realize for yourself too. There's no need for you to harbor so much. I'm here for you, no matter what."

"I know you are."

"Char, don't get the wrong impression, but could I…can we share your bed tonight? I promise not in *that* way, but just so I can stay close to you?"

She felt her face light up, and she nodded.

"I'm going to hit my workout room before bed, so I'll be a while. I need to let off some steam first."

The look on his face told Charlotte he was more affected by her story than he was letting on, and she felt bad.

Asa pawed at the front door again. "Poor little guy; he's being patient, but I'd better get going," he said, making his way to the door.

What Emmett had said about needing to work out bothered her. Would she ever stop feeling like baggage? "I'm sorry, Emmett. You had a long week. Maybe I should have waited to tell you." In reality she worried she shouldn't have told him at all.

Emmett turned to her. The look on her face must have revealed her inner doubts because he rushed back to her side. The warmth from his nearness comforted her. "No, absolutely not, Charlotte. I'm proud of you. You don't know how much it means to me that you trusted me with this. I'll be honest; it's hard to imagine anyone laying their hands on you. The thought drives me crazy," he said, gritting his teeth before quickly calming back down. "But it's nothing for you to worry about. Go lie down, sweetheart; I'll be in later."

She couldn't wait for him to get back so she could feel his arms around her once again, but as soon as her head hit the pillow, she was off to sleep, drowsy from the wondrous feeling of acceptance after all she told him. It made her feel warm and light, not so burdened. Emmett gave her hope that maybe she wouldn't be forever beholden to the past.

Morning mom, Chloe's dad's side of the family is awesome.
Having great time. Hope u r 2. miss u xoxox Aub L

Aubrie's text woke Charlotte up. She'd briefly stirred when Emmett came to bed and had slept even better knowing he was there all night, but after she read the text, she looked over to see he was already up for the day.

After she texted Aubrie back, she lay in bed thinking about the talk she had had with Emmett the night before. She knew she couldn't have asked for a better outcome. She had made it through with Emmett there by her side. He didn't make her feel embarrassed or ashamed. He just listened and supported her. If ever there was a perfect man to fall in love with, Emmett might just be it, but thinking this scared her to no end.

She hobbled to the kitchen on her crutches, and there was Emmett. As always he looked scruffy and sleepy, but his eyes lit up as he saw her come into the room. Her heart fluttered.

"Well, don't you look like a bowl of sunshine this morning?" he said, kissing her on the head. "How did you sleep?"

"Better, knowing you were there."

"Same here, babe. Thank you for letting me in."

"How was your workout?" she couldn't help but ask.

He grinned. "My punching bag's seen better days, let's just say that."

For some reason at that moment she felt especially drawn to him. She walked up and put her arms around his waist, hugging her body into his. He set her crutches against the counter and pulled her in close.

"Charlotte, after last night's conversation, I was left with only one question." He looked serious.

"Yes?" she said, looking up at him.

"After our talk I feel like we took a step forward in our relationship. Would you say we're a couple now?"

She had to think about it before answering, knowing Emmett was waiting with bated breath. She reminded herself the reason why she'd been so brave with him the day before. She didn't want to lose him. She told herself not to be afraid.

"Yes, I think we can safely say that we're together."

Emmett startled Char with a loud whoop before calling out, "Hot damn!" She was laughing at his exuberance when he went in for a kiss. He held her face, taking possession of her mouth. It was a celebratory kiss that could have gone on forever, but for a small cough from Anna, letting them know she was coming through with a load of laundry.

Char knew she and Emmett both looked like cats that swallowed the canary, but Anna pretended not to notice. She said good morning to Char and continued on her way like nothing was out of the ordinary, though Char thought she saw Anna smiling as she passed into the laundry room.

. . .

Emmett told Charlotte his Mondays were usually filled with anticipation for the week, since he loved his job, but confessed that now, instead of looking forward to work, he longed to spend the day with her. At her insistence, however, he did the right thing and dropped her and Asa off at her condo before going to work. Moe was finally coming over for a visit and had offered to walk Asa for her.

Charlotte was happy that at least Emmett would have to carry her up the stairs. They kissed good-bye and tried to pretend they weren't sad about spending the day apart.

Charlotte told herself to just focus on the tasks at hand and not act like a forlorn teenager. She wanted to have the condo just perfect for the girls, and there was still so much to do. Lots of boxes still needed to be emptied and clutter to be picked up. Before starting in on the boxes, however, she decided to call her daughter.

Aubrie said the trip was going great and that they would be leaving for California Friday morning. They would take two leisurely days to get to Malibu. Char said she thought that was a great idea, but told her to be careful of where she decided to stay, to pick a bigger town with decent hotels. Aubrie promised she would.

She'd been working for several hours straight when she heard Moe calling up from downstairs; Char had asked Emmett to leave the door unlocked for her. *Perfect timing.* She was ready for a break. "Hi, Moe, come on up."

Moe jangled up the stairs as Asa ran in circles at the top, anxious to greet her.

"Well, hello, my furry friend! And how are you, Charlie?"

"I'm good. I'm getting my boot off Friday, and my niece and daughter will be home Saturday, so things are nice. I have a lot to look forward to." She wanted to divulge more but being so private, held back.

"Oh, Charlie, I saw you go somewhere else for a second, somewhere romantic. Do tell!"

Char hesitated, but decided to be honest. "Well, Emmett. He and I, we're, I guess you could say we've taken the step beyond friendship." She searched for the right words, and that was the best she could come up with.

"But of course you have; a match made, that's what I said when I first saw you two together. And I'm not just talking about both your movie-star good looks! No, your chakras complement each other perfectly!"

"Our chakras?" Char said dubiously.

"It's all very scientific; I don't want to bore you with the details, but yes. What each of you is lacking, the other clearly holds the ability to provide. You've had love, but the aloof kind. Emmett's heart yearns to embrace a woman fully. I think he's been taken advantage of a time or two. Your heart doesn't have a superficial spot whatsoever. You two could create a pure love together. It's all quite magical," Moe said wistfully.

As exciting as it was, Char couldn't help but have the twinge of worry that she could still mess things up; she was holding in so much.

"Oh, but now I see worry on your face. Is something troubling you? Are you afraid to be in a relationship, my dear? You know, if you ever need to talk to anyone, I should let you know, I've been a licensed psychologist for over thirty years, and just recently I've begun incorporating holistic approaches. I'm what they call a sensitive, not in the ghostly way, but I can read people's chakras, gauging their current psyche, which nine times out of ten is an indicator of their past, be it peaceful or traumatic. I've learned to take it all into account, and I've been successful helping those who have suffered any sort of trauma."

Charlotte listened to Moe and knew that she knew. She thought of Emmett and all that stood in their way. She wanted to be rid of her past, so she could move on with Emmett in her future. She decided to take a brave step.

"I think I might know someone who could use your services."

"We could get started right away, my dear Charlie."

Charlotte smiled appreciatively and felt hope crowding out her doubt.

Moe clapped her hands together and looked down at Asa. "Well, what do you say, Asa? Shall we go smell the roses?"

Asa looked up at Moe with his head cocked as if to say, "I'm not familiar with that euphemism," but then he seemed to figure it out. He started spinning around at Moe's feet, excited for a walk.

Charlotte set about unpacking more boxes and was interrupted by a text from Emmett.

> *Trying to concentrate at work today but can't seem to get you off my mind. Tons to do but I haven't made a dent. Look what you're doing to me.*

She smiled and texted back.

> *Boo-hoo, how do you think I'm doing? Not much better. But you'll get more done if you don't waste your time texting complaints to me!*

He sent back an emoticon sticking its tongue out.

She laughed and sent him the same, plus a smiley face blowing a kiss. She took in a deep breath and enjoyed feeling so light and carefree.

Moe returned with Asa after a long walk, and he went straight for his water, making a huge mess and giving Moe and Char quite a show. While cleaning up after Asa, they agreed to meet twice a week for Char's therapy. Charlotte decided to keep it secret from Emmett and surprise him with the news once she felt she'd made significant progress. They agreed to meet at Moe's downtown office until her ankle healed, since it had an elevator. Once her boot was off Charlotte was welcome to come to Moe's home office.

When Emmett got to her condo, he didn't wait for small talk and instead went straight for a kiss. It caught Charlotte off guard, but she reciprocated wholeheartedly.

As he carried her down the stairs, he joked, "You know I love any excuse to have you in my arms, but you've got to be itching to get out of this boot. What did the doctor say last week?"

Char's eyes lit up. "Oh my gosh, I can't believe I forgot to tell you. I've got great news: the boot comes off Friday."

"Babe, that's great news; this Friday, the Fourth of July?"

Charlotte couldn't believe she'd been in California for a month already; she had to check her phone to confirm it. "Wow, you're right."

Emmett's eyes danced. "You'll be footloose and fancy-free, with fireworks to boot. I'll call Lou, and the four of us can celebrate."

Thursday snuck up on Charlotte; she was nervous for her first appointment with Moe. Anna had agreed to give Charlotte a ride to Moe's office and promised to keep Charlotte's therapy a secret, saying she couldn't think of a better surprise for Emmett.

A receptionist checked Charlotte's name in her computer before buzzing her into the hallway. She found Moe's suite and, with some trepidation, opened the door. Moe was sitting behind her desk typing intensely, a pair of glasses perched on the end of her upturned nose. When she looked up, she greeted Charlotte with her typical exuberance, and that settled Charlotte's nerves.

Moe's office was done up in muted tones of sand and khaki, and there were thoughtfully placed aloe vera plants and ferns throughout. A simple desk, a couple soft chairs with end tables, a coffee table, and a zero gravity chair were all that occupied the space.

"Welcome. How are you, Charlie? How about I pour you some tea before we get started?"

"Do you have coffee?" she asked as smoothly as possible.

"Sorry, no. But the teas I have are wonderfully aromatic and calming, something that helps during sessions. What do you say?"

Charlotte nodded while wringing her hands and looking around the office.

"Oh, Charlie, it's going to be all right. Go on and have a seat," Moe said as she handed her a teacup and sat down.

"Thank you. I'm sorry. I'm really, really nervous though," she said as she sank into the soft chair. It seemed to envelop her, and she liked that. It made her feel less vulnerable.

"It's perfectly fine to be nervous, but it'll get better, I promise," Moe said with an easy smile.

"Your office; it's different than I expected. It's calming."

"You thought it would be loud like me," Moe said, laughing. "No, I know better than that. This room should inspire us to relax physically on the outside so that we can focus on what's going on on the inside. So many times in life we focus on the logistics, outside stimuli, where we need to go, what we need to do, and we forget to check in with ourselves to simply see how we're feeling, and that's just as important as everything else."

"But I think some people prefer to focus on the logistics, as you put it."

"Oh, many do, yes. But some of our most treasured parts of ourselves can become lost if we don't face our feelings. Think back to some of your best memories as a young child. What were they?"

"As difficult as my childhood was, there were bright spots—one of them was probably playing with my brother. We could laugh for hours. We found humor in everything; we had so much fun together. People thought we were twins. We were only ten months apart and inseparable."

"And now?"

"We haven't spoken in years. We both did our best to run as far away from home as soon as we could, and we just lost touch."

"And how does that make you feel?"

"Sad. I miss him; I wish we could go back to that time. But I couldn't imagine reaching out to him now. And he hasn't reached out to me, so I guess we feel the same about it."

"While you can't go back to that time, my posit to you is: if you and your brother could have stayed in touch with your truest selves and held on tightly, you likely wouldn't be separated now. But you know what? There's hope. If you can do the work and get in touch with your authentic self, you might find the gumption inside to reach out to him."

"So much happened to us growing up that I think we just don't want to face the past, and I think that's what we'd see if we were to stand face-to-face again."

"And what about now, Charlie? Are there things in your more recent past that you're hiding from?"

Charlotte felt a heat rising in her chest and toward her ears as a bead of sweat crowned at her hairline. She put her tea down.

"Charlie, I'm certified in what's known as EMDR. That stands for eye movement desensitization and reprocessing. It's a light-aided therapy to help with traumatic memories. I won't lie, it's not easy. It requires accessing those darkest of memories during therapy. But the light stimulation to the eye, just as its name implies, desensitizes you to them and reprocesses the brain so that they can't immobilize and haunt you further. My intuition says that's what you need."

"It doesn't sound fun."

"It's not, Charlie, but it's likely your best bet at reclaiming your life. Don't worry, we'll work slowly. I won't push you too far too fast. And that's not all we'll do. There's talk therapy, massage, herbs. We'll run the gamut until we find what works best for you."

Charlotte thought about the night that her life changed and all that was involved. She wasn't sure she could or should share every detail.

"You look concerned about something. Are you worried about confidentiality?"

Char nodded and felt her stomach turn.

"Under California law, I do fall under the duty to report." She went to her desk and rummaged through files before finding a pamphlet. "Here's the gist of what I'm required to divulge."

Char looked it over and read the criminal activity clause that said only if the subject is still engaged in criminal activity and poses an active threat to herself or others would there be a duty to report. She resolved that if she were going to try to heal from that night, that in time, she would come clean with Moe.

"Don't worry, your secrets will be safe with me, and there's nothing, and I mean nothing, you could say that would shock or unnerve me. Believe me, I've heard it all. And let me tell you a little secret of mine. Many lifetimes ago when I was a young woman, I dated a mob boss for years. When I tell you I've heard it all, well, my dear Charlie, I've seen it all too. How do you think my hair got so white? No wonder I started going gray before I turned thirty."

Charlotte and Moe laughed, and Char felt much better about her decision.

Charlotte had the condo in tip-top shape for Aubrie by Friday afternoon and was excited for Emmett to pick her up for her doctor's appointment. Later that night they planned to head downtown to meet Kat and Lou at a chic hotel where they could enjoy the view of the fireworks.

As they were leaving the doctor's office and making their way down the hall and out of the building, Charlotte said to Emmett, "Wow, this feels scary."

"Feels fragile, doesn't it? But it's just weak, honey. As much as I've loved carrying you in my arms for the last month, and as much as I'd love to sweep you up again right here, right now, it's best you work on building its strength up."

"Ha, don't worry, I wasn't hinting for help. In fact, I'm looking forward to being in the driver's seat again," she said, swiping the keys from Emmett's hand when they got near the car.

"What? A man always drives his lady."

"Not today he doesn't. This lady's celebrating." She looked at him with a bright smile, challenging him to disagree.

He acquiesced and opened the driver's door for her. She smiled in victory.

Charlotte headed downtown and was giddy all the way there. She noticed Emmett staring at her. "What?"

"Nothing; it just makes me happy to see you happy," he said, his smile bright.

"I feel so free right now. I can't wait to go swimming again."

Emmett chuckled and said, "Just make sure you don't push too hard. Give your ankle time to gain strength."

"You're always looking out for me—thank you," Char said sincerely.

"I wouldn't have it any other way." He put his hand reassuringly on her thigh. Charlotte couldn't have felt happier.

The rooftop view of the city was breathtaking. Emmett brought a chair out for Charlotte, and as he did, bent down and gave her a tender kiss at her temple. Char reached for his hand.

Kat and Lou looked on and smiled. Charlotte could swear that they were watching her and Emmett more than they were the fireworks.

When the show was over and the couples said their good-byes, Emmett held his hand out for the keys. "I'm driving this time, babe," he said with authority. "You're a decent driver, but you do know you can get a ticket just as easily for impeding traffic as you can for speeding, right?"

Charlotte playfully slapped his arm. "Whatever. What's the hurry anyway? Are we up past your bedtime?" she teased.

"No, I just can't wait to get home with you."

Charlotte hoped he didn't have any expectations, but since she'd already made unfair accusations at him once, she decided to give him the benefit of the doubt.

When they got home, they shared a bed again. Charlotte was hesitant, but willed herself to trust him. He pulled her in close, his lips at her ear. "This is what I was anxious to get home to. Charlotte, I don't care that we haven't taken things to the next level. I just crave being next to you. The smell of your hair, your soft skin, and the way you fit perfectly against me—I just enjoy being close to you." He kissed her shoulder, and in no time, Emmett was fast asleep with his arm over her protectively. As she lay in his arms, a small tear of happiness hit her pillow.

. . .

It was about one in the morning when Char thought she heard her phone ringing, but when she managed to open her eyes, she didn't hear anything. She closed her eyes, and her phone lit up again. Emmett patted her shoulder. "Babe, I think your phone's ringing."

She fumbled around for it. "Hello?"

"Mommy! Chloe and I are here at the condo. Where are you? I need you! Oh, Mommy!" It was Aubrie, and she was sobbing.

The terror in her voice snapped Char awake, and she felt a rush of adrenaline laced in fear. "Aubrie, what's wrong? Oh my God, what happened? How are you already here?" Charlotte's panic fully woke Emmett. He sat up and turned on the bedside lamp.

"We were at my dad's." Aubrie's voice trailed off into sobs again.

"You were *where*? Aubrie, why, what happened? Are you all right? What did he do to you? Is Chloe all right?"

"Everything was fine the first night, but tonight he got drunk and angry. Mom, he wasn't making any sense and just came after me. He kept calling me Charlotte. Oh, Mommy."

"Honey, I'll be right there, don't worry. Mommy's on her way." She shot out of bed and threw on a change of clothes.

Emmett got out of bed too. "What happened, Charlotte? Is Aubrie okay?"

"She went to her father's house. She hasn't seen him in, I don't know, twelve years. It sounds like Aubrie saw the worst side of him tonight. He got drunk, and oh my God, if he hurt her..." Char couldn't imagine. She refused to let herself cry; she knew she'd have to be strong for Aubrie when she got there.

Emmett asked if he could go with Charlotte, but she couldn't allow it. She was afraid of what condition Aubrie might be in and what Aubrie might say. "I think it best that you don't. She doesn't know about us yet. It's not the right time for introductions. I'm sorry, honey."

Disappointment showed on Emmett's face. "You're right; I understand. But that creep doesn't know where your new condo is, does he?"

"No, I'm sure he doesn't. Aubrie knows better. I'll text you later, Emmett."

"Be sure you do. I want to know you're all safe."

Charlotte was distracted with her fearful thoughts. "Yeah, I will. I have to go." She made for the door, but Emmett had other ideas.

"Charlotte." Emmett's gruff tone startled her enough to make her stop her in her tracks and make eye contact with him. "I mean it—you need to call me. If I don't hear from you within half an hour, expect to see me at your door. Got it?"

She could see in his eyes he hated letting her go alone, but him coming just wasn't an option.

Char stammered, "I…I will. I promise."

She held it together on their way to the condo. When she made it up the stairs, Aubrie ran to Charlotte.

"Mommy!" she cried and threw her arms around her mother. Char was horrified to see that Aubrie had a swollen eye, sure to turn black by morning.

"Oh, Aubrie, what did he do to you? What happened, honey? And why in the world were you at his house in the first place?"

"I'm sorry I didn't tell you, Mom, but I knew you'd be against it. I just wanted to see for myself who my dad was."

Aubrie explained how she and Chloe decided to make a pit stop in Reno where her father and his fourth wife, Mona, lived. The first night was great. Aubrie didn't like it that they both smoked and drank quite a bit, but she felt safe because she and Chloe had their own hotel room a few miles away. However, on the second night, Aubrie said he started going down memory lane and became more hostile as the evening wore on.

"Eventually, Chloe and I just looked at each other. We knew it was time to go. But he could tell, Mom, I swear. He started pacing back and forth right by the front door. And he was ranting all kinds of bad things about you. But he was talking to me as if I were you, accusing me, you, of being a money-grubber, saying you left him and stole his kids from him because you wanted to whore yourself out to the highest bidder. It was awful. Finally Chloe and I had enough, and we told Mona to get him out of the way because we were leaving. Then she started in on us too!"

Chloe put her hand on her hip, her silky dark hair swinging over her shoulder. "Then Mona was saying we were snobby little rich bitches just like you, Aunt Charlie. I told her to shut the hell up, since it was obvious she was just jealous, and that's when it went really bad. Mona attacked us, then Mike jumped in, too. I'm sorry, Aubrie, I think it was my fault you got hit in the eye." Chloe started to cry.

"Girls, girls, no, it's neither of your faults. Those people have real problems. Come here. There, there, you two," Char said as she pulled Chloe and Aubrie in for a hug. "How did you get away?" She couldn't believe the girls had experienced what she had so many times.

"They live in an apartment complex, and some neighbors were having a Fourth of July barbecue. Some of the guys heard us and helped us out. Actually, one of their girlfriends helped too. She was pretty badass," Chloe said, impressed.

"It was kind of funny, actually; she pulled Mona off me by the hair!" Aubrie said, her dimples that were identical to Charlotte's flashing at the memory.

"Yeah, Mona was crying about her weave." Chloe giggled as she snuggled her small frame into the sofa and pulled a throw over herself.

"Aubrie, looks like you got it pretty good in the eye. Let me get some ice for it," Char said, heading to the kitchen, thankful that the girls were finding the humor in an otherwise awful situation.

When she returned, Aubrie said, "Before the neighbors came, I said something to Mike, and he backhanded me, hard." She looked down, as if she were ashamed. "It wasn't your fault, Chloe—it was mine."

"What did you say?" Char asked softly as she sat down and gently put the icepack to the side of her eye.

"That he wasn't my dad. That he was just a loser sperm donor. And I thanked him for letting me finally understand why you left him all those years ago. I told him you obviously left to find a real man." Aubrie peered up at her mom, unsure how she'd react.

"Oh, honey!" Charlotte pulled Aubrie in close for another hug. "And just so you know, it doesn't matter what you did or didn't say to him; it's not your fault. None of this is." Charlotte felt a familiar guilt wash over her. She knew ultimately it was her fault that her precious daughter was hurting.

The two girls were tired after all they'd been through, so Char led them upstairs and let them sleep with her in her king-size bed that night. They didn't want to sleep alone.

Char finally texted Emmett once the girls were settled in, but he ignored her text and called her. She answered quickly and spoke softly so as not to wake the girls.

"I thought I told you to call me. I need to hear in your voice that everything's okay."

Charlotte realized she was a bit rusty in the give-and-take of a relationship. She knew she would have to work on thinking outside of herself. "Sorry, Emmett. The girls are a little shaken up, but they're going to be fine. I just got them to bed. Can we talk about this tomorrow? I'm drained. But everything's fine, considering."

"Sure, babe, I can imagine. But, hey, you've locked the condo up tightly?"

"Of course I have," Char said. Though her eyes darted around the room, and she couldn't help but become spooked. Years ago she'd been home during a random break-in, and it had been traumatizing even though the perpetrator fled as soon as he saw her. She shook her head and reminded herself of all the features of her complex that would ensure their safety. She had to trust the technology. It was the only option if she ever wanted to sleep soundly.

She knew she needed to convince not just herself, but Emmett too. "Mike's not the type of guy to go chasing anyone in the middle of the night anyway, Emmett. That would take too much effort. Plus, if he got as drunk as Aubrie said he did, he's likely passed out. And Aubrie confirmed she didn't give him our address."

"That's a relief. Either way, be careful tonight and call me in the morning, will you?"

"We have the best security here, so I'm not too worried, Emmett. But I will, thank you. Good night. I'll talk to you in the morning."

Char wept quietly throughout the night, but she thanked the heavens that Aubrie hadn't been hurt worse and that Chloe had been with her. Otherwise, she could have been stranded, a hostage almost. It sickened her to think of how much worse it could have been.

When morning rolled around, everyone slept in, and then Char and the girls had a late breakfast together. Aubrie didn't know what to do about her black eye and complained she was embarrassed, but she didn't want to stay stuck in the house hiding. She and Chloe had wanted to hit the beach. Instead, they decided to hang by the pool at the condo and hope for privacy, but Aubrie borrowed Char's big Chanel sunglasses, and they hid her black eye perfectly. Aubrie and

Chloe had fun looking through Char's collection of wide-brimmed sun hats. It amazed Char that the very next morning they could have fun putting together disguises for themselves. *Thank God kids are resilient,* she thought.

Finally she called Emmett. It was just before noon, so technically she was doing as he'd asked.

"There you are—good morning. So what exactly happened?"

Char explained only that her ex, Mike, had become drunk and combative. She wasn't sure how she was going to tell him that he had struck Aubrie. She only said there was a commotion that alerted some neighboring kids, who had come to their aid.

"Thank God those neighbors cared enough to step in. But I have to say again, babe, this is another example of why you, and the girls, of course, need to take self-defense classes. The boys and I have a great mixed martial arts gym we go to a few times a month. I'm taking you three with me next time, okay? No argument."

"It didn't seem like an issue until now. To think, the girls were on that road trip with no way of protecting themselves. Guess I'm out of the running yet again for the Mother of the Year award."

"Babe, it's nothing to blame yourself for. Let's just do something about it here and now, all right? I'd love to see you tonight. Can you come for dinner? The girls are welcome, too; I'd love to meet them."

Charlotte grimaced at the thought of Emmett seeing Aubrie's black eye. "I'm not sure the girls are up for a visit just yet, but I'd sure like to see you tonight. I think they'll be fine for a couple of hours if I come over for dinner."

"Whatever you think is best, though I can't wait to meet the girls. I'll see you tonight around six."

The girls asked Charlotte to come to the pool with them, so she agreed. She was excited to finally be able to swim. The girls threw their stuff down indiscriminately and jumped right into the water. Charlotte came behind them, picking it up and setting it at a table for them. She did so almost absentmindedly, all the while observing Aubrie and Chloe.

Charlotte never tired of watching the girls interact, nor would she ever get used to how opposite Chloe and Aubrie looked from each other. Aubrie was taller than Char, but with the same peaches-and-cream complexion and strawberry blond hair, but her green eyes had a touch more blue to them. Chloe was a full five inches shorter than Aubrie, with a beautiful tan complexion, long dark hair, and the deepest brown eyes, with thick long lashes. They were both beautiful girls but in totally different ways. On the inside, however, they were like sisters, completely in sync and the best of friends.

"Ha-ha, Chloe! You have a total wedgie, oh my God! You *crack* me up!" Aubrie teased.

"Yeah, I'm meaning to do that, duh, Aub. Tan lines much?" Chloe rolled her eyes in mock annoyance.

"Girls, the neighbors might hear us. Please, can you pretend you have a little class?" The girls made faces at Charlotte, and she just laughed. Over the years, the girls had gotten used to Charlotte giving them a hard time once in a while.

Char sat at the deep end and reveled in the feel of both feet in the water. She kicked her legs gently, testing out how the drag from the water would feel on her weaker ankle. Aubrie floated by on a noodle. "So, Mom, Chloe and I have a question. When we got to the condo so late last night, you weren't here. Where exactly were you?" Aubrie pulled her sunglasses down and peered up at her mom.

"I was with a friend I've met here in the area." Char wasn't comfortable saying much more to Aubrie.

"What's this friend's name?"

Chloe swam up, treading water, paddling fervently. "Yeah, Aunt Charlie, we told you where we were yesterday. Now it's your turn to tell the truth." Chloe gave her a big smile and wiggled her eyebrows, looking goofy.

"Yeah, speaking of that, I trusted you girls on this road trip. You were hundreds of miles off course. What if something had happened and I didn't have a clue where you were? What then, Aubrie?"

Aubrie elbowed Chloe and mouthed, "Thanks a lot," before turning back to Charlotte. "Mom. Seriously. I have a right to see my sperm donor, regardless of how jacked up he is."

"Absolutely you do. Which is why you had no need to lie about it."

As Charlotte spoke, Aubrie trailed a finger in the water, watching the ripples instead of making eye contact with Char.

"Whatever, Mom. You know you wouldn't have told me, 'Go ahead honey, have a splendid time!' No way you'd have been all chill with it."

"We would have had a conversation about it, of course. But it would have been on how to keep your boundaries and stay safe, physically and emotionally, Aubrie. That's all. I know the man; you don't."

"Well, looks like I know him now too. So thanks for the warning, Mom."

Aubrie's words stung. "All the books and professional advice say not to bash your children's father in front of them. I didn't think you needed to know since he lost custody and had no rights to see you. Like I said, Aubrie, if you'd have told me your plans, I would have filled you in a bit more. But remember, we're talking about you. You haven't been known to take my advice anyway. You just do what you want, regardless."

"Anyway," Aubrie said dramatically. Charlotte was sure she had rolled her eyes, even though she still had on her sunglasses. "I'm fine, Mom, so I think we can close the subject. What we *need* to talk about is you. Please tell me you're not dating someone, because I swear I'll freak."

"Aubrie. I'm an adult, and I can actually choose when and if I date anyone." Char put up a strong front. She hoped Aubrie would never know how insecure she actually felt.

"So you *are* dating someone? Un-frickin'-believable, Mom. It hasn't even been a year since you broke up with that freak, Ash."

"Oh, you mean Ash-hole," Chloe chimed in, and the girls threw their heads back in raucous laughter. Obviously Aubrie had told Chloe everything.

"Aubrie Elle, that's enough. I mean it. And watch your language, you two. If you have any respect for me whatsoever, you wouldn't—"

"I know, I know, Mom, no one's allowed to bring that freak up. But after seeing firsthand what a whack job my sperm donor is, things are beginning to make sense. Between him and Ash, you clearly have a type: psycho. Can't wait to meet this one."

While she wanted to, Char resisted the urge to defend Ash. They'd argued about him a million times, and it was no use. Defending him required her to start with, "I know you think you saw him manhandling me once or twice." She had to stick with the facts that were black and white.

"You know better than to throw Beau into the mix, Aubrie. He was a gentleman through and through, and you know it."

"Of course he was, but he could have been a fluke."

Charlotte's embarrassment grew. Aubrie knew how to line up her mistakes one by one. It was a long list. She grasped at anything to somehow defend herself. "You know the circumstances of how I ended up marrying your dad at such a young age," Char said, as a fleeting sadness passed over her.

"Mike. The sperm donor. Beau is my one and *only* dad. Yeah, Mom,

I know you were raised by a violent, alcoholic stepdad, which is why I'm worried now. Your good-guy radar might be a little whacked."

"Emmett is sweet and kind, Aubrie. We've formed a great rela—friendship." Charlotte was suddenly afraid to share the whole truth of what Emmett meant to her. She thought she'd better ease Aubrie into it.

"His name's Emmett? Well, I want to meet this guy, Mom."

"I'm going over there tonight, but Aubrie, don't you think after everything that's happened that you might want to stay home and take it easy?"

"Not on your life," Aubrie said as she smiled not so sweetly and floated by. "Chloe and I are coming with."

"How about I come along too?"

"Grandma!" Aubrie and Chloe shrieked as they got out of the pool and ran past Charlotte.

Charlotte turned in disbelief to see her mother hugging Aubrie and Chloe. She hadn't seen her mother much in the last two years since Beau passed away. In Charlotte's times of need, the last thing she ever wanted was to have her mother around. Pam only ever served to make her feel worse. Charlotte had asked the kids a million times to please try to keep their family affairs private. Blake did a much better job keeping things from Pam than Aubrie did.

Pam laughed loudly with a voice only Char knew was a touch deeper than it used to be from over forty years of filling her lungs with cigarette smoke. "Girls, girls, you're going to get Grandma all wet. Go get your towels, sillies." She smiled and smacked Chloe on the butt.

Char rolled her eyes and heaved a sigh. She always felt a pang of jealousy when she saw how fun and nice her mom was with everyone else. Pam never afforded the same to her. Despite the fact that she was turning forty soon, Char still longed to even just once feel the warmth of a mother's love.

"Mom, what are you doing here?" she asked flatly, but she didn't have to ask, not really. It shouldn't have been a surprise to Charlotte. Her mother always seemed to conveniently pop up during times of distress in her family, should she catch wind of it. Pam wouldn't think of missing an opportunity to come cast judgment.

"Aubrie called me, frantic, last night. I tried to convince the girls to stay put in Reno and that I'd come to them. They shouldn't have been driving after all that commotion. But they insisted on coming here to you." The disdain on Pam's face was all too familiar to Char. "So of course I jumped into the car and headed on down. I needed to see for myself that my girls were in good care."

Pam stood there with her arms wrapped protectively around both girls, who stood there, wrapped in their towels, soaking up the attention. Charlotte couldn't help but feel Pam's stance implied she felt the girls needed protection from her, that it was all her fault. That had to be why Pam had driven all the way from Eastern Oregon, to witness Char's failure as a mother yet again.

She didn't want to fight with her mom; it was never a fruitful venture, so she tried to placate her. "Thanks, Mom, but you really didn't have to. As you can see, the girls are fine. We're out here enjoying the pool, and they're going to put it in the past and check it off as a learning experience."

Pam dropped her protective grasp from the girls, who said they were going back to the condo to make lunch. Pam called after them to bring her a drink, whatever Char had on hand, while she dug her cigarettes out of her purse. Once the girls were out of sight, Pam's whole demeanor changed.

She had her eyes fixed on Charlotte as she tapped the pack on her palm and didn't take her eyes off her daughter as she deftly popped a cigarette into her mouth, shielded the lighter from the breeze, lit it, and took a long drag.

Internally Charlotte cringed, and she looked away. For as long as she could remember, Pam had a knack for making her feel simultaneously worthless and coldly detested with not a word spoken.

Out of the corner of her eye, Charlotte watched her mom saunter over to sit at a shaded table. Even though she was in her early sixties, Pam still tried to exude a sexual vibe, and she dressed accordingly. She had on a scooped tank, low enough to show what little cleavage she had, tucked into a skirt too short and too flouncy for her age.

If she'd taken better care of herself over the years by avoiding alcohol, tobacco, and the sun, she may have been able to pull it off. She was still thin with a decent figure, but her skin had become creped in places, and her chest was covered in deep wrinkles and a plethora of freckles. Charlotte and her mom shared the same fair skin and strawberry blond hair that Charlotte had passed down to Aubrie, though Pam's hair had long been more white than blond.

Pam kicked off her three-inch wedge sandals, wiggled her chipped painted toes, and sighed. "You know why this happened, right? You never should have left Mike in the first place. The only reason he and Aubrie got into their little tiff is because of his years of resentment toward you. The way you treated him, abandoning him and taking up with Beau." She eyed Char sideways as she flicked her ashes into the wind and took another drag.

As she exhaled the plume of smoke, Pam started in on Char. "You always were putting on like the princess and the pea, wanting to be treated like royalty. You couldn't be happy with a hardworking blue-collar man. No, you wanted a snooty rich SOB, and you destroyed a family to get it. Can't wait to see who you've hooked this time." Pam chuckled to herself and shook her head as a sneer lingered across her face.

The familiar sting of tears burned the corners of Char's eyes. Pam's outrageous defense of Mike was also familiar. "Little tiff? How would Aubrie feel to hear you make light of what happened last night? And if you were taking a swipe at Beau with your rich SOB comment, I have to warn you that Aubrie won't appreciate your slamming the man who raised her and loved her unconditionally."

"Oh, Char, you always were the drama queen, and now poor Aubrie is taking after you. Mike was a hardworking man who took your snotty little nose in after Keith and I had about had it with your smart mouth. He took care of you and the kids and put food on the table, which is more than I can say for a lot of men these days," she said with a disgusted huff.

"He also drank away our money and—"

Pam cut Char off, pointing at her with her cigarette between her fingers. "Charlotte, let me tell you something. You're not the easiest to live with. I raised you. I should know. And you drove me to drink on more than one occasion with that mouth of yours and your snooty attitude, walking around like you were better than the rest of the family."

Charlotte was actually grateful Pam had cut her off. She had been about to break her own cardinal rule and share details of her marriage with Mike, and she would have sorely regretted it. Any personal information shared with Pam would most certainly be used against her.

"I left Mike with not a penny to my name, just me and the kids. And it was a struggle being a single mom. We were penniless for those years, but I promise you I couldn't have been happier." Charlotte's voice rang a couple octaves higher than normal, revealing the exasperation she was trying to shove down.

Pam snorted as if about to laugh and lit another cigarette. Char received Pam's message loud and clear: she thought Charlotte was full of it. Her mother may as well have slapped her in the face. She bit her lip and shook her head. She wanted to tell Pam off and tell her to get the hell out of her life, but she held back for Aubrie's sake. They didn't need any more drama at the moment.

"Believe what you want, Mom. I'm done defending myself to you." She grabbed her towel and marched back to the condo, and Pam just let her go.

Aubrie and Chloe were heading down the stairs with a tray of food and some drinks when Charlotte came through the door. "Mom, we've got drinks and sandwiches. Are you coming back out?"

"No, honey, let's just say it's getting too heated out there."

Aubrie and Chloe looked at each other knowingly. It was no secret in the family that Char and Pam didn't get along.

"Here, Aubrie, let me take the food out to Grandma, and you and Aunt Charlie can talk." Chloe widened her eyes at Aubrie as if to say, "Have fun; glad I'm not in the middle of that."

Before she closed the front door, Charlotte had a thought. "Chloe, can you do me a favor? If Grandma asks you to get her another glass of wine, can you please tell her that was the last of it?"

"Sure, Aunt Charlie. See you out there, Aubrie," she said. Chloe didn't look shocked by her aunt's request. Pam had caused many a scene at many a family gathering from getting drunk. Everyone but Pam agreed she had a problem.

"Is Grandma getting on your nerves already, Mom? I'm sorry. I shouldn't have called her, but it's not like I knew she was going to hop into her car and come all the way down here."

Char hated to ask, but wanted to know. "Why did you call Grandma? As fast as she got down here, you must have called her hours before you called me."

Aubrie looked down at her toes. "I mean, I'll be honest. My first thought was I didn't want to get in trouble. I knew you'd be so mad. But I also knew this was the last thing you needed on top of everything else you've been going through."

Several heavy tears fell down Charlotte's cheeks. She quickly wiped them away and wrapped Aubrie in her arms. "Oh, Aubrie Elle." She held on tightly, and Aubrie latched on just as tightly.

"I'm so sorry, Mom." Aubrie's voice was just a squeak.

Charlotte rubbed her back. "No, honey; I'm the one who should be sorry. No matter what I was going through these past couple years, it was no excuse. I know I let you down. But please believe that I'm strong enough now to be the mother you deserve, the mother I was until—" Her voice cracked, so she sucked in a breath. She closed her eyes, pursed her lips, and willed herself to focus. She grabbed Aubrie's arms and looked her in the eye. "I'm back on my feet. You can depend on me again, okay?" Char gave Aubrie a bright smile in an effort to convince them both.

Aubrie smiled back. "I know you took a big step coming out of your cave back home and agreeing to come down here with me, so I guess I should believe you."

Watching as Aubrie smiled, Char felt relief. She didn't want Aubrie to feel as alone and without a support system as Charlotte had when she was her age. It was hard for Charlotte to fathom that when she was Aubrie's age, she had been married with a newborn. In many ways Aubrie was still a baby herself. And for that, Charlotte was thankful. She still had time to right most her wrongs.

"Yes, you should believe me," Charlotte said with a laugh. "Don't worry about me, honey. You need to just relax today. Why don't you go out and have a nice time with Grandma and Chloe? I need to work on a contract for a new client, and it's due Monday. If you can, though, will you try to convince Grandma not to come with us to Emmett's tonight? Would you be willing to stay and keep her company here? I'm just not sure about having all of you over at once. That's asking a lot of Emmett."

"Mom, you don't really expect me to sit this one out, do you? Like I said, after what just happened with my sperm donor, I have to meet this guy and make sure he's not another creep. And you'll hurt Grandma's feelings if you don't let her come too."

Charlotte didn't understand her daughter and Pam's relationship. She'd never admit it to Aubrie, but she suspected Pam's main interest in Aubrie was just to use her to torture Charlotte. Many times Pam had been the primary source of tension between the two of them, helping to fan the flames of contention between mother and daughter. Blake had even been brave enough to say as much out loud on more than one occasion, but Aubrie didn't see it that way. She had never understood Charlotte's and Blake's mistrust of Pam.

"You're a sweetie, Aubrie, for thinking of Grandma's feelings," Charlotte said as she rubbed at her brow, resolving not to argue. "Dinner's at six tonight, so just make sure that you guys are back here, showered and ready by five thirty." Charlotte wished Aubrie could see that Pam never took her feelings into consideration, but for some reason Aubrie was oblivious.

"Well, don't think I'm too sweet, Mom. I'm not going to dinner tonight to be nice. I'm going to make sure Emmett's going to be nice to you."

"But you need to be respectful, Aubrie. Please don't embarrass me."

"I'll respect him if he deserves it," Aubrie said in a singsong voice as she headed out the door.

Charlotte groaned on the inside. Before she settled into her work, she texted Emmett the "good news" that the girls were coming after all, and surprise, her mother would be joining them too. Emmett called her right back with a barrage of questions. Was this a planned visit? How was she feeling about it? Would she be okay tonight?

Char almost forgot she'd shared with Emmett bits and pieces of her childhood, specifically that her mom and stepfather had been abusive. She could hear the concern in Emmett's voice. A new wave of embarrassment spread over her. She hated talking about it.

"It was a surprise. She just popped in on us at the pool like she owned the place. Of course, the girls are happy to see her. She's their grandmother after all. But, Emmett, it's already gotten rocky. I really don't want my mom to come tonight, but Aubrie wouldn't hear of it, and she's insisting that she meet you sooner rather than later. I couldn't say no to her after all she's been through."

"I understand."

"You don't sound like you do. I'm sorry I didn't think to ask. Are you okay with my mother coming to dinner with us?"

"I'll be honest; it's going to be hard, knowing how she treated you growing up. What she allowed to happen to you. But I can put on a good show and pretend I don't know any of it if that's what'll make you happy. For Aubrie's sake."

"Thank you. I can't promise tonight will be barrels of laughter."

"But we'll get through it together. What do they say—forewarned is forearmed, right?" Emmett laughed.

Charlotte laughed too. "Right. I like that. Thank you, honey, for understanding."

"Don't you worry—I'll have your back. We'll see you tonight."

She hung up feeling a little less nervous and was able to immerse herself in work until it was time to go.

Thankfully, since Pam wanted to smoke on the way over, she said she'd follow in her own car. Char thought it was a good idea so if, God forbid, things went sideways, Pam and the girls could leave early. It was out of the same precaution that she decided not to take Asa with them. He didn't like being around tense situations, so just in case, she left him home safe and sound.

Pam pulled into Emmett's driveway right behind Charlotte. Before getting out of the car, Charlotte lectured the girls, looking at them both through the rearview mirror. "Listen, Aubrie, I want you to be on your best behavior. I don't want you to be disrespectful in any way. And girls," she said, pausing for effect, "please do not bring up Ash, okay?"

"What are we, in third grade? Chloe and I are adults, Mom. We're both eighteen now. I just want to get to know the guy. Don't worry, we're not going to air your *very* dirty laundry to him, promise," Aubrie said as she got out of the car.

Charlotte eyed Aubrie as she came around the car. "Aubrie, I thought we just had a nice conversation back at the condo. Why are you being so snotty to me now?"

Charlotte realized the answer before she even finished her question. Aubrie had just spent the afternoon with Pam. It never failed that Aubrie would have an attitude toward her after spending any amount of time with Pam. She took it in stride, knowing that Aubrie would invariably shuck the attitude off once she was away from Pam again, though the timing at the moment couldn't be more inconvenient.

"Oh, Charlotte, lay off of Aubrie. She's been through enough," Pam said as she stubbed out her cigarette into the potted plant by the front door. Char wanted to protest, but thought better of it and made a mental note to clean it out later.

She made a concerted effort to ignore Pam and gave Aubrie a look letting her know she meant business; then she took a deep breath and walked in, her stomach in knots.

"Whoa, you can just waltz into this guy's house without knocking already? This must be more serious than you're letting on, Mother."

"Don't you know your own mother by now, Aubrie?" Pam rolled her eyes, and Aubrie stifled a giggle.

"Guys, stop," Chloe chided.

Charlotte gave Chloe a thankful glance as she called out to Emmett, not sure if he was outside at the grill or still in the house. "Hi, Emmett, we're here."

. . .

Emmett came out from the kitchen. Charlotte forced her best smile possible. She had wondered if he would be nervous, but saw he was as relaxed and cheerful as ever. "Hi, honey. Come on in, everybody," he said before he looked at Pam. "I thought you said your mom was coming, but this must be your sister, right?" He winked at Charlotte and held his hand out to Pam, who instead went in for a tight hug.

"Emmett, this is my mom, Pam." She tried to sound upbeat, but cringed inside when she saw her mom pressing in on Emmett.

"Oh, a Southern charmer, are you? Isn't this a surprise. Charlotte usually goes for the stuffed-shirt types. Nice to meet you, Emmett."

"Pleasure is all mine, ma'am."

"Oh, you can call me Pam," she said, looking up at him with her hands on his chest. Charlotte half expected her mom to start trailing her fingers up his chest. She was mortified, but Emmett took it in stride and subtly escaped from Pam's clutches to say hello to the girls.

"And you must be Aubrie. I've heard a lot about you." He reached out to shake Aubrie's hand.

"Funny, I know nothing about you." Aubrie tilted her head to the side and flashed an obviously fake smile, which was all the more dramatic since she still had her oversized black sunglasses on.

"Well, I look forward to changing that." He didn't miss a beat, giving Aubrie a warm smile before turning to Chloe. "And you must be Chloe, Charlotte's niece. Nice to meet you."

Aubrie interrupted. "A Southern boy, Mom? You really have a thing for accents, don't you?"

Charlotte shot a warning glare to Aubrie. Emmett missed it and only looked amused.

Chloe was congenial and ignored Aubrie's jab at Emmett to say, "Nice to meet you too," with a giggle and a blush. She looked at Charlotte and mouthed, "Oh my gosh!" Clearly she approved of his looks, but thankfully she was much more subtle than Pam.

Charlotte flashed an uneasy smile at Chloe and prayed the night wouldn't become a complete disaster. She had little faith it wouldn't.

Emmett offered everyone drinks. Charlotte stuck with iced tea, but to her chagrin, Pam asked for a gin and tonic while the girls helped themselves to pop.

"I hope everyone's hungry, because I went a little overboard on the grilling tonight. Why don't we all head out to the patio?" Emmett said before grabbing a tray and leading the way outside to dish up the chicken, steak, and bratwurst.

Anna had taken the afternoon off, so Charlotte brought out the side dishes, silverware, and napkins from the kitchen. "Wow, it all looks great, Emmett. Thank you for having us over tonight." She smiled at him appreciatively.

"Well, look at you, Char, helping set the table and everything. Quite a change from your life with Beau, what with his team of servants at your beck and call."

"And your point, Mom?" Charlotte asked as she took her seat, bracing herself both physically and mentally.

Pam drank down her gin and tonic before saying, "Oh, no point, really. It's just funny seeing you actually working for once in your adult life. Chloe, go make your grandma another gin and tonic, would you, please?"

Charlotte gave Chloe a glance that said, "More tonic, less gin," before answering her mother's jab. "Mom, I have a career. As an attorney, if you don't remember."

Pam looked at Emmett and waved her hand dismissively. "Oh, pffft. Wearing silk suits every day, gabbing, and lunching is not the same as managing a household. It can be backbreaking work, and thankless too," Pam said, her eyes boring into Charlotte's.

Shifting in his seat, Emmett looked as if he were about to say something, but Aubrie, who had her own agenda that night, interjected. She was clearly intent on changing the subject and, Charlotte noticed, not the least bit concerned with defending her mother from Pam's attacks.

"So, Emmett, how did you and my mom meet?" Aubrie asked.

Emmett's eyes brightened, and he smiled at Charlotte. He seemed relieved that Aubrie had changed the subject. Charlotte knew better, though, and wished she had thought to warn him earlier to keep his guard up, even with Aubrie.

"We met on the Solstice Canyon hiking trail. I was coming down the trail, and from far away, I saw this little red fur ball running at full speed toward me. At first I thought it was a rabbit or something, but as it got closer, I could see there was a leash trailing behind. I figured it must be someone's little pup that got loose. I prepped myself to catch him. I was willing to take a dive if I had to. He saw me, and knew I was prepared for him. He juked left; I juked right. I thought he was going to make it past me, but at the last second I was able to just catch the end of his leash, and I got him. Boy, was he a mess, all covered in grass and panting like crazy. He sure gave me a run for the money," Emmett said, laughing.

Aubrie couldn't help but smile. "But didn't he, like, try to bite your face off? He doesn't like strangers, especially men," she said, looking pointedly at Char.

Her look toward Charlotte didn't go unnoticed by Emmett, and Charlotte cringed, but Emmett just smiled at Aubrie. "Well, no, he didn't. Actually he started licking my face. We were buddies right off the bat."

"And you brought him back to Mom, it was love at first sight, and you want to tell me you've set a date, right?"

"Aubrie," Char said, embarrassed.

Emmett didn't skip a beat. "No, actually I don't think your mom wanted my help. If anyone wanted to bite my face off, it would have been your mom," Emmett said with a laugh.

Char smacked his arm. "That's so not true!"

"Help her with what? I'm confused." Aubrie looked between Emmett and Charlotte.

Emmett nodded to Charlotte in a gesture to allow her to take over. The look on his face showed he knew he'd just messed up, since it was obvious Charlotte still hadn't come clean with Aubrie about her injuries.

"I had a fall and twisted my ankle. Emmett offered to help me get back up, that's all."

"That's Char for you, always playing the damsel in distress," Pam said in annoyance.

"Actually, Grandma, that's not true. Mom keeps everything from us." Aubrie cocked her head to the side in exasperation. "Mom, you're a horrible liar, and you always downplay things. If I didn't know better, I'd say you probably broke your leg and just didn't want to tell me. That's your MO."

Emmett shifted uncomfortably in his seat and cleared his throat. "Well, what's important is your mother's all right now."

"So it *was* worse than she's trying to say. That's Mom for you, isn't it, Chloe?"

"Totally. Remember the time she cut her finger at Thanksgiving and said it was no big deal, but she actually needed stitches?" Chloe's eyes danced at the memory. Aubrie nodded in agreement.

"Well, I wouldn't know about that, since I'm never invited to her Thanksgiving dinners. Chloe, another drink for Grandma—little less tonic this time, honey," Pam said, holding her swaying glass obnoxiously high.

Chloe obeyed her grandma, but looked to her aunt for help. However, Char was more worried about defending herself from Aubrie.

"I don't think Emmett wants to hear about that. Not exactly polite dinner conversation. And other things are just better left unsaid," Charlotte said to Aubrie, her tone sharp.

Aubrie slumped back in her chair, crossing her arms. "Well, all I'm going to say is it's so funny how you expect me to tell you everything, but you don't tell me anything. Ever."

"Why don't we move on from this conversation? Aubrie, you and I can finish it at home, *later*."

Clearly in an effort to help, Emmett interjected, "So, girls, how was your road trip?"

Aubrie leaned an elbow on the table and looked at Emmett, making sure she had his undivided attention. Pulling off her sunglasses with flourish, she said, "Well, if this is any indication, the trip didn't end so well, thanks to dear old Dad."

Aubrie's eye had worsened from the night before; it was swollen nearly shut with a black-and-blue halo that was painful even to look at.

Char's eyes darted to Emmett. He had put his head down, closing his eyes for a moment before taking a deep breath, clearly in an effort to keep himself composed. The table had gone silent.

"Aubrie, I'm sorry," he said, his voice low, before looking at Charlotte, who avoided his eyes, knowing he must be upset with her for not telling him about it earlier.

"Well, so am I. I'm sorry my mom refuses to share pertinent details that might actually be helpful for me to know. Like, don't go looking up your sperm donor; he's a violent alcoholic. I don't know, seems like I should have known this before planning a trip with my cousin and taking her along for the ride," Aubrie said, staring Char down.

Chloe tried to cut the tension. "It's okay, Aunt Charlie. I've tried to tell Aubrie you were only trying to protect her. I'm sorry we lied about the trip."

"Don't apologize to her, Chloe—gawd! I think I've lost my appetite. Come on, Chloe, let's go. Grandma, will you take us home?"

"Sure, honey. Your mom really knows how to make a mess of things. Let's take you home, and Grandma will make it all better." Pam stood, looking a bit shaky on her feet as she dug into her purse for her keys.

Charlotte was mortified. She thought it best that the girls leave, so she didn't argue, but clearly her mom had had too much to drink. She needed to finagle a way to get one of the girls to drive without angering Pam. Char knew from experience it would take great delicacy.

Emmett got up from his chair; Charlotte saw he looked uneasy. He had a hand at his hip and the other gripping his neck. "Uh, listen, Pam, why don't you let one of the girls drive. The police out here are real sticklers for drinking and driving. It doesn't take much out here to get nabbed."

The girls' mouths dropped open. Charlotte stood and tried in vain to come up with something quick to mitigate Emmett's third unwitting faux pas. She also wanted the girls to leave before things got ugly. It was a lot for Char to juggle, and she felt a pounding headache coming on.

"Are you calling me a drunk?" The vitriol in Pam's voice put a chill throughout the patio.

Crossing her arms, Charlotte turned toward the girls and whispered, "I want you two to wait for Grandma in the car. Now, please. Tell Emmett good-bye."

"We're leaving now, Emmett. It was nice to meet you. Thank you for dinner," Chloe said politely but quickly.

"Yeah, nice to meet you. You better not be a violent psycho like the rest of the guys my mom ends up with. Grandma, you coming? We want to get out of here."

"I'm right behind you, girls. Here are the keys, start the air-conditioning, won't you? Just give Grandma a—a minute." Pam was now hiccupping, her words slurring.

Charlotte wanted to die.

Emmett looked like a deer trapped in the headlights. He looked from Aubrie, stomping out, to Pam, glaring at him. He was hit from both sides, and Charlotte couldn't do anything about it.

Pam took an uneasy step backward, and her head bobbed. She

theatrically craned her neck back to look up at Emmett. Pam was shorter than Charlotte, so Emmett towered over her, even with her in heels.

"You still haven't answered me. You really have the nerve to stand there in your fancy clothes and call me a drunk?"

Emmett stammered. "Um, no, no, ma'am. I—"

Pam interrupted Emmett to address Charlotte. "This is all your fault," she said, glancing back to jab a finger toward Charlotte, her voice rising. Charlotte sighed; she had been able to see the blame coming. "Here you go again with another pompous asshole passing judgment on your own family," she said before turning toward Emmett again. "And you—you stand there in your fancy house looking down on me, but you don't know anything but the lies Char has told you. She's the liar and the fake and the superficial fraud. But birds of a feather, I guess."

Emmett walked around the table to Charlotte, put his arm around her shoulders, and gave her a sympathetic look.

"Oh, the damsel in distress," Pam said in a high-pitched voice, fanning her hands out and feigning daintiness before putting them back on her hips. "Don't let her fool you. She's walking destruction. She's ruined two of my marriages and one of her own. She plays a good victim, but just so you know, anything that's happened to Little Miss Fancy-Pants here, that's called karma. She's brought it upon herself."

"Pam, I'd like to help you to the door." Emmett went to take Pam by the arm, but she jerked it away from him.

"Oh, you go to hell. You too, Charlotte—I'll find my own way out." Pam stumbled to the French door and slammed it behind her. They watched to make sure she was headed the right way, toward the front door.

Emmett kissed the top of Char's head and then gripped her

shoulders. "Wait here. I need to make sure she doesn't drive." He heaved a sigh and jogged out the side gate. Charlotte sat in stunned silence.

A few minutes later, Emmett was back. "Chloe was in the driver's seat, and Pam was talking to her, I bet trying to get her out, but she knew better when she saw me coming around the corner. She scurried to the backseat. The girls are fine. The question is, are you?"

"I am. I'm sorry about this, Emmett. I'm so embarrassed. My mom and Aubrie had no right to be so rude to you. I really should go." Charlotte turned to go inside and gather her purse, but Emmett caught her arm and spun her back around.

"Whoa there, you're not going anywhere, Charlotte." He was smiling, but it didn't reach his eyes, which concerned Charlotte.

"Why not?" Char hoped against hope that Emmett wasn't mad at her too.

"Babe, if you think I'm going to let you go running back to that viper's den for more belittling from your mama, you've got another think coming. Sit down here and let me pour you a drink."

Relieved, Charlotte acquiesced and sat down. "Water. Just water."

Emmett smiled. "I understand. If you don't mind, though, I'm going to pour myself a scotch."

Charlotte managed a small smile. "I understand."

Emmett came back with their drinks and took a gulp of his. "Okay, that's better," he said, and then looked at Charlotte with sympathy in his eyes.

"I'm so sorry about all this, Emmett," Char managed to say quietly.

"No, I'm the one who should be apologizing. First I outed you about your injury; then I brought up the trip, and that really got Aubrie going. I was trying to diffuse the tension between you two, and I just blurted the first thing that came to mind. Then I offended your mom and got her started. I messed up tonight, and it all fell on you."

"It's a lot of dysfunction, and I'm sorry you were witness to it."

He waved his hand dismissively. "Don't worry about it. I'm forty-two years old. I've seen and heard much worse. Families have issues, I get it. And I'm sorry to see your mom has some issues. My parents raised me to respect my elders, and I'm sorry here, but, Charlotte, that woman tested my patience to no end."

"That's an understatement. But you handled it perfectly. You didn't engage."

"I took that cue from you. You didn't say much yourself. I figured you must have learned how to best manage her over the years."

"I have. We've never gotten along. She just doesn't like me." Char bit her lip, trying not to cry.

"Your mom's issues are her own. I don't see it as a reflection of you, and I hope you don't either. My heart goes out to you; I couldn't imagine having to grow up like that."

"It is what it is. Don't feel sorry for me, I've learned to deal with it. I don't want to be the damsel in distress. I really don't."

"I've called you a damsel in distress before, and I meant it to be endearing. Your mom kind of spoiled that. But, Charlotte, truly you aren't. You're strong. No offense, but you'd have to be, growing up with a mom like that."

"I try to be strong; it's just hard sometimes."

Emmett stood and grabbed Charlotte by the hand, pulling her close to him. She allowed herself to be enveloped in his arms. She felt safe.

"But, babe, do me a favor and don't try to be too strong. I think out of all of this, what really bothers me is Aubrie's black eye." He pulled back to look into her eyes. "Honey, I wish you would have told me. Your ex-husband gave Aubrie that black eye, didn't he?"

Charlotte teared up and cast her eyes down. She paused for a moment before garnering the nerve to answer. "He did, and it's all my fault. I may as well have hit her myself. Oh my God, Emmett, this is horrible. What have I done to my children?"

"What are you talking about, Char? You're not responsible for what that lowlife did to Aubrie."

"I married that animal. Because of me, that abusive man is their father. It is my fault. It is!" She felt borderline hysterical.

Emmett took her firmly by the shoulders. "Charlotte. Knock it off. This is not your fault. You've got to get your mom out of your head. Would you ever raise a hand to either of your kids?"

"No! Of course not, but that's not the point!" Charlotte wouldn't calm down.

He gripped her shoulders tighter. "Charlotte! That is the point! Now cut it out!"

He pulled her in close and let her cry into his chest. He kissed her head and stroked her hair. He kept his arms around her until she calmed down, though it took a few moments more for her shuddering to stop.

"I'm sorry, Emmett. Seems since we've met, there's been one issue after another. I don't blame you if you're getting second thoughts about us. I mean, if I think it's too much, I can only imagine what you're thinking."

"Please, don't apologize. Every family has issues. And while I'm not too sure you and your mom have any easy answers, I am sure that you and Aubrie will patch things up soon."

"I'm sure you're dying inside to say, 'I told you so.' After knowing me for only a few days, you'd already admonished me to be more honest with my kids."

"Charlotte, I already said I was wrong for butting into your business."

"But you were right."

Emmett said, lifting her chin, "Nobody's perfect, including the two of us. I'm not passing judgment. But I do wish you would have told me first thing about what your ex did to Aubrie. Remember your promise to trust me, Charlotte? It's important to me. I want to be here for you. And I don't like you keeping things from me, you got it?"

Her face burned hot. She had so many secrets, she realized she'd defaulted to just keeping everything a secret. It may have worked and even been encouraged in her past relationships, but it wasn't going to work with Emmett. He expected the truth.

"Emmett, it's been tense since Aubrie came home, and I haven't been in the best frame of mind. Yes, my first instinct was to put off telling you, but when I think about it today with a clearer head, Emmett, I realize it's not my story to tell—it's Aubrie's. She's an adult now, and it should be her choice whether or not to keep it private."

"Fair enough. I hadn't thought of it that way. But what I said still stands. I hope you're still working on the trust factor between the two of us, okay?"

"I think about it every day," Char said truthfully. She laid her head on his chest, feeling a jumble of emotions: love, guilt, and worry.

"Can I take an opportunity to test your trust in me?" Emmett pulled back from Char to look her squarely in the eye, keeping his hands on her shoulders. His voice was soft. She could tell he was doing his best to be gentle, but for what reason?

"Um, yes, I guess." she said. Her heart fluttered with foreboding.

He began slowly. "I want clarification. Something Aubrie hinted at on her way out the door. Was your ex-husband, her dad—did he ever put a hand on you?"

Her stomach dropped. She broke from his embrace and walked to the edge of the pool. She stared into it, wishing she could jump in and hide from his question. It wasn't necessarily hard for Char to talk about him, but she had a lot of shame attached to the abuse she'd suffered throughout her life. She wasn't sure it would ever stop. She secretly felt she was somehow responsible, and she refused to believe it was just an idea put in her head by her mother.

She folded her arms in and pushed herself to be honest. Emmett came up beside her and put his warm hand on the back of her shoulders. She knew he already had the answer.

"You know none of what has happened is your fault."

"I know," she said without conviction, staring blankly at the water.

"I'm not sure you do. I see now how you may have gotten the idea that's how you deserve to be treated. But you must know deep down that you don't. Proof in point: you did leave him." His voice hitched as though he had another disturbing thought. "Please tell me your second husband wasn't abusive too."

A cool evening wind swept over her, but their talk was so intense she barely felt the chill.

She closed her eyes and shook her head. "No. Beau was nothing like Mike. Mike's biggest problem was alcohol. Sober, he was a philanderer who spent what little money we had on beer and women. Drunk on tequila, he was enraged and violent." Charlotte felt empty reliving those memories, though she preferred that to feeling pulled down by emotion.

"Charlotte, your strength amazes me, you know that? You should be so proud of yourself. Despite your past, look at the life you've forged for you and your children. I can't wait to meet Blake. I just know you've done a great job."

"My kids are great in spite of me, not because of me. I've made so many mistakes."

Emmett turned Charlotte so they were looking at each other. His hands were warm on her shoulders.

"That's not true, Charlotte. Granted, we all have dark times we'd rather forget. I'm not perfect, and I wouldn't expect you to be either. I don't see anything about you I can't accept. You're loving and honest, and you fought for the best for your children. I love that, and I think, no, I know, I'm falling in love with you, Charlotte."

Charlotte couldn't believe her ears. Here was the kindest, most patient man she'd ever met, standing in front of her with open arms, professing his love no less. Could she be as honest as he was being in that moment? She'd avoided so many truths for so long, and she was tired of lying to herself. She craved to tell him even just one truth. She wanted to feel free even if just for a moment.

"I…I'm falling in love with you too, Emmett. And it scares me."

"Don't be afraid," he said softly as he dipped his head to gently take her lips. She surrendered to his kiss with the passion that had been building since their first kiss weeks before.

Emmett pulled her face from his. "Babe, do you want to take this to the bedroom?"

She knew she was falling in love with Emmett, and she knew she could trust him, but she was still scared, so she hesitated to answer him.

Emmett blushed. "I'm sorry, I shouldn't have asked. I know tonight has taken a toll on you." His face went dark. "You didn't deserve to be treated the way you were earlier, and I just…I want to make you feel better." He pulled her in tight.

"You've been perfect tonight, Emmett, thank you. I'm so sorry. You're not mad, are you? I just…I'm not ready."

"I couldn't be mad at you. I made you a promise to be patient. It's too soon. I jumped the gun."

"Tonight was such a wreck, and I'm worried about Aubrie. She's clearly worse off than I thought. I should get back to her, make sure she's settled down and that my mom hasn't gone berserk on them, God forbid," she said as she looked around for her purse. "And really, I'm kind of worried now how Aubrie's going to take us being together. You saw her earlier. Adult or not, she's dealing with a lot, and I don't want to throw this in her face."

Guilt weighed on her for enjoying the safety and security of being with Emmett while her daughter was home with a drunken grandmother after having just been beaten by her drunken father the night before. She began to feel a strong pull to get back to her daughter and help make her see everything was going to be all right for her too.

Emmett walked her to her car. "You're taking a big step with me, and I'm not ignoring that. But Aubrie doesn't want you to be alone, Charlotte. She wants the best for you. She'll come around; she just needs to get to know me."

Char couldn't look Emmett in the eye. She hated herself for leading him to believe she hadn't been with anyone since Beau passed away. But if she told him the truth about Ash, it would lead to questions she couldn't answer. Char knew she was getting in over her head. Here she was, lying to the man she was falling in love with, but she didn't know what else to do.

"So, you'll tell her about us, right?" He leaned against her car and crossed his legs.

"Maybe." She pretended to look for her phone in her purse.

Emmett groaned and ran his fingers through his hair. "Charlotte. You need to tell her. I'm a grown man. I'm not going to hide our relationship, from a kid, no less. Sorry: adult."

Charlotte's feelings of déjà vu filled her with foreboding. It wasn't the first time Aubrie had been a source of contention between Char and a lover.

"No, you're right, Emmett. I'm sorry. I'll tell her. I just—let's not throw it in her face, please?"

"All right, I understand. I can do that. And what about your mother? Do you think she'll be calmed down when you get home? If not, I want you back here. You're not going for round two with her."

"I'm sure she's probably passed out on the couch by now. It'll be fine; don't worry."

He pulled her in for one more kiss. "Please be safe. Let me know you got home and that everything's okay there, all right?"

"I will. And, Emmett, thank you for being so great about tonight."

He smiled at her. "You're worth it. I love you, Charlotte."

"I love you too."

. . .

Hoping everyone was asleep, Charlotte opened her front door quietly and tiptoed up the stairs, but a light was still on. Thankfully, she found Aubrie, not Pam, on the couch.

Aubrie still looked pouty. Charlotte reminded herself to be patient with her, but really just wanted to go up to her room, climb into bed, and pretend the night hadn't happened.

"You got the couch, and Grandma and Chloe got the bedrooms?"

"No, it's just Chloe up there. Grandma was so burning mad she had us bring her back here to get her stuff so she could check into a hotel. She didn't have much cash on her, so we had to put her room on your card. I hope that's okay," Aubrie said, risking a glance at Charlotte through her thick lashes.

"Yes, of course. I'm sorry to say I'm relieved she's not here. Did she give you two much trouble?"

"No, I mean, it's annoying when Grandma gets that way, but Chloe and I know how to deal with it. We're going to see her in the morning, say good-bye. She has a job interview Monday, so she needs to get back home."

Pam went through jobs like she went through men and money. She just couldn't seem to make much of anything last, but Charlotte wouldn't make any snide comments about it. She'd long tired of having anger and irritation toward her mother and was only left with the sadness of it all.

"Anyway, I'm curious about something, Mom. You sure stayed late at Emmett's for having just met. What's that all about?"

Charlotte shifted on her feet. The soft glow of the lamplight warmed the living room and highlighted the fresh hydrangea bouquet in the center of the glass coffee table. There should have been a cozy feel to the room, but instead the stress of the night permeated the space.

"Aubrie, I'm not in the mood to go back and forth about my personal life, especially after you were so rude to Emmett tonight. I understand you're upset with me, but there was no reason to take it out on him."

"Mom, if you haven't realized, I've had to be along for the ride during your misadventures, and I'm freaked out now. I don't know Emmett, and you have to admit I have good reason to be suspicious."

"I know it hasn't been easy on you, and I'm sorry for that. But you're going to have to trust me when I say Emmett is truly special. I've spent a lot of time with him. He's trustworthy, kind, and patient. I have my eyes wide open."

"Mom, you defended Ash when you were practically on your deathbed because of him. You didn't leave the house for months, and it's been a year since your 'accident,'" Aubrie said, making air quotation marks and rolling her eyes.

"Aubrie, enough. We've been over and over this. Let it go. We broke up as couples sometimes do, end of story. Now forget Ash because, honey, I have." Her children could never know the truth. It would be much too painful and risky, though Charlotte knew she was overstating the facts. She hadn't quite forgotten about Ash, but with her therapy sessions, she was confident Moe would help her extinguish the pain of the past like rain to a fire. She could only hope it would happen sooner rather than later.

"Really? You're over him?" Aubrie said skeptically.

"Yes, really. It's been a year, Aubrie. I wasn't looking to fall in love, but if you give Emmett a chance, you'll find out why I did. And you'll like him too—I promise. We can trust him."

"You love him?" Aubrie said, taking a breath.

Charlotte hadn't realized she'd blurted that out and could have kicked herself.

"Mommy, I'm scared for you. And I'm sorry, but I don't believe you've forgotten Ash," Aubrie said with teary eyes.

Charlotte sat next to Aubrie and put her arms around her. "To be honest, it scares me too. I didn't plan on this. I'd planned on taking much more time to myself. And I worry sometimes I still should, but Emmett really is a wonderful man. Look, he already cooked you a meal. Did the one who shall not be named ever cook for you?"

Aubrie laughed and looked up at Charlotte. She could tell Aubrie wanted to believe her.

"Emmett's already said more words to you than Ash ever did during our entire time together. Doesn't that tell you something? Not that Ash was without reason for his distance; you weren't exactly the easiest teen to be around, Aubrie. In fact, you should get the Ms. Congeniality award for how you're treating Emmett, compared to how awful you were to Ash."

"Well, he proved he deserved it all in the end, didn't he?"

"Aubrie, you're so exasperating. Enough about Ash. Emmett's

a kind man with an open and loving heart. And meeting him has helped me forget you know who. You'll see. Please trust me, or at least give me a chance to prove to you everything's going to be okay. Please, sweetie?"

"Mom, I hope you're right. I'm tired of worrying about you all the time. But I won't stop until I know for a fact you're not going to get hurt anymore."

"I can promise you I'm not. Just give us a chance."

Aubrie looked at Char sideways. "I'll try. But the first red flag I see, it's not going to be pretty, Mom. Just forewarning you."

"Oh, I believe you, Aubrie," Char said with a touch of annoyance, "but you won't see any red flags, not with Emmett. I promise."

"We'll see. I love you, Mom."

"And I love you, Aubrie. I've put you through a lot, not on purpose, but I have, and I'm sorry. No more, though. I promise. And I'm really sorry I didn't tell you more about your dad."

"His name's Mike. Beau will always be my dad."

"I'm sorry, honey. I just didn't want you or Blake growing up with any kind of complex. You two are beautiful, wonderful kids. That your dad—sorry, Mike—has his own personal issues is no reflection on you. I hope you see that."

"I know. I felt like I was looking at a complete stranger when we met. It didn't even seem real. And his wife, Mona—yuck! Seriously, Mom, how did he end up with you? You're so above his league. What were you thinking?"

Charlotte laughed. "I wasn't thinking, Aubrie. I was escaping. I've made a lot of mistakes, and I hope you learn from them and don't fall into my footsteps. Promise me you won't."

"Grandma filled me in on what a jerk your stepdad was to her. I totally understand why you wanted out from under that craziness.

And no offense, Mom, but yeah, you don't have to worry. My plan's to do pretty much the opposite of a lot of things you've done."

Charlotte hadn't realized Pam had ever spoken with Aubrie about Keith. But it didn't surprise her that Pam would leave out the other half of the story and blame it all on him. Yes, her parents had had a tumultuous relationship, but in Char's eyes they had shared equally in the blame. And of course Pam wouldn't speak of the abuse Charlotte suffered at both their hands. But she had to let it go to focus on Aubrie's needs. The pain of her childhood had dulled over the years but the anguish of failing her kids held fast, though she kept it well hidden.

"When I should have been my strongest for you two, I crumbled. But it gives me some peace to hear that you know better. I love you so much, Aubrie."

"Actually, despite your horrid, awful, stupid mistakes with guys, you've been a pretty awesome role model, so don't be too hard on yourself. And, Mom, I love you too." Aubrie threw her arms around her mom.

Anytime they were close, Charlotte just soaked it up. Growing up where affection was essentially nonexistent, she cherished each moment of closeness with her children, even if after all the years it still caught her off guard.

"Anyway, Mom, it's been real, but I'm going to bed now. I'll see you in the morning. And don't worry; I'll start being nice to Emmett. Well, I'll do my best, anyway," she said with an impish smile.

She gave Aubrie a faux-stern look. "Do better than your best, honey. Good night."

Char woke early and took Asa on a long walk. She thought back to the night before and smiled. Despite her attempts, her mother hadn't succeeded in ruining the evening entirely, and Char had made strides in being more honest with Emmett. They'd professed their love for each other; she had to pinch herself to be sure it was real.

Charlotte was relieved Aubrie had agreed to give Emmett a chance to prove himself. She knew he'd pass with flying colors, and while she was looking forward to having them all spend time together, Charlotte wanted to spend some one-on-one time with Aubrie and Chloe, especially after realizing the previous night that Aubrie hadn't bounced back as quickly as she'd thought. She texted Emmett and let him know she wanted to have Sunday to herself with the girls once they got back from saying their good-byes to Pam. Charlotte was thankful she wasn't in the least bit expected to go with them.

Emmett texted her good morning and complained it was becoming difficult to spend even one day away from Char, but he told her if he had to, he'd put his Sunday to good use, that he'd go to the office and put in some hours as well as FaceTime his boys. He reminded her they'd be coming home Thursday and gave her a heads-up that he wanted to throw them a homecoming party. The prospect of meeting his close friends and family both excited and intimidated Charlotte, but she told him she'd be honored to help in any way with the party.

Charlotte took the girls to the restaurant where she and Emmett had had their first lunch together. She worried they might run into Leann, Emmett's ex, but of course that was a long shot. The girls loved the restaurant, sitting right out over the beach at high tide, the waves crashing in just below. They took lots of pictures and posted them for their friends.

They stayed out at the beach most of the day, and Charlotte was happy it ended up being a light and carefree time with the girls. There was no mention of Pam, Emmett, or anything else contentious; they just laughed and talked and played around in the water. These were the days that truly sustained Charlotte.

When Monday rolled around, Emmett asked Char if she would meet him at a restaurant near his office for lunch. Emmett sounded serious, so it made her nervous. She wondered if he'd had time to think about the multiple fiascos with her family over the weekend and gotten cold feet about her after all. She also worried he could be upset about them not sleeping together yet. She didn't know what was going on, but she knew in her gut that something wasn't right.

He was already at the table when she arrived. He stood to give her a kiss and told her she looked lovely. He seemed happy to see her, but she also felt tension in the air.

They made easy small talk, but all the while, Charlotte kept her guard up. She asked him about the boys coming home and shared some ideas for the welcome-home party.

"Speaking of the barbecue, Charlotte, I have to talk to you about something." His lips were scrunched.

Charlotte knew this must be the reason for the tension. She couldn't imagine why.

"I invited the boys' mother to the barbecue. We've always included each other in holidays and special events like this. I know it can be uncomfortable for the new people in our lives, but Dara and I have remained friends. Pretty close friends, to be honest. We've worked hard to keep it that way for the boys' sake. I just thought I'd give you heads-up. But it's something that won't change, regardless of how you might feel about it."

"Emmett. No, I completely understand. Your boys are lucky to have two levelheaded parents who've been able to get along for their sake. By all means, invite her."

"Well, like I said, I already invited her. I wasn't asking; I was telling you." He looked wound up and ready to spring at her. She didn't like the vibe, didn't understand it.

"Listen, Emmett. I don't know why you're speaking this way to me. I'm not giving you permission. I guess that came out wrong. I'm trying to show you I have no problem with her coming."

"And that's what I'm telling you; I don't care if you do or not. It's happening anyway."

Charlotte stiffened. "Surely this can't actually be about the barbecue. Regardless, I'm not staying around for it. And if this attitude is because I wouldn't make love to you the other night, you need to grow up." She grabbed her purse and left Emmett at the table.

She felt blindsided by his behavior. Her feelings were hurt, but her pride wasn't going to let her hang around and hope for an apology or an explanation. She stormed outside and through the tree-shaded parking lot to her car; she had just taken hold of the handle when she heard Emmett behind her.

"Charlotte, wait." He grabbed her arm, and she spun around and tried to jerk it from his grasp, but he held tight.

"Let go of me. I'm done with this conversation." She wouldn't look up at him; she didn't want him to see how hurt she was.

"Charlotte, I'm sorry. Look at me. I really am sorry. I didn't handle this right, but can you let me explain?" he said, letting go of her arm and holding his hands up as if in surrender.

She looked up at him and saw his face was pale, his eyes pained. She could tell he felt defeated, and it softened her anger. "Fine, go ahead."

"I'm sorry. I think I'm just still reeling from all the drama Leann caused between me and my boys, and with them coming home soon and knowing I have to introduce you all to each other, including Dara, their mother, I'm just nervous. I can't go down that road again, Charlotte."

"I'm not Leann, Emmett." Charlotte wouldn't look at him.

"I know, I know, I'm sorry. I should know better. I think this stress is affecting my rationality. Do you understand? Can you forgive me?" He bent his knees to meet her eyes. He looked so handsome, and he seemed truly worried that she might not forgive him, but she understood, far more than he'd ever know, how one's past could cloud judgment in the present.

"Of course I'll forgive you. You've put up with so much from me; it's the least I could do." She laughed when he put his hands together and looked up to the sky, mouthing, "Thank you, thank you."

He pulled her in close one last time. "But, Charlotte, can you do one thing for me in return?" His voice was stern. Char looked up at him, puzzled.

His arms were around her, and he pulled her in tightly. "Don't ever, and I mean ever, accuse me of being mad at you for not making love to me."

Charlotte blushed crimson. "I'm sorry for that."

"You know me better than that. Babe, I'll wait for you 'til the end of time. Don't ever say or think that again."

"I said it before thinking. I know you'd never think of pressuring me."

"Not on your life." He playfully brushed at her nose and kissed her forehead, and then he looked at his phone and sighed. "I gotta get going, babe. I have a meeting in twenty minutes. I'll get the door for you," he said, and he helped her into the car and leaned his arm on the door. "I really am sorry, Charlotte. Here you had a rough weekend, and come Monday I just piled more on you."

"Maybe we're both just under a little stress right now. But please know I fully support your relationship with Dara and your boys. That it's important to you to keep a good relationship with her just makes me love you even more."

He put his hand over his heart with a beaming smile. "And that right there is how I fell for you so hard. Drive home safely, honey."

As she pulled into her parking space, she got a text from Emmett, telling her not to worry about dinner, that it was on him that night to further make up for being such a jerk. She told him it wasn't necessary, but he wouldn't hear of it.

Instead of going to her condo, Char knocked on Moe's door. They had a session scheduled, and now that her boot was off, she was able to get up Moe's stairs. Moe welcomed her in and poured them each a cup of tea. Charlotte told her about the weekend, with all that had happened to Aubrie and the fiasco with Pam coming for a visit.

Moe suggested they do a Reiki session, saying that certain areas of the body acted as portals for energy, and that, with fluid movements of her hands held just above Charlotte, she'd be able to release the negative energy, helping Char let go of the tension and stress. Charlotte wasn't convinced the therapy would work, but she trusted Moe, so agreed.

By the time Charlotte was back in her own condo, she felt lighter and clearer headed. At times, talking was difficult for Char, so she appreciated the noninvasive therapy and was surprised at how well it actually worked. Best of all, she felt refocused and was able to delve into her work and get the papers sent back to the firm even before they were expected.

Emmett showed up at the door that evening with a full grocery bag, a bottle of expensive wine, and an extra-large bouquet of flowers. He looked so cute with his arms full of apology.

She grabbed the flowers and wine. Together, they set the small table out on Char's back deck that overlooked the palm-tree-dotted path to the pool. Flowering trees lined the next condo over, and she had a small two-tiered birdbath in the corner that bubbled and trickled water. Flowerpots filled in any open spaces. It looked like an English country garden and smelled divine. In the distance, the sounds of the ocean rolled softly. Charlotte loved spending time on her deck.

"Babe, I have to say again I really am so sorry about earlier. I don't know what came over me. I was such a class-A jerk. Deep down I knew without even asking that you would never cause a problem between the boys, their mother, and me. I was being ridiculous."

"Yes, you were," Char said flatly as she set the forks and napkins out. Emmett laughed at her frankness. "Don't worry about me being jealous. I think a good sign of a great man is when he has a close, loving relationship with his mother and healthy relationships with other women. And as far as trying to keep you from falling for another woman, the way I look at it, I can't worry about whether or not you're looking at, or even wanting, another woman. If I don't mean enough to you to stay faithful, then adios, amigo, and don't let the door hit you on the way out."

"Really? You're not willing to fight for me? Blow to the ego!" Emmett said, laughing and clutching his chest, but Char wondered if there was a little truth to his proclamation. Men did seem to enjoy a jealous woman, but to her it was game playing and she wanted nothing to do with that.

"I just believe there are more important things to fight for than to convince a man that I really do mean something to him. That just seems counterintuitive."

"Oh, I see. So it's *your* ego we're talking about."

"If that's what you want to call it," Charlotte said dismissively.

Emmett stepped in close. "Well, sweetheart, I have to tell you, there's no one else I'd rather be with. I can't stop thinking about you, and I miss you like crazy when we're apart," he said as he nuzzled Char's ear and put his hands at her waist.

He made Char's knees weak, but she worried about Aubrie coming around the corner. "Honey, not here. I think the girls are coming upstairs." She broke away to head to the kitchen to get what was left for setting the table. Emmett made no reply, but sighed heavily as she walked away.

As she was gathering extra napkins and a couple of serving spoons, Charlotte heard the girls coming through the front door. "Girls, Emmett's here. He brought us dinner. Go get changed, and let's eat, chop, chop!"

"We're starving, Mom. Any chips out there?" Aubrie said, hanging on to the beach towel draped around her shoulders and eyeing Emmett standing out at the table, working to get the bottle of wine open.

Charlotte smiled. "Yes, there are chips out there, and no, Emmett won't bite, Aubrie."

Aubrie rolled her eyes. "Well, you never know, Mom."

Charlotte was about to reply, but Chloe did the honors. "Oh, get a grip, Aub, come on." She grabbed Aubrie's elbow and pulled her through the sliding-glass door.

Char watched the girls, hoping to see Aubrie and Emmett have a pleasant exchange. Chloe wore a smile, but Aubrie had her arms crossed defensively. Emmett was pulling at his neck like he did when he was uncomfortable, though he smiled and seemed to chuckle as the girls came back into the house.

"See, he didn't bite, did he?"

"I think it's Aubrie you need to worry about, Aunt Charlie."

"Chloe, don't be so dramatic," Aubrie said in a huff, which made Chloe and Charlotte laugh, since the entire family knew Aubrie was the one with the dramatic flair.

Char went to check on Emmett, who, sure enough, didn't look as cheerful as he had before she went to the kitchen.

"So, what did Aubrie do?"

"Nothing, really. But sometimes I wonder if I'm ever going to measure up with you women."

"What do you mean?"

"Oh, I just think I won't be using flowers as a mea culpa ever again," Emmett said as he raked his hands through his hair.

"Why not? I love them."

"Aubrie just came through and hit the nail on the head. She asked what I did to you that I had to apologize for with the flowers. That girl isn't going to let me get away with anything, is she? Not that I deserve it, after earlier today." He looked like a schoolboy being sent to the principal's office. She couldn't help but laugh.

Char was disappointed that Aubrie wasn't holding to her promise to give Emmett a chance, but she wanted to put Emmett at ease. "What happened at lunch wasn't a big deal, Emmett. You were grumpy, and you've apologized. You told me Saturday night you didn't expect me to be perfect because you yourself aren't. I want you to know I don't expect perfection from you either."

"I appreciate that. But you must have standards. You excused my jackass behavior today, but what's your deal breaker?"

"Emmett, I don't want to think about us breaking up." Char didn't want to hear his deal breaker, for fear she might have already committed it.

"But I think it's important to know where we each stand. I want you to know," Emmett said, crossing the patio to stand close to Char, "that above all, I value honesty. Just don't lie to me. Leann lied about wanting to have children with me, and it about killed me. I don't want to go through that kind of betrayal again."

"How can we even be together now? I can't talk with you about my scars." Charlotte's voice began to crack.

"No, no, Charlotte, I don't mean that kind of thing. It's not like you made up a story about it; it's just painful for you to talk about. That's totally different from a direct, 'look me in the eye' kind of lie. No, I understand that we're still getting to know each other. I hope I never stop learning more about you."

And I hope there are things you never learn about me, she thought.

"What's for dinner? We're starving," Aubrie said, interrupting. Char lit up at seeing the girls. She was happy for the distraction.

"There you are. We've got curried chicken salad, and you can either make it into a sandwich or pair it with a green salad. Emmett was also kind enough to bring dessert for us: your favorite, Aubrie, lemon meringue pie." Charlotte watched Aubrie, hoping she'd be nice.

"Thank you, Emmett. What a fortunate accident for me."

"You're welcome, Aubrie. But I have to admit it wasn't an accident. I texted your mom. I wanted to get you something to sweeten your day. You've had a rough couple of days, and for that I'm sorry. All you girls deserve to be treated with respect, and I'm sorry that hasn't always been the case," he said as he looked at all three of them, "but over time I plan on proving to you that I'd never hurt Charlotte, or any of you, for that matter. You have my word."

Aubrie studied Emmett before allowing a small smile. "Thank you for the lemon meringue. It's been my favorite since I can remember."

Charlotte could tell Emmett had actually reached Aubrie with just this tiny effort to show he cared. She had a good feeling they would be able to bridge the gap between them.

When it was time to say good night, Charlotte walked Emmett to his car, so they could have some privacy. Emmet said, "I hope I made some progress with Aubrie tonight. She seemed to thaw a little by the end of the night, don't you think?"

"I do. She'll come around, Emmett, sooner rather than later, I'm sure. But the girls have been through a lot, so I'm planning a little surprise for them, and we'll be out of town a couple of nights. I think they really need this."

"Selfishly, I'm going to miss you, but I think that's a great idea. You'll be home in time for the boys' welcome-home party, Thursday, right?"

"Wouldn't miss it."

"You're a wonderful mom and a special woman, Charlotte," Emmett said, pulling her in close and kissing her with a tenderness that left Charlotte speechless. Emmett pulled back to look into her eyes and just smiled. He gave her a soft peck on the lips before getting into his car. With her arms around herself and a smile, she walked back to the condo.

The next morning at breakfast, out on the deck, Charlotte told the girls to pack overnight bags. Aubrie was midbite but put her spoon down. "We just got here, Mom, and we have a lot of unpacking to do. Why would we go anywhere?"

"Because we need a break. It was scary what you two went through and then stressful for me when Grandma came. I think we all need a little dose of Disneyland. A quick trip. Just two nights, what do you say?"

Charlotte saw Chloe's eyes light up, but Aubrie slumped in her chair and said, "Aren't we a little old for that?"

"I know I'm not. I'd love to go, Aunt Charlie," Chloe said with enthusiasm.

"You're never too old for Disneyland, Aubrie. Anyway," Char said, smiling conspiratorially at Chloe, "we have a two-thirds majority. It's decided. We're going." Chloe squealed and gave Charlotte a big hug.

Aubrie's faux irritation at having to go to Disneyland lasted all of about three minutes. As soon as they got there, both the girls were just as excited to be there as they had been when they were kindergarteners. Charlotte remembered when Beau had surprised them with their first trip to Disneyland, and he'd let Blake and Aubrie each bring a friend. Of course Aubrie brought her cousin, and they had been on cloud nine the whole time. Charlotte was warmed to see the same light in their eyes now that they were much older, especially Aubrie, after all she'd been through in her young life.

Their stay didn't seem nearly long enough, but when it was time to go home, Charlotte reminded the girls that they now lived only sixty miles from the park. They could hop into the car and go whenever they wanted, even if just for a day.

Charlotte called Emmett when they got home. "Hi, honey, how was Disneyland?"

"Perfect, as always. We must have gone on Peter Pan ten times," Char said, laughing.

"And the girls?"

"Oh, it was like stepping back in time with them. They were so happy and carefree. Best of all, there was no tension between Aubrie and me, not one bit. It was nice."

"I'm happy for you, honey. And tonight you get to meet my boys. I can't wait to see them, and I'm looking forward to introducing you."

"I can't wait either. I'll see you soon, Emmett."

Charlotte and the girls got to Emmett's early to help Anna prepare for the party. Charlotte knocked on the door as she opened it and called out to Anna. She didn't want to startle her. "Anna, we're here."

Anna came to the door, and if she were stressed from preparing for the party, no one would be the wiser. She had her blond hair in a bun, and not a hair was out of place. Her big brown eyes got even bigger when she saw Aubrie and Chloe.

"Dios mio, this is your daughter and niece? Nice to meet you, Aubrie Elle. And you too, señorita Chloe. You two are *muy bonitas!*"

"*Mucho gusto*, señora Anna," Chloe said proudly. She'd taken three years of Spanish by the time she'd graduated from high school.

"Nice to meet you, Anna," Aubrie said as she shook her hand.

Charlotte put her hands on her hips and looked around the room. "So, what can we do to help?"

Anna put them all to work setting out drinks and décor. The girls put up a *Welcome Back* sign and hung balloons around the house. In fewer than five minutes, Anna and the girls were like old family friends. Anna was so easy to get along with, very maternal. The girls took to her right away.

As the minutes ticked by, Charlotte became more and more nervous. She'd be meeting some important people in Emmett's life, his boys and ex-wife. It was nerve-racking. All she could do was make sure she looked good and bake an out-of-this-world berry pie, apparently the boys' favorite. She thought she'd reciprocate after Emmett's overture to Aubrie.

When the doorbell rang, announcing the arrival of the first guest, Anna let in a strikingly beautiful woman. They exchanged pleasantries before Anna turned to Charlotte.

"Señora Charlotte, this is Kai and Noa's mother, señora Dara," Anna said in a formal tone.

"Nice to meet you, Dara. I imagine you're counting down the seconds until your boys come through the door," Charlotte said. She was trying to act as natural as possible, but she could barely contain her feelings. This woman was gorgeous, much more than even Leann, who could have taken nearly anyone's breath away. She was tall, with long legs and perfect curves, a heart-shaped face, full lips, and beautiful, deep brown eyes. Charlotte felt the absolute polar opposite of Dara.

Dara nodded and said, "Oh, I miss my boys terribly. I hear you have a son and daughter?"

"I do. My son's going to school in New York, and my daughter, Aubrie Elle, is here somewhere, along with her cousin Chloe. Maybe they're out by the pool. They're looking forward to meeting your boys."

"Emmett tells me your daughter and niece just graduated? My boys graduated last year, and their freshman year went really well. We're so proud of them. But I'm thankful they were able to take some time away from the team and experience the world as they *don't* know it," Dara said with a laugh.

Even her laugh is gorgeous, Charlotte thought. She had never considered herself a jealous person, but maybe now she was beginning to understand where part of Leann's insecurity came from. Dara seemed genuinely sweet and beautiful. *What's not to be insecure about?*

Before she could answer, the doorbell rang, and Anna welcomed in a larger group of people. Charlotte didn't know any of them, but then, lagging behind, Kat and Lou came through the door, and Charlotte was happy to see some familiar faces. Dara hugged Kat and Lou before Kat found Charlotte.

"You have your daughter and niece here? Please, I must meet them." The longing in Kat's voice reminded Char of Kat's harrowed past and that she was robbed of the chance to have children of her own. Char's heart went out to Kat.

"By all means, Kat, let's go outside. I think they're by the pool," Charlotte said as they walked outside. When the girls saw them approach, their eyes about popped out of their heads.

Charlotte smiled. "Aubrie, Chloe, please meet my friend Kat."

"What? You've been on magazine covers, like, a hundred times, right?" Aubrie asked, astounded.

"Yes, that is me; and you're my friend's daughter," she said looking at Aubrie and Chloe. "And you her niece? You two are gorgeous. We must be friends too. When your mother is too busy with Emmett, we shall go shopping together, no?"

"Oh my gosh, totally!" Chloe squealed.

"I can't believe we're meeting you. I got in my first fight ever with a boyfriend because he'd pasted your pictures all over his locker," Aubrie said in amazement.

"My dear, men are visual creatures. You must get used to it. We'll go shopping. I'll show you what to buy so he looks only at you."

Aubrie and Chloe both reached for their phones at the same time to get Kat's number. Charlotte's heart warmed to see the girls and Kat hitting it off.

She left them in their huddle and Anna called over to introduce Char to some of Emmett's employees, who seemed overly eager to meet Charlotte. She felt a little on display as Anna made the introductions, and was thinking of how to remove herself when she heard a commotion.

She turned and saw, to her relief, Emmett coming in with his sons. Both boys were tall like their dad, and, like him, they clearly worked out a lot too. Char guessed that came with the territory of playing college football. She had known they were fraternal, not identical, twins, but she wasn't prepared for how opposite they were. One took after their mother, with a decidedly Hawaiian look, while the other was a near spitting image of Emmett.

Char hung back to allow their mother to greet them first. As she watched the happy family reunion, Charlotte noted how comfortable Dara and Emmett looked around each other. They almost looked as if they still shared an intimacy. Charlotte told herself that surely it was an innocent closeness and to knock it off and not be like Leann, so she pushed those thoughts aside and reminded herself how the boys were blessed that their parents were still close and that that was most important. Dara waved at someone and left the circle.

Emmett caught Charlotte's eye and waved her over. "Noa, Kai, this is Charlotte, who I told you about." Emmett was sporting a proud smile.

"Nice to meet you, Charlotte, I'm Kai, and this is Noa." Kai's deep brown eyes twinkled just like his mother's. He looked like he had a sweet disposition.

"Nice to meet you, Charlotte." Noa's voice sounded much like his dad's. Char thought Noa seemed a bit more reserved than Kai but still pleasant.

Katena came up to the boys and gave them both hugs.

"Boys, let me introduce you to Charlotte's girls," Katena said, motioning the girls to step closer. "Kai, Noa, this is Aubrie, Charlotte's daughter, and Chloe, her niece." Katena wore a mischievous smile as she stood back to watch the kids' interaction.

Char and Emmett did the same. Aubrie and Noa went for each other's hands the same time as Kai and Chloe locked eyes to do the same.

Katena obviously was trying to help with some sort of love connection, because she said, "Boys, where are your manners? Why don't you offer the girls a drink?"

"Oh yeah, totally. Here, this way, guys," Kai said. He surreptitiously gave Katena a thumbs-up.

"Katena, what are you trying to do to Char and me?" Emmett grumbled, clearly irritated.

"Introducing your children? Where's the crime in that? As if they weren't going to meet. Don't be ridiculous, Emmett." Katena huffed. She patted his shoulder and sauntered off.

Dara walked back up and asked, "Are those your girls? Our children are about the same age, aren't they? Your girls are beautiful, Charlotte. That could spell trouble down the road," Dara teased.

Emmett and Char knew what she was thinking—what all the adults were thinking.

"Not if we don't let it." Emmett sounded serious, but Charlotte couldn't be sure.

"What, really? Tell the kids they're off limits to each other?" Charlotte asked.

"You'd better believe it."

"And that's my cue to leave—been there, done that. Believe me, Charlotte, I don't envy your position." Dara gave Charlotte a sympathetic look and made a hasty retreat.

"What does Dara mean by that?"

"She was admitting she's much too easy on Noa and Kai. I set strict guidelines for my boys and expect them to toe the line. She always had a problem with that," he said as he huffed an irritated sigh. "Listen, I just don't want any nonsense coming from our kids. We have enough issues to deal with, and as their parents, we have every right to have a say in whether they can see each other or not."

"Enough issues? What do you mean by that? Am I an 'issue' to deal with?" Char kept her voice low and was thankful for the bustling talk drowning out their somewhat heated conversation.

"No, Char. I'm sorry—that's not what I meant."

"Then what did you mean?"

"I don't know. I shouldn't have said that. I just…I don't want unnecessary problems complicating our relationship."

"Well, I agree that I don't want anything coming between us, but I also trust my kids. Aubrie, Chloe, they're good girls. I try to choose carefully which hard lines I draw."

"See? That sounds like you're too intimidated to set boundaries. That's ridiculous. You're the parent. What you say goes. That's the way it is. If you're afraid of that, then they'll take advantage and run all over you. Come to think of it, maybe that's part of Aubrie's issue. The way she stormed out of here the other night—I would have had either of my son's asses if they'd disrespected me like that."

"Emmett, I'm not sure how you think I should have 'had Aubrie's ass,' but I can assure you I don't even like that phrase, so I'm sure I don't agree with you. We've had our issues in the past, but Aubrie's her own person, and she has a right to her opinions." Charlotte was afraid a fight was brewing between her and Emmett. This wasn't the appropriate time for an argument, of that she was certain.

"Her disrespecting you is an issue she shouldn't be allowed to have in the first place. That's my only point there, Charlotte. Tonight's about my boys, so if you don't mind, I'd like to focus on them for the rest of the evening," he said, sounding as brusque as he did the day at the restaurant.

So much for the apology, Char thought.

"There you go again, Emmett, just like the other day, pretty much accusing me of getting between you and your family, which I certainly haven't done. Please, by all means, focus on them and not the way I parent my kids, thank you very much."

Charlotte left Emmett and went to find the girls. It was clearly time to go, but before she could get very far, Dara stopped her.

"Charlotte, hey, can I talk to you? If I'm intruding, you can tell me to mind my own business, but I couldn't help but notice you two likely went a small round about parenting?"

"We did." Char wasn't sure she should be talking to Dara about their private conversation, but she let her continue.

"If the past is any indication, he was touting being a tough disciplinarian while admonishing you for being too lenient?" Dara asked with a wry look on her face.

"That's about right. I'm afraid to say we aren't seeing eye-to-eye at the moment. It's an awful feeling having to defend your parenting skills," she said, taking in a big breath.

Dara nodded in agreement. "Well, just so you know, Emmett talks a good game, but give him a little time, and he'll usually soften his stance."

Charlotte looked at Dara, surprised. She was lending help for Char and Emmett, and Char could tell she was being sincere. Now she felt even guiltier for her earlier suspicion. Charlotte sighed. "I appreciate your insight, Dara, thank you. I think the best thing to do is gather the girls. I think I'll leave and give your family some time together."

Dara offered a kind smile. "It was nice meeting you. I think Emmett is lucky to have met you, Charlotte. I hope to see you at more family gatherings."

"Thank you, Dara. I hope to see you again too." Charlotte was happy that at least one good thing had come out of the night: meeting Dara and seeing what a lovely person she was and knowing she was supportive of her and Emmett, completely the opposite of Leann.

Charlotte found the kids but hesitated, knowing her announcement wouldn't go over well. The only other alternative was to stay and, after Emmett snapping at her, that just wasn't an option. She put a smile on her face and stepped up. "Girls, hi, sorry to interrupt, but it's time to go."

"Mom, seriously, didn't we just get here?"

"Please, Ms. Charlotte, just a little longer?" Kai begged.

"No, I'm sorry, but we'll get together soon, I'm sure." Charlotte hoped that was the truth.

"I think Dad was going to take the day off tomorrow so we could go deep-sea fishing. Maybe you guys could come with us," Noa suggested.

"Oh, that's nice of you boys, but your dad's waited weeks to finally spend some time with you."

"No, Dad's cool—we'll talk to him," Kai said confidently.

"Well, we'll see. Thank you, boys. Nice to meet you. Have a good rest of your night."

Charlotte said good-bye to Kat and Lou and Anna. She saw Emmett in the corner but felt they'd said all they needed to say, so continued toward the door, hoping he wouldn't notice. However, he was at her side before she knew it.

"Charlotte, you can't leave, not like this. Let's talk, please." He set his drink down to focus on her.

"Now's not an appropriate time, Emmett. Spend time with your family, your boys. I don't want to intrude any further on your first evening back with them."

"Charlotte, you're not intruding. You know that's not how I feel."

"I'm not sure I agree. I think it's best I leave now." She forced a smile, trying to appear pleasant in case there were any observers.

His eyes dropped to stare at the floor as he accepted defeat. "Here, let me walk you to your car." He put his hand at the small of her back and walked her out. Char waved the girls over, who were still hanging back, not wanting to leave until they absolutely had to. Begrudgingly they caught up to Charlotte.

Emmett looked at both the girls and said, "Sorry to see you go, you two, but I'm glad you could make it tonight."

"Thank you so much for inviting us, Emmett. We hope to see you soon too," Aubrie said enthusiastically, with Chloe agreeing. Char wondered at Aubrie's change in demeanor toward Emmett.

Emmett waited until the girls were in the car and out of earshot. His hands in his pockets, he shifted his feet, looking up to the sky. "What infuriates me about you, Charlotte, is if it gets even the slightest bit uncomfortable for you, you just up and leave. Why can't we be real, have real discussions, and actually work it out in one sitting? You're always taking off. It's kind of juvenile, if you ask me."

Char looked down at her feet, rocking back a couple of times. "Hmmm, wow. I didn't know you felt that way about me. Maybe you've hit on something, Emmett." She looked up at him. "Maybe I'm leaving because you're always pushing me. How about I delve a bit more into my compulsion to leave you? Maybe that's an indicator of future failure of this relationship." Char, once again, didn't believe what she was saying to him, but her defense mechanism just kicked in and made her go for the jugular, the best mode of defense. She figured she'd better leave before she said anything worse.

"Char, I hope you don't mean that. Don't go, please?" Emmett begged. He looked so handsome in his pale-yellow linen button-up that made his shoulders look particularly sculpted. It made what she was saying to him even more painful, because she could feel that pull to be with him as she was pushing him away. Charlotte was tired of feeling conflicted, especially since she thought she'd overcome so many of her objections, making a huge step forward in their relationship, but she also didn't want to be a pushover, and he hadn't been the nicest to her lately.

"I need to go. This is too much. Good night, Emmett." She got into the car and shut the door.

"Mom, seriously, what are you doing? You better not be fighting with Emmett, because Chloe and I just fell in love tonight, and you can't ruin it for us!"

"Oh, that's real rich, Aubrie. Just a couple of days ago I was asking you not to ruin things with Emmett and me. But you didn't care, and you've been on Emmett's case every chance you get."

Charlotte saw Chloe in the rearview mirror give Aubrie an imploring look as if to say, "Please, fix this, Aubrie." Aubrie gave Chloe a reassuring nod. She looked up at Charlotte.

"Mom, I'm sorry. I thought I was being protective. But after meeting everyone, I know I made a mistake about Emmett. Chloe and I *really* like Noa and Kai. We really, really, really want to go fishing with them tomorrow."

"See? Your mom's radar isn't, what did you say, 'totally whacked,' is it?" Charlotte felt even worse for getting into the argument with Emmett now that she saw the girls were being affected. She didn't have the heart to tell the girls that Emmett was putting his foot down about the four of them.

"No, Mom, I think your radar is actually working pretty well right now. So, can we go fishing tomorrow with them?" Aubrie and Chloe looked hopeful.

"Girls, that's up to Emmett. Like I said, his boys just got back home. He may want one-on-one time with them, just like when you two got here, we took some time to ourselves. Don't be shocked if the boys can't take you along tomorrow, okay?"

Charlotte didn't hear from Emmett that night. It hurt her feelings, and she began to think Emmett may have taken to heart the hurtful things she said. She worried he might be agreeing that things just couldn't work out between the two of them.

To Char's surprise, at eight o'clock in the morning she got a text.

> *Morning. Apologies again. My fault. Again. Plz accept my apology. Again. ☹ The boys and I would love for u girls 2 join us out on the high seas. Plz?*

Charlotte felt relief wash over her, and she wondered at Emmett's seeming change of heart. She'd thought when she didn't hear from him that perhaps he'd decided that the whole lot of her and the girls was just too much trouble, but after reading his text, she remembered what Dara had said about him, and she had been right. He talked a good game, but in reality, he truly was a softie at heart, and that was comforting to her and brought a smile to her face.

She figured she'd better accept, or the girls would never let her hear the end of it. She enjoyed waking them up so "early" to give them the good news. They went from grumpy to ecstatic in a nanosecond. The only thing they were still unhappy about was the minimal time to get ready. Charlotte assured them they could go without a stitch of makeup and they'd still be gorgeous, but they wouldn't hear any of it.

Emmett picked them up in his SUV. He took them through a coffee drive-through. The boys each got three breakfast sandwiches. The girls got a fruit plate to share and skinny lattes. Charlotte laughed to herself because she knew they would normally have ordered almost as much as the boys.

They drove down to Marina del Rey, and while they waited for their boat to be readied, the girls enjoyed the boys' showing them around all the different kinds of boats and talking about their purposes.

Char liked seeing Emmett in his casual clothes: khaki shorts, a T-shirt, and a ball cap. With his five o'clock shadow, his strong jawline stood out, and all she wanted to do was kiss it, but of course she was still mad at him for being so brusque and accusatory with her twice in just a week. She hoped they could talk it out and come to a better understanding of what had happened and why. She appreciated that she could already take for granted that they would talk. She already knew she could trust Emmett to open up to her and allow her to do the same.

It was ten in the morning, but the July sun was already heating up. Thankfully the slight breeze on the dock would become stronger out on the ocean, offering relief from the heat.

Once they boarded, the boys took to showing the girls how to work the fishing poles and what to do if they were to get a fish on the line. Within the first hour of their fishing trip, it was obvious that the developing couples were Aubrie and Noa, Chloe and Kai. Charlotte laughed to Emmett that it seemed a bit narcissistic that they paired up with the person with whom they shared the most physical similarities. Emmett laughed and said he should have figured. Kai had always gone for women who looked like his mom, while Noa always seemed to go for blondes.

Charlotte had a thought, and though she was reluctant to reveal her insecurities, she couldn't help but ask. "Seems after meeting

Leann and Dara that you have a type—the complete opposite of me?"

"Yeah, I have to admit, I've never dated anyone seriously who was even remotely like you, on the outside or inside. But I want you to know I've never been happier.

"Listen, I don't know what's gotten into me lately. I want you to know how sorry I am. And it's definitely not you; it's just backlash from Leann. Our divorce is almost final, but you're the first one since our breakup that I've brought around my family, and I'm finding I have some stuff to still work out from that fiasco. I felt like I almost lost my man card to her." He pulled his hat down lower, as if ashamed. He was leaning back against the railing, and he crossed his arms, looking down at his feet. "But I can't reclaim it at the expense of your feelings or, God forbid, at the expense of our relationship. Will you please accept my apology?" he asked, shyly looking up to meet Char's gaze.

"I will. If you can do me a favor and count to ten before you react so defensively. You get angry at me when I haven't even done whatever you think I have."

"I will. Can you do something for me in return?" He unfolded his arms and brought his shoulders back as he asked, signaling to Char his confidence was returning.

"What's that?" she asked in mock suspicion.

"Can *you* count to ten before running? I know I praised you the other day when we met at the restaurant for high-tailing it out of there when I was being a jerk to you, and I still stand by that. But when we're simply having a disagreement, can you find it within yourself to finish it out with me instead of taking off?"

She heaved a big breath as she looked out over the expanse of the deep, sparkling blue ocean, feeling like his request was as difficult a challenge as asking her to swim back to shore. "I'll try. I don't know;

it's just a strong visceral reaction of mine. It'll take some work, but I'll try my best."

Emmett put an arm around her and leaned his head on hers. "We'll get this figured out. I have a lot of faith in us."

"No way! Oh my God, I think I got a fish!" Aubrie squealed. Char and Emmett went over to watch as Noa ran to her side to show her how to reel it in. Charlotte noticed Aubrie was paying more attention to Noa helping her than to the fish on the line. She enjoyed watching them from afar and noticed Emmett seemed proud of how Noa was stepping in to help Aubrie.

Chloe and Emmett were the only two others to get a fish all day, but no one missed out on the fun. They had a quick bite to eat back at the boardwalk before calling it a successful day.

On the drive home, the boys seemed to be trying to show off for the girls, arguing about which one could bench-press more, who was quicker, and who could kick whose butt.

"Last time on the mat I had you tapping out in about thirty seconds," Noa said to Kai.

Not missing a beat, Kai replied, "BS, Noa, you cheated. You went for me before we slapped hands. You took a cheap shot—admit it," he said, glancing at Chloe, clearly hoping she wasn't buying his brother's side of the story.

"What are you talking about? You two box?" Chloe asked, already looking impressed.

The boys laughed. "No way. We've been studying jujitsu for about ten years. We've almost got our black belts. Noa's behind me a bit, though," Kai said, as he flexed his biceps.

The girls exchanged smiles.

"Now you're talking BS, Kai. We've got the same belt, and you know it."

"Speaking of, guys, why don't we take the girls with us tomorrow. We can get a refresher course in self-defense. It's always good to review, regardless of level, and it would sure be great for the girls. What do you say, girls? Would you be up for a self-defense course?"

Aubrie and Chloe looked at each other, unsure.

The boys clearly saw it as another opportunity to show off their prowess. "Aubrie, seriously, you have to come. It'll be a blast. Promise," Noa said.

"Chloe, I can show you the ropes. With my help, I'll get you primed to kick butt in no time," Kai said, winking at Chloe. Noa rolled his eyes.

Emmett and Char enjoyed listening to the kids banter, but Emmett wanted an answer. "So what do you say, girls?"

Clearly they realized it was another great excuse to spend time with the boys, so they heartily agreed, and the boys fist-bumped each other.

Emmett pulled into their condo and reminded the girls, "We'll text the address for tomorrow, and it starts at nine in the morning. Don't be late."

"It's a date," Aubrie said with a smile as she and Chloe jumped out of the car and the boys walked them to the door. Char wanted nothing to do with it but decided to keep it to herself. Before she slid out of the car, Emmett caught her hand and held it gently.

"Char, I saw the look on your face. You don't want to go to the gym with us, but I think it would be a big mistake not to. You need to do this just as much as the girls. I expect to see you there, okay?"

The pit in her stomach assured her she wouldn't be going, but she didn't have the nerve just yet to say no. "I...okay, Emmett," she lied, hiding behind the best smile she could muster before sliding out of the door. It hurt to see the smile on his face, though she still wished he weren't so demanding. He wasn't giving her the space she needed, and she wasn't ready or brave enough to be honest with him.

That evening the girls made a spaghetti dinner at home, and Charlotte invited Moe, who accepted with gusto. The girls thought Moe was a riot. She seemed to put on a show whether she meant to or not. She ended up with Asa in her arms all evening. He hadn't forgotten it had been Moe who had walked him when he was stuck inside with Char.

"I understand you're both starting college in the fall. Have you both declared a major? Wait, don't tell me yet. I'd like to guess. I'm getting a lot of blue aura from you both, so I'm thinking something in the arts," Moe said, gazing at Aubrie and Chloe with a look of intrigue.

"You guessed right for me. I'm getting my degree in creative writing," Aubrie said with a smile of surprise.

Already used to Moe's sense of perception, Charlotte smiled knowingly. "As soon as she learned to write, Aubrie's never put the pencil down," Charlotte said to Moe.

"It's therapy to get my feelings down on paper. And more often than not, they morph into wild stories," Aubrie shared as she twirled spaghetti noodles onto her fork.

"Wild, yes, but funny too. Since we were little, Aubrie has kept me in stitches," Chloe said.

"Yeah, unfortunately not all of them are, shall we say, appropriate?" Charlotte said, giving the eye to Aubrie.

Moe batted her hand through the air. "Pfft, if we stifled ourselves by only saying and doing what was appropriate, it would be a mighty boring world, wouldn't you agree?"

"My point exactly, Moe," Aubrie said in triumph.

Moe turned to Chloe. "And what about you, Chloe? What creative endeavor are you embarking upon?"

Chloe nodded and eagerly answered, clearly impressed with Moe's confident prediction. "Santa Monica College has a great associate degree in fashion design. I mean, there were others closer to home, but this one was exactly what I wanted. I'll start there, then see about transferring to a four year."

"But I sense there was some apprehension about your decision. Was that about your career path or something else?" Moe asked Chloe.

"No, I almost didn't agree to come with Aubrie to go to school down here. I wasn't sure about leaving my mom. But so far I'd say I made the right decision, and now I couldn't imagine not being here," Chloe said happily.

"Otherwise she wouldn't have met her future husband. It would have been tragic," Aubrie said with a giggle.

"Aubrie! Shut!" Chloe said.

Char smiled at Chloe. "So, you and Kai have really hit it off?"

"Who's Kai?" Moe asked.

"One of Emmett's twin sons," Charlotte said with a mock-serious expression.

"Oh, good heavens. What about the other twin?" Moe looked right at Aubrie.

"Yeah, Aub, your turn. What about Noa?" Chloe asked her tauntingly. "You know, the one you're texting back and forth with every 1.5 seconds."

Aubrie rolled her eyes. "Well, I haven't declared Noa my husband-to-be like you have with Kai." She hesitated, then added softly, "But I think we like each other, a little."

"A little. Hmm, that's not what it looked like when you two were locking lips on the other side of the boat this morning," Chloe teased.

"Now it's your turn to shut, Chloe," Aubrie said with a glare.

Charlotte stepped in. "Girls, I hope you're pacing yourselves here.

Aubrie, you've known Noa all of twenty-four hours. Kissing him today may have been a little soon, don't you think?"

"I'll have to meet these boys, gauge their chakras against yours. I'll let you know if it's a good match or not," Moe said, trying to help.

"Huh?" the girls said in unison.

Char tried to help out. "Their energies," she said, but the girls kept staring. "To see if you guys are a good fit or not." Char enjoyed watching the girls' reactions. They were at least trying to be respectful.

"Ohhh, cool," they said again in unison. Moe looked pleased.

"But chakras or no chakras, I still say it's a bit too soon," Charlotte reiterated.

"Mom, who are you to say I'm moving too soon? Noa said he went into his dad's bathroom and found some women's stuff in there, and apparently your crutches are out in the garage. So your little ankle twist wasn't so little, was it? But that's beside the point, because more importantly, it sounds to me like you were staying with him while Chloe and I were on our road trip. You knew him for what, not even a month, and you were already having overnighters? Please!"

Moe slid out of her seat and stood nervously patting the back of the chair. "Dears, it's getting late. I want to thank you for the wonderfully enjoyable meal. It's my turn next. Thank you and good night. I'll show myself out," she said with a flourish; she hugged each of them and jangled her way down the stairs to her condo.

Char looked on in disbelief as Moe left. "Aubrie, you just scared our guest out of our home. You can be very inappropriate sometimes, and I don't appreciate it." Full of nervous energy, Char started clearing the table. The girls followed suit.

"Inappropriate? So you can shack up with Emmett while we're out of town and then lecture us about taking things slow?" Aubrie said as she gathered her and Moe's plates.

"Aubrie, you don't understand. There were extenuating circumstances—" Char was going to tell Aubrie and Chloe the extent of her injury, but Aubrie cut her off.

"Oh, there always are, Mother, aren't there. Save it. I know, I know. I wouldn't understand, it's private—I've heard it all before with Ash. You treat me like a baby. I'm so tired of it. I can deal with a lot more than you give me credit for, Mom. You know, I'm beginning to think us all living together isn't such a good idea. I know I'm the one who convinced you to come with us, but it looks like you've moved on quite well on your own. I think if we want to keep getting along as mother and daughter, you should get your own place now, not later."

"Aubrie, don't be mean. No one kicks their mom out, seriously," Chloe said, shooting Aubrie an incredulous look. She turned to Charlotte. "She doesn't mean it, Aunt Charlie."

"Chloe, you and I are both going to college. We need that third room for studying. I should take Mom's room and you take mine; then we've got a place to do our papers, and we preserve our relationship with Mom, right? I'm not trying to be mean; I think I'm just being practical. Plus, it's always been Mom's plan to either get her own place here or move back to Oregon after we were settled. I think she should get a place here, now. Problem solved." Aubrie stood there in the kitchen, hand on hip, asserting what she thought was right.

Char listened to Aubrie as she got out the broom and dustpan and set to work. "You may be eighteen, Aubrie, but I'll always be your mother. You have to admit I've afforded you quite a bit of independence over the years. I'm not exactly a smothering mother, wouldn't you agree, Chloe?" Charlotte looked to Chloe for a little backup.

"Definitely. You know how hard I had to work for my mom to be okay with me going to school down here. She's still not 100 percent okay with it. Talk about a smotherer!"

"See? I'm not so bad, Aubrie," Char said, as she emptied the dustpan into the trash.

"I know, but I hate feeling like I'm always catching you in lies, Mom."

"Aubrie, if I've ever lied to you, it was to protect you or someone else. And sometimes you may ask me things you have no right to know. Lying by omission, I understand, hurts, but sometimes it's out of my hands." Char was hurt by the truth of Aubrie's accusation but tried to dilute it anyway.

"I don't think this question is out of your hands. Noa knows his dad dates—big deal. He and Kai don't care; why do you? Come on, I know you stayed with Emmett while we were on our road trip, just admit it, Mom."

"Aubrie, who's the parent here?"

"Who's not a kid anymore here?"

Charlotte sighed as she wrapped her arms around herself, feeling exposed and not wanting to answer, but knowing she had to if she didn't want their relationship to implode again.

"You are right: the injury to my ankle may have been a bit more serious. I'm sorry I didn't tell you the whole story, but, Aubrie, you and Chloe had just left on your trip, far away. I didn't want you to worry about me or, worse, cancel your trip when I knew I was fine."

"Mom, that should be my choice, whether I feel I need to be there for you or not."

Char had a sense of déjà vu, remembering Emmett had said nearly the same thing to her early on.

"It wasn't a big deal, really. As I said, I did just slip. But it was a grade-two injury, and I had to wear a walking boot for a few weeks and a brace on my wrist. Yes, I did end up staying with Emmett. He and Anna helped me and Asa out. I couldn't get up and down these stairs in my boot and crutches. But he took one of the boys' rooms upstairs and gave me his, which is why his boys came across something I must have left there."

"Mom, that's your trick—you leave out details. Yeah, Emmett may have given you his room to *begin with*, but it's clear that didn't last long. Seriously, don't even try." Aubrie looked at Chloe, rolling her eyes. Chloe stifled a laugh.

"Girls, I am not obligated to share my entire life. That would be inappropriate on too many levels. That part is none of your business."

Part of her wanted to tell Aubrie she hadn't slept with Emmett, but she couldn't see how that would be appropriate. Aubrie was her daughter, not a friend.

"See! Chloe, I knew it! Oh my gosh, I'm going to bed. Nice job lecturing me for one little kiss when, well, gross. Never mind. 'Night, Mother," Aubrie said and stomped upstairs.

Chloe said good night with a quick hug to Charlotte and then skipped up the stairs to catch up to Aubrie.

It pained Charlotte to have any kind of tension between her and Aubrie. She was still so young, and yet they'd already gone through so much together. Blake had escaped the brunt of it, since he was older, and when he left for college, he managed to escape the worst. Maybe getting her own place was a better idea than she'd thought. She didn't want the girls to know every private detail of her life, and she didn't want any more fodder for fighting. She had a lot to think about.

・・・

Saturday morning Charlotte did what she did best and lied to the girls, telling them to send her regrets to Emmett that she wasn't feeling well enough to go to the MMA gym with them. Aubrie had long stopped arguing with her mom about whether or not she was really under the weather. Claiming recurring pain from her "car accident" had been Charlotte's go-to excuse for not venturing out for over the last year, so Aubrie didn't blink an eye and even brought her mom an ice pack before she and Chloe left.

Charlotte fully expected to get some sort of admonishment from Emmett, so when she heard an incoming text message from her phone, her heart sank.

> *I nearly broke my promise. I won't push you to do this, babe, though I'm sorry you can't. The girls are going to Dara's with the boys, so can I pick you up afterward? Spend the day together, any way you want?*

Relief and elation flooded over Charlotte. She'd expected some sort of argument later. Instead, he was being supportive. There was no way she could have gone to the self-defense class. Just imagining someone coming up behind her or holding her down threatened to throw her into panic mode. Her heart swelled at Emmett's understanding. She smiled as she looked forward to the day ahead. She looked at Asa snuggled in the corner of the couch and knew just how she wanted to spend the day.

. . .

Emmett let out a hearty laugh when he saw the dog park. "This is smaller than my master bathroom. How can they call it a dog park?"

Charlotte smacked his arm. "Cut it out. Look, it's got the cute little fire hydrant, a little play structure for him to run around on, and there are only a few other dogs just his size. See the size limit? Twelve inches," she said, pointing to the posted sign. "It's not like it's a dog park for Great Danes and Saint Bernards. He'll be safe and happy," she said as she unclipped Asa's leash and let him through the gate.

He laughed heartily again. "Twelve inches—is that height or length?"

Char playfully rolled her eyes at him. She refused to let him make fun of her perfect little park for Asa.

There was a pair of black Chihuahuas running around together as if they owned the place, a white moppy-headed teacup poodle, and a tan pug. They were all ignoring each other until Asa joined the group. Suddenly, excitement was in the air. Asa began running like lightning around the perimeter of the park. The other dogs took notice and soon joined in. Everyone was laughing as the other dogs tried to catch up to Asa, who would occasionally look back to see if any were gaining on him. If any got too close, as fast as he was going, he'd somehow push himself faster. He was a caramel-colored streak zooming round and round.

"Wow, Asa's got quite the turbo boost," Emmett said with a laugh.

"I know, and look how competitive he is. He won't let anyone pass him."

Eventually they all tired, and the dogs settled into a loping game of tag. Char and Emmett decided to leave the fenced area and sit at a table under a shade tree, just outside the fence. It was a perfect place to enjoy themselves away from the dogs but still be in view of Asa. Char had brought a full picnic basket for their lunch, and as she was laying everything out, Asa realized they were gone and pawed at the gate. Emmett laughed, telling him not to worry, that they weren't abandoning him. He brought him out, and soon Asa was under the table, settled in for a little siesta.

Emmett opened their sparkling waters, and as he sat down, he looked up sheepishly at Charlotte.

"What?" she asked.

Emmett rubbed his face. "It's just—you're so happy right now. And I love seeing you smile. You're in your element when you're having a picnic, going on a hike, or just spending time with your family.

I was trying to put you in a really uncomfortable situation. And I'm sorry."

"I have to be honest: given a choice, I'd have chosen the cold November rain over going to that gym with you," Charlotte said with a mischievous smile, hoping to lighten the mood. It was getting heavy, and she didn't want their beautiful day darkened.

Emmett laughed, "Maybe you don't detest the cold November rain as much as you think."

"I want you to know I do understand, though, Emmett. You meant well. The girls went, and you said they had a great time and learned a lot. I'm really thankful you included them. And who knows, maybe someday I'll get there." Char could only hope that she'd get to a place where fear and panic were no longer lurking just around the corner.

"Me too, babe, though like I promised, I won't push," he said as he took her hand in his.

Charlotte smiled as the warmth of his hand on hers went all the way to her heart.

As they started to eat, a young couple with a teacup Yorkie in a doggie stroller came along. The girl was dressed to the nines, in heels, with hair done and makeup painted on perfectly. They were a handsome couple. The guy had on the latest designer jeans, which hung low on his hips, paired with a casual-cool V-neck tee, which was supposed to make it look as if he hadn't given the day's outfit much thought, but of course that couldn't be further from the truth, what with the perfectly sloppy spiked hair, designer shades, and neatly trimmed five o'clock shadow.

The girl exclaimed, "Oh my God, Jace, I forgot her bottle of water back in the car. Can you please go get it?"

"There's a fountain here she could use," the guy suggested helpfully.

"Uh, gross, I think *not*. Baby isn't going to get grodie germs from these other fur balls. Puleeze. Oh, but first, can you get her out of her stroller and put her in there? I am so not going inside. I don't want anything to get on my heels. Wait, let me kiss her!" He handed Baby to her, and she puckered up big, letting Baby lick all over her Botoxed face and filler-injected lips.

Emmett and Char couldn't help but stare. "She's worried about germs, but doesn't she realize where her dog's tongue's been?" Emmett drawled flatly.

Charlotte tried her best to stifle a laugh. The poor guy had to go back to the car to get the designer water. His girlfriend or wife toddled in her heels over to the farthest bench possible. When he came back with the water, she whined that her shoes had sunk into the grass. He unlatched her heels for her and worked to clean them off. The guy didn't look as if he were having much fun, yet every order she barked at him he was at the ready to fulfill.

"That poor guy; I can barely stand to watch him. That's been me in about every relationship until you, Charlotte."

Char had been picking at her salad but looked up in shock at his admission. "That was you? I don't believe it." It was the second time she had seen Emmett appear not so self-assured. She couldn't get used to it.

"Well, it was. I mean, if the guy's happy, more power to him, but I think you and I would both agree from the look on his face that's not the case."

"I'm sorry, I just can't see you washing my heels for me and pushing a puppy in a stroller." She shook her head at the thought.

Emmett laughed. "I guess I was lucky enough not to get recruited for that kind of thing. And had I been, I would like to think I'd have refused. I never said my man card was completely revoked," he said, smiling and giving Char a nudge.

"Well, you don't have to worry about me acting like lips over there," she said, making Emmett laugh. "I'm more the autonomous type. You do what you need to do, and I do what I need. Space and autonomy, two good things."

Emmett pulled her in close, putting his head on her shoulder from behind, and Charlotte leaned into his chest. "Well, I like autonomy to a point, Charlotte, but I'd gladly give up some freedoms to have you in my life."

"Thank you. Me too," she said, wrapping her arms over his.

When Charlotte dropped Emmett off at home, he told her to plan on a pool party at his place the next day. Char thought that sounded like a relaxing way to spend their Sunday. She couldn't wait.

Charlotte and the girls pulled in to a grocery store on their way to Emmett's for their planned get-together. Aubrie said, "Barbecue Saturday at their mom's, pool party Sunday at their dad's. Some of the benefits to split families: double Christmases and double parties!" Chloe, whose parents had also long been divorced, laughed with Aubrie.

"The poor kids caught in the middle have to have some consolation, right?" Char said to the girls in agreement.

They loaded up on all things college-aged kids would like. The boys were inviting a handful of friends, and Kat and Lou were coming too. Soda, energy drinks, chips galore, and various dips; Char insisted on a veggie and fruit platter, but the girls teased her, saying she was just wasting her money.

When they got there, the boys were already out by the pool. They were tossing around a ball, but when they saw the girls, their attention turned to them. They grabbed chaise lounges and put them where the girls pointed, saying they wanted the best angle for their tan. The four of them talked animatedly with lots of laughter, and Charlotte was happy to see the kids so happy.

Emmett came out with a tub full of ice and pop, and when he saw Charlotte, he slung it down in haste and made a beeline for her.

"Good morning, sunshine," he said to Charlotte as he went in for a kiss, but she shied away. Char remembered she still had yet to talk with Emmett about her and Aubrie's argument. The day before Emmett had been so understanding about her skipping out on the self-defense class, she hadn't wanted to broach any other sticky situation.

"Emmett, the kids are right there," she said as she looked back at the group too engrossed in each other to notice their parents on the patio. Gaining some distance from the kids, she walked to the kitchen to unpack more groceries, and Emmett followed.

"Charlotte, we talked about this. Plus, it's no secret; the kids know we're together. I need to be able to touch you, kiss you, on occasion." Emmett's hands wandered down Char's back, resting at her hips as he nuzzled the back of her neck.

She grabbed his hands and pushed them away, turning to face him. "And I want that too. But for the kids' sake at least, let's take the PDA slowly. They weren't around while we were really getting to know each other. This is only the third time we've all been together. It'll appear to have happened much too quickly. Aubrie grilled me a couple nights ago about her discovery that I had been staying with you. I've been meaning to talk to you about it."

"What do you mean? What's the problem?" Emmett asked, leaning against the counter as he crossed his arms and cocked his head to the side. Charlotte couldn't tell if he was irritated or just listening intently.

"The boys apparently found my crutches in the garage and some of my stuff in your bathroom, and they told Aubrie and Chloe about it. Aubrie gave me the third degree about not trusting her and making dubious relationship decisions myself. She suggested that I move out, so she and Chloe can live their lives peacefully without my, as she put it, 'judgmental interference.' And, well, I think she may be right—I should probably plan on moving. She deserves her space. This was probably a huge mistake to begin with."

He stepped toward Charlotte and braced his hands on the counter with her in between. She felt trapped. His face was mere inches from hers.

"You're kidding, right? First, you need to put Aubrie in her place. That's your condo, not hers, and second, who's the mother here?" Char could see Emmett's jaw tighten as he looked into her eyes; yes, he was clearly irritated.

She instinctually leaned back. "Emmett, you don't know our history as mother and daughter. I can see, partly, where she's coming from."

"So, what, you're going to move back to Oregon? Not if I have anything to do with it. You're not going anywhere, Charlotte."

In a past life, she would have been flattered that Emmett took such an interest in where she might choose to live, but not anymore. Her defenses came up, and she wasn't going to put up with his controlling behavior. Fighting about her daughter wasn't unfamiliar to her, but this time she wouldn't fail Aubrie the way she felt she had with Ash. Aubrie would come first this time.

"Emmett. Wow." She put a finger to his chest, pushing him back. "Let me set you straight here. If I do choose to move, I will. No one can stop me, not you, not anyone." Charlotte spat those words without thinking. Had he forgotten when she made the move she'd been undecided about staying? Or, as private as she was, had she failed to mention that little fact to him? As mad as she was, it was of little significance either way.

Emmett held his hands up, stepping backward. "Damn, Charlotte. Sorry to break it to you, but you aren't anyone's hostage. And you'll never be mine, I can guarantee that. You're making this a hell of a lot more dramatic than it needs to be. You read Katena's book, right? Those are scars of having all your freedoms stripped. Having a boyfriend who doesn't want you to move a thousand miles away is not a hostage made."

Emmett's words were like a stake through the heart, bringing her back to the most horrific night of her life. She knew from habit she was about to throw up. Her stomach churned, and she covered her mouth and ran to the powder room.

Charlotte threw up only once; that was an improvement. The self-calming techniques Moe had taught her were working. She focused on the here and now, reminding herself that she was no longer there, that that horrific night was long over.

Emmett knocked on the door. "Babe, are you alright?"

"I...I'll be fine. Just give me a few minutes," she called out. She took some deep breaths, and, feeling more present, she was able to fumble through the cupboard and grab a washcloth. She soaked it under the cold tap and put it on the back of her neck. She sighed from the welcome relief, feeling calmer, and knew her best bet was to get out now.

When she opened the door, Emmett was waiting right outside and jumped to attention when she came out. "Charlotte, what's going on?"

"I think I need to go home. Stomach bug or something. When I woke, I didn't quite feel right, but I thought it would pass. I guess not," she lied. "I don't want the girls to worry. Could you or one of the boys give them a ride home later?"

"Are you sure you're not just running from our argument?"

"No, we can talk about our disagreement later. I just don't feel well. I need to go home and lie down. If I have to throw up again, I don't want to be here." She was fairly certain she wouldn't be sick again, but she needed her out.

"I understand. Are you sure you don't want me to drive you? The girls can take your car home."

Charlotte needed to be alone. "No, thank you. I don't want to get sick in your car. I need to go, Emmett. I'm sorry."

She made for her car, and Emmett stayed on her heels. "Charlotte, wait."

"No, I have to go."

She left Emmett looking confused and dumbstruck standing in the driveway. She cried all the way home. She knew she'd made a lot of progress with Moe, but this episode revealed the shocking truth that she still had a long way to go.

She'd been largely unaffected personally when she'd read Katena's book, not having seen many similarities between their situations. They'd seemed so completely different, but Emmett's off-handed comparison brought Charlotte's tragic night right to the forefront, and she felt raw all over again.

Charlotte had pulled out every trick in her book to suppress her memories by time she pulled into her condo's parking garage.

She saw Moe heading toward her front door; she must have heard Charlotte coming up the walk, and she turned around. "Hello, dear, all alone today? Well, so am I, what a surprise, ha-ha. Want to come over for some of my famous lemonade? It's delicious; I mix one part lemonade and one part orange juice. Whaddya say?"

Charlotte couldn't even fake a half smile. She was spent. "Not today, but thank you, Moe."

It was then that Moe calmed down enough to really look at Charlotte. "Oh dear, what happened to you? Your chakras are all but drained."

Charlotte thought that word, "drained," was apropos. She didn't have the energy to deflect, and thankfully she trusted Moe.

"You couldn't be more right, Moe. I just had a bad moment. And I just wanted to come home and sleep it off."

"Interesting choice of words," Moe said as she assessed Charlotte. "Are you sure you didn't have a bad *memory*? You know, trying to sleep it off isn't a very reliable coping method. The rest of my day is open; why don't we talk for a while, and then have a light-therapy session, clean out more of those cobwebs?"

"Yes, I think I'd like that. I'll let Asa out and be right back. Moe, thank you."

. . .

Once the session was over, Charlotte still felt tired, but clear-headed.

"Remember what I said, Charlie; there's nothing wrong with taking time on difficult decisions. There's no need to rush. You go get some rest. Maybe you'll feel different by tomorrow."

Char checked her phone before letting herself fall asleep and saw the girls and Kat had texted several times wanting to know if she was okay. She texted the girls back she'd be fine, had gotten home safely, and was going to nap, and to tell Kat she'd call when she could. She felt so exhausted; she had no idea when that would be.

Emmett texted Char asking if he could come by once his guests were gone, but she told him no, that she was much too tired, which was true, but he wouldn't ease up and begged to come over with coffees on his way to work the next day.

She texted him yes, but knew in her heart it likely wouldn't be a happy morning for either of them.

Charlotte slept like a rock all night and barely woke to the sound of Emmett coming up the stairs, Asa bounding after him. She'd made a decision after talking with Moe the night before, even though Moe didn't exactly agree with the decision she came to. Moe cautioned her that she thought Char was throwing the baby out with the bathwater, but Char disagreed, though she dreaded breaking it to Emmett.

He knocked on her door that was slightly ajar before poking his head in cautiously. "Hey, babe, did I wake you?"

"No, no, come on in," Char said as she sat up and rubbed the sleep from her eyes and focused them on Emmett. He still looked handsome as ever, though Charlotte noticed he must have been in a rush to get to her place. His hair wasn't combed into place with any pomade, and he wasn't wearing even casual work attire, just jeans and a T-shirt.

He came in and sank onto her fluffy bed, leaning toward her, looking into her eyes as he handed her a cup. "Here, I brought you a coffee. How are you feeling this morning? Better?"

She knew he was trying to sound upbeat, but his brows, knitted together in worry and tension, betrayed him. He tucked a wayward lock of hair behind Char's ear. "You look beautiful. You must be feeling better."

"I am, thank you, and thanks for the coffee. I'm sorry about yesterday."

"When you left sick yesterday, I was left hanging, and I've worried all night about it. I have to know. Are you moving back to Oregon or not, Charlotte?" Charlotte wasn't surprised Emmett was jumping right into the conversation.

She took a sip of coffee first, delaying what she knew was the inevitable. "You didn't give me a chance to explain before you lit into me. What I would have told you was that I had no intention of moving back to Oregon. Not yesterday, at least."

His head dropped. "Don't tell me you've changed your mind."

She fiddled with the fringe on her bedspread. "I...I don't know, Emmett. I know we talked and agreed that we'd be patient with each other, but maybe it's too much. Since the kids returned, it's been rough. On both of us."

Charlotte's stomach flipped, and suddenly she wasn't in the mood for coffee; she set it down on her nightstand. Her silver-framed picture of Aubrie caught her eye, reminding her why she needed to stay strong.

Emmett's eyes were soft. He quietly said, "We've had our fair share of bumps, but honestly, most of it was my fault, all the unresolved issues about my and Leann's messed-up relationship. I promised you I'd get over it, and I'm going to hold myself to it, Char, I am." His eyes were pleading.

"But what about our differing parenting styles? I did what you asked and came clean with Aubrie about us, but I'm still not comfortable flaunting our affection. And now, it seems the kids all like each other, and I think you might be right. We can't be up in each other's parenting business, but that's nearly impossible if our kids all start dating. I mean, that's what yesterday's issue was about, our kids. We've had two fights already about parenting styles. Those fights had nothing to do with Leann."

"I've never been one to be afraid of hard work. We have some complications, yes. But is the fight worth it, Charlotte? I happen to think so." He paused for a moment. "I don't know about you, but I think I'm getting déjà vu here. We've had this conversation before, haven't we?"

"We did. That's kind of what's making me take a second look at our situation. We keep saying we can weather anything with a little patience. And I love that you feel what we have is worth fighting for—but, Emmett, I hate fighting. And we've been doing a lot of that lately."

"But we make up quickly. We're not having huge blowups."

"That doesn't mean it's not tearing me up inside. Emmett, I've been thinking, and I think I've decided I may not be ready for a relationship right now. After Beau and everything, I'm still not—I'm just not as strong as you are, Emmett."

Emmett stared straight into Char's eyes, his voice flat when he finally spoke. "How many times have we discussed you not running?"

Pinpricks pained her stomach, and Charlotte pulled her arms around her torso and knew she had to find relief. "We should have seen it as a red flag to our whole relationship. I'm sorry, Emmett." She shrunk into the covers. She hated to do it, but she still felt so fatigued from the day before and simply didn't feel strong enough to fight for what they had.

Just then the girls interrupted to call up to Char that they were heading out. She called back to them to have fun and text her later. She tried to sound upbeat. In reality, Charlotte felt so low, but she didn't know what else to do. Yesterday, the way she almost fell apart at the seams—it scared her and showed her how weak she still was. She looked at Emmett, and the hurt in his eyes showed his love for her.

He stood, widening the space between them, and Char didn't like the feeling. It confused her even more.

"You're saying you never want to see me again? We're over? Are you sure about that?"

The thought of never seeing Emmett again tore at her heart, but the threat of her cracking under the pressure was lurking just under the surface, and it scared her to the core. She needed more time. Moe promised her she was making strides, but she needed weeks, maybe even months, and with the pace their relationship was going, she didn't have that kind of time.

As Char looked at Emmett, her feelings for him welled up, weakening her resolve to call it off for good. "Could we take a break? I just feel I need a breather. Everything's progressing so fast."

A spark of hope lit Emmett's eyes, and he eagerly agreed, returning to sit down next to her. He leaned forward. "Absolutely, we can do that. Let's take a break. Maybe it's just too intense. We've barely given each other any breathing room. I mean, I can't say I want much breathing room from you, but if that's what you need, I can do that. Just please don't shut the door on us entirely."

"No, I don't want that either, Emmett."

His pleading tore Charlotte up, but she knew a break would be for the best. Was she weakened with guilt and giving in just to placate him, or did she really believe taking a break would help repair things? She couldn't be sure.

"How do we do this?" he asked softly. Clearly just the thought of being away from her was tearing him up inside.

She could barely look at him. "I don't know. Could we take a week, and see if we miss each other horribly or not and go from there?"

"Well, I already know I'm going to miss you. But this is what you need, and that's okay, Charlotte."

Immediately she felt like a giant weight had been lifted, and she could kind of breathe again.

"I'm sorry. But thank you, I do need this." Was she being weak or strong? Charlotte was so confused, but at this point she had to follow her gut, and if she needed a break from the intensity, that's what she was going to give herself.

"What do we tell the kids?" he asked, looking to her to take the lead.

"They don't need to know much. A week can go by pretty quickly, especially if we're immersed in work, right?" she asked Emmett, hinting at what their excuse could be.

"That'll be an easy enough excuse for me; what about you?"

"We're bringing on a couple more clients with unique needs. I'll have to write new contracts. In fact, I may need to fly to Portland for a few days to handle it. It'll be good, give me time to think about us."

He grabbed her hand. "Can we agree to meet in a week, say, Monday night? And we'll either say our good-byes or hash out a way to make this work?"

"I like that idea, Emmett. We'll text Monday and see when and where to meet."

The room got quiet. Neither knew what to say.

Finally, it was Emmett who broke the silence. "I guess I'll be going. I don't want to, but I think the sooner I leave to give you time to yourself, the sooner we'll get this over with and hopefully be back together. Can I kiss you good-bye?"

She wanted him to, desperately. She reached for his hand and pulled him closer. He leaned in, and as their lips touched, it was achingly pleasurable, bittersweet.

When he pulled back, his voice was husky. "Our chemistry doesn't lie, Charlotte. I know we're meant to be together. In time you'll see it too. Take your break—I'll wait for you."

He kissed her on the cheek and left without ceremony. Charlotte couldn't bear to see him go. She rolled over and buried her head under her pillow and let herself cry when she knew he was gone.

When her phone rang early the next morning, she was certain it would be Emmett breaking the rules, but it wasn't. Her heart sank, but she tried to ignore it. She answered as brightly as possible. "Jonathan, hi, you must be calling about the Torson contract. Have they agreed to the terms?"

"We're close, but that's not why I'm calling. I have to come to LA this weekend for a family thing I haven't been able to get out of, so I thought I'd save you a trip to Portland and come a day early so we can meet up Friday. Does that work for you?"

Charlotte had been looking forward to a change of scenery, especially with what was going on between her and Emmett, but knew it made more sense to let Jonathan save her a trip.

"Sure, that works great."

"Super. I have to say, as much as I'm dreading mixing with my fam, I'm looking forward to seeing you. I know this great bar we can hit. Don't worry; it's more a restaurant, but they have great drinks and big comfy booths. We'll still be able to get our work done, more or less," he said, laughing. Jonathan was in his late twenties and had the exuberance of a teenager, and Charlotte loved him for it.

"Looking forward to it. The office has my address; I'll let you pick me up."

"I get in Friday afternoon. I'll pick you up at five; we'll beat the dinner rush."

"Great, see you then, Jonathan."

. . .

Two days went by without even a text to or from Emmett, and it felt strange. Even when they'd had their first argument and Emmett went away to Denver, he'd still texted her. She knew in her heart it must be killing him not to have any contact. When Wednesday rolled around, she almost broke and texted him; she wanted to see how he was feeling. Maybe she was wrong and the radio silence for so many days meant that he was getting along fine. Maybe he was actually enjoying his time without her.

By Thursday she had to admit she missed him, terribly, but she knew if she chose to get back together with him, she'd have to suffer along until she was healed enough to be completely honest with him. If she wanted to find her strength, which choice was the coward's way? Was she being strong by holding it in and keeping her secret, protecting those who had protected her? Or would she be strongest by utterly baring her soul to Emmett? Was staying away from Emmett proof of being strong or weak?

On Friday, Aubrie must have thought she seemed the latter. Charlotte was tying her shoes at the bottom of the stairs with Asa bouncing around her when Aubrie came down. "Hey, Mom, can I join you and Asa on your walk?"

Char looked up at Aubrie, grateful for the company. "Sure, honey, let's go." They headed out the door and followed the meandering walking path that wound throughout the complex.

"Mom, is something going on with you and Emmett? It's been days since you two have seen each other. And you haven't seemed yourself. I'm starting to worry."

Char had hoped Aubrie wouldn't notice. "Honey, no, nothing to worry about. We've both been busy with work stuff this week, that's all."

"Hmm, that's exactly what Emmett said, yet Noa said he's been home every night like clockwork this week, and so have you. So what's up?"

Charlotte couldn't tell her that Emmett had inadvertently caused a horrible flashback, about which neither Aubrie nor Emmett was the wiser, and she wouldn't tell her the argument at the barbecue had started because of her and Aubrie's fight about getting her own place. Aubrie would feel horrible if she knew she were the cause, at least now that she liked Emmett.

"The older you get, the more complicated life seems to be, Aubrie. I don't know what more to say." Charlotte felt that was her best bet: saying something without saying much of anything.

"Mom, I've been meaning to talk to you about this, and now I'm worried I've waited too long. I hope you're not cooling it down with Emmett because of me. I've been watching you with him, and I know you're trying to not make me uncomfortable, but you don't have to do that. You were honest with me that you guys are together, and I'm great with that, so why would I be mad if you two, you know, kissed or hugged around me?"

Charlotte was amazed by Aubrie's perceptiveness. "Honestly? You were so angry with me when you found out I'd already been staying at Emmett's. I just don't want to hurt you more. And when you said I should get my own place, I did worry a part of it was because you were uncomfortable seeing Emmett and me together."

As the path took them alongside the pool, they passed several young kids splashing and giggling, with two moms chatting together as they watched over them. Charlotte thought the scene looked so simple, happy, and uncomplicated, but she knew better than to make such an assumption. As they walked by, one of the moms smiled at Char and Aubrie. Charlotte mused about whether she was assuming the same about the two of them, seeing only a mother and daughter out for a lovely walk without a care. If only in her dreams.

"You were lying to me about it," Aubrie said, snapping Charlotte back to her complicated reality. "That's the only reason I was so angry. But really, you were right, Mom. Either way, it's none of my business. Emmett makes you happy, and I don't want you to push him away on my account."

"I'm not—"

"You are. I've seen how you react to him when you think I'm not around. It's clear you two are one way with each other when I'm around and another when I'm not. And now you haven't seen each other in days. I'm just saying if this has anything to do with me, you can stop worrying. I mean, you stayed at his house for weeks, for God's sake. Don't stop on my account. Cat's out of the bag, Mom," Aubrie said, dipping her head toward Char pointedly.

Char blushed. "Well, no, not exactly." She wanted to tell Aubrie that they hadn't taken their relationship to the next level, but had no idea how to say such a thing to her daughter. Thankfully, Aubrie took the hint.

"Stop. Enough said. But thank you; glad to know you're taking things slowly," Aubrie said with her hand held up, leaning away from Char and laughing.

Charlotte laughed too. "And I hope you're taking things slowly too."

"Mom, ugh. Yes, I am. But we're not talking about me and Noa," Aubrie said. It was her turn to blush.

"Just thought I'd ask," Char said a bit defensively before getting serious again. "But thank you, Aubrie, for this. I'll take what you've said into consideration."

"Of course you will," Aubrie said confidently. As they arrived back at the condo, Aubrie said, "I'm going to head out. Chloe and I are going to the mall, and she should be ready now. We've both got appointments to get blowouts." She leaned her head through the door and yelled, "Chloe, time to go. Can you grab my purse?"

When Chloe bounded down the stairs, they both said bye, and Aubrie gave her mom a hug and let her eyes stay on Charlotte's a bit longer than needed as she squeezed her shoulders. Charlotte willed herself not to cry and instead gave Aubrie a grateful smile.

• • •

Charlotte readied for the day and then did a little paperwork in preparation for her meeting with Jonathan. She was excited to see Jonathan that evening. They'd been pretty close friends before her nightmare began and she had had to go on sabbatical from the firm. She knew she had hurt him when she'd refused to see him, or any other visitors, for that matter. Even when she started working for the firm again, she hadn't had the courage to go back into the office, so seeing him tonight would be a big deal.

He texted her when he was on his way, and she went outside to meet him. After parking, he jumped out of his car and gave her a big hug. "Charlie! You're a beauty to behold. I can't believe it's been a year. I think I almost forgot how breathtaking you are," he said, eyeing her up and down.

Charlotte laughed. "And you look as sharp as ever. Love the suit." He was wearing a trim navy pinstriped suit with a bold navy-and-pink striped tie and pink paisley handkerchief. He was always dressed to the nines, and the ease with which he expressed himself was one of the many things she loved about him.

Despite missing Emmett, Charlotte was excited to go to one of Jonathan's favorite haunts, a popular bar and restaurant in West Hollywood with a rich atmosphere.

Once they were seated, they wasted no time catching up with each other. Jonathan knew the rules with Charlotte, how much she would and wouldn't talk about when it came to the past, but he was one who liked to push the limit, dance around the danger zone, all the while measuring Charlotte's reaction. She knew he'd test the limits again, but she put up with it because he had proved time and again to be a loyal and true friend.

"Sweetheart, that sabbatical did you good, I must say," he said, looking intently at her. "After your car accident, I prayed up and down that your beauty hadn't been marred. You scared me so, not letting me come see you. My imagination got the worst of me, imagining what kind of scars you were hiding." His tone was fun, but Charlotte saw the look in his eye. He was anticipating her reaction.

She faked a laugh. "Well, as you see, you have an overactive imagination. I was in a lot of pain. I wouldn't have been good company, Jonathan—that's all." She didn't lie to him. She could look him in the eye, a win for her tonight. She silently toasted her victory, taking a long sip of her martini.

"Yes, I believe you were. By the way, I saw Ash the other day at a commerce mixer downtown. He asked about you."

Charlotte choked on her drink and started to cough.

Jonathan quickly handed her a napkin. "I'm sorry, should I not have told you?"

"No, it's just the martini. It's a bit tart," she lied. No more toasts for her, but she needed to get Jonathan off the subject of her and especially Ash. "We've been broken up for a while now. I'm sure he was just making nice. But enough about me; I want to catch up with what's going on with you."

He looked at her for a moment, tapping his finger on his wineglass, seeming to weigh his options, but to her relief, Jonathan decided to take the hint. He took a deep breath and delved right into catching her up on the latest happenings in the office and telling her all about the pain-in-the-butt clients. He'd always been the office gossip, and Charlotte was happy to see that hadn't changed. He filled her in on his dating trials and tribulations being a gay man in the too-small city of Portland. He lamented the fact he wasn't living in LA, though he loved his job at her firm, he promised.

Charlotte told him how her kids were doing and how she felt about living in LA. She kept mum about Emmett. It was too complicated a story, and since she wasn't sure how the ending would turn out, she didn't want to even touch on it. They enjoyed their drinks and shared some appetizers. Eventually Jonathan begrudgingly suggested they start digging into work.

Char moved their plates and drinks aside, wondering where their waiter had gone, and scooted closer to Jonathan. He brought out his laptop and pored over the details with Charlotte, who took copious notes.

"So, two more things before we can put this away. First, good news. Torson did agree to the financial terms, but they added a few new performance addendums. We did the numbers and are confident we can do even better than they're asking. These guys don't understand the goldmine they're sitting on. But we'll show 'em soon enough. I'm looking forward to a fat Christmas bonus," he said smugly. Charlotte laughed.

"The last thing is, and it's the stickler: we're going to need your negotiation skills on the intellectual property they're so worried about. They won't let it go, and they want all of our asses on the line, personally. We never agree to that, but they won't budge. We're going to need a face-to-face in a couple of weeks' time. Are you going to be around?"

"Of course, anytime, I'll be there."

"Perfect, that's all we need. One more drink, how about it? We need to celebrate. We're so close to closing this, I can feel it in my bones." He waved to the waiter for another round and put his laptop away.

When they finished their toast, Jonathan said in barely a whisper, "Oh, Charlie, look at this hunka-munka coming our way."

Char scanned the room and was surprised when her eyes landed on Emmett, and he didn't look happy. He was several tables away, marching toward their booth. Even from that distance, she could see the tension in his shoulders, his brows drawn tight. Stopping at their table, he narrowed his eyes, looking back and forth between Charlotte and Jonathan.

"Hi, Emmett, what are you doing here?"

He seemed to tower over their table, and with the look on his face, Charlotte felt small.

"I'm sorry, am I interrupting something here?" he asked as he shifted on his feet, one hand in his pants pocket, the other gesturing toward the both of them. The tone in his voice carried a possessiveness she hadn't experienced from him, and it was also accusatory. It was then Char realized she hadn't moved back since scooting close to Jonathan to look over the notes on his laptop. She could only imagine how it looked.

Charlotte felt her cheeks flush. She was about to answer in defense when an attractive Asian woman with long red nails came up to Emmett, putting her hand on his shoulder. "Em. I got us a table and ordered up champagne—no rush, though." She patted his shoulder and gave Char and Jonathan a once-over. Emmett nodded thanks to her and turned back to Char with an expectant look. He waited for Char to answer him.

"Excuse me?" Charlotte said, her eyebrow arching in disbelief. She couldn't believe his nerve, demanding an explanation from her when he obviously had some explaining of his own to do.

Jonathan grabbed his satchel and scooted out of the booth. "I'll give you two a moment and go pay the bill." He was gone before Charlotte could protest. She was in no mood to be left alone with Emmett while he was being so hypocritical.

"Actually, Emmett, you're not interrupting anything, because I was just leaving. Please, don't let me keep your date waiting." She gathered her purse and briefcase, expecting Emmett to step aside so she could leave the booth, but he didn't budge an inch. She was determined to leave either way and made up her mind to squeeze past him, but Emmett took her by the arm.

"Charlotte, wait," he said, pulling her close.

At mere inches apart, despite the hurt she felt, Charlotte couldn't help but feel their chemistry. She had put her hands on his chest but couldn't push him away. Emmett opened his mouth to say something, but instead could only look into Charlotte's eyes for a moment before bringing her lips to his. With not a word spoken and Emmett's mouth on hers, Char was swept up in a rush of relief. Trailing her hands up further, Charlotte could feel the tension in Emmett's shoulders relax as they eased each other's worries with their kiss.

He pulled back with a smile. "Now would I be drawn this way to you if I were on a date with someone else?" he asked, his voice still gruff.

"Would I?" Charlotte managed to whisper.

"Is your car here?"

"No, Jonathan picked me up."

"I'll be the one taking you home."

"Uh, Charlie." Jonathan sheepishly caught Char's attention.

"Oh, Jonathan," Charlotte said, prying herself from Emmett's territorial grasp. "It looks like I won't be needing a ride home tonight."

"You can say that again," Jonathan said with a smirk.

Besides blushing, Charlotte ignored his commentary. "It was wonderful seeing you tonight. And I'm looking forward to closing this deal."

Jonathan smiled. "Me too, Charlie. I've missed you. I'll call you when we set a date for hopefully what will be our last negotiation."

"We'll talk soon, and try to have a good time with your family this weekend," she said, giving him a hug.

"Thank you, Charlie," he said as he eyed Emmett. "Looks like there'll be no *trying* to have a good time for you tonight. Good for you," he said with a wink. "Take care now, Charlie. We'll talk soon."

When she looked up at Emmett, he was staring at her and looked as if he wanted ask her a question. "Are we ready to go?" she asked Emmett.

He collected himself for a moment before saying, "Yeah, let me first say good-bye to Lijuan."

"Your date?" Char asked in a prickly tone.

"No, ma'am. As you see, her husband was also joining us," he said as he pointed to the handsome couple at the table they were coming up to. "Lijuan, Dishi, as much as I appreciate your invite tonight, I've made a change of plans after bumping into Charlotte. Thank you so much for all of your hard work. I really do appreciate it." He looked at Charlotte and took a big breath before saying, "Charlotte, these are my divorce attorneys. We came here tonight to celebrate my divorce. It's finally over."

Charlotte threw her arms around Emmett in celebration. "Emmett, I'm so happy for you." Her arms still around Emmett, she turned to his attorneys and thanked them. Emmett told them the champagne was on him.

On their way out of the restaurant, Charlotte and Emmett kept their arms wrapped tightly around each other, looking more at one another than paying attention to where they were going. They nearly ran into the door leading out to the back parking lot, and Emmett let out a hearty laugh. He opened the car door for Charlotte before rounding the car and, with a beaming smile, sliding behind the wheel. Charlotte's heart warmed at how happy Emmett was with their turn of events.

He was about to put the key into the ignition but instead turned toward Charlotte. "That kiss back there," he said, putting his hand over his broad chest, "told me all I really need to know, but I can't help it, babe. Before I start the car, I have to clear one thing up first."

Char studied his face; it was still full of the high of their kiss, but there was a slight edge to his voice.

"Who the hell was that guy, and why were you sitting so damn close to him?"

Char laughed, thankful that even when Emmett was actually irritated, he still had an easygoing vibe. She was happy to tell him she was, in fact, as innocent as he was. "That was Jonathan, an exec at the firm. I've known him for years. Remember I told you I might have to go to Portland? Well, he had to come to LA this weekend anyway, so he met me here, saving me a trip."

He continued to look at her suspiciously but with the smallest hint of a smile. "That still doesn't explain why you were practically sitting on his lap."

Char rolled her eyes, although she secretly enjoyed seeing him riled up. "He had his laptop with him. We scrunched together so we could go over his notes. We'd just finished when you came barreling toward us."

He looked at her sideways. "Well, how's about next time when you're done working, you can scoot back off his lap."

Charlotte rolled her eyes again but couldn't help but smile. "Sure, if you then agree to not let women practically massage your shoulders right in front of me. How's about that?" she said, mocking him.

Emmett huffed and started the car but didn't pull out of the parking lot. "That's not what happened, and you know it, but that aside, let's talk the serious turkey, okay? Can you admit that this little experiment of yours isn't working? One look at each other, and we're all over the other, marking our territory. I think that's proof enough we're just going to have to work this all out."

Charlotte smiled and knew it was the only answer. As tough as it got between them at times, she knew she'd just have to keep working at it. She wondered if she were clinging to Emmett as a life preserver or being strong in claiming a love for herself, but either way she knew she cared for him immensely and tried to convince herself that was what really mattered.

"So, babe, we're back together 100 percent, right?"

"I would tend to agree with that statement," she said, causing him to laugh at her formality.

"Good, good to know. Can I ask, were you going to make me sweat it out until Monday if we hadn't bumped into each other tonight?"

"Were you sweating it out this week? Since I never got even one text from you, I figured you were living it up while we were apart. And then when I saw you with Lijuan…"

"I thought the same when I saw you with Jonathan. I have to admit, I saw red, Charlotte." As easygoing as Emmett was, Charlotte had to remind herself he was still a quintessential red-blooded male. There was nothing to say about it—she too had seen red when Lijuan came up to Emmett, and it wasn't just Lijuan's nails.

"This week was hard on me, Emmett. But there was a bright spot.

Aubrie had a talk with me. She was worried about us. We weren't snowing her with our 'We're both just busy this week' mantra. She let me know in no uncertain terms she likes us together and gives us her wholehearted blessing. We had probably our most mature discussion to date. She let me know she has no problem with us, you know, showing affection to each other, et cetera, et cetera," she said, blushing.

Emmett flashed a blush of his own before asking, "So, that's how Aubrie feels, but what about you?"

"I realized I need to do better at treating her like the young adult she is. If she says she's okay with us, then I need to trust and believe her, and I guess start acting like a normal, nearly-forty-year-old human being."

"So, if I were to, say, ask you to come home with me tonight, would you be more likely to say yes now, since you don't have to worry about weirding Aubrie out?"

Charlotte gripped her hands together and looked down at her laced fingers.

"Not that I expect us to be completely intimate; that's not what I'm asking. I just miss you. I want to make up for not being with you at all this past week. I want you by my side tonight."

Charlotte smiled. "I think, if you were to ask, I might be more inclined to say yes."

"Will you, please?" His eyebrows shot up, and hope was written all over his face.

Charlotte took her cell phone out. She wanted to make double sure Aubrie meant what she'd said. She texted, saying she might stay over at Emmett's. She could barely breathe as she waited to hear back. The reply was short and sweet.

So happy you guys are back together. Chloe and the boys and I are going to a movie. Tell Emmett they'll be home around midnight. Have fun, Mom. See you tomorrow!
Xoxo

She breathed a sigh of relief and looked up at Emmett, who was patiently waiting. She smiled. "Yes. I will."

He put the car into drive, sporting the happiest smile Charlotte had ever seen.

The next morning Emmett suggested they go for a hike at the Solstice Canyon trail. They left before the boys were up for the day. It was just as well, Char thought, knowing she'd still be uncomfortable around them after having stayed the night with Emmett, regardless of how everyone else actually felt.

"This hike is just what we needed," Charlotte said once they were on the trail.

"I agree," Emmett said as he took Charlotte's hand, lacing his fingers through hers before looking at her.

"I have to tell you something amazing that happened last night, and I'm just not sure whether I was dreaming or not. Aside from the pleasure of having you in my arms all night, I dreamt that you and I actually got back together. Is that true? Are we really back on?" She thought Emmett was being facetious, but when he wouldn't take his eyes off her, she realized he was clearly waiting for an answer, his shoulders tight in anticipation.

She thought about it honestly for a moment. "Were we ever really off?"

His body relaxed, and the twinkle in his eye returned. "Not in my book. But I don't know, you and Jonathan…"

"Emmett, you're so mistaken. I'm not on the right team for him to even be interested, okay?"

"Ah, I see, well, good to know. I wanted to kick his ass."

"Emmett Waterman!"

"I know I already said this last night, but I think it bears repeating: if we're together, then we're together 100 percent with no ambiguity, right?"

"I'm a one-man woman, so don't worry about that on my end. And you'd better be too."

"Absolutely not," he said. Charlotte shot him an icy glare. "I'm a one-*woman man*," he said, laughing.

She rolled her eyes and smacked his arm. "That's what I meant."

They came to the spot where Emmett had found Charlotte, and they agreed they couldn't believe it had been two months already.

"I wasn't lying when I told Aubrie that if anyone would have bit me the day I found you and Asa, it wouldn't have been the pup. You wanted nothing to do with me," he said as he threw an arm around Charlotte, looking down at her with a grin.

"The first of about twenty times I've tried to push you away or give you the brush-off."

"It's not something that's happened to me too often in life. But you sure made up for lost time."

"Special me, huh?"

"Very special," he said sincerely.

They topped their afternoon off with a romantic dinner at a cozy restaurant tucked in near Malibu's Country Mart, and started off with a toast. "Here's to nothing standing in the way of us being together," Emmett said warmly.

Though she was happy about his divorce, his words unknowingly caused Charlotte to feel a cold sensation deep inside. Would the foreboding ever stop?

Emmett stretched his hand across the table to take Charlotte's into his. "I have no idea how you might feel about this, but I wanted to ask you something, Charlotte. I wanted to know if you'd consider moving in with me."

Charlotte was caught completely off guard. She knew she was completely in love with this man but wondered if moving in was the right thing to do. "Wow, Emmett, I wasn't expecting this. Can I…I don't know. I need to think about it."

"What's to think about? I think it makes perfect sense. We're serious about being together, and if you're really going to leave the condo to Aubrie and Chloe, why waste all that money finding a place of your own?"

"I don't need to shack up with you to save a buck, Emmett. My autonomy at this point doesn't have a price on it."

"Autonomy? What's autonomous about a committed relationship? Autonomy's for singles." He pulled his hand away and picked at his straw, stabbing it into his ice-filled glass.

"Autonomy just means my own person, my own space. It has nothing to do with trying to hang on to an identity of being single. I just…like I said, since Beau, I'm still trying to figure out who I am and learning to trust myself. I'm not saying no, or yes, just yet. But needing to think on it doesn't negate my love for you. I just need more time."

"I'm sorry. Maybe because I'm a guy, I don't understand the difference. It sounds to me like you're saying no. If you were sure about us, you wouldn't be hesitant or confused about it." Emmett looked away, running his hands through his hair.

"Please don't be mad, Emmett. Remember your promise not to push me? This would be one of those opportunities to pull back a little." Char reached for his hand, but he grabbed for his drink instead.

Charlotte sighed. "Are you afraid it will stall our progress if I say no? That we'll never get to enjoy our nights together?"

"Don't try to equate this to sex again. It's not about that," he said in a tone Char wished were more of hurt than anger.

"I'm not being flippant. I'm honestly trying to clarify a point. Let me finish, please. Emmett, I promise we'll continue to become closer. If I get my own place, it won't mean I'll never stay the night with you, and of course I'd have you stay the night with me. In fact, it may be better for you to stay over with me because of the boys."

"They stay in the dorms, and they'll be moving back, soon in fact. That's another reason I want you at home with me. It's going to be quiet and lonely."

"I didn't realize that." She wondered if the girls knew when the boys were leaving, and worried it would be a tough blow to them, but she tried to focus on appeasing Emmett. "Honey, either way, we'll spend plenty of time together, I promise. Just let me get the girls situated for school. I likely only have a few more weeks with them before they'll be completely consumed. I want to make the most of it and not have this hanging over my head. You're not really mad, are you?"

"No, just disappointed." This time Emmett reached for Charlotte's hand and took it in his. "I really love you, Charlotte."

"I love you too, Emmett. And I love that you're thinking about the future with us in mind."

...

At Emmett's behest, the boys invited Charlotte and the girls over for Sunday dinner that night. The girls made sure to look nice since the guys were going to the effort to prepare dinner all on their own. They were impressed with how well the boys did. Noa claimed responsibility for the garden salad, and Kai proudly showed off his perfectly toasted garlic bread. Emmett bragged he didn't have anything to prove, as he claimed supremacy at the grill.

"I do have to say, Emmett, I love your salmon. People tend to overcook it, but you keep it a perfect medium rare. It's delicious," Char said after her first bite.

"Remember when Aunt Charlie and Blake tried to grill salmon on her birthday trip last summer in Sunriver, and we ended up having to go out for Italian instead?" Chloe said to Aubrie, laughing.

"Ugh, don't remind me. You and Blake need to stay far away from the grill, Mom. You know what? We haven't even talked about your birthday yet. I hope you didn't book Sunriver this year. I mean, I know it's tradition, but I just feel like celebrating here, in LA."

Emmett paused from cutting into his steak and interjected. "Wait a second, your birthday. I hate to admit, I don't even know when it is."

"Mom's turning forty in, like, less than two weeks. Could you imagine being forty, Chloe? OMG, no thank you," Aubrie said with a grimace.

"Well, we're not, so let's just focus on that," Chloe said in all seriousness.

Char was aghast at the girls' exchange but kept it to herself, hoping the conversation would end—soon.

"Hold up, no one's answering me. When's your birthday, Charlotte?" Emmett's fork and knife were suspended in air as he waited for her to answer.

"Emmett, is that really important?" Char asked, tight-lipped.

"Uh, actually, yes," Emmett said. He set his utensils down while shooting a challenging look at Char. Still, she hesitated.

Aubrie was happy to answer for her. "The fifteenth, so, Friday after next."

"Wow, well, I'm glad I found out. When were you going to tell me?" Emmett said, looking at Char with a hint of a smile.

"I don't know; maybe I'd have forgotten," she said, taking a gulp of her water, wishing it hadn't been brought up at all.

Emmett reached out, resting his arm on the back of Charlotte's chair and tilting his head toward her. "Even if you think it's no big deal, it's not fair to rob me of the chance to do something nice for you."

"Fine, but just so you know," Char said, lightly dabbing her lips with her napkin, "I truly appreciate a low-key approach. A lovely dinner would be more than enough."

Emmett leaned back in his chair confidently. "Oh, we'll go out to dinner, that's for sure. But I have to surprise you with something one way or another. What kind of example would I be setting for the boys here? It's another chance to show them how it's done." Emmett grinned around the table.

That got the boys going, and soon the kids were all sharing their birthdates, and the boys were calculating how much time they had to prepare before the girls' birthdays came around. It appeared the kids were getting more serious about their futures together. Emmett and Charlotte exchanged knowing smiles.

"I've pored over Charlotte's communications since her move. We have updates."

"And?"

"She's taken a lover. He may be of interest to us. I've sent you an encrypted PDF of his dossier. He's planning her birthday. Her family will be in LA soon."

"Of course she has a new lover. That harlot wastes no time setting a new trap for some unfortunate bloke, don't I know. And check your facts. The only other family she'll be inviting is her son, Blake."

"Sorry, Boss, you're right."

"I know who should be gathered to LA for her big day. It's time to steer everyone in. Maybe we, me included, can help Charlotte take a trip down memory lane. We'll have to follow everyone closely to orchestrate this just right."

The morning after the dinner at Emmett's, Kat texted Charlotte, saying she'd be out of town for a week but asking if they could meet for a drink as soon as she got back. Kat unabashedly explained she wanted to hear all about their latest developments. While it was a bit intrusive, Charlotte still held Kat in high esteem for all she'd been through and for the support she'd lent to her and Emmett as a couple, so she agreed.

They met a week later for drinks. On the way to meet Kat, Charlotte realized her birthday was that coming Friday. She couldn't believe how fast time had flown. She mused over the saying that time flies when you're having fun. For her and Emmett, it certainly rang true, and she was thankful that they'd decided not to give up. Things between them were only getting better and better.

"Hello, my Charlotte, you look radiant," Kat said as she gave her a kiss on each cheek. They were led to their table at a chic bar nestled in an oasis of flowering plants and shrubs. It was a beautiful warm August night, and Charlotte still felt as if she were floating on air.

"You and Emmett are back together, I hear," Kat said, looking as if she were trying to stifle a smug smile.

"Yes, and it's going well. I think we've smoothed a lot of our bumps," Char said, unwilling to share more than absolutely necessary.

Unfazed, Kat pressed on. "Lou tells me you're contemplating moving in with Emmett. Does that mean you've told him everything about your scars, the ones on your back? You look like a weight is lifted; you must have revealed that secret, no?"

Charlotte stiffened. Of course it was still looming over her, but things had been going so well she had all but completely pushed down having to tell him someday. She still marveled at how cold and direct Katena could be, and felt a little resentful that she was even bringing it up.

Katena watched Char closely. "If you can't tell him yet, why not tell me? I think I could help," she said, her voice soft for once.

"Katena, it's not just my secret I'm keeping. There are other people involved, and I'm committed to protecting them. If I tell anyone, ever, it'll be Emmett, and no one else. So, please, stop asking."

As soon as Char said it, she was angry with herself for saying too much, but she wanted to make it clear to Kat to drop it. Despite the fact that Ash had hurt her so deeply, to the point that she almost didn't survive, she wasn't someone who took pleasure in revenge. She wasn't willing to take everyone down with her, and she assured herself Ash was no longer a threat; mind, body, and soul, she was getting stronger. Proof was all around her: the move, the new friends, and her growing love for Emmett. No, Ash was fading fast in the distance.

Kat leaned back, eyeing Charlotte up and down as if trying to get a read on her. "That's all very mysterious. I'm only human, so of course I find myself highly intrigued. I'd love nothing more than to know the whole story. But I'll refrain from asking again. I apologize. But you must, and I mean must, at least answer me this one question. This person, are you still in love with him?"

"What? No. Who says I'm talking about a past lover?" Char said defensively.

"You."

Charlotte looked away; she knew it was futile to try to deny it to Kat. "No. I'm not in love with him anymore."

Emmett and Char were snuggled on the couch, about to watch a movie, when Emmett casually told her to be ready for her first present the next morning and to clear her schedule.

"Tomorrow? Emmett, my birthday's not until Friday. I'm not one to subscribe to birthday-month or even birthday-week celebrations. That's just too over the top," Charlotte pleaded. Not only was a several-days-long birthday celebration ridiculous, she also felt maybe she didn't deserve it. Her conversation with Kat the night before had put her in a sour mood.

"Trust me, you're going to love your first gift."

"If you say so," Charlotte said, unconvinced.

"I've had a blast planning this. The boys will realize they have nothing on me, come Friday."

Charlotte couldn't help but laugh at Emmett's exuberance. "Is everything a competition to you?" she asked, tossing a handful of popcorn at him.

"Where would the fun be in life if it wasn't? I strive for the best, and I think I've found it with you, babe, and I'm looking forward to this bringing us closer."

Char wanted nothing more than to be so close to Emmett that it would shut anything and anyone else out.

. . .

Char was up early the next day. With her nervous energy over what Emmett may have planned for her, she swam laps in the pool, had her first coffee, gave Asa his walk, and was showered and ready for the day by seven thirty. Soon afterward, she heard a knock at the door. She was excited despite herself.

She opened the door and gasped, wide-eyed. Her son, Blake, was standing in her doorway, sporting a big, gorgeous smile.

She threw her arms around him. "Blake, you're here. How? When? Oh, honey, I'm so happy you're here." Char couldn't help but get emotional. She was worried her mascara would run, and she needed a tissue, but they were all happy tears.

"Happy birthday, Mom. It's your big four-oh. You think I'd let some little major motion picture get in the way of seeing you on your birthday?" Blake smiled big, his white teeth made even brighter, Char noticed, by the deep tan he'd obviously gotten from spending so much time outside filming.

"Honey, I can't believe this. What a birthday present." She wrapped her arms tightly around her son.

"Well, you can thank Emmett and Aubrie. They worked hard to get a hold of me. Literally, Mom, I've been the middle of nowhere. I'm still not sure how they tracked me down, but they did. I can't wait to meet Emmett; he must be a keeper if he went to all this trouble for you," he said, hanging an arm around Char's shoulders.

"Blakey!" Aubrie squealed. "Come up, there's no room down there for me." Char and Blake hadn't moved from the entry.

As soon as Blake stepped to the top of the stairs, Aubrie jumped onto her big brother and wrapped herself around him. It was a sight Charlotte hadn't seen, she realized, in far too long. Tears escaped again.

It had been almost six months since the last time they were together, but in that time her boy had not only become more handsome, but also she couldn't believe how much he had matured. *My goodness, he looks like a man now,* she realized. His brown hair had grown a bit longer, probably due to working long hours and being out in the wilderness without much time for a haircut. He had wide-set, large brown eyes with dark, curly lashes any girl would be envious of. His thick, shapely brows gave him a brooding look, yet he was one of the kindest, most upbeat, and gentle souls Charlotte had ever known. Her love for him was an ache deep in the pit of her soul. He was patient and nonjudgmental. All he seemed to be capable of was love.

It was always Char's worst fear that Blake and Aubrie wouldn't understand that the depths of her love for them knew no bounds. She was so grateful for this moment that Emmett worked so hard to give her. Her heart was overfilled.

"Oh my gosh, you've gotten, like, bigger. Not taller, Blake, but beefier." Aubrie laughed and gripped his biceps.

Blake gave Chloe a big hug too. "Hey, cuz, how are you? Good for you, moving down here with Mom and Aub. You're going to be the next big designer, I just know it. Can't wait to see you make it, Chloe." Blake and Chloe had always had a close relationship. It was funny how they looked more like brother and sister than Aubrie and Blake did. Chloe was just another sister to Blake, as far as he was concerned.

The girls gave Blake no elbow room, crowding around him, hanging on his every word as they talked. Aubrie and Chloe had always idolized Blake, and to Char's delight, it appeared things still hadn't changed.

Charlotte was so grateful that Emmett had ordered her to clear her schedule. The three girls in Blake's life wouldn't be letting him out of their sight from now until he left again for Canada.

"How much time do we have with you, Blake? I know you said filming wouldn't wrap up for another month," Char said.

"Friday night I'll take the red-eye back to Canada. Emmett has Friday planned for the two of you, but don't worry, I want that day with my sis and cuz. But we're all meeting up for your birthday dinner, and I'll head to the airport after that."

"So that means we've got today and tomorrow. Let's make the most of it. What would you like to do, Blake? You're the one who's been in a rustic environment the past five weeks."

Blake scratched his head for a moment, thinking. "I'd love to just hang at the beach, really. But I would also like to sit down to some civilized meals. We've been subsisting on food similar to military MREs. I could use a break from that. Last, I'd love to meet Emmett. I need to thank him for organizing this."

"What am I, chopped liver?" Aubrie said, her mouth hanging wide open, waiting for her due credit.

"No, really, thank you, Aubrie. This is awesome. You're a good sleuth, tracking me down," Blake said with a laugh.

"You better believe it. Come on, peeps, let's get our stuff and hit the beach," Aubrie said with excitement.

Charlotte was on cloud nine. As she waited for the kids to get ready, she called Emmett.

Emmett answered on the first ring. "Happy early birthday, sweetheart."

"Emmett, are you kidding me? You've just made my birthday. Cancel anything else you had planned. This is so—I just don't know how to thank you. I've missed Blake so much." Charlotte had to stop talking. The lump in her throat was coming back.

"Well, I felt it was the least I should do for you on your birthday. So, you're welcome. It makes me happy to make you happy."

"It's my absolute favorite gift, I can tell you that now. Our plans are to spend the day at the beach. It's Blake's request. He's worked so hard filming on location that he wants nothing more than to indulge in rest and relaxation. How about you meet us for dinner tomorrow night at the condo? Blake wants to meet you before Friday."

"I'd love to. I'm looking forward to meeting Blake too. I'll see you tomorrow after work. Enjoy your time with the kids."

"Oh, I will. Thank you so much, honey."

The day with the kids filled Charlotte with such a sense of gratitude. The kids let loose on the beach, playing volleyball with anyone who would join in, and they also brought kneeboards and had a lot of laughs trying to get the hang of it. When they tired of that, Blake played catch with some children who had been building sandcastles.

College-aged girls kept walking past Blake, trying to catch his eye. Chloe and Aubrie acted as his sentries, glaring at any girl who gave him so much as a second glance. Even though Blake seemed oblivious to it all, Char had to finally call the girls over and ask them to cool it.

"Mom, we're not going to let any skanks get their claws into our Blake," Aubrie said in defense.

"Girls, you have to allow him to be able to meet and talk to people. Look at you two; Blake's not glaring down any guy who walks by the two of you. Be fair," Char said in exasperation.

"Whatever, Mom. You don't know what we're saving him from."

Char shook her head and figured she'd let it go, since Blake seemed either unaware or uninterested. When the game fizzled with the kids, Blake came and sat by his mom.

"So, honey, tell me, how's life been going? You've kept me in touch more or less about how film school's going, but what about your personal life? Anyone special in it?"

Blake smiled and hung his head a moment and then glanced up at her, looking almost shy. "Actually, Mom, I've met someone on the set. She graduated last year, and this is her first real job. I've met some great girls, but no one like her, ever."

"Are you in love?" Charlotte's heart skipped a beat for her son. She'd never seen him talk of a girl with anything more than a casual air.

He blushed. "I mean, I wouldn't go that far, Mom. We've only known each other a couple of months, but she's pretty amazing. I'd love for her to meet you. Thanksgiving maybe? She's actually from California. Her dad has a vineyard about forty-five minutes from here, so yeah, I think it'd work out great." Blake beamed from ear to ear.

Charlotte was elated to see Blake so happy. "That sounds perfect. I can't wait to meet her."

"Blakey, get your tan butt out here and swim with us," Aubrie called to Blake.

"That's my cue. I'll be back, Mom." Blake shot up and ran to the water. Charlotte could see all eyes on the beach go to him. There was just something about Blake that drew people to him, and she felt so much pride knowing he was just as beautiful on the inside as he was on the out.

It made her think of Emmett. She felt so fortunate to have found him, right when she'd felt there was no hope for her to ever find love again, let alone a love that was so all-encompassing. He, too, was a kind heart: patient, loving, and protective, but not in a controlling way. In a way, he was like Beau, in that he wanted her to find her confidence, but he didn't keep her at arm's length the way Beau had. Emmett picked up where Beau had left off, and worked to truly know Char, as tough as that now was sometimes. Despite her repeated re-proofs, he never stopped trying to achieve a deeper connection with her. She knew she had something special with him. Charlotte sat in reflection until the kids informed her they were starving and asked to go to a drive-through.

When they got home, Char and Blake stayed up late into the night catching up. They had always been close. Blake had no qualms about sharing his innermost feelings with his mom, and although it had been months since they'd last seen each other, to Char's relief, nothing had changed.

. . .

The next night Charlotte was exhausted from a full day. She had taken the kids down to Balboa Bay, where Emmett had taken her on their first weekend together, and they did everything under the sun they could while there. They kayaked and tried the paddleboards, and for lunch rented one of the Duffy boats for an hour. As much as Charlotte just wanted to relax on the couch, Emmett was on his way over to join them in their family dinner.

Charlotte let Blake choose what she'd make, and he wanted tacos. Char was happy to do such a small thing for him that would give him such a big smile. She made fresh salsa, corn-and-jalapeño salad, handmade tortillas, and a taco bar with every topping imaginable laid out on a giant lazy Susan in the middle of the table.

When the doorbell rang, Charlotte answered it and threw her arms around Emmett in a flash. Emmett laughed, pulling her into a tight hug. "Well, hello to you too, babe."

Charlotte felt teary as she thanked him again for bringing Blake home. "You don't know how much this means to me," she said softly into his ear.

He rubbed her back and kissed her cheek, then said, "Oh, I think I do, honey."

They walked up the stairs holding hands, and Charlotte enjoyed feeling so fulfilled at that moment. She squeezed his hand tightly, hoping Emmett knew just how happy she was.

Blake was on the deck on his cell phone, and when he saw Emmett and Char, he ended the call and came in to meet Emmett.

"Hi, I take it you're Emmett. Listen, I appreciate you getting me down here for my mom's birthday," he said as he reached out to shake Emmett's hand.

"So great to meet you, Blake," Emmett said, shaking Blake's hand. "I was happy to do it. Love seeing your mom smile." Charlotte blushed and told them they could take a seat, that dinner was about ready; then she called up to the girls, who sounded like a herd of elephants coming down the stairs.

"Finally! We're starved," Aubrie said as she and Chloe took seats.

"So, Blake, I have to ask, why aren't you on a college team? You're as big as my boys," Emmett said with exuberance.

"Basketball and football aren't my thing. I love a game of pickup ball, but I've always been drawn more to creating rather than competing, in a physical sense anyway. Believe me, I'm going to be competing to make the best films when my time comes," Blake said confidently.

"See, Charlotte, a man loves a good competition in any form. It's what feeds us," Emmett called over his shoulder with a laugh.

"You're right—I see that more clearly every day," Char said, smiling, bringing a pitcher of water to the table.

Emmett jumped up to pull Char's seat out for her. "Well, I don't know if Charlotte told you, but I own a sports-media production company, so if you need another internship or a job straight out of college, remember me, okay?" As he pushed Char's chair in, he kissed her on the cheek, and Char smiled up at him. Blake and Aubrie smiled at each other, clearly happy to see their mom happy.

"I appreciate that, Emmett, thank you. I will," Blake said.

Blake and Emmett talked for the majority of the dinner, hitting on a variety of interesting subjects that the whole table could partake in. Everyone was getting along great, and Charlotte couldn't have been happier.

"Charlotte, you've been keeping a secret from me," Emmett said with a straight face as he set his fork down on his empty plate and threw his napkin on top of it.

Char felt a little adrenaline and hesitated. "What do you mean?" She slid out of her seat to clear her plate and gain some distance.

The kids laughed, thinking Charlotte was feigning anxiety.

"You're a fabulous cook. What I wouldn't give to have a home-cooked meal like this every so often." He gave her a big smile as he leaned back and rubbed his stomach, and then he got up to help Char clear the table.

"Mom's a great cook, but don't let her fool you with her 'I'm a simple girl at heart' nonsense. She loves to be pampered. And she much prefers to go out to dinner than to cook and clean at home," Aubrie said with authority.

"Oh, I promise, if she cooks, I'll clean," Emmett said with his hand over his heart as he came back to take more dishes to the kitchen.

"Lies, all lies, Aubrie. Back me up here, Blake, Chloe, someone…" Char said as she looked from Blake to Chloe.

"Sorry, Mom, no can do. You do like to be pampered. You're a Leo; you like to be catered to. Don't they call that a lazy Leo?" Blake teased as he jumped out of his seat to avoid Charlotte snapping him with her kitchen towel.

"You just start clearing the table, Blake, and mind your own business," Charlotte said in mock anger.

"See? She wants everyone else to do the work," Blake cried as he joined in helping clear the table.

"Well, if your mom wants to be pampered, pampered she will be tomorrow for her birthday. Charlotte, I'll pick you up at eight in the morning. We have a fun-packed day planned. Start off in jeans, okay?

Oh, and bring a small overnight bag. I thought it'd be nice to stay over where we're having dinner. Anyway, that's all I'm going to say. And I should go. I have a few more things to do tonight before our day tomorrow. Bye, kids. I'll see you all at dinner tomorrow. Don't be late," he warned with a smile.

"Not for Mom's birthday, we won't be," Aubrie said, with Chloe nodding in agreement.

Blake put his arm around Charlotte and kissed her cheek. "This is the one official day of the year we can show our mom how much we love her. No way we'd be late to that."

Charlotte blushed at the attention.

Emmett gave Blake a hearty pat on the back. "You remind me a lot of myself at your age. You just keep on respecting your mom the way you do, and you'll end up with a woman as great as she is."

"I would be so lucky," Blake said, smiling at his mom.

Charlotte gave Blake a big bear hug and, before she could tear up, walked with Emmett to the door, where they stepped out into the warm night. The ocean waves crashed in the distance while the crickets chirped in the potted greenery in the courtyard.

"This was a great night. You've got a great son there, Charlotte. I see a lot of your heart in him. I'm touched to be included in your time with your kids. Thank you."

"It wouldn't be the same without you here with us. You know you've made my birthday already. Thank you for bringing Blake home." She went onto her toes to give Emmett a quick kiss.

Emmett told her good night and to get a good night's sleep, but instead she stayed up late with Blake again; they both wanted to make the most of their time.

Julian was just hanging up the phone when Taryn came into his office and said good morning. Julian stood and gathered his money clip and keys; his luggage stood at his feet.

"You've got your suitcase? Where are you going?" Taryn asked Julian as she stepped close to give him a quick morning kiss.

"LA. Something's come up. Some of the guys and I need to spend a few days there." He stepped back with a distracted smile.

"Are you working a detail? You don't normally accompany the guys. Must be a big deal." She eyed him carefully.

"Not at all. Nevertheless, it's confidential." As if to shush her, he put his finger to his lips in mock irritation. He hated lying to such a sweet girl but was thankful he was so good at it. He gathered his things.

"I'll miss you. And, Julian, whatever you're doing, have fun."

"Oh, I always do," he said as he turned to go, but she caught his arm.

"Wait, I have a surprise for you. I'd actually planned a dinner for us tonight, but since you're leaving…I've been wanting to tell you for a while now that I…I love you, Julian." She stood there with flushed cheeks and waited for his reaction.

Julian stiffened slightly before grabbing both her hands and bringing them to his lips for a kiss. He gave her as good a forced smile as possible before letting go, and as he did, his expression turned to regret as he walked out.

He wasted no time refocusing as Jameson joined him in the elevator and they headed to the airport, where they would take his six-person jet. He had already ordered the other men on his team to take the helicopter to LA; they'd be slower getting there, but he wanted to be prepared.

"You've done great work, Jameson, fleshing this out. We couldn't have positioned ourselves better. It's been a long time coming, but there will be payback this weekend. You mark my words."

The sun streamed in through Charlotte's balcony window, waking her the way she loved, hearing the sound of birds in the trees and feeling the warmth on her face from the sunrise. Blinking in the light and with a smile, Char wondered how she could have a better birthday than she'd already been having with her kids under one roof the past couple days.

She enjoyed a breakfast in bed, thanks to the girls and Blake. They had even clipped a couple of pink and yellow roses from her flowerpots.

"Avocado omelet, heavy cream in your coffee, and a garnish of berries, just what you like if you're going to have a, ahem, as you call it, big breakfast," Aubrie said as she set the tray down and blew Char a kiss, her eyes twinkling with delight. Aubrie loved surprising people and watching their happy reactions.

"It's the least we could do for you, Aunt Charlie. Thank you for being such a great aunt. Happy birthday." Chloe gave Charlotte a peck on the cheek.

"We all pitched in to get you a birthday present, but it wasn't in stock. But we picked you out a covered swing. We know how much you love being outside, but there isn't a whole lot of shade on the back deck. Now you can enjoy the birds and flowers even in the heat of the day. It'll be here tomorrow, courtesy of Emmett's delivery service," Aubrie said, laughing.

"Oh, I know I'm going to love it. Thank you so much—you're the sweetest kids anyone could ask for. I hope you three know how much I love you all. You give me such love and support, and sometimes I don't even feel I deserve it." She beamed at them, blinking away tears of love.

"Mom, of course you deserve our love. You're the best. And we hope you have a great birthday today," Blake said, squeezing Charlotte's hand.

"Thank you, sweetheart. I guess Emmett's taking me out for the entire day. I feel bad not spending your last day with you, Blake."

"Mom, Chloe and I want some alone time with him too. You've had tons more time with him. We could hear you guys laughing and talking 'til, like, the middle of the night. It's our turn today."

"Well, I don't think Mom hogged me," Blake said, shooting a look Aubrie's way, "but I do think a little sister-brother-cousin bonding time's in order. They're about to start college. I'm in my senior year. I can give them some important pointers. Like how to steer clear of the primo jerks I've come to be able to pick out a mile away," Blake said with a look of disgust.

"Oh, we're prepared for creepers, Blake. We're been going to MMA self-defense classes with Emmett's sons. Mom, you've got to get in there too," Aubrie said, to Char's discomfort. "But anyway, we'll be prepared to kick butt should we need to." Aubrie got in the offensive stance she had learned and demonstrated her best don't-mess-with-me face.

Chloe joined in and demonstrated her best one-two punch move.

Blake laughed. "I see. I'm impressed. Good on Emmett for getting you into self-defense classes. But you two might want to think about avoiding ending up in those kinds of situations in the first place."

"That's true," Aubrie conceded. "We've talked a bit about that at

MMA, but yeah, we should hear your perspective too, Blakey. See, Mom? We need this time. You go have fun with Emmett, and we'll see you tonight at dinner."

Charlotte sighed and looked lovingly at her kids. A smile came over her face. "Okay, okay, then. I'm going to jump in the shower. Emmett should be here in no time. I have to wear jeans. I have no idea why, but why don't you guys skedaddle out of here so I can get ready."

The kids mock shoved and elbowed each other, playing as if they were being rushed out of her room. Char laughed and threw a pillow at them.

"Ouch, the abuse," Aubrie called out as they shut the door, their laughter filling the condo and Charlotte's heart.

Soon, Charlotte was ready for Emmett, and she could hear he was downstairs. She came down wearing a pair of skinny jeans rolled up just above the ankle, a white fitted V-neck tee, and some silver sequined Sperrys. Something told her they must be going out on a boat, so she dressed accordingly.

Emmett laughed when he saw her. "Happy birthday, sweetheart." He put his arms around her and gave her a peck on the lips.

"What? Why are you laughing at me?"

"That's what you're wearing? Can you at least run up and bring a pair of socks with you?"

"They won't fit with these shoes, Emmett."

"That's okay, it doesn't matter. Just grab a pair," he said, grinning at her.

Char ran upstairs to grab socks and realized she must have made the wrong assumption about his plans for the day.

She said bye to the kids, socks in hand. Emmett carried her overnight bag, and they loaded into his convertible.

Her phone rang; it was Jonathan. She spoke to him briefly, agreed to a time to meet, and got off the phone, not before he wished her happy birthday. She smiled, touched that he remembered.

"Who was that?"

"Jonathan. You met him that night at the restaurant," she said, slipping her phone into her purse.

"Oh, the guy I wanted to pummel, I remember him. Sounds like you guys were making plans."

Charlotte smacked him again, rolling her eyes. He only laughed. "I have to meet him tomorrow afternoon. He's hoping I can allay our client's fears about one last detail before we sign. At the moment they won't do it until we accept personal liability should there be any breach of confidentiality. It's an outrageous demand, but so far they won't budge."

"And you're the big guns, so to speak, that Jonathan's relying on to change their minds?"

Emmett had no outward sign of doubt, but Charlotte knew what he was thinking. "You don't think I'm strong enough to change their minds, do you?"

"I didn't say that, Charlotte." He wouldn't explain further what he actually meant.

"I don't conduct myself as 'big guns,' obviously, Emmett. But brute force isn't always the most effective strategy. Sometimes what it takes to turn a situation around is simply the facts. Our clients are letting the fear of what-ifs cloud the facts, and at the moment, it's like they can't see the forest for the trees. I know because I end up doing the same thing myself, often; even being self-aware can't save me from it sometimes. But, somehow, with work, I seem to have a knack for unknotting the doubts and fears of our clients and getting everyone where they need to be. No posturing, no threats, just the honest truth."

Emmett tilted his head and looked at Charlotte thoughtfully, but he didn't say anything.

"What?" she said to him.

"Just thinking how lucky I am to have such a beautiful, intelligent woman in my life," he said, reaching over to give her shoulder a warm squeeze.

As hard as it was for her to take any kind of compliment, Charlotte allowed herself to accept Emmett's with gratitude, a big step in her healing. Emmett put her at ease, made her feel confident, and that's what she needed in her life. She needed him.

"But back to Saturday's plans: I need to pick up your swing in the morning. It's in its box, so I'll bring my tools and set it up for you. It's a thoughtful gift the kids got you. I hope where we're going will be just as appreciated."

"Yeah, so are you going to tell me where in the world we're headed?"

"I'm not spoiling the surprise. Where would the fun be in that?"

Charlotte rolled her eyes and let Emmett have his fun. He patted her leg and assured her the surprise would be worth the wait.

When they had been driving for about thirty minutes through the Santa Monica Mountains, Emmett turned onto a gravel road.

Charlotte took in her surroundings. There were rolling hills all around, covered in tall grasses swaying in the wind. It was a beautifully rustic scene. "I've got it. I know what we're doing; we're going hiking. But you should have told me, honey. I would have dressed much differently."

"No, ma'am, that's not what we're doing," Emmett said with a stifled laugh as he turned a corner, following the road up a small hill.

Charlotte sagged in defeat. "You're really enjoying this, aren't you?" she said through gritted teeth.

Emmett laughed even harder. "I'm not trying to torture you. I promise."

Charlotte's stomach dropped, and suddenly she felt a foreboding. Was it Emmett's offhanded remark about torture? No, she didn't think that was it, but she couldn't explain her sudden feel of dread, not until they crested the hill where Char was hit with an eerily familiar site, one she had never wanted to lay eyes on again. Ahead of them on each side of the driveway were green fields lined with white fences with several horses galloping gracefully together. In the distance was a horse stable nearly identical to the one in her nightmares. Charlotte was in a state of shock.

"Look at them go. Aren't they beautiful?" Emmett said.

Char couldn't answer. She bent forward, one palm to her chest, the other gripping the door handle. She wanted out. She stared at the floor, trying to comprehend how it was they had ended up there, of all places, but her mind was taking her to a memory from many months ago, a night of horror. She felt her chest seize, barely able to breathe. Brutal scenes flashed through her mind. She grabbed the V of her shirt into a fist, and a flush of perspiration whipped over her.

Emmett turned toward Charlotte, who was curled forward, clutching her chest. He put on the brakes. "Charlotte, are you okay? What's wrong?"

Charlotte didn't answer and instead bolted out of the car, flinging the door open and falling to her knees on the gravel and grass. Her stomach turned, and she thought she might get sick. She squeezed her eyes shut. She told herself she could get through this without a major freak-out. She focused on all she had learned from Moe on how to stay in the present and not get carried away.

Emmett ran to her side. "Charlotte, what's wrong? What can I do?" He knelt by her and put his hand over hers. She grabbed it like a lifeline. She didn't dare look him in the eyes, afraid he'd see the rabid fear she'd been hiding for months.

"Charlotte, talk to me." The panic in his voice brought her back to the present. She struggled to win control, for her and Emmett's sake. After taking several shaky breaths, she was relieved to find she wasn't going to be sick. She focused on her breathing and fought to catch her voice. "I'm sorry, I'm not feeling well. I'll be okay, but please, you have to get me out of here."

Emmett didn't argue. He didn't say a word. He helped Charlotte to the car, his brow knotted in confusion and concern. When Emmett put the car into drive, Charlotte saw they were going toward the stables. They couldn't go to the stables. She gripped the door again, feeling caged and desperate. It took all she had not to scream at Emmett. "No, we can't go down there. I said get me *out* of here. Please, Emmett."

"All right, all right, I'm sorry. I can do that." He stomped on the brakes and threw the car into reverse. He backed out of the half-mile driveway as fast as he could, kicking up clouds of dust.

Once they were on the road and headed away from the stable, Emmett looked over at her. She was still trembling, and her lip was covered in perspiration. She could feel her hair sticking to her temples, and her shirt was damp.

At the first opportunity, he pulled over. "What the hell happened back there? Charlotte, look at me. Are you sure you're okay?"

She had to think of how to explain it away when all she really wanted to do was slip into a catatonic state. She fought to stay lucid. All the sessions with Moe helped her stay in control, though just barely.

"Charlotte?" he said, louder.

"I'm so sorry, I'm fine. I just needed to catch my breath. I panicked. I…I had an allergic reaction. You shouldn't have brought me there."

"Allergies? Why would Aubrie suggest horseback riding if you're allergic to horses?" he said, pausing for a moment. "No, that makes no sense. Aubrie said you've been riding for years."

Char bit the inside of her lip and thought quickly. "I didn't say I was allergic to horses. There are certain molds and grasses I'm allergic to, some trees even. I guess that stable was in the wrong area for me."

She stared out the window and told herself to take long, slow breaths. She had to do whatever she could not to cry. She was aware she needed to play this off right, or she'd be caught in the lie she'd been telling Emmett since they'd met. She fought to garner all the strength she could to be strong for Emmett and not let the entire day be ruined.

"You're still shaking, Char, and you're pale. Hey, look at me." He gently tugged on her arm so she'd look at him. "Are you telling me the truth? Shouldn't we go to the doctor?"

"No, no, this fresh air will be fine. I just need to catch my breath. I felt like I couldn't breathe, and I panicked. Just give me a little time to calm down. I'll be fine." She gave him a weak smile.

"I'm sorry for this, Charlotte. Let's go back to my place so we can kind of regroup and hopefully move on with your birthday plans." He reached for her hand, and she soon fell asleep in the car from pure emotional exhaustion.

When they arrived back home, Charlotte awoke to his whisper that he was going to carry her to his bed. She managed a faint nod.

An hour later, Char fully woke. She showered and put on a change of clothes but was still reeling from what happened. For the last year she had avoided riding and anything related to horses, but she had no idea she'd have such a visceral reaction to being near a stable.

It was frightening how similar the place had been to Ash's rural property near Portland. The long winding driveway, the style of fence, even the stable was the same style and color. It all brought her back to that night. She told herself she would have to push it all down and be stronger than she'd ever had to be to not ruin the rest of Emmett's birthday surprises for her.

As bad as her reaction was, she knew it could have been much worse. She realized that with Moe's therapy she'd made progress in leaps and bounds, and knowing that helped her get out of Emmett's bed, something she wouldn't have been able to do even a couple months earlier.

Anna must have heard Charlotte get up, because she came in to check on her. She gave Charlotte a big, yet gentle, hug. "*Feliz cumpleaños*, señora. How you feel? *No bueno?*" Anna said, inspecting her. She grabbed Char's hands, holding them out and looking her up and down.

Char smiled weakly. "*Gracias*, Anna, I'm fine. Just a case of bad allergies." Char cringed inside, feeling sure Anna could see right through her.

"And on your birthday, no less," Anna said with a sympathetic yet knowing look. She gathered Charlotte's discarded towel and clothes and noticed Char's jeans marred with the grass stains and assured her she could get them looking brand-new again. Charlotte thanked her, but all she really wanted to do was burn them, ridding her of the reminder. She startled herself, recalling that someone from her past had thought along those same lines. Her stomach fell again. She pushed it out of her mind as she finished getting ready and hurried out of the bathroom to find Emmett. It scared her to the core that she was thinking of Ash.

She padded out to the kitchen, where she found Anna unpacking the picnic lunch she'd prepared for them to take on their horseback ride.

"Oh, Anna, you went to all that trouble to pack a lunch for us, yet we're right back here eating it at home," Char said, her voice small and sad.

Anna looked at Charlotte with concern impossible to hide. "When things don't go as planned, we must push forward, counting our blessings along the way, no? You're safe here with señor Emmett," Anna said, patting Charlotte's shoulder warmly.

Charlotte knew how right Anna was and marveled at how she knew just the right thing to say. Emmett had proved himself time and again to be a man she could trust. He was patient and kind and a soft place to fall, away from the past. That's what she would focus on to help push forward.

When Emmett came out to the patio, Charlotte couldn't help but rush into his arms. She was beginning to see Emmett as her protector, and what she desperately needed protecting from at that moment were her thoughts of Ash. She knew she was a glutton for punishment, and hoped against hope that Emmett would save her from herself.

Emmett caught her in his arms. "Hey, hey, are you okay?"

"I am. I just wanted to be in your arms. I hope I haven't ruined our day, but I'm feeling better now." She buried her head in his chest. She reveled in the feeling of safety she felt with his strong arms wrapped around her.

Thankfully, he seemed to know that he needed to keep her in his embrace. He kissed her head and rubbed her back. "I'm glad you're feeling better, sweetheart. Don't worry, the day is still young, and we have plenty more to look forward to."

Char felt better after they had lunch. Emmett checked his watch and told her they could still make their next appointment if she felt up to it. He promised her it was nothing outdoors, so no risk of allergies, and that it should be relaxing.

She agreed, and they were in the car again, headed to downtown LA. Emmett couldn't keep his hands off Charlotte while he drove. He either had his hand on her thigh or on her shoulder, or he held her hand, kissing it every so often, and while they didn't talk much, it was a comfortable silence.

Charlotte mused how they'd been practically inseparable all summer long. She thought about his standing offer for her to move in. Even though she already had a couple of surprises in store for him, she decided to add one more.

Eventually they made their way to the heart of LA, and pulled up to the portico at the Ritz Carlton.

"Is this where we're staying, Emmett?"

"It is, and I thought we could spend some relaxing hours together before our dinner here. The food is great, plus Blake will only have a twenty-minute cab ride to the airport, so it's a win-win. I'm hoping the rest of the evening will make up for earlier. I'll never live it down, will I?" he asked sheepishly.

"Actually, I'd prefer that we keep this morning's fiasco to ourselves anyway. No need for everyone coming tonight to know, right?" *Liar, liar, liar!* Char yelled in her head.

Emmett looked relieved. "Good point. It'll be our secret. The rest of the night will go off without a hitch, I promise." Charlotte could only hope that Emmett would be able to keep his promise, and that the earlier events of the day weren't actually a harbinger of things to come.

"Blake *may* have been joking when he said you prefer to be pampered, but joking or not, that's exactly what I have planned. We're going to spend the rest of the afternoon at the spa until our friends and family join us later. Shall we?"

Charlotte took his arm, and after checking in, they were shown to a couples' spa suite, where they could get ready and later relax with a glass of champagne after their treatments. Suddenly Charlotte realized that a massage generally meant being fully undressed, having one's back exposed, touched. She began to panic once again.

Emmett watched her as she set her robe out and nervously fiddled with the tie. He walked over to her.

"Sweetheart, I know you're self-conscious about getting undressed. Among other things, I've ordered a hand, scalp, and foot massage for us. You'll be able to keep the towel wrap on the whole time today."

Charlotte's shoulders relaxed, and she stopped biting her lip. She looked down with a small smile. "Thank you, honey." *Someday I'll tell him. Someday soon. He deserves that trust and honesty from me.*

There was a knock at the door, and they were led to their treatment room. Soothing music was playing as they got onto their tables. Char looked over at Emmett. He was so tall and muscular, the robe barely fit him. The deep V in the robe exposed his pecs. He looked so sexy with his long, muscular legs stretching the whole length of the table. He had his hands laced together over his abdomen. His biceps were bulging through the robe. As hard as the day had been, Charlotte found herself luxuriating in the sight of him. Emmett looked over, catching her staring.

"What?"

"Nothing. You're just nice to look at." Char was embarrassed to be caught.

"Hmmm, thank you. So are you." He smiled and closed his eyes. Charlotte realized he surely needed to decompress from the day as much as she did. The technicians dimmed the lights and put lavender-scented puffs on their eyes and brought them both to a calm and relaxed state. Char remained nearly asleep until the last step, a cold mist meant to awaken them.

The attendant led them back to their suite, where they were told they could stay as long as they needed. They had run a bath for them in the couple's tub. Red and pink rose petals floated in the water. The only light was the soft illumination from candles set beautifully around the room.

Emmett poured them each a glass of champagne. Without apology, he downed his first glass in one gulp. He looked at her sheepishly. Char laughed and decided to follow suit. Emmett grinned as he poured them both refills. He gave her a wink, and they clinked their glasses.

"I see they assumed we might want to have a bath together," he said, glancing at the tub. "If you brought a swimsuit, maybe we could relax in the warm water together?" Emmett smiled, and his eyes twinkled in the candlelight. Char felt no pressure from him, only love.

"I'd love to take a bath with you. Let me get changed. I'll be right back."

Emmett was already in the tub when Charlotte came back in her robe. She had her strawberry blond hair piled high, thrown into a messy bun, and Emmett watched her come over, not taking his eyes off her for a second.

Char smiled and untied her robe. When she let it fall to the ground, she wasn't wearing anything underneath. Emmett caught his breath and sat up taller in the tub, reaching out for her as Charlotte stepped in. She knelt in front of him. She felt full of life, abuzz with the step she was taking.

Emmett was in awe as he pulled her in close. He searched her face. "Charlotte, I don't know what to say."

Staying silent, she put her arms around his neck and pulled in closer. She put his arms around her. Charlotte simply laid her head on his shoulder and waited. Her pulse quickened as he gingerly rested his hands on her back; then, slowly, his fingers gently explored the puffy lines that crisscrossed this way and that. She heard him suck in a breath, telling her that he realized they could only be one thing, whipping marks.

He wrapped his arms tightly around her and buried his head next to hers. To her surprise, she could still breathe. They sat entwined in silent truth, silent trust, comfort.

He pulled back to cradle her face and kiss her ever so gently. Eventually their eyes met. "Charlotte, I don't think I could love you any more than I do right now—thank you, thank you for trusting me."

"I'm ready to trust you more, Emmett. Now."

Emmett took her mouth in his and kissed her with a hunger ever so tender. Charlotte let go, let everything go so that she could come to Emmett with the same desire that she'd been denying for too long. They explored each other with only pleasure in mind until neither could wait any longer. He took her hand and they made their way to the daybed, where they delved into their honesty: his love, her revelation. It drew them together like the moon pulling in the high tide, each thirsting for something precious from the other. Emmett was gentle, Char relaxed. They fell into an easy rhythm as if they'd been intimate for years. He filled her with the deepest pleasure of true acceptance, and she knew she quenched his desire for the most intimate of truths.

Emmett wrapped her in his arms afterward. "I could stay like this with you forever. I never want to let you go. Happy birthday, Charlotte." He kissed the top of her head sweetly as he tenderly trailed his hand up and down her arm. She had a smile she couldn't subdue. For a moment, all her fears and worries had completely evaporated, and all she felt was love.

"Thank you, Emmett, for everything." She couldn't let him know the extent to which his steady support had helped her overcome so many obstacles. One day she would tell him, of that she was sure.

"Babe, I've forgotten—is it my birthday or yours, because I have to tell you it sure feels like mine. The trust you gave me today…" He tried to finish, but his voice hitched in emotion.

She smiled up at him and kissed him softly.

They relaxed together in a comfortable silence, each lost in their own hopeful thoughts until the attendant knocked on their door to let Charlotte know her makeup and hair appointment was coming up in fifteen minutes. It was yet another surprise Emmett had scheduled for her.

She didn't want to, but she had to get up, shower, and gather her things together for her next appointment, and when she came out of the shower, Emmett had one more surprise.

"Before you go, I want you to know, Charlotte, you're a true gift to me. And speaking of gift, I have one more surprise for you." He opened a pocket in his bag, brought out a small blue box, and put it in her hands.

Char's eyes lit up. "What is this? Why did you do this? You've already done so much. This is too much." She looked at him, confused.

"Babe, you're worth so much more than I'm giving you."

She opened her mouth to protest again, but he held his hand up, "Just open it."

She sat down and opened the box. Inside were three gold bangles. Each had three stones, peridot, aquamarine, and amethyst.

"Emmett." Charlotte was at a loss for words. "This is so sweet. It's my, Blake's, and Aubrie Elle's birthstones. This means so much to me. Thank you, Emmett, thank you," Char said as she stood and threw her arms around him.

"I knew that would be something you'd appreciate. So, have I so far made up for the earlier snafu?"

"Let's just forget that even happened, please," Char said with a flash of anguish before her eyes were bright with excitement again. "Yes, absolutely, I'm going to wear them right now."

"I want you to know, Charlotte, these bracelets represent what you mean to me, because the proof of how special you are lies in the two wonderful kids you've raised. The unconditional love you've given them is what you deserve too."

In that moment, Charlotte was overwhelmed with the love Emmett gave her. She wanted to give him something in return. She realized she could tell him one more truth, another step.

"Emmett, this birthday you've given me, it means more to me than you know. I have a surprise I wasn't planning on giving you until sometime in the future, but you deserve to know now after all you've done for me."

"Charlotte, you don't owe me anything in return. Today, baring yourself, being with me. God, I couldn't ask for more."

"But that's just it. Today, how strong I was, actually is because of the surprise I've been working on."

"I don't understand." Emmett searched her face.

"Emmett, meeting you and seeing this unconditional love you have waiting right here for me, mine for the taking, was too much for me to ignore. I wanted it. I wanted you. So my surprise is that for weeks now I've been going to intense therapy sessions to work through my demons. I don't want to hide anymore, especially not from you. I want to talk with you about everything. You've fought for me and convinced me I'm worth the fight. My surprise is I'm fighting for us."

Emmett shook his head in amazement. It took a moment to sink in, and then in a flash, Charlotte was in Emmett's arms being spun around the room. He called out a whoop, set her down, and planted kisses all over her face and head. She could see his eyes had watered, though he was beaming from ear to ear. She couldn't help but tear up too. They both laughed as Emmett brought her a tissue.

Char felt more and more confident that he'd been right all along, and it felt so good to throw fear overboard and just immerse herself in his love. Another knock came through the door. Charlotte was expected in the salon.

"Babe, let me get in the shower, and I'll see you at dinner. I'll take care of getting our bags sent up to our room. I invited Kat and Lou to come early, keep me company, and have a drink with me while you're getting ready. I'm so happy with all you've told me. Do you mind, honey, if I tell them what you've been working on?"

"You know I'm a private person, but yes, I'd love for them to know I'm fighting for us too. I want them to share in the celebration. I'll see you soon. I love you."

Once in the salon, the stylists went straight to work on Charlotte. Her hair was set in loose, beachy curls. Her strawberry blond hair looked much lighter after all her time in the sun, and the stylist made the most of her natural highlights.

The makeup artist played up her peaches-and-cream complexion but kept it natural; Charlotte loved that she still looked like herself, just enhanced. She put on her black strappy heels and a lace cap-sleeved dress in a beautiful sea-green hue that complemented her complexion beautifully. It hugged her in all the right places and fell just below the knee. She smiled in the mirror at how the dress fit her like a glove, and her wavy hair tumbled past her shoulders, while the large gold hoop earrings glinted here and there. She wasn't a conceited person by any means, but she had to admit she'd never felt more beautiful, and she knew in her heart it had to be because of Emmett's unconditional love. Even with all of their ups and downs, he was right by her side with patience and understanding.

By time she was ready to meet her party upstairs, Char was excited. Usually she would be self-conscious, but instead, she was floating on air. She marveled at her ability to focus on the positive and look forward to the night, despite the horrid trip down memory lane earlier. She shut that out and remembered with a blush the beautiful moment she and Emmett had shared in their suite earlier, and looked forward to part two later, when she would give him her last present, agreeing to move in with him.

Everyone was at her table. They all rose to greet her. She wasn't sure who, but someone called out, "Charlotte, you're absolutely glowing." She smiled at the table and was touched to see Emmett had invited Moe and Anna.

She got hugs and birthday wishes from everyone as Emmett stood watching intently from the other end of the table. When Moe wished her a happy birthday, she stopped Char from moving on. "Oh, Charlie, before I forget, I need to give you your gift."

"Moe, you didn't have to," Char whispered, embarrassed.

"Nonsense!" Moe said as she fussed around in her billowy caftan, which apparently had pockets, somewhere. "Ah, here it is," she said as she fished out a long gold necklace with a small gray crystal. "I'm so proud of you and all of your progress. Emmett tells me you finally told him about your therapy work—I'm so proud of you! You're doing so much on your own. You may not necessarily need this, but it can lighten your load, help you fight any fear, and bring clarity to any situation you find yourself in. That kind of help never hurts anyone, now does it? May I?" Char nodded, and Moe put it over Char's head and gave her a peck on the cheek as she patted her shoulders.

It wasn't the right moment, but Char couldn't wait to tell Moe that her therapy was working, that she'd never felt so strong and alive. "Thank you, Moe, really," Charlotte said. She was touched by Moe's gesture. Moe patted her hand and took her seat.

Char greeted the boys and girls and finally made her way to

Emmett, who looked to be enjoying watching her genuine excitement.

She stopped for a moment just to take him in. He wore a soft coral button-up. His strong chest, kissed by the sun, was barely visible, but enough to jump-start her heart. His broad, strong shoulders always seemed to beckon her. She craved feeling his strong, safe arms around her.

Emmett came to her and put his arms around her. How had he known? He bent down and whispered happy birthday. The sensation of his breath on her ear sent a shiver down her spine.

He held her chair out, and a server came with a lemon drop for her. Emmett told her he had seen to it ahead of time, and she thanked him for his thoughtfulness.

Their server came and took the table's orders, and after he left, Emmett got everyone's attention. "I'd like to make a toast to our guest of honor, Charlotte." He looked at her. "You have a full table here of people who think the world of you. The beauty is that some of us have only just begun to get to know you, but we're here, and we're not going anywhere. That's a testament to your character. You're a wonderful woman, a gentle soul who has done a fine job of raising two amazing kids," he said, looking at Aubrie and Blake, "which is also a testament to you as a person. I only hope that your birthday today has been even half as special as you are to all of us. To Charlotte: happy birthday," Emmett said, beaming at Charlotte.

Char was embarrassed but knew someday she'd be all that Emmett thought she was. She smiled at everyone and thanked them as they toasted to her special day. Charlotte felt a humble gratitude as she took in the large table of truly wonderful people there to help celebrate her day.

Their meal was served, and the table was full of laughing and raucous chatter. Moe hit it off with Anna; they were talking nonstop.

Blake, Noa, and Kai got along well, and the girls seemed to be in deep conversation with Kat most of the night.

Dinner was over, and the party beginning to wind down at the table, and Blake let his mom know he had to step away to make a call for a cab. Her heart sunk a bit as she thought of him leaving, but she was so happy to have had her unexpected time with him. When Blake got up, Aubrie scooted over to his chair and put her hand on her mom's arm. "Don't worry, Mom. Thanksgiving break isn't that long to wait, and then we'll we see Blakey again," Aubrie said.

"You're right, honey, the time will fly by," Char said with an appreciative smile. Everyone at the table began gathering their jackets and purses, saying their good-byes.

Char stood as well and waited for Aubrie to do the same, but she sat, seemingly frozen, her face ashen. "Aubrie, what's wrong? You look like you've seen a ghost."

Instead of answering her, Aubrie shot up out of her seat and grabbed Char's arm with both hands in a protective grip and glared straight ahead. Her face had initially gone pale, but now Charlotte could see her cheeks burning crimson. She was angry.

Charlotte followed Aubrie's glare only to have the floor fall out from under her with dizzying force.

There was Julian Donatello Ashbourne III—Ash, as she'd always called him—being shown to a table just across from them. Despite her mind blazing into frenetic chaos, Charlotte managed to pray he'd sit down and not see her, with a hope that by then she could muster enough strength to flee. So far Charlotte could only stand there. She realized that some in his group were the very same security detail that had worked for Julian that fateful night when they saved her. Jameson, Ash's right-hand, noticed her first, giving her a quick nod of acknowledgement. To her dread, he turned to whisper something into Ash's ear. Time seemed to stand still in that moment. With a cool demeanor that didn't betray any emotion, Ash's eyes met hers, knocking the wind right out of her.

His all-too-familiar British accent poured through her ears like smooth butterscotch, and her heart ached. "Charlotte, my, it's been a while, has it not? I wouldn't figure any chance of seeing you here, of all places. It appears you're having a fine time, and I wouldn't want to interrupt your evening, except to say happy birthday."

Char felt Emmett stiffen next to her. Aubrie whispered something into Char's ear, but she hadn't a clue what she said. Char managed a feeble, "Thank you" to Ash. Aubrie gasped and ran off in a huff, with Chloe and the boys at her heels.

When she finally had the presence to unlock her gaze from Ash, Charlotte realized she was holding onto her clutch for dear life; her knuckles had grown white with tension.

She gathered the courage to look around, and saw Emmett looked ready to pounce on Julian, but she could only stand there, still paralyzed. She wasn't the only one; everyone around her had stopped in their tracks to watch, the tension in the air unmistakable. She saw Katena was just as transfixed and, like Emmett, was shooting an icy glare toward Ash.

Charlotte knew Ash hadn't noticed, because when she looked back at him, their eyes locked once again, and she knew in her heart his had stayed fixed on her and her only.

This had all happened in the blink of an eye, but before the brief silence became awkward, Blake came back and unknowingly broke the tension, though it also served to prolong Char's agony.

"Julian! No way, are you here for Mom's birthday?" Blake said as he walked up and threw his arms around Julian, who returned in kind with a fatherly hug. Char willed herself to keep it together.

"Blake, my dear boy, how are you? No, no, I actually had no idea your family was here visiting," Julian said pleasantly but stiffly, his eyes scanning Charlotte's party, blinking with each calculation. No one could tell except Charlotte that Julian was just as uncomfortable as she was. He was a trained spy, a master at self-control.

"Yeah, well, didn't you hear? Aubrie was accepted at Pepperdine, and she and Mom have moved down here. Emmett's been showing her around the area," he said, innocently pointing toward Emmett.

Julian cooly refused to look Emmett's way. "No, I didn't hear. Tell your sister congratulations." Char noticed he didn't make eye contact with Emmett.

"How's business? You making sure all the millionaire-billionaires and their assets are safe and sound?"

"That I am, Blake. As well as protecting my own," he said smugly, clearly for Emmett's benefit. "Thank you for asking. And your film school? Last we spoke, you'd just been approved for an internship, were you not?"

"That's right; in fact, I'm on location now. I've just taken a few days to come celebrate Mom's birthday. But I'm going back up tonight, and soon I'll be directing a feature film of my own," Blake said, expanding his chest.

"Good for you, Blake. That I do not doubt. It's too bad you're returning tonight. I'd have loved to catch up with you more, but listen, I must get back to my dinner guests. However, I do have business this winter in New York. Let's make plans to hit the slopes again, shall we?"

Blake agreed, and they shook hands before Ash turned to Charlotte again. "Charlotte, you look well." He gave her a surreptitious once-over that wasn't lost on Charlotte; she could feel the heat of his gaze, to her utter chagrin. "A pleasure, as always," he said stiffly and turned his back on her again, leaving her cold.

Charlotte couldn't believe her ears. It wounded and worried her to hear that Blake and Ash had stayed in contact. She swallowed some air and turned to Blake. She grabbed his arm and pulled him away. She threw hurried good-byes to the group and mumbled something about wanting to find Aubrie so the kids could see Blake off. Like Ash, she wouldn't look at Emmett. She knew her eyes would betray her.

When Char saw Aubrie, Chloe, and the boys huddled outside the bathrooms, the boys turned to stare. Char realized God only knew what Aubrie had or hadn't filled them in on, or what Aubrie might say to her in front of everyone, so she didn't dare approach. Instead, she went around the corner to ask the hostess to call her a cab and have her bag sent down from their room; foreboding was in the air, and she knew to trust her gut and plan her escape.

Turning around, she saw Emmett making his way toward her, looking determined to get some answers. She shrunk inside, but thankfully Noa and Kai intercepted him to say they were going to head out with the girls, who'd just gone up to make their tearful good-byes to Blake. Aubrie still hadn't so much as looked Charlotte's way.

Emmett nearly had a moment to start his inquiry, but mercifully it was Blake's turn to interrupt Emmett. "It's time for me to head out. Do you guys want to walk down to my taxi with me?"

Charlotte hung her head for a moment, sad to have to say good-bye. "Of course we'll walk you down, honey." She reached for Blake's hand and gripped it for dear life.

Blake gave her a knowing look. He whispered into her ear, "You'll be okay, Mom. Sorry, that must have been awkward earlier." He was referring to her seeing Ash, and it was the understatement of the century, but she couldn't begrudge him for his ignorance since it was of her own creation.

"It was, but you're right, Blake, I'll be fine." Charlotte wanted to believe that more than anything, but she felt as if she were walking the plank. She knew that once Blake left, Emmett would have her all to himself. She felt further dread with each step she took, but she tried to stay focused on her son.

They stepped out to the portico into a gust of warm August wind to find Blake's taxi already waiting. Charlotte and Blake hugged, and she cried a little. Blake's eyes seemed watery too. Emmett grabbed Blake's oversized duffel and helped load it. Blake thanked Emmett again for bringing him out as he shook his hand and got into the cab. He rolled down the window and said to his mom, "I love you, Mom. I'll see you soon. Don't worry about Aubrie. I don't understand what her deal is, but she'll get over it. She always does," and then the cab pulled away.

Charlotte wished she were in the cab with him. *Now what?* She was supposed to go back to their hotel room with Emmett, but she knew better than to back herself into a corner for an all-night interrogation. Emmett had sworn to be patient, but she knew without a doubt that after the awkward interaction with Ash, another man, he wouldn't be so patient anymore. He'd want answers she wasn't yet prepared to give. She didn't know how to start a conversation when the crux of it would be an admission to lying to him since the day they'd met.

"Come on, babe. Let's go check out our room." He was playing it cool, but Charlotte knew Emmett couldn't wait to get her up in their room to start the cross-examination. He put his arm around her and took a step forward, but Char stayed planted.

"Emmett, I can't," was all she could blurt out.

Emmett didn't blink, as if he'd expected her reaction. He stepped in front of her. "And why is that?" His voice was low, and it sent a shiver down Charlotte's spine.

"I just, you know it's been a long day, and I think it's caught up to me. Saying good-bye to Blake is weighing on me, and I think I just need to go home. I'm sorry, but with what little energy I have left, I know I won't be much fun tonight after all."

"I'm not trying to disrespect your feelings for your son, but are you sure this doesn't have something to do with that guy?"

"What guy?" Charlotte asked as innocently as possible, but the look on Emmett's face told her she'd just blown it. *Wrong approach, Char.*

"What *guy*? Is that how you're going to play this? Don't BS me here, Charlotte. What is he to you?"

He stood with his arms crossed, staring down at her. Char glanced around the portico and hoped they weren't causing a scene, before turning back to Emmett. He jutted his head forward and shrugged as if to say, "I'm waiting."

Grasping for an explanation that wasn't entirely a lie, she came up with "He's an old friend of Beau's. He came to the United States to expand his business, and when Beau died, our firm was handling his merger with another company. That's all."

"Really." His tone dripped of sarcasm, clearly not believing her.

She folded her arms. "Yes, really, Emmett. Listen, I told you I'm not feeling well, yet you're sitting here with this interrogation you want to conduct, and I want to go home."

"Actually, you didn't tell me you were feeling sick, you said you were tired. So which is it? Are you sick or are you tired?" he said, completely unapologetic. Charlotte had never heard him so acerbic.

Knowing there was no right answer and not wanting to provoke him, she stormed off and made her way to the valet counter to ask about her taxi and retrieve her luggage.

Emmett stayed at her heel and waited until she'd finished with the valet. "You're making a big mistake running away this time, Charlotte."

"Is that an ultimatum?" Char turned to him, her eyes blazing. She tried to show strength, but inside she was scared to death.

"Double-oh-seven and you just had a moment up there in front of the whole table, while I stood by, invisible, and you have the nerve not to give me one iota of an explanation?" Emmett's voice rose, causing people to look over.

Charlotte looked around, embarrassed by the scene they were making. "Emmett, shhhh,"

"Babe, you're not going to shush me. I deserve some answers."

Char felt her head swim and feared she might pass out from the stress.

"Ma'am, your taxi's here—right this way," the valet said as he approached timidly. He motioned to the cab, clearly hoping to usher them out before their argument escalated.

As soon as Char made for the taxi, Emmett changed tack. "Wait, Char, you don't have to take a taxi. I can take you home," he pleaded, softening his tone.

"No, thank you. I need some air." She kept her tone brusque, but inside was relieved to see his anger abate.

He followed her to the cab. "Can I still come over tomorrow? I'm supposed to deliver your birthday present from the kids."

Just that little request brought Char back to the present and reminded her how much she loved this man and how much he loved her. She acquiesced.

She got into the cab, and the valet loaded her bag into the trunk. "Of course. I'm sorry. I don't mean to have the night end on a sour note. You went above and beyond to make my birthday special. We can talk tomorrow, I promise. I have to come back into town to meet Jonathan in the afternoon, but I'm free before and after."

"Thank you. I'll be there around noon. Remember, I do love you, unconditionally." He shut the door and reluctantly watched the taxi pull away.

As soon as the cab dropped her home, Charlotte just wanted to get inside and pass out on her bed, but Moe caught her before she could even get the key into her lock.

"Dear, are you okay? Oh my, everyone's chakras were in overdrive at your dinner. That man, he's at the crux of your emotional blockage, isn't he? Oh, Charlie, if he's back in town, we need to up your sessions, double them to four a week. I don't want to sound like an alarmist, but, dear, it's gravely important. You can't keep hiding now. You've got to face this down and reclaim your life."

Char's head dropped, and she wept. "I know, I know. I don't know what to do, Moe. I'm so at a loss. I felt like dying right there when I saw him. I don't know how I made it through."

"You're stronger than you think, Charlie, remember that. The strength to deal with all of this is inside you. It's there. Give yourself some credit. You kept your strength up the whole time when you two came face-to-face. I was so proud. But I must say, that man, I know he hurt you deeply, but I have to tell you something, and I hope it helps rather than hurts you, but the chakras? You know what I saw in his? Love for you. He was frightened when he saw you, but he also was brimming with love."

Char broke down even harder, the pain in her chest almost unbearable. Moe stayed at her side. "There, there, let it out; let it out. Let me help you upstairs to your room."

Asa followed them upstairs to Char's room and pawed at the bed. When Moe brought him up, he curled next to Charlotte, licking away her tears. "Charlie, could we do a short session? It could really be of benefit right now."

"I just can't, Moe. Thanks for being here for me, but I need to be alone."

Moe looked at her with concern, but didn't argue. "Okay, Charlie. Call me if you need anything at all."

Charlotte curled into a ball with Asa, and the tears came in a never-ending stream. She slept very little. The ramifications of seeing Julian were infinite. She tried in vain throughout the night to push out all the swirling worries, the most immediate of which was the conversation she'd have to have with Emmett later. She still wasn't sure what she would tell him. She couldn't tell him everything but had to figure out a way to placate him until she could get her footing. Charlotte felt as if she were trying to tread water with weights on her ankles. She could only pray she'd be strong enough to make it through.

In the morning she checked her phone. It was late morning and there were no messages from Emmett. She wondered if he still planned on coming over later. Maybe he'd changed his mind after last night. She couldn't think about it; she was in desperate need of caffeine. She had to will herself to get out of bed, not because of sleep deprivation, but because of the strong pull of avoidance. She knew as soon as the day started, she'd have to face what was coming. Whatever it was, she knew it wasn't good.

She got herself out of bed and padded down to the kitchen to start the coffee. Aubrie and Chloe were at the dinette, still looking sleepy. Char had heard them come home well after midnight.

Chloe said good morning to her, but Aubrie didn't say a word and instead gave a pouty grimace, grabbed her bowl of cereal, and went out to the deck. Looking uncomfortable, Chloe followed.

Charlotte didn't have the mental energy to deal with Aubrie and decided against having her morning coffee at home. She needed to get away. She went back to her room, showered and got dressed for the day. Because she was feeling so meek and timid, she knew she needed to dress the opposite to have any hope of being successful in her client negotiations later and, more importantly, when she would have to come face-to-face with Emmett. So she put on an off-white jumper with a gold belt, strappy gold heels, and a navy blazer. Looking good but feeling awful, she grabbed her purse and went downstairs.

She called to the girls that she was leaving and would be back later, then headed out the door. She was looking forward to the coffee with the hope that it would clear her head and give her some strength.

Julian sat in stunned silence, his eyes bloodshot and his head pounding from working through the night with his team. "I want assurances from all of you that you're on board with this plan. If any of you aren't comfortable with the risks, I won't hold it against you if you want out."

Jameson looked around the office in Julian's presidential suite, getting a nod from the other men on the team before saying, "Boss, we've been in this since the beginning, and we're going to see it through to the end, whatever you decide to do."

Julian sucked in a breath of relief. "So be it. Jameson, Turk, you come with me. The rest of you stand by. It shouldn't take long at Charlotte's, but time is not on our side, so let's get a move on."

Their driver was ready at the portico, and in no time they were at Charlotte's complex, the location of which wasn't hard to uncover, and simple gate codes were no obstacle in their line of work.

Julian nodded to his men as they went to the back side of the condo. He hoped for the best but worked to keep his composure as he rang the doorbell. He thought he heard footsteps come down a set of stairs, then a "What the hell?" come through the door. His hackles went up. It wasn't Charlotte; it was Aubrie Elle.

He shoved his hands into his pockets, leaned his head toward the door, and willed himself to sound genial. "Aubrie, please, it's important. I need to speak to your mother. She's here, is she not?"

"Why the hell would I tell you?"

Julian looked up in exasperation before clamping down on his bottom lip. "Aubrie, please. I know I'm not your favorite person, but I'm here out of concern for your mother. I need to speak with her. Is she here?"

The door flew open and Aubrie got right into Julian's face. "Concern? Where was your concern after mom's quote-unquote *accident*?"

Julian's stomach dropped as Aubrie brought up the most brutal night of his entire life. He couldn't allow himself to revisit his regrets and instead let some of his anger, of which there was plenty to go around, take over. Julian raised his hand to jab a finger toward Aubrie, and as he took a step toward her, he was suddenly rushed from the side and slammed against the wall. Julian was stunned, but quickly refocused. He recognized his attacker as the man who had been with Charlotte the night before. Emmett, if he remembered correctly.

"Why don't you back up there, buddy?" Emmett said through gritted teeth; he kept a firm grip on Julian's suit jacket, with his forearm pinning him against the wall. They were nose-to-nose, eyes narrowed at each other. Julian saw nothing but red. He knew he needed to check his emotions. They would serve no purpose but to weaken him at the moment.

Before he could work a leg sweep and subdue Emmett, both Jameson and Turk were back and yanked Emmett off Julian, their hands like vise grips on his arms.

Aubrie was having none of that and lunged at Jameson and Turk, flailing at their backs. She knew them well, and despite their size and what they did for a living, they didn't seem to scare Aubrie one bit. "Let him go, Jameson. Turk, get your hands off him!"

"Gentlemen, it's all right. He was defending Aubrie." When they still held tight to Emmett, Julian had to say, "Release him." They obeyed Julian's command, and he smoothed down his jacket from Emmett's attack. Jameson and Turk stepped back, and Jameson snorted a small laugh at Aubrie. She'd always amused him, and they used to get along great, but with Julian nearby, she continued to glare.

"What the hell is going on, and what are you doing here?" Emmett asked, breathing hard but looking ready to pounce again.

Since he felt no compulsion to answer him, at least not in a timely fashion, Julian took a moment to study Emmett. He hated to admit, but the guy was damned good-looking and about the same height as him but, bloody hell, quite a bit bulkier. He also liked the look in Emmett's eyes; he saw fierce protectiveness, which he knew all too intimately would serve Charlotte well.

Aubrie, with her arms crossed and shooting a fevered stare at Julian, answered Emmett, breaking Julian from his thoughts. "I was just asking this creep to please get out of here and leave my mom alone. He's done enough damage."

Julian finally answered. "Listen, I mean no harm. That's God's honest truth. But as I was trying to explain to Aubrie, which is quite hard, what with her histrionics and such, it's imperative that I speak to Charlotte immediately. Please, if you could set aside your American-Neanderthal impulses and give her my card, it would be greatly appreciated. Where is she right now, by the way?"

Aubrie laughed. "Like we're going to tell you of all people."

Julian sighed. "Please, you must let her know I have to speak with her," he said as he looked back and forth between Emmett and Aubrie, neither of whom looked welcoming or trusting.

"I think you need to leave. You're upsetting Aubrie," Emmett said as he begrudgingly took Julian's business card and read it. He looked up at him. "Julian."

Julian could tell Emmett was learning his name right then and there. Good girl: proof that Charlotte had never discussed him with Emmett.

"I'll let Charlotte know you *and* the men you bring to do your fighting for you stopped by," Emmett said, holding Julian's stare, clearly still trying to get a read on who he was.

Once Aubrie saw that Julian was really leaving, she shut the door.

Seeing again the protectiveness Emmett felt for Charlotte and her daughter, Julian softened a bit. "I thank you. Please do; it's imperative that I speak to her. Please let her know I'm staying at the Ritz, downtown, in penthouse one."

Emmett nodded and then went inside Charlotte's condo, though not before he glanced over his shoulder, looking reluctant to leave Julian standing there at her entryway.

When Emmett shut the door, a woman a couple of doors down came out of her condo. She looked quizzically at Julian, maybe because he was still standing at Charlotte's door.

"Can I help you, young man? You look lost," the woman with bright eyes and white, messy hair asked. Never one to forget a face, Julian knew she'd been at Charlotte's dinner the night before.

The lady was right. He'd never felt more lost in his life. His world was turning more upside down than he thought possible. He pulled out another business card and handed it to her. "I was here to see Charlotte, but she appears to be out. If you could give her this and let her know I desperately need to speak with her, I would be forever in your debt. You don't happen to know where she is at the moment, do you?"

The woman gave him a sympathetic and seemingly knowing smile. Had Charlotte actually spoken to her about him? His head spun at the thought. "I'm sorry, I don't know where she is, though I think the two of you having a chat would be a wonderful idea. I'll be sure to give this to her, Ash."

Good God, she knew the nickname Charlotte had given him. She had talked about him to a stranger. How much did this woman know? To his relief, he deduced not much, since she was smiling at him instead of glaring like she certainly would be had she known everything.

...

As Charlotte sat under the bright canopy on the coffee shop's back patio, she began to think her head was as clear as it was going to get, though she felt no more prepared for talking with Emmett than when she'd first gotten up. She checked the clock and found she shouldn't waste any more time lost in thought if she wanted to get to her meeting with time to spare.

As she grabbed her purse, she shuddered. Why hadn't she brought her briefcase with her too? Her plan was to avoid Emmett until after her meeting downtown. Now she had to go home and risk seeing him.

She had to wonder, though, if subconsciously she'd done it on purpose. As scared as she was to have it out with him, she loved him and hoped against hope that she'd be able to fix their relationship without revealing anything about Ash. If he kept his promise to come set up her birthday present, he'd likely be there.

With hope and trepidation, she headed back home.

"Are we online now? Did you get it done?"

"We should be able to pick up all audio throughout the condo, even on the deck."

"Damn it, what are you waiting for? Flip the switch. Turn the damn thing up; I don't want to miss a word."

Emmett's voice came through the speaker. "Aubrie, are you all right? They didn't hurt you, did they?"

"No, no, they didn't. I hate that guy, I hate him, I hate him. My mom is such an idiot. Why didn't she tell him off when she had the chance last night at dinner?" Aubrie sobbed.

"Why? What's Julian done? Who is he to your mom?"

Silence.

"I can't say anything."

"I think you need to, Aubrie. I don't want to betray your mom's trust, but this situation seems to be getting out of control, and I want to help put a stop to it. And you seem to be carrying other people's burdens. That's not fair to you. Why is your mom an idiot?"

"She's an idiot because she was in love—no, infatuated—with that man. She loved him more than Blake and me. I had to practically raise myself after Beau died. She became so wrapped up in Ash that I was all but invisible. You felt that way, too, at the table last night, didn't you? It's what happens when they're in the same room. No one else matters to the two of them."

More silence.

"At least Blake got to go away to college. That's why he and Julian are buddies. Blake had no clue what was really going on, and afterward, he believed Mom's version of events and not mine."

"None of this makes sense; your mom said she hadn't dated anyone since Beau died."

Aubrie laughed. "Oh, that's rich. The truth is, she started her affair with him *before* Beau died. That's right. My mom, the adulteress."

"Aubrie, are you sure?"

"Mom and Beau were fighting tons just before he died. He was spending more and more time away from home, and Julian had come to town, and he and Mom were glued at the hip. It was obvious."

"So, the damage Julian is responsible for is that he broke your mom and Beau apart?"

"Oh no, that was just the beginning. I mean, to be honest, at first I thought he was pretty cool. But after Beau died and they got together, I saw things I didn't like. He was controlling and obviously abusive to Mom, a total asshole, but she would never leave him. Well, that is, not until he beat her almost to her death, and then *he* left *her*."

"He…what?"

"Yes, Emmett. He beat her, badly. Mom was devastated afterward and didn't leave the house for months and months. But she still wanted him back even after that. I could hear her leaving these pathetic and desperate messages for him. It was sick. I'm sorry, Emmett. My mom has some real issues, and one of them is her infatuation with that freak. I thought maybe she really was over him until I saw her reaction to him last night. I'm sorry to drop this bomb on you, Emmett."

"No, don't be. You needed to get this off your chest. And I needed to know."

Aubrie suddenly sounded overly bright. "Oh, hey, Chloe."

"Hi, guys. Am I interrupting something?"

Emmett said, "Hi, Chloe. Aubrie and I just had a pretty serious talk, and now I need to wait here to talk with Charlotte. Alone."

"And that's our cue to leave. Don't worry—I don't want to be here anyway. Emmett, I'm sorry. I'm sorry I had to tell you. But I do love my mom; please don't be too angry with her. I don't know for sure what that guy's hold on her is all about, but I know she loves you too, Emmett. A lot. I think she's just confused."

"I love your Mom too, don't worry. I'm not like some of the men in her past. Your mom is always safe with me."

"I know, Emmett. Thank you."

The front door shut; then the sound of pacing started, along with several huffs. Then came the crash of glass shattering into a million pieces.

"Temper, temper, Emmett. I hope that wasn't something expensive."

"Boss, are we ready for the next phase?"

"Before we make another move, let's throw the guy a bone and let Charlotte and Emmett have one last tête-à-tête for old time's sake, shall we?"

As Charlotte came through the front door and made her way upstairs, she noticed the girls hadn't opened all the drapes yet, and the lights were off. It was nearing one o'clock, and it was usually much brighter, but there was just enough light coming through the drapes that she noticed strange sparkles all over the floor. It wasn't until she took a step into the room that she realized it was shattered glass.

Scanning the room for an explanation, she caught her breath and stepped back when she saw Emmett's silhouette at the dinette. He was sitting motionless in the chair, glowering at her, one arm outstretched on the table.

"I didn't see you there—you scared me. What happened here?" she asked, looking at the glass. She felt the hairs on the back of her neck stand up.

"You had a visitor earlier."

"I did? Who?" Charlotte flushed. Deep down, she knew.

"Julian," he said, slamming his arm onto the table.

Charlotte jumped, and her stomach dropped. Questions quickly ran through her head: What did Ash want? Why had he come? What did it all mean? She had a sick realization that they must have come face-to-face. Emmett was obviously angry. As far as she knew, anything could have happened.

"What? Why? I don't understand," she said, not sure if she really wanted to know.

Emmett stood and made his way toward her, glass crunching under his feet. "You know, the man you didn't introduce me to last night at dinner, the one who sent Aubrie running from the table." Emmett's voice tightened. "The one you had an affair with while you were still married, the one who beat you 'til you nearly died, then deserted you, leaving you still wanting him, wanting more?" Emmett was in her face at that point and grabbed her arm. He paused, lowering his voice, and said through clenched teeth, "Does. That. Ring. A bell?"

His eyes were brimming with tears, but Charlotte couldn't see anything past his outward anger; she felt her knees almost buckle under her. She had thought Emmett was angry last night, and that had unnerved her, but today was much worse. She didn't understand why he was making such disgusting accusations. She had to get out of there. She jerked her arm out of his grasp and marched to the stairs.

"There you go, hightailing it out of here when the truth gets to be too much. If I mean anything to you at all, you'll stay here and give me an explanation, Charlotte."

Charlotte couldn't respond. She could only think of leaving. She grabbed the banister, but paused when she heard his voice again. "Charlotte, you walk out that door, and we're over. I mean it."

She couldn't stay, and she knew when the front door shut, so would Emmett's heart.

Charlotte was neither physically nor mentally ready to come clean. If Ash had never come to LA, she could have taken her time, everything would have been fine, and none of this would have happened. She was angry and sad—another relationship stolen. Tears escaped left and right as she made her way to her car.

Moe was coming out of her car and stopped Charlotte. "Dear, that man from last night, Ash. He was at your condo this morning."

"Moe, I know. I'm sorry. I can't talk right now."

"Wait, he talked to me for a moment and insisted I give you his card. Here, I promised him I'd give it to you," Moe said, frantically fishing out Ash's card and handing it to her as if it were of the utmost importance.

Char grabbed it and shoved it into her purse and unlocked her door.

Moe held her finger up to say something, but Charlotte ignored her and jumped into her car.

Tears streamed down her face as she made her way out of the security gate to the main road. She barely paid attention to her driving as she tried in vain to make sense of what was going on. She knew Ash would never say anything to Emmett about the two of them. He'd always said rule number one was never reveal more truth that you needed to. It must have been Aubrie. She had accused Char of as much over the past year. Poor Aubrie; Char wished she could tell her the truth, but it was too dangerous.

She turned on her blinker to make a turn, and her navigation system unexpectedly came on with its familiar *ding, ding, ding.*

"I wouldn't make that turn if were you."

Only it didn't sound like her navigation system. It was coming through the speakers, but clearly it was an actual person. Had someone hacked into her car? The last thing she needed to be dealing with was some prankster.

"What? Who is this? Whatever kind of game you're playing, it isn't funny." She pulled over to a side street so she could figure out what was going on. She thought the man's voice was eerily familiar, but she couldn't place it.

"Oh, it's no game, Charlotte. This is all quite serious. Now listen to me carefully: do exactly what I say, and be sure not to make any sudden moves. Your very life depends on it. You see, Charlotte, there's a bomb strapped securely to your vehicle."

Charlotte unlocked her seatbelt and frantically went for the door, but the unlock button had malfunctioned. The voice overhead spoke again, chilling her to stillness.

"Ah, ah, ah, Charlotte, you make any move to get out of the car, and I'll detonate the bomb. You'll be blown to smithereens. But do as I instruct, and not a hair on your strawberry blond head will be hurt."

Charlotte sat there in a daze, having gone numb from head to foot. She looked up desperately at her emergency response button but knew better than to test his threat. As if he could read her thoughts, he told her, gloating, that her phone, car locks, GPS, and emergency services had all been rendered useless. She was all his.

"Who is this? What do you want?" Her mouth had gone completely dry. She was surprised she could even speak.

"Charlotte, I'm offended. Don't you remember me? It's Mr. Wolfe. Carl Wolfe."

A jolt of fear shot from her head to her feet. This couldn't be happening; he should be long dead, retribution courtesy of Ash's security detail. She had heard Ash give the very order, having said it was the least Carl deserved after abducting Char and viciously torturing her until Julian and his men tracked them down.

"You, you're supposed to be…" She couldn't finish.

Carl's sinister laughter filled her car. "Sunk at the bottom of a river, never to be seen again?" He laughed more. "No, no, darling. I'm a wolf. Wolves don't die; they attack again and again. And you see, you, Julian, and—no, wait, what was your pet name for him? Ash, was it? You, Ash, and I have unfinished business. So, here's what you're going to do. You're going to put that car into drive, and you're going to follow every direction I give you to a *T*. If you don't, that car bomb will be deployed before you can say, 'horse stable,' got it?"

Charlotte just sat there. Her mind swirled with a myriad of

thoughts and emotions. How was he not dead? Someone from within Ash's own detail must have been paid off by Carl to help him pull it all off. Her body shuddered as she took in the gravity of her situation.

Carl screamed his order. "I said put the fucking car in drive!"

Charlotte jumped. She started the car and followed Carl's commands. She felt as if she weren't even in her own body. She had no idea how she was driving the car, let alone following his directions.

"Sorry for the outburst. It's just there's so much to do in so little time. You see, the more quickly you get here, the sooner Julian will be here. Then we can get down to business. I don't want to give away the surprise, but you do have a bit of a drive ahead of you. Why don't I keep you company?"

Charlotte wanted to tell him to stick it, but, for one, she couldn't because of the burning lump in her throat, and for another, she knew better than to provoke him.

"Charlotte, I must extend my apologies. I have to take full responsibility for breaking the two of you up. You were quite the pair, weren't you? Heads turned whenever you walked into a room together. The sexual tension between you two was nearly palpable. You couldn't keep your eyes off each other; to be honest, it was nauseating. Oh, but I digress; my point is to apologize. I just want to say I'm sorry I took it a little too far that night with you cross-tied in the stable. Your Ash had much better restraint. He liked the control, and you sure wanted to give it to him, didn't you? But the whole thing was so confounding. How is it that with you so willingly shackled, he never so much as took even a small crop to you? And really, where's the fun in that? But when I saw that whip hanging on the wall, what can I say? When I go for it, I go all the way. Oh, where are my manners? I'm sorry to bring that awful night up—it must be a sore subject for you." Raucous laughter filled the car, and Charlotte went green with repulsion from the memories, from him.

His macabre jokes aside, Charlotte knew he was dead serious about having unfinished business with her and Ash, and here he was back from the dead for round two. Carl had been one of the top executives in Beau's firm, a trusted friend and business partner. About a year after Beau died, Carl had snapped in a jealous rage and abducted Charlotte, which had been easy to do. They were friends, or so she thought. She'd willingly gone with him in his limo. But soon she had realized that getting into the car with him was a big mistake. He was drunk and angry about things she was completely caught off guard by. Carl took her to Julian's stable, where Charlotte and Julian had enjoyed many days riding together, and as many evenings locked in heated passion. Carl had equal hate for the two of them and had explained he felt the stable was the perfect locale to exact his revenge.

His sick laughter came over the car speakers again. "Did you enjoy your field trip to the horse stable on your birthday? And the surprise later, at dinner? If I could have, I'd have loved to have had Ash jump out of a birthday cake for you. Nevertheless, it was still an amazing shock, wasn't it? And your new lover sure got an eyeful, now didn't he?"

"How do you know about that?" Charlotte demanded, though a wave of nausea washed over her before he even answered. She knew. That sick bastard had been spying on her, and Ash had obviously been his pawn too. Bile came into her throat at the thought as she realized he'd orchestrated the whole thing, playing all of them just to watch her squirm.

"Your Ash isn't the only one with expert stalking skills."

"Ash has never stalked anyone. His whole career has been helping people." Charlotte couldn't believe she was defending him. But Carl agreed.

"How ironic. You, defending Julian. After all he's done to you? How much help was he to you after our little dalliance? And, honey, he's been stalking you for the last year, except for the last several weeks. So you can knock him off that high horse you put him on. Julian's no better than I am, and you know it. You just haven't admitted it to yourself. I'll leave you to stew on that. Keep driving. Don't forget, one wrong move and kaboom."

The car went silent, and Charlotte was left with a knot of information to unravel. Ash had been keeping a detail on her? Why? Why would he care? And Carl—if he had gotten her in his clutches, what on God's earth did he have planned for Ash? She had no answers.

Charlotte squeezed her eyes shut for just a moment as she gripped the steering wheel and then tried to focus on the road and the cars in front of her. There wasn't much more she could do. The silence in the car dragged on, and Charlotte felt it wasn't a good sign. She wondered how long she'd have to drive and where she was being directed.

Eventually Carl came over the speakers again to give her further instructions. He directed her to I-15 north and told her he and his associates would be monitoring her. He warned again against making any sudden movements.

Charlotte compelled herself to think. *Is there any way out of this?* She decided she'd try to negotiate with him. "Carl, let's talk this out. What can I do for you? You don't have to do this."

"Charlotte, I do. I really, really do." The way Carl drew out his words made her skin crawl.

"Listen, I have money. Julian has money. How much do you want? All you have to do is name your price."

He laughed at her, which told her that was not what he was interested in. "Charlotte, didn't you learn anything from our first go-around? Think, Charlotte. You have a law degree; you can't be that dense."

It wasn't money he wanted. They'd bruised his ego; he had felt slighted. Only a psychopath would take his hurt feelings to that level. No, money wouldn't help her out of this, but what could she do?

She checked the time and couldn't believe she'd been on the road for several hours already. She thought she'd try to appeal to his ego instead. "You're right, Carl. I forgot. You're a much more principled man than someone who can just be paid off. We slighted you, and I'm sorry."

"Slighted? Slighted? What you two did to me was far worse than a mere slight," he said, nearly screaming, his anger vibrating throughout the car.

Char cringed, realizing that was the wrong word to use with a psychopath. "No, no, you're right, you're right. We completely disregarded your intelligence. I'm sorry, Carl. We got caught up in our own egos and couldn't see straight. We messed up, big time."

"You were caught up, all right—in the sheets. You're a little vixen, Charlotte. Oh, who am I kidding? 'Vixen' is too kind a word. You were quite the whore, actually. So, I can't say I blame Julian entirely. Women using their feminine wiles to get men to do their bidding—it's a tale as old as time, now, isn't it?"

Charlotte didn't understand what Carl could possibly think she needed to manipulate Ash for. Beau's consulting firm was set to make millions on the deal, regardless of which company was chosen. It made no sense. She appeased Carl anyway.

"You're right, I completely manipulated him, and I did you wrong, horribly wrong. What can I do to make it up to you? How can we spare each other any more grief?"

"Well, that's why the first round I chose you for the brunt of the punishment, but in a way that would bring Ash to his knees as well. For whatever reason, he had actual feelings for you. But I digress. He ordered my execution. It's too bad they didn't use a silver bullet, isn't it? Never underestimate the cunning of the Wolfe—that was your Ash's fatal mistake. But I realized there are so many advantages to being dead. Everyone's guard is down when they think you're a ghost. I've plotted long and hard for my revenge on him. He's already suffered much. He's taken quite a hit to his business this past year. I've brought his company down to its knees, and his reputation is following suit. Oh, I've had so much fun, but now it's time for Ash and me to have a face-to-face, shall we say."

Char hated that Carl was using her nickname for Julian. He had been her Ash back then. As angry and hurt as she was at him for turning his back on her when she needed him most, she didn't want him to suffer. She was afraid for him. She felt a new wave of desperation come over her.

"Carl, please, don't do this. What can I do? Anything, I'll do anything."

"I have something you can do for me. Up the freeway about a mile is the exit for Highway127, also known as Death Valley Road. Take it."

This is it, Charlotte thought. *I'm driving to my death.* She couldn't even cry. Her eyes burned; her palms, gripping the steering wheel, were clammy. She thought of her kids. How would they handle losing her? Did they understand how much she loved them? Had she raised them with enough love to last them the rest of their lives? Would the loss of their mother cause them to end up scarred and timid, like Char had been most her life?

Char's desperate thoughts reminded her of Katena's story, something her mother had told Katena repeatedly: that it would be better to die fighting for her freedom than to live like a trapped animal.

Through her grief and panic, Charlotte fought to think of a way out, willing herself to be like Katena, to not give up. Her mind quickly ran through every puzzle piece until she came to a stark realization.

Carl wanted her alive, not dead—not yet anyway. Blowing her up before she reached his chosen destination wouldn't fit into his grand plan. He'd simply been manipulating her emotions, preying on her worst fears with a lie. If she was the bait for Ash, Carl's real target, then there was no bomb.

She made a split-second decision and committed to it.

"On second thought, Carl, I think you can take Highway 127 and shove it up your ass."

She checked her rearview mirror and, without hesitation, whipped the car across both lanes of traffic and through the open dirt median, screeching into the southbound lanes of I-15, cutting off an old Nissan Sentra. The driver flipped her off and honked like crazy as he passed her.

Carl came over the speaker again, "Charlotte I'm disappointed in you. I thought you had more sense. I'll give you ten seconds to turn around."

Hearing the tension in Carl's voice, she felt even more confident that there was no bomb in the car.

"I don't need the ten seconds. Fuck off, Carl."

"Oh, and we were going to have so much fun. Very well. How about we do a countdown to the big boom, shall we?"

Charlotte felt quite confident in calling his bluff, but fear and doubt did their best to seize her.

"Five."

She thought of her kids and prayed to God to watch over them. She only wished that if there really were a bomb that her kids could somehow know how brave she was finally being in that moment.

"Four."

She thought of Emmett. She looked at her wrist. She was still wearing the bracelets he had bought her, with her and her kids' birthstones. He was so hurt when they last talked, and now she might never get the chance to make it up to him.

"Three."

She realized if the car really did explode, that she'd better steer clear of all other cars to spare them. She looked around. Her best bet was to pass the Nissan she'd already cut off once. She floored it past him, and he honked and flipped her off again. He probably thought she was a nut.

"Two. It's not too late, Charlotte. You can still turn around and save yourself."

"Thanks, but what's that saying? 'I'm going to live free or die trying.'" Charlotte gripped the steering wheel; sweat was now trickling down her temples. She sucked in air.

"One."

Nothing.

No boom, no bang; Charlotte was still driving.

Without even thinking, she saw a truck stop exit and took it. Her whole body was shaking. She pulled in and found it had a twenty-four-hour diner. Just in case the car wasn't safe, she drove over the rocks and scrub past the diner, far from the gas station.

Charlotte checked the locks, and they were still overridden—she couldn't get out of her car. If she didn't get out quickly, she'd bake to death. Her phone was still shut down too. She took off her heels and leaned back, readying herself to kick the glass out with all of her might when she remembered she had an emergency kit and was pretty sure it came with a window-breaking tool. She found it buried at the bottom of her glove box and had never been more elated. It only took two quick hits before she was brushing the glass away and climbing out.

She reached in and grabbed her purse and made sure she still had Julian's business card. When she started toward the diner, her legs were wobbly from the stress and adrenaline, and she had to walk carefully and deliberately. Gaining strength as she went, she made her way inside and asked the one waitress where the restroom was. The waitress looked her over dubiously before telling Charlotte she had to make a purchase to use it. Char gave her a ten-dollar bill and ordered an iced tea. The waitress gave her the key, chained to a large plastic board.

She made her way into the bathroom and locked the door, and as was her habit, she ran the faucet and then sunk to the floor. But instead of sobbing like she had assumed she would, she let a slow smile come across her face.

Charlotte realized she had stared down her demons and won. She was victorious. She looked up to the ceiling and shook both fists. *I did it, I did it.* She suddenly felt a rush of adrenaline. She felt good. She felt strong. She felt free. She put a hand to her throat and took a deep breath. She was in amazement at herself. She smiled so hard it hurt, and she laughed. She laughed and laughed until she cried, but they were celebratory tears.

She slowly stood, then checked her makeup; her eyes were smudged, but otherwise it was still there, despite the major perspiration from the drive. She took off her jacket, which had been clinging to her, and cooled the back of her neck down with cold water. Soon she felt great, energized, but she knew what she had to do next.

The waitress showed her to a booth and set down her iced tea. Charlotte took a sip and then looked up at the waitress. The drink was loaded with rum.

"Oh, you'll get your ten dollars' worth here, honey. Sure looked like you could use it," she said with a wink. "Anything else I can getcha?"

"Thank you. Actually, yes, there is one more thing. Could I borrow your phone?"

Back at the penthouse, Julian was becoming more worried by the second. With his hands in his pockets and his head down, he couldn't help but pace the floor, racking his brain to figure out exactly how dire their situation was. Time wasn't on their side, and at the moment they had little intel to go on. Jameson stood there, watching Julian pace.

Julian said, "Despite the fact we haven't yet been able to talk with Charlotte to confirm our suspicions, I think we already know the answer. One, there's no way running into Charlotte last night was a coincidence, and two, the men last night were bogus. Here we thought we were coming face-to-face with the company that was trying to bring us down. They were two-bit chumps. It was all a ruse, a bloody setup just to get us in the same vicinity as Charlotte. Why? Who would go to such lengths for seemingly inconsequential nonsense? Carl Wolfe, that's who. That bloody bastard is still alive. And damn it, we must get to Charlotte before he does."

"Boss, we're doing all we can to canvass the area for Charlotte. We tried putting a trace on her phone, but to no avail. The only good thing is, though they wouldn't say where she was, Aubrie and Emmett definitely didn't seem worried about her whereabouts."

"It's not enough, Jameson. Damn it, we never should have stopped tailing her."

"We'll get him, Boss. I'm sorry I cancelled Charlotte's detail. I know you, and I struggled with following through on your orders. I should have known better," Jameson said.

"You're not the only one." Julian wouldn't say more. The day Taryn had challenged him about Charlotte, Julian had followed through on cancelling her tail. At that point, so much time had gone by, his judgment had become muddled. By then he wasn't sure who the true threat was, the ghost of Carl or his own feelings for Charlotte. That day he'd convinced himself that he was the threat to the happiness Charlotte so deserved. He hoped against hope his decision wouldn't prove to be a grave mistake.

Jameson hesitated, hemmed before blurting, "You know, you two really were remarkable together—"

"Jameson. Stop." The room seemed to drop ten degrees from the icy stare he gave Jameson.

"Sorry, Boss," Jameson said, his body tensing. He was clearly frustrated with the whole situation.

"Jameson, why don't you go check the data logs again, make sure we haven't overlooked anything," Julian said, giving Jameson some needed busywork. Jameson's wife, Natalie, and Charlotte had been best friends before that awful night, and Jameson had nearly as much vested interest in finding Charlotte as Julian, and his nervous energy was about to drive Julian over the edge.

Another member of the detail rushed in. "Boss, Emmett—Charlotte's, er, friend—is in the lobby. He wants to talk."

"What are you waiting for? He could have information. Get him up here. I'll speak with him in the office." He abhorred the thought of Charlotte having a boyfriend and knew he could only tolerate being in the same room with him for as long as he was useful in helping to find Charlotte.

Emmett stepped into the office, American swagger to the hilt.

Julian was repulsed and jealous. What was Charlotte doing with a meathead? The painful realization struck him that she had moved on with someone completely the opposite of him.

"Yes, how can I help you? Emmett, is it?" Julian said as he held out his hand. Emmett didn't offer his. He looked worried and worn. Julian braced himself for bad news.

"Where's Charlotte? I need to speak with her."

"What do you mean, where's Charlotte?" Fear struck Julian's core.

"I mean, it's been hours since anyone's talked with her. She had a meeting at two o'clock downtown, but she never made it. Her employee Jonathan tracked down Aubrie to see if she knew where she was, but none of us do. I thought since you were so desperate to talk to her that maybe you got a hold of her and she was with you."

Julian could tell it pained Emmett to even suggest Charlotte might be with him. "I'm sorry. I've not had the pleasure of her company today." Julian tried to steady himself. He didn't want to show the slightest hint that something might have been terribly wrong, but of course he knew it was. Checking his watch, he knew Charlotte had been unaccounted for now for at least three hours, meaning Carl could likely have Charlotte. He needed to get rid of this Emmett character and get with his team to figure out what happened, but first he needed to glean any helpful information from Emmett that he could.

"Did you see her this morning at all after I left?"

"I did. She came back around twelve thirty, I think. We talked; then she left." Emmett avoided his eyes and shifted on his feet.

Being a trained spy, Julian could tell from a mile away if anyone was hiding something, and he knew to dig deeper, though he acted indifferent, casually tapping a pen to the desk.

"Did you two by chance have an argument?"

"That's none of your business."

Julian got his answer from Emmett's reaction. They clearly had.

"Have you called her friends to see if anyone is with her or has at least seen her? If they've said no, do you think they'd be lying to cover for Charlotte if she perhaps didn't want to speak to you?"

"No, no. We've called everyone." Emmett appeared to be thinking down the list of each person he'd asked. "No one would lie to me."

"And she left in her car?" Julian spoke with detached professionalism while Emmett became more agitated.

"Yes. Is something wrong? Is there something you're not telling me?" Emmett asked, running a hand over his harried face.

There was plenty Julian wasn't telling him. He knew enough that it was time to smoothly get rid of Emmett and get to finding Charlotte. "Well, I'm sorry, Emmett, but I suspect that you two did in fact have a fight. I know Charlotte; she's a bit flighty, that one. Doesn't like conflict. I'm sure she's just at a shopping center somewhere, blowing off steam. She'll come to her senses and be back once she hits your card's limit. Something she tried to do to me on several occasions—but alas, that's just not possible." Julian smiled slyly. Even in the most stressful of situations he couldn't help playing mind games, especially with someone who had claim to someone he had once treasured more than anything in the world.

Emmett snorted in response. "I might not be a billionaire, but she'd have a hard time breaking my bank. But regardless, she's not that kind of woman anyway. She doesn't come for my credit card; she comes for me," Emmett said, looking straight into Julian's eyes, smiling with smug satisfaction.

Before Julian could one-up Emmett, Jameson interrupted. He gave Julian the look that said he had something important. Julian held a finger up to Emmett and turned to Jameson, who spoke low into Julian's ear. "We have Charlotte on the line, and she has information.

She wants us to meet her."

Overwhelming relief flooded Julian's body. "Is she okay? Is she safe?"

"Yes, but we need to head out, the sooner the better. I'm getting the heli ready."

Julian nodded and Jameson left. Staying cool under pressure, repressing the urge to run for Charlotte immediately, Julian looked at Emmett, the corners of his mouth tugging at a smile. "Charlotte just called. She's fine. She's asked to see me. I'm sorry she didn't call you," Julian said, relishing being disingenuous. "Now, if you'll excuse me."

Emmett grimaced at the news but clearly wasn't ready to leave. "Not so fast. Can I speak with you alone first?" he said, looking at two of Julian's bodyguards. "Unless you're afraid?"

Julian hated to waste time, but he knew Charlotte was safe and was curious what Emmett wanted to discuss. He waved the guards toward Emmett, seizing the opportunity to put him in a humbling position. "Of course, so long as you don't mind a quick pat-down? Never can be too cautious."

Emmett rolled his eyes. "Pat away," he said as he spread his legs and put his arms behind his head. After patting him down, the guards gave a thumbs-up. Julian gave a nod, and they were out the door.

"I had a talk with Aubrie today. She made some pretty shocking allegations against you, Julian. I wanted to give you an opportunity to refute them."

Julian let out a huff. "Aubrie Elle. I wouldn't trust much of what comes out of her mouth. The problem with that girl is her parents didn't give her a proper beating now and again."

Without warning, Emmett's fist came at Julian, but he was able to duck with his lightning reflexes. Emmett came right back and lunged for Julian, pinning him to the desk, and yelled, "I'll kill you if you even so much as think of laying a hand on Charlotte again. Ever." Emmett pulled his fist back to deliver a blow, but Julian managed a leg sweep, taking Emmett off his feet. In a blur, the doors to the office flung open, and Jameson and Turk rushed in, pulling Emmett back and slamming him against a wall.

Again, Julian had to order the men off Emmett. He understood why Emmett would be so furious, but was livid at the accusation. He marched up and got right into Emmett's face, grabbing his shirt collar and pointing a steady finger at him, his breath labored after their scuffle. "I may not be perfect, but I can promise you this: I would never lay a hand on Charlotte, or any woman, for that matter. I don't know what Aubrie said to you, but it's a bloody lie. That insolent teenager has got an issue or two. I wouldn't trust a word she says." He shoved at Emmett's shoulders and took a step back, maddened that Emmett would be so gullible and believe such a melodramatic teen. He straightened his back and fixed his tie as he addressed Emmett. "Now, Charlotte is waiting for me. Do you think she'd really be calling for me if I were her abuser? Think about that," Julian said with both hurt and sincerity in his voice.

Julian nodded to his guard, and they showed Emmett the door.

It was a mad scramble, but within twenty minutes, Julian was in his helicopter with his team. They briefed him on the way. Charlotte had made it clear that if Julian didn't come, she wouldn't divulge what she knew of Carl and his plans. Deep down, he'd known this day of reckoning would one day come, though he had no idea how, but what he did know was that it scared him to death.

Once Julian and his team had planned all they could on their way to get Charlotte, Julian sat in quiet reflection, not that he wanted to. Memories of Charlotte were quite painful, and he'd shut them out as best he could, but knowing he was on his way to her weakened his resolve.

He'd been a longtime friend of Beau's, and he would never have betrayed his best friend, but when he met Beau's wife, Charlotte, to his chagrin, he had known he would never be the same. For years Beau had joked that he would never allow his wife and best friend to meet, which was easy to prevent, since they lived on different continents. He had said that they were both too attractive to lay eyes on each other, for fear they'd fall for one another.

One day, out of the blue, Beau had dropped his edict and insisted they meet. Julian wondered at times if his friend wasn't almost pushing them together because at the same time Beau had started growing more and more distant to Charlotte. She was left fragile and confused, and Julian was there for her but did his best to resist it going any further than friendship, emotionally or physically. Resisting the physical was easier than he thought, despite how attracted he was to Charlotte. He knew she'd sooner die than betray her husband, and he felt the same about his best friend, but to his dismay, he had failed miserably in controlling his emotions and had fallen deeply in love with her.

At the time, he couldn't have fathomed the tragedies and chaos that would ensue, even though he'd stayed faithful to his friend until the end—but how could he have known an employee and good friend of Beau's would have a psychotic break and enact a misplaced revenge? But who was Julian kidding? He hadn't stayed faithful to his friend until the end. He had absolutely broken Beau's trust. Beau had asked Julian to protect Charlotte if something ever happened to him, and in the end, he had failed miserably, and Charlotte had tragically paid the price.

It had been dreadfully painful to see her the night before at the restaurant; she'd never looked more beautiful. If he'd been a weaker man, he'd have fallen to his knees and begged for forgiveness and pleaded with her to give him another chance. Or maybe to do so would have taken a strength he didn't have; Julian wasn't sure.

What he did know was it was going to kill him to have to be so near to her, hear her voice that was always so soothing to him, and smell her unique scent that was all hers and drove him crazy. He'd be seeing her within the hour; he needed to pull himself together.

Charlotte tried to sip the spiked tea slowly, but the alcohol was helping calm her nerves. It was euphorically empowering to call Ash's men and make demands. She dimly remembered a time when she had taken her assertiveness for granted. What had happened to her strength? She couldn't wait to finally have her say with Ash. She realized something inside her must have snapped while she was facing down death in that car. She wasn't afraid anymore. When Ash turned his back on her all those months ago, she wouldn't have dreamed of insisting on a face-to-face—groveling for it, maybe, but not demanding. Now she just couldn't fathom what she had been so afraid of all this time.

Before she realized it, the waitress had served her a second drink. She sipped away, lost in thinking of all the ways she would tell Ash off.

She was enjoying her reverie when it was interrupted by a familiar sound, a distant quick-paced thud-thud-thud. It became louder and louder, which caused the waitress and the few other patrons to run to the windows to see what the commotion was all about. What they saw was Julian's black thirteen-seat helicopter. It was a sight to most, but to Charlotte, old hat. She smiled wryly.

She paid for her second drink but asked the waitress to hold her table and went out to meet Ash. She walked tall this time, ready to face him without the negative visceral reaction.

The team piled out first; then she watched Ash. His long, lean frame ducked out of the helicopter, and when he straightened, he looked simply regal, like a king ready to hold court. He was a beautiful man, of that there was no doubt. Her pulse quickened, but this time from neither fear nor apprehension.

Before he could even approach her, his team surrounded her, peppering her with rapid-fire questions. She held her own and told them all she could about Carl, what he'd said, that he was out for revenge, his bomb threat, and where she'd been headed at his command. They pulled out a map and set it on a truck in the parking lot, much too old to need a car alarm. The team discussed possibilities.

Char looked at the map and knew instantly where he'd intended on taking her. She pointed to it.

"That's where he was waiting for me." She pointed to a national park.

"Did he tell you this?" Jameson asked.

"No, but it would have meant something to me. It's a play on words. I was supposed to take Death Valley Road, and it's obvious he meant for me to head to Ash Meadows National Wildlife Refuge. You all know Ash is what I liked to call Julian." The men were quiet. She hadn't realized Julian was standing right next to her. They locked eyes. A heat wave came over Charlotte, as well as a torrent of mixed emotions. She blushed painfully. Stupidly, what stood out most in her mind was the question of whether or not she had any business calling him Ash anymore.

Julian seemed unaffected and ordered her around just as he had before whenever he was in work mode. "Go inside the diner. Carl or his men could still be coming after you. I need to talk to the team."

"We need to talk, Ash…Julian," she said uncomfortably. She was irritated at herself. Here she was trying to be assertive and instead faltered over his name.

"We will, but go inside for a moment please. I'll be right there." He turned to the team, looking determined, focused on the threat at hand.

Charlotte hesitated, but decided she'd better do as he asked. She went back to her booth, and soon she heard the rotor blades start back up. She turned to watch as the team piled back into the helicopter. When it took flight, Char's stomach dropped. She knew he had left her again—but then the glass door behind her swung open. She turned, and there he was, making his way back to her. He had kept his promise. Her body flushed, but she told herself it was only from the tea.

As always, he was in a suit, cut to perfection over his tall, lean but hard frame. While he was the same height as Emmett, he didn't have nearly the bulk Emmett did. They were equally alluring, but in completely different ways. Emmett moved with an almost cocky strength, whereas Julian moved with a confident grace. They exuded completely different vibes, though they were both alpha males. The waitress eyed him with lusty awe.

When he reached Charlotte's booth, he was all business. "So, what we need to do is get the hell out of here, but your car's likely still being tracked. We need to pay someone off for their vehicle." He scanned the restaurant's patrons for the easiest mark.

Charlotte interrupted his search. "I'm not going anywhere just yet, Ash. We need to talk first," she said, drumming her fingers on the table as she looked up at him.

"I'm sorry?" He was indignant; his eyes narrowed. "We've got a madman on the loose, after us both, and you'd prefer to stay here like sitting ducks? What, to chitchat?" He shoved his hands into his pockets and leaned his head to the side.

"That was my condition for telling you what I knew, that you and

I would have a talk. Are you going back on your word?" She knew that would get him. Ash had always prided himself on being a man of his word.

He heaved a sigh of frustration. "We will; be patient. Please, let's get on the road first."

Charlotte smiled in triumph.

He paused to look her over. He bent down and came within an inch of her face. "Have you been drinking rum?" He pulled his head back with a sneer.

"If you had the day I just did, you'd be drinking too," she said defiantly. Gone were the days she'd feel guilty for having more than he or anyone else deemed appropriate.

"Fair enough. However, you need to get some food. Place an order to go." He threw down a hundred-dollar bill, then looked around. There were only a few patrons there at the moment, but Charlotte knew Ash always carried a minimum of two thousand dollars. He'd be able to throw a thick enough bundle of cash to get what he wanted.

Sure enough, he came back in a few minutes, having paid a wiry farmer five hundred dollars for his car keys with the promise to have the truck back by morning with a full tank of gas. From the looks of the beat-up truck, they could have bought it outright for less, but it started right up, and the lights worked, so they couldn't complain. Julian did look completely out of place behind the wheel of the squatty truck. His head nearly hit the roof. She had to stifle a laugh and decided she'd better keep eating the fries she'd ordered. The situation they were in was no laughing matter. She needed to sober up.

After they filled up, they headed in the direction of home. Julian said he felt pretty confident they'd be safe from then on, as long as his guys were able to track down and, as Julian put it, "neutralize the target."

"I must say, you're surprisingly composed, given the circumstances," Julian said as he looked Charlotte up and down. She felt tiny butterflies in her stomach. She put down the fries; there was no way she could continue eating with him looking at her that way. She grabbed for her water instead. He was checking her out like he always used to, right before telling her how beautifully seductive she was.

That was then, and this was now, she told herself. She had a lot she needed to get off her chest. It likely wasn't going to be pretty, but strangely she was no longer intimidated—not by Ash, not by death, not by truth. She felt so strong, almost invincible. She was exhilarated by her newfound sense of freedom.

She thought before speaking this time, choosing her words carefully. "Julian, thank you for heeding my request and actually coming, and for staying with me so we could talk. I'm shocked that you did, but thankful."

He didn't say anything. He wasn't going to speak about the two of them easily. Char decided to change tactics, but before she could ask her next question, Julian got a text message. He flipped his phone over, and Char saw the picture of a striking woman. She was maybe a few years younger than Char, with medium-brown hair, a cute angular nose, and rosy cheeks. Her smile was radiant and kind, and for some reason it made Charlotte feel sick to her stomach.

He didn't read the text, and he quickly flipped his phone back over.

"Who's that?" Char swallowed hard and her cheeks flushed. Why did she have to ask? And why did her stomach hurt all of a sudden? Was it jealousy? No, of course not. They were long over, and she prided herself on not being the jealous type, but maybe it was just the realization that he had moved on from her, just as she had from him. She assured herself that her confusing feelings were only due to the fact that they had been robbed of a proper closure to their relationship. Or were they? Charlotte wondered if what she actually felt was sadness that they had been robbed of their relationship in the first place. Their relationship had only ended because of what Carl had done.

"She's a friend. Much like your dinner date last night, I assume," he said, only managing the slightest look her way.

She decided to be more forthcoming. "Yes, that was Emmett. We're more than friends, though." Saying it made her feel brave.

"Emmett." Julian said his name as if he had a bad taste in his mouth, but true to form, said no more.

Charlotte ignored his reaction. She remembered she had started out as one of his "friends" too. The pang in her stomach came back, and she knew better than to press Julian Donatello Ashbourne III, at least on the topic of that woman.

It was a warm August night, but the air-conditioning was blowing too cold, so she went to turn it down. Julian must have thought the same thing and reached for the dial too. When their fingers accidentally touched, he pulled back as if he'd been burned. It stung Charlotte to feel the all-too-familiar rejection from him. She felt like a leper in his presence. He treated her as such, but she tried to ignore it and press on.

"Do you think your guys will find Carl?"

"We'll find him."

"I can't believe he's been alive this whole time. He could have gone to the police."

Julian remained cool. "Attempted murder? There's no proof. Anyone who might know anything has no reason to come forward, or they'll be implicated in a hundred other crimes. Not to worry."

"What about what he did to…" Charlotte meant to say, "me," but couldn't bring herself to. Julian had never spoken to or even looked at her again after he found her in a bloody heap in the stable.

Julian went rigid. She could see he was gripping the steering wheel. There was a tiny vein that pulsed at his temple any time he was angry. "We won't discuss that." His voice was hard. He sounded downright contemptuous.

It angered Charlotte that it angered Julian. Her fearlessness returned, and she remembered Kat's defiant words from weeks ago at their first lunch together. They went through her head like a mantra.

I'm not the ugliness that the other people perpetrated against me.

"Stop the car," she yelled. Julian looked at her in disbelief. "I said pull over. Stop the car, Ash." This was it. They were going to have it out once and for all.

He said not a word but cut off a string of cars to pull over to the shoulder. The truck bumped over the dirt, rocks, and sagebrush. He stopped safely off the freeway.

"I'm assuming you don't have motion sickness," Julian said rhetorically; he obviously knew what was coming.

"No, Ash, get out of the car. Now." Judging by the look on his face, her authoritative tone had taken Julian by surprise, but he obeyed without argument.

He came around to her side of the truck. By then the sun had gone down, and the only light was from the occasional car zooming past.

Julian stood almost statuesque, hands in pockets, staring her right in the eyes like a soldier bravely facing a firing squad, ready to take whatever she had to give.

"Ash, after all I thought we meant to each other, you're going to apologize to me, today, right now, for how you've treated me. I'm not a leper, Ash. I didn't ask for what happened. What Carl did to me is not who I am." Heavy tears escaped her eyes, but she kept on.

"When you turned your back on me, never to speak to me again, it hurt worse than anything that Carl could have ever done, don't you understand?"

Julian couldn't respond.

"Talk to me, say something, explain yourself. Why can't you apologize for what you did to me?"

Julian snapped. He marched closer, his finger pointed toward his own chest. "That's right, Charlotte. You said it right. What *I* did to you! This was entirely my fault. You wouldn't have been there in my stable—it was because of me. You're not the leper, Charlotte; I'm the monster!"

Charlotte was shell-shocked by Julian's admission. The sadness and desperation in his voice nearly broke her heart. It all made sense to her at that moment. He had been suffering just as much if not more than Charlotte had. The irony wasn't lost on her that they had both suffered alone the whole time. It could have been so different had they had even one honest conversation.

Julian's voice was weak, broken. "After what happened to you, the guilt that ensued—I wasn't sure I could go on." His voice cracked with pain. He paused to regain composure. "It rocked my world, all the agony and devastation I know I caused you. You're so beautiful, Charlotte. The torment I feel when I look at you, it's unbearable; it kills me to be so near you. What you suffered should never have happened. Why do you think I burned my stable to the ground?" He choked back emotions Charlotte had never known were possible for him to feel. She only knew him to be stoic and in charge, rarely one to lose control.

Charlotte couldn't believe her ears. "I…I thought you were destroying evidence."

"No, Charlotte. The anger I had, I couldn't deal with it. We'd built something so beautiful, and I failed us both."

"So, you weren't disgusted by me?" Charlotte asked in wonderment as she stepped toward him.

"Charlotte, I never could be." Julian took another step toward her.

"I didn't listen to you that night. I didn't believe you that someone was out to get us. You don't blame me?" she said, taking another step.

He closed the distance. "Not in a million years."

At that moment they came together in a kiss burning with a desperate passion. Julian had an arm around her waist and a hand at the back of her head, entwined in her hair. Charlotte's hands gripped his back. The synergy between them was palpable.

As quickly as it started, they both pushed each other away as if they'd been struck by lightning. They stood in a daze.

Emmett flashed through Charlotte's mind, and guilt settled in her gut, and so did confusion. They'd built a solid relationship, yet it hadn't barred her from standing there with Julian, it didn't stop her from feeling the way she did, and it hadn't stopped her from acting on it. And yet she knew she loved him.

Julian stalked away into the darkness. She saw him pick up a large rock and throw it, heaving a guttural yell as he did. Char wondered if he was thinking of the girl who had called on the phone. She decided to give him some time and went to wait for him back in the truck.

He stayed outside a good ten minutes. When he came back, his hair looked a mess, but he seemed at peace. They sat in silence. He didn't start the truck.

Finally, he turned to her. "I'm extremely thankful, Charlotte, that you requested—no, commanded—that I come to you. You seem to have turned a corner and have a newfound confidence. I like it; it's always suited you," he said, looking her over again. "Can we thank your Emmett for coaxing this out of you?"

She noticed Ash now said his name without the sour expression. "No, actually, as supportive as he's been, I've continued to be a timid weakling until tonight. I stared down death tonight, Ash. I fought for myself for the first time in a long time, and I've come to realize that I'm worth the fight."

Julian smiled, almost laughing as he started the truck and pulled back onto the freeway. "That you are, my dear. That you are." He reached out and held her hand. Charlotte knew it was his gesture to her that they were all right now. A warm sensation came over her, and they sat in silence much of the way back.

They'd been driving for some time when Julian's cell rang.

"Aren't you going to get that? It's probably your friend again." She desperately needed to know what that woman meant to him. She held her breath, knowing if he took the call in front of her, the woman meant nothing. But if he refused to take it, Charlotte knew it would mean he'd moved on. She knew protecting the privacy of those he cared for was a priority of his.

"I'll call her after I get you home safely."

Her heart sunk, and he didn't let his eyes off the road. Char got her answer.

It was nearly midnight when they reached Charlotte's condo, giving her time to come to an acceptance of all that had happened. A couple of residents did a double take when the rickety old Datsun pulled through the security gate. Charlotte and Julian couldn't help but laugh.

Just then his cell rang, and he answered it. It was a quick call.

"They got him." Julian took a deep breath.

Charlotte leaned her head back. "Thank God."

"I knew they would. My men did a sweep of your car. It's clean. They'll have the window repaired and bring it back to you by morning."

He tilted her chin toward him, and her eyes met his. "Charlotte, he'll never hurt you again, I can assure you."

Charlotte had a sickening thought. "You're not going to kill him, are you?" Her voice shook.

Julian closed his eyes ever so briefly and lightly touched his brow, but Charlotte knew. He was grieved. "The messages you left. Afterward. You were pained by many things, but the fear in your voice—no, Charlotte. Despite it all, you didn't want his blood on our hands. I won't do that to you again. But he will get his. We've kept meticulous records of every federal crime he's committed against my company. Be assured, he's in police custody, and with the charges he's facing, he'll be locked in federal prison for a long, long time."

"What about when he does get out or, God forbid, escapes?" Charlotte couldn't look at Julian. She only wanted him to see her as strong and fearless now because, for the most part, that's how she felt.

Julian tilted her chin up to again look her in the eyes. "On my life, he'll never hurt you again. We'll keep up on his prison whereabouts on a daily basis if need be. And when or if he's ever released, you'll be guarded, Charlotte. You have my word."

Charlotte felt a tightness in her throat, and her eyes welled. "Thank you, Ash."

He cast his eyes down and drew his brow. "Charlotte, I didn't say it outright, but I hope you understand now how terribly sorry I am for all you've been through. I'm sorry I wasn't the man you needed me to be. Please know, as much as I tried to push you out of my mind, not a day has gone by since that you weren't in my thoughts, in my—" His breath hitched, and he wouldn't finish. He looked up at her with a sadness that vanished so quickly she thought she might have imagined it. "I hope Emmett is the man you deserve. Take care, my dear."

Charlotte couldn't speak. She wouldn't even know what to say, but she willed herself to smile as a tear escaped. Julian put his hand to her cheek, his thumb catching her tear as he leaned in and gave her one final kiss.

Charlotte got out of the truck and walked away.

Despite her worry about Emmett and the cold shoulder from Aubrie again at breakfast, Charlotte was on cloud nine. She'd slept surprisingly well and woke feeling lighter; a burden had finally been lifted. She couldn't get over the feeling of wonderment about all she'd overcome, and she kept luxuriating in the newfound knowledge that Ash hadn't been repulsed by her this whole time, that sadly he'd been repulsed by himself and his guilt for what he felt he had allowed to happen to her. She knew she would have to stay stoic and strong to resist the temptation to play what-if with their past. It was a moot point. Ash had made it clear he had moved on.

Sadly, Emmett may have done the same. She winced at the memory of her and Emmett's last moments together when he was so angry and told her it was over, but she knew it was due to the love they shared and his hurt from the misinformation Aubrie had told him. Charlotte regretted now not taking care to explain more to Aubrie. She just hadn't had the mental energy at the time to figure out what she should and should not say to her young, impressionable daughter.

The more she thought about it, the more anxious Charlotte was to get to Emmett and explain everything, confident it would repair their relationship. She got ready quickly, and as she headed out the door, Asa insisted on going with her. She laughed and grabbed his leash, happy to have a companion. As promised, her car was back in the parking garage, the window repaired like new.

On the way, she called Emmett. She was excited to tell him everything now. She knew he'd understand and imagined the relief he'd feel to know the whole story, but he didn't answer her call. She figured it was just as well—better to have a face-to-face with him.

She pulled into his driveway and, grabbing Asa in her arms, rushed to his door and rang the doorbell. While she was confident they wouldn't have another argument, she was still happy to have Asa with her. Either way, she'd need his support. She felt silly waiting for Emmett to answer the door, since she'd been coming in as if it were her house for weeks, but for some reason she couldn't bring herself to let herself in.

Finally Emmett opened the door. Charlotte was stunned to see Emmett looking like hell, far worse than he'd looked after their disastrous night in Montecito. His clothes were rumpled, he hadn't shaved, his eyes were swollen and bloodshot, and he smelled like old liquor. Char knew then he must have been drinking all night.

"What do you want?" His tone stung.

"I—I wanted to come in, so we could talk."

"Charlotte," he said with a tired sigh, "we have nothing left to talk about. I know you were with Julian all night. That's all I need to know."

She took a step forward, eager to tell him everything. "Emmett, let me explain."

"No," he said and grabbed her arm. He pushed her back a step, and Asa let out a whine. "Save it. I'm not going to sit here and allow you to spin another one of your lies. I know you've gone through a lot in your life, and for that, I'm truly sorry, but the choices you've made here and now, I can't understand. And I won't. I'm sorry, Charlotte, but we're done." And with that, he stepped back and shut the door.

Charlotte stood at the door stunned. She couldn't think of anything else to do but turn around. As she got back into her car,

Charlotte felt as if her whole world were crashing down on her, and she knew she had to fight back. Before starting the car or buckling Asa, she called Kat.

"What do you want?"

"Kat, hi. I know you're angry with me. I just lost Emmett, and I don't want to lose you, too. He didn't give me a chance to explain."

"And neither will I, Charlotte. I warned you, and you failed. You didn't see Emmett last night. You were off with your English lover. Lou and I had to console him as best we could. He's had enough hurt, and you won't be using me to try to get to Emmett. It's over, Charlotte, with the both of us."

Kat hung up on Charlotte, and her shoulders slumped. Kat's tone alone had been devastating. It had been just like Emmett's: empty. She wanted to call Anna but ultimately decided against it. She didn't want to put a strain on Anna and Emmett's friendship and working relationship. Though she felt that Anna would have understood completely and likely would want to help, Charlotte just couldn't bring herself to reach out to her.

No, Charlotte told herself in the end, she shouldn't be fighting against people, but for herself, and if Emmett were serious about ending it, she'd have to accept her part in it and decide what she wanted to do with her life. She flicked a few tears away but told herself that was all she was allowed.

Asa whimpered again and climbed into her lap to kiss at her neck. She laughed and pulled him away. "Don't worry about me, Asa, I'm going to be okay. This hurts, and I feel pretty alone right now, but we'll get through it. After last night, I know I can get through anything."

It seemed a little demented, but she was thankful for the threat Carl had made against her life. She embraced feeling so strong and invincible. It wasn't that she felt nothing could hurt her now, but that she wouldn't let it. No more would she turn against herself. She knew she would be able to stand tall and refuse to let anything take her down. She refused to crumble like she always had in the past. She buckled Asa up next to her and said, "It's time go home, Asa."

Aubrie begged Charlotte not to go when she announced that she was moving back to Oregon, but she wouldn't be giving in this time. She did assure the girls that she would fly out to see them every four to six weeks. She had booked her flight a week earlier, and now her bags were packed and it was time to go.

Though Charlotte had either run away or hidden so many times in the past, she didn't feel weak about her decision. This time it was a logical decision, not an emotional one.

When Char said good-bye to Moe, Moe promised to look after the girls in her stead, and she made Char promise to check in with her and to plan for therapy checkups with her whenever she came for a visit with the girls. Moe also promised to send her a couple of referrals for therapists near Portland and said in the meantime they could Skype their therapy sessions.

She sent Anna flowers with a note saying good-bye and thanking her for being so kind. Perhaps it would be awkward that she would receive them at Emmett's home, but she couldn't be concerned with that; they were about Anna, not Emmett.

She wanted to but knew better than to try to contact Kat again, and that really hurt. She knew Aubrie and Chloe didn't want to throw it in her face, but Charlotte had overheard Chloe on the phone with Kat, making plans to go to dinner together. Though she wouldn't be a part of it, she was happy to see Kat wasn't abandoning the girls. She wondered if it meant there was a sliver of hope for them to be friends again someday, but realistically she knew better than to hold her breath.

She had just been getting to know Emmett's boys. She hoped they didn't think the worst of her, although she imagined they did. The consolation was that they too, like Kat, would be there for the girls. Char was hopeful that she hadn't ruined everything.

Her luggage sat by the door, Asa's carrier at the ready, but there was one important thing she had left to do.

Before leaving for home, Charlotte wanted to finally come clean with Aubrie. She'd chickened out so many times in the last week that it came to telling her the day of her flight. Maybe not the best timing, but Charlotte had a plan to sweeten the departure: she would be giving Aubrie the keys to the convertible after saying good-bye. Charlotte couldn't wait to give her the surprise; she hoped to leave the girls with a smile. But before then, mother and daughter would have to share a few more tears.

She found Aubrie in her room with her earbuds in, completely immersed in her homework. She tapped on her shoulder. Aubrie looked up and took an earbud out. "Aubrie, can we talk?"

"What's wrong? You look serious." Aubrie sat up straight.

Charlotte forced a smile. "Everything's fine, honey. But what I want to talk about is serious. Can we shut the door?"

She didn't know how to start, so when she sat on Aubrie's bed next to her, she decided to jump right in. "I want to come clean with you about that night." She didn't have to tell Aubrie what night she was referring to; she had her daughter's complete attention, and she looked shocked.

"Really, Mom?"

Char answered with a weak smile. As hard as it was going to be for her to share, Charlotte knew it was the right thing to do for their relationship going forward. Without hesitation, Charlotte delved in.

"Your suspicions have always been right, Aubrie. I wasn't in a car accident. You remember Carl Wolfe, one of Beau's executives, and that before Beau died, we had been helping Ash's firm with their merger?"

Aubrie nodded.

"When Beau died and I was appointed as his successor, Carl didn't take it so well, but I tried to be understanding and thought we'd worked it all out. But I was wrong, and he continued to hold a grudge for months. Later, when we made the final selection for Ash's firm, it was the opposite of what Carl had been campaigning for. That pushed him over the edge, and he completely lost it. Honey, that night, to get his revenge, Carl took me hostage, and he beat me." Charlotte couldn't bring herself to tell her how, that he'd taken a whip to her and tortured her. It didn't matter, and would only add to Aubrie's pain.

Upon hearing the truth, Aubrie sat stunned for a moment before her eyes welled and her chin quivered. Finally she threw her arms around her mom before bursting into tears. Charlotte held her tightly and rocked her gently, telling her it was all okay now, though she couldn't help but cry on her daughter's shoulder too.

Once she gathered her composure, Aubrie peppered Charlotte with questions as she thought back to that time and worked to put all that Charlotte had shared with her into perspective. As Charlotte caught her up on the latest developments, she felt Aubrie was doing surprisingly well and gave an internal sigh of relief.

"Wait, this happened last Saturday? The day Jonathan called saying you missed your meeting? Oh God, Mom, where were you? We all thought you were with Julian. Carl didn't abduct you again, did he?"

"No, Aubrie, I never laid eyes on Carl. I was always safe. But he did try to lure me to the desert, and for a while I complied, thinking I had no other choice. But I came to my senses and called his bluff, and sure enough, I was free from him all along." Charlotte didn't want to relive either night and hoped Aubrie would be satisfied without every sordid detail.

"Then you called the police?"

"No, I called Julian. I knew he'd be successful in apprehending him. His team has been involved since the beginning, and they deserved to be the ones to get him in the end."

"So, let me get this straight: Carl's in custody now and should be in prison for decades. That's great and all, Mom, but it must have been hard for Ash to not to just off the psycho. He must still really care for you to respect your wishes," Aubrie said, before clapping her hand up to her mouth. "Oh, Ash. I've blamed him this whole time."

"Ash is the one who rescued me that night. He would never, ever raise a hand to me, Aubrie."

Aubrie took a moment before replying. "But he still hurt you. How could he desert you after that? It killed me to hear you afterward, calling him and leaving messages, begging him to talk to you."

Charlotte smiled and grabbed Aubrie's hand in reassurance. "Some couples can claim their shared tragedy as a bonding experience, but for many, it tears them apart. We were one of the many. He carried unimaginable guilt for failing to protect me. I can't blame him for how he felt and how he dealt with his pain."

Aubrie pulled her hand away, troubled. "I don't know, Mom. On one hand, I feel for him and wish that he could have been stronger for you, but on the other, I can't just wipe away how messed up your relationship was. First, you two had an affair; then, after Beau died and you guys went public as a couple, he was controlling, Mom. More than once I saw him grab your arm or push you against a wall."

Charlotte gently took Aubrie's hands again and leaned in to look her in the eye. "Aubrie, I'm only going to say this once. Ash and I. Did.

Not. Have. An. Affair. We both loved Beau very much; we would have never disrespected him that way. I loved Beau fiercely until the day he died, and still do. No, that never happened, Aubrie. You believe me, don't you? I wouldn't lie to you about this. It's much too important."

Aubrie teared up again and took a deep breath, clearly relieved. "Thank God," she whispered.

Charlotte smiled. "You loved Beau so much, and he you. He would be proud that you're so protective of his memory." Charlotte blushed and knew she had to tread delicately for the next issue she had to clear up. "As far as your thinking Ash was abusive, honey, with any of those times, had you heard us arguing, or did it look to you like we were fighting?"

Aubrie thought for a moment before answering. "Well, no."

"And those few times you saw us that way, you may not remember this, but you were supposed to have been out of the house."

"Okay, so?"

"So, honey, all I'm going to say is, what you saw between us was us being frisky. It was passion, honey, not abuse." Charlotte's face was in a full crimson blush from embarrassment, but she knew she had to set things straight so Aubrie could finally drop her misconception that Julian was an abuser.

Aubrie studied Charlotte for a moment, clearly trying to understand, before squealing, "Oh my God, Mom, fifty shades of TMI!" Aubrie grabbed a pillow and buried her face in it. She lifted her eyes to peek at Charlotte before shaking her head and burying her face in her pillow again, squealing some more.

Charlotte laughed, and so did Aubrie. "I'm sorry, but I couldn't let you continue to think I'd fallen in love with another abuser, Aubrie. I have to set the example for you and certainly don't want you thinking your biological dad is the precedent. Beau, Ash, Emmett—they've all been great men, Aubrie, gentle and kind."

Char could tell Aubrie was still trying her best to get serious, the wry smile not quite leaving her face, but when Aubrie could finally look Charlotte in the eye again, she spoke with confidence. "You may not be perfect, Mom, but I know you've always done your best for me and Blake. I'm so sorry I wasn't there for you, Mom, after that night. I was so angry, and I knew you were lying to me. I just didn't understand why."

"You were a young teen who had recently lost her father. I didn't want you hurting or in fear. But it was a big mistake, keeping you in the dark. That's why I'm coming clean with you now. I'm so sorry, Aubrie," she said before pulling Aubrie in for another hug.

"Mom, I'm sorry if what I told Emmett caused you two to break up." Aubrie looked at Charlotte and dabbed the remaining tears from her cheeks.

"Honey, no, it wasn't you. Emmett and I had our own issues, for the most part stemming from my dishonesty. I see now that I was making the same mistakes with him that I made with you. I didn't trust our love for each other. If I had, I'd have been honest with the both of you and allowed you two to be there for me, each in your own way."

"Do you think there's a chance you two could get back together?" Aubrie sounded hopeful.

"Sadly, no. I lied to him about Ash, granted, mostly by omission, but a lie is a lie. He had so much faith in me, and I shattered it. Trust is hard to get back, but Aubrie, I've learned a lot from all of this, and I feel stronger for it. I'm okay. No, I'm better than okay. I'm unafraid now, and it's a wonderful feeling."

"If you're not afraid anymore, then why don't you go fight for Emmett?"

Char smiled. "I went to him, and he pushed me away. I respect him and myself enough to not make a scene. What's done is done. How he feels is how he feels. I'm able to accept that and move on."

"But aren't you dying inside?"

"Oh, it hurts, honey. And if he were to change his mind and be willing to at least hear me out, of course I'd jump at the chance. But I don't see that happening, and like I said, I'm strong enough to accept it."

"Are you and Ash getting back together then? You can't let him off the hook for abandoning you when you needed him most. I don't know how you could forgive him."

"No, sweetie, we could never get back together." Again Char felt the sting of love stolen. "That book is closed. He did hurt me more than words could ever express, but he was hurting too. We loved each other deeply. But just before Carl was arrested, Ash and I had a moment together and were able to bring closure to that tragic night and to our relationship. It was healing for us both, and I think we're finally at peace with ourselves and with each other."

She didn't tell Aubrie about the lingering, bittersweet love for Ash that would likely never abate. Their love had fallen victim to grief, but she found solace in knowing that what they had had wasn't thrown away by disgust but by despair. The small pain in her heart for her loss somehow gave her a sense of peace, made him feel near, and that was good enough.

"I understand that you must want space from Emmett, but why go back home? What's the difference? Either way you'll be near someone you can't be with. You may as well stay here with me and Chloe."

A small part of Charlotte was tempted to give in, but she knew she couldn't allow their mother-daughter codependence to go on any longer, and that it really was time for her to stand on her own two feet.

"After Ash, I shut myself out from the world. But I've come out from the other side stronger and truly ready to embrace life. I feel like it's my chance for a do-over. I'm actually excited to go back to Wilsonville. You know, some of my close friends back there, they've never given up on me. They still reach out every so often, and I feel I'm finally ready to reconnect."

"Yeah, they freaked out when they heard you were moving down here."

"What do you mean? How'd they know?"

"Mom, all this time people have kept in contact with me so they could keep tabs on you. I'm always assuring them you're fine and promising them I know you'll reach out to them soon, especially Natalie. Seriously, I think she's obsessed with you, as much as she calls and e-mails me."

Charlotte laughed. "I had no idea you've been acting as my social gatekeeper. That time's over, Aubrie. I can take over now, I promise," she said with a sympathetic smile.

"I can't believe I'm saying this after all you've been through, but I'm happy for you, Mom. Despite all the loss you've experienced, you really do seem okay. And I can see this whole new confidence all over you. It's weird." Aubrie laughed.

"Weird? Thanks, honey," Char said, looking sideways at her daughter.

"Not in a bad way. I'm just—it's going to take some getting used to, that's all." Aubrie slid in closer to her mom and gave her a big hug.

"Ohhh, honey, thank you. I love you so much." Char squeezed Aubrie tightly and told herself to enjoy this moment. Her daughter was growing up, and they had finally been able to have a mature heart-to-heart.

"I love you too, Mom."

"Come on, Asa, ready for your walk?" Charlotte made her way to the utility room to get Asa's leash. Asa stayed close at her heel, excited for his walk. She knelt down to buckle his harness. With a laugh, she struggled against Asa's lunging at her face for kisses; he never tired of showing his gratitude. He wouldn't stay still for her, but nevertheless, she got him buckled. She slipped on her rain boots, went for the door, and paused to look at the calendar hung on the wall. Was it really November already?

She couldn't believe so many weeks had gone by. With the amount of time she spent with Jonathan and Natalie, her best friend who was overjoyed to finally reconnect with Charlotte, she had stayed much busier than she could have imagined. And Aubrie and Chloe had come for a visit not once but twice already. Chloe blamed their trips home on her mom, but Charlotte suspected it was just as much Aubrie's wanting to check up on Charlotte. Their visits had been wonderful and bonding, and Charlotte felt redeemed for many of her mistakes with Aubrie and was thankful that in its own strange way, time really was healing all wounds.

She only wished that time would also help to fade certain memories, but it hadn't. The violent nightmares had resurfaced since she moved back home. Those were already happening less often and becoming much less disturbing, thanks to her continuing therapy sessions with Moe via Skype and her occasional visits to a local psychiatrist. Both told her not to look at the dreams as a setback and that they were to be expected, due to the move and recent turbulence in her life.

What hadn't quieted yet was her unabated pining after her lost love. She put her hand to the calendar and wished that someday soon, time would be on her side in helping her move on once and for all.

She and Asa stepped out onto the back patio and made their way around the house toward the walking trail. It was a gray day, and she felt the chill in the air and lamented the fact that, unlike in Malibu, there was no bright-blue sky and warm sun to welcome the day. She turned back to look through the large arched window into her cavernous, empty home and wished for the old days when the house was full of family, friends, and love. Now it was just her and Asa. She felt as empty on the inside as her home now was. She tried to shut out those thoughts and turned back to the burgeoning clouds hanging low in the sky. It was cold and drizzly, so she zipped her jacket and pulled her scarf snug under her chin.

She made her way down the loop that headed toward the garden, pausing often to let Asa sniff this plant or that leaf. She'd learned long ago to have patience with Asa on his walks in the woods. Everything interested him; it reminded her of her kids when they were young, and she found it endearing.

They made their way back to the house through the oak grove. Moss hung in curtains off the oak trees, and a misty fog that was so thick she could barely see fifty feet in front of her had settled in. The mist tickled her face and blurred her vision.

Her eyes scanned the trail up to the house, where she thought she saw a figure standing in her yard. She blinked hard and wiped her eyes but saw clearly there was a man there. He started walking toward her. She would have panicked, but she had two security gates, and someone would have to know both codes to get through. She was confident it had to be someone she knew, so she kept walking and realized the figure was familiar. She stopped in her tracks. Ash?

No, she realized with a pang deep inside, it wasn't Ash. It was Emmett. She smiled.

"Emmett?" she called out through the mist.

"It's me, Charlotte. I'm here." The way he said it told her all she needed to know. He was back. For whatever reason, he had forgiven her; she could hear the love in his voice.

She let go of Asa's leash and ran toward Emmett, but Asa was beating her to him. Emmett laughed that same joyful, hearty laugh she loved so much, and he ran to her.

She threw herself into his arms. Asa was barking in happy excitement the whole time. Emmett brushed her wet hair out of her face and kissed her everywhere he could.

"Oh my God, I've missed you. I'm so sorry," he said, barely above a whisper.

"But how? Why? What made you change your mind?" Char asked, searching his face for answers.

"It was Aubrie. She could see how miserable I was, and I was getting worse every day. She didn't want to betray your trust, but she had to set me straight. She said you'd fill me in on the rest but promised I'd easily forgive you. She said it was complicated but that you weren't with Julian by choice that night. It was all I needed to hear. Babe, I've missed you so much," he said as he squeezed her tightly.

"Emmett, it was so hard to leave you. You have no idea how happy I am. I wanted to tell you everything weeks ago." She would tell him the whole truth, and she knew he'd love her still.

"Charlotte, we're back together, and I'm not going anywhere."

It started raining. Charlotte, still wrapped around Emmett, threw her head back and laughed.

"What's so funny?"

"I've never been happier to be caught in a cold November rain!"